"What flight of womanly fancy is this?

"I have never broken a pledge!"

"That kiss last eve was no flight of fancy and neither was it welcome!"

The knight glanced to either side, then he leaned closer and lowered his voice. "My lady, this is neither the place nor the time for this discussion."

"Ha! I will wager that you will *never* find the time or the place to discuss your breach of our agreement."

"Breach?" Yves visibly ground his teeth, then continued with low urgency, his gaze boring into Gabrielle's own. "I made no breach of our pledge...."

"No? That kiss was far beyond the terms."

"That kiss," Yves said through his teeth, "was for your benefit alone."

Gabrielle nearly gasped aloud at his audacity. That he would put such a thought into words astonished her. "Well, you do have a lofty opinion of your charms, sir!"

Dear Reader,

Since she published her first book during our premier March Madness promotion in 1992, Claire Delacroix has gone on to pen numerous tales that continue to "wow" the critics. She returns with *My Lady's Desire,* a "5 Bells!!" story says *Bell, Book and Candle.* In this compelling medieval novel, which is a sequel to *Enchanted,* a handsome blade for hire and an exiled noblewoman marry to reclaim a lost estate, and together find an unexpected passion.

When a prim young spinster falls for a very improper cattle rancher who she thinks is in love with her sister, tempers flare in the adorable Western *Prim and Improper* by Liz Ireland, who is fast becoming known for her skillful weaving of humor and romance.

Ruth Langan returns with *Malachite,* the final book of her popular THE JEWELS OF TEXAS series. In this emotional story, the wild heart of Malachite, long-lost Jewel brother, is captured by a gentle widow and mother. And keep your hankies out when you read Susan Spencer Paul's *Beguiled,* an endearing Regency about a much-sought-after earl who learns the power of unspeakable love when he's blackmailed into marrying a silent beauty.

What a terrific lineup we have for you this month! Whatever your tastes in reading, you'll be sure to find a romantic journey back to the past between the covers of a Harlequin Historical®.

Sincerely,

Tracy Farrell
Senior Editor

Please address questions and book requests to:
Silhouette Reader Service
U.S.: 3010 Walden Ave., P.O. Box 1325, Buffalo, NY 14269
Canadian: P.O. Box 609, Fort Erie, Ont. L2A 5X3

Claire Delacroix

My Lady's Desire

Harlequin Books

TORONTO • NEW YORK • LONDON
AMSTERDAM • PARIS • SYDNEY • HAMBURG
STOCKHOLM • ATHENS • TOKYO • MILAN
MADRID • WARSAW • BUDAPEST • AUCKLAND

ISBN 0-373-29009-8

MY LADY'S DESIRE

This edition published by arrangement with Harlequin Books S.A.

® and TM are trademarks of the publisher. Trademarks indicated with ® are registered in the United States Patent and Trademark Office, the Canadian Trade Marks Office and in other countries.

Printed in U.S.A.

Books by Claire Delacroix

Harlequin Historicals

*_Romance of the Rose_ #166
Honeyed Lies #209
†_Unicorn Bride_ #223
*_The Sorceress_ #235
*_Roarke's Folly_ #250
†_Pearl Beyond Price_ #264
The Magician's Quest #281
†_Unicorn Vengeance_ #293
My Lady's Champion #326
Enchanted #366
My Lady's Desire #409

*The Rose Trilogy
†Unicorn Series

CLAIRE DELACROIX

A confessed romantic dreamer, Claire Delacroix always wove stories in her mind. While working as a technical writer, she decided to write a book—just for fun—and unwittingly started upon a new career. A year and a half and many rejections later, Claire sold her first book, _Romance of the Rose._ When her second book sold, Claire left her day job to write full-time and never looked back. Many historical romances later, she still thinks she has the best job in the world.

Claire makes her home in Toronto, Canada, with her husband, far too many books and a variety of undisciplined houseplants. She is an avid needleworker and often works out plot tangles while knitting intarsia sweaters. Claire travels as much as possible, rides her bicycle everywhere and cooks with enthusiasm—as long as someone else washes the dishes!

For Karen Kosztolnyik,
who likes her heroes with baggage.

Chapter One

Court of Burgundy—Easter, 1114

Yves stepped into the blessedly private shadows of his silk tent and deliberately ignored the cheers of the crowds. They were chanting his name, but Yves had no intention of returning to the fields again.

Ye gods, but he hated tourneys.

Yves doffed his helmet and ran one hand through his damp hair, letting the exhaustion of the day slide through him. If it had not been by his lord and patron's particular request—and to that man's honor—he would not even have competed this afternoon.

Tournaments, to Yves' mind, were a spectacularly useless waste of time.

He dispassionately examined the tear in the black tunic that protected his skin from his hauberk and hung to his ankles. His only wound of the afternoon looked to be readily reparable.

"God's wounds, my lord, but you showed him!" Yves' squire, Gaston, burst into the tent with characteristic enthusiasm.

The boy was grinning from ear to ear, his excitement mak-

ing him look markedly less than his sixteen summers. Typi-
cally, he was unkempt, his curly hair tousled, his tabard wrinkled and graced with more than one food stain. It was hardly
appropriate for the squire of the count's own marshal—and
the count's only nephew—to appear in such a state.

Would Yves ever make a knight of Gaston? Even after a
year together, everything he told the boy seemed to go in one
ear and directly out the other.

"Language," Yves chided, choosing one issue of many.

The pinkening of Gaston's ears revealed the boy's recollection of past tutelage on the subject. His smile faded as he
took his master's helmet with a gesture that lacked the care
Yves might have preferred.

"It is just an expression," he argued.

Yves arched a brow. "And a blasphemous one." He turned
his attention to the lace of his hauberk, a slight frown crin-
kling his brow. "As we have discussed before."

Gaston sobered, then stepped to his knight's side. His expression had turned defiant, though he was quick to unbuckle
Yves' sword. "All the squires say it," he insisted.

"And if all the squires took to thieving, would you join
their ranks in that, as well?" Yves inquired mildly.

Gaston flicked him a mutinous glance, as though he already
suspected he would lose this argument. "No. That is clearly
wrong."

"Yet the priest at Château Montclair did not teach that
blasphemy was wrong?" There was no anger in Yves' tone
as he referred to Gaston's home estate, for this knight had
learned long ago that emotion had no place in a thinking
man's life.

Gaston's ears burned a fiery red and he could no longer
hold Yves' gaze. "It is not the same," he protested, but there
was no conviction in his tone.

Yves was encouraged to see that the boy at least understood
when his reason had failed a test.

"A knight must be honorable in all he says and does,"

Yves counseled in a low voice. Gaston nodded and laid his master's blade aside with greater care than he usually showed, then straightened to help Yves with his hauberk.

And this without being asked.

Yves hid his relief that the boy's training might finally be showing signs of progress. Only the soft clink of the mail sounded for a few moments as buckles were unfastened and armor unlaced, then Gaston could hold back his words no longer.

"But you were wonderful on the field this day!" he exclaimed, the words bursting forth like water from a broken dam. "Four knights downed in but a twinkling of an eye!" He parried in the air with Yves' sheathed quillon dagger, blithely unaware of his knight's quelling glance.

"Had they not been men of such repute and in such foul temper over their losses, I would not have believed it possible," Gaston continued. His eyes shone with the telling, and he mimicked each grand gesture as he recounted it.

Sadly, it was not just with language that Gaston was careless, or even with equipment. Indeed, the boy did not pay sufficient attention to anything other than fighting itself.

It was clear to the most casual observer that Gaston lived and breathed for the excitement of battle. His knowledge of such feats had fed mightily upon troubadours' tales, those sweeping sagas that oft had little to do with reality.

Yves had begun to fear that the boy cared more for the romance of knighthood than its arduous fact and this account of the day lent weight to his suspicion. Battle was but a small part of a knight's obligation to society, after all.

Perhaps it was time to set matters straight for Gaston.

Yves shed his boots and considered what to do.

The squire, undeterred by his knight's silence, waved his hands in the air as he continued. "The crowd was shouting, the count saluted you, and the countess, the *countess* even cast her sleeve onto the field!"

Gaston sighed with longing while Yves donned a simple

linen shirt, his own heart unstirred by these tributes. "If only I could one day be as effective a warrior!"

"A tournament is a far cry from the truth of battle," Yves said firmly.

Gaston gaped at him, yet again forgetting his tasks. "But how can it be? Tournaments are wonderful!"

Yves flicked an impatient finger toward the pitcher and ewer. Gaston jumped, then hastened to fetch the water he should have already poured. As Yves scrubbed his face, the boy stared impertinently at him.

Yves shook the water out of his hair and eyed the boy's obvious curiosity. "Do you understand nothing of this business?" he asked evenly.

"You fought to show that your skill was the greatest of all."

"I fought at the whim of my lord the count, who planned these tourneys to please his wife and lady fair. It was his will that I, as his marshal, take to the fields, and so I did."

Gaston's eyes glowed. "And you succeeded wondrously!"

"All to the greater glory of my lord and patron."

"And to you."

"To my lord the count alone," Yves corrected sternly. "The skill of the knights in this keep is to *his* credit, not to their own. Humility, after all, is a trait a knight does well to cultivate." Yves dried his face with a length of linen.

Gaston, though, stared at his knight in amazement. "You truly care nothing for the bounty you have won, do you?" He gestured to the field beyond. "You must have gained half a dozen steeds and a chest of gold, not to mention the favor of any number of ladies!"

Yves shrugged. "Steeds and gold, as well as women, come and go, Gaston. The only thing of merit that a man can own is knowledge of who he is. That alone tells him where his place is in this world."

If nothing else, Yves knew both of those things, though neither of them were pretty tales.

The trumpets sounded anew from the field, and the announcement of another contender's name could be heard but not distinguished. The crowd cheered and Gaston, looked longingly toward the tent flap, his toes tapping with his desire to return and watch.

It seemed Yves' lessons would fall on deaf ears this day. He glanced pointedly about the simply appointed tent, but Gaston was too busy straining his ears to notice.

Yves folded his arms across his chest and watched the inattentive boy. If nothing else, the boy had a charm that made it difficult to be overly harsh with him.

But still, he should not forget his tasks.

"Is there wine?" Yves asked finally.

"Oh!" Gaston jumped guiltily. "Yes, my lord." He scampered to fetch vessel and cup, but could not completely restrain himself from glancing at the flap again as the challenger was announced on the field far beyond.

Yves sank onto a simple wooden stool, sipped his wine and despaired of ever having the boy's attention long enough to teach him what he needed to know. Gaston's head snapped up as the crowd roared, and Yves knew this battle was long lost.

"Go," he said quietly.

There was no need to issue the command twice. Gaston was gone in the twinkling of an eye.

Yves shook his head. Had he ever been so young? He sipped his wine, savoring his fleeting privacy as the count and his guests watched another contest. Soon there would be a thousand deeds to be done, but for these few moments, Yves would enjoy the warm gold of the afternoon sunlight, fanning through the stripes of the silken tent.

The wine was robust and lightly spiced with cloves, its rich flavor welcome after the hard labor of the match. Yves flexed his tight muscles and considered the training of the irrepressible Gaston.

Even banning him from listening to the minstrels would

accomplish little, for it seemed the boy had memorized vast tracts of romantic tales. His imagination was boundless and his memory astonishing. There certainly were those—Gaston's dame included—who thought the boy would made a good minstrel himself.

Yet there was a determination about Gaston when he had a blade in his grip that made Yves certain that the count had chosen his nephew's path rightly.

If only Gaston weren't so impetuous.

Yves' thoughts were interrupted by the sound of a throat being cleared portentiously near the tent flap. His head snapped up and he smoothed the linen of his shirt as he stood. Congratulations from the count, no doubt.

"Who comes?" he called.

"Chevalier Yves de Sant-Roux?" demanded a man whose voice was unfamiliar.

"Yes," Yves acknowledged with a frown. "Who calls?"

"The Lord de Tulley!" interjected a second voice, though this impatient one was an unwelcome echo of the past.

Not Tulley!

Yves glared across the tent just as that very lord swept inside. Any ease the wine had brought disappeared immediately. Yves felt pulled as taut as a bowstring as he met a frosty blue gaze he had never forgotten.

The Lord de Tulley was still the same small, wiry man, though the dozen years since their paths had crossed had made him even more wizened than Yves recalled. Tulley's hair was now as white as the driven snow, his face gaunt, the hand gripping his newfound cane gnarled yet determined. His eyes shone like fiery sapphires as he appraised Yves, who felt himself once again an uncertain boy of Gaston's age.

It had been a long time. And their parting had been less than sweet. An anger Yves had not known he nursed flared to life within him and burned with a cold heat. He held the old man's gaze stubbornly, even as he forced himself to maintain his usual impassive expression.

Manipulative old cur.

The men stared at each other in silence for a long moment, each assessing the mark of the passing years upon the other. Tulley's manservant lingered in the shadow of the tent flap.

"You fight well," Tulley acknowledged finally, his words uttered in the same biting manner that Yves recalled. The older man stepped farther into the tent and nodded dismissively to his servant. "Leave us."

The servant made the mistake of hesitating to obey. "But, my lord—"

"Now!" Tulley did not even turn to look before he snapped the command. The man's eyes widened, then he darted from the tent, hastily closing the flap behind him.

And Yves was left alone with a man he had never wanted or expected to meet again. How dare Tulley come here and so casually awaken the ghosts of the past!

But Tulley—as Yves had learned long ago—was a man who would see the world turn to his own advantage alone, regardless of what he had to do to make it do so. Everyone was but a pawn to Tulley, a tool that could be used to bend matters to the old lord's will.

Tulley's cane tapped as he advanced into the tent, his appraising gaze undoubtedly seeing more than most had the opportunity to see in the marshal's eyes. But Yves did not care whether Tulley saw the embers of his fury. He needed nothing from him now—for when he had, Tulley had failed to provide it.

And a woman with a rare enthusiasm for life had paid the price.

Yves would never forgive Tulley for that.

"Simple accommodations," the lord pronounced. He poked the second stool in the tent with his cane as though assessing its strength. It must have met with some approval, for he harrumphed, then lowered himself to sit.

Tulley folded his hands across the top of his cane as his

bright gaze locked with Yves' once more. "I approve of that."

Feigning indifference to this visit, Yves shrugged and sat again himself. "I cannot see that your approval is of particular import," he said, knowing full well that his words were bold.

The old lord stiffened, and those blue eyes blazed. "I had forgotten your impertinence," Tulley snapped. "Though I suppose it was not overly foolish to imagine the count might have set you straight."

"Why are you here?" Yves asked silkily.

Tulley took a deep breath and his gaze narrowed shrewdly. "I want to hire you, to recapture a besieged property of mine."

Yves leaned back, sipped his wine and leisurely regarded the older man, now come to seek a favor from *him*. He would not have been human if he had not savored this moment just a little.

Tulley needed him.

The only question was how quickly to refuse.

Then Yves' heart skipped a beat. Recapture a property? Surely Tulley would not ask him to do the unthinkable? Yves would never return to Sayerne, *never*, not under any circumstance!

"Which property?" he asked, as calmly as he could manage given the hammering of his heart.

Tulley arched a white brow. "Perricault. My most easterly holding and one with wondrously rich hunting grounds."

The wave of relief that coursed through Yves was frightening in its intensity. What had happened to his self-control? Clearly the awakening of that old wound and his exhaustion were combining to make him uncharacteristically emotional.

Yves took a deep breath. "Besieged by whom?" he asked, as though he might be considering the offer.

Tulley's features contorted with rage. "Philip de Trevaine!"

Yves shrugged. "I know nothing of him."

"I know too much of him!" Tulley pounded his cane on the floor of the tent with agitation. "I made that worthless upstart what he is this day! It was *I* who quietly ensured he won the estate of Trevaine, and he rewards my aid with the theft of a prize holding!"

Tulley growled under his breath before he found the words to express his outrage further. "And there is no sign that he will be contented with Perricault! No sign at all! Philip must be stopped!" He jabbed a finger through the air toward Yves. "And you—*you* will be the one to strike the fatal blow."

"My blade is sworn to the count," Yves said mildly. "It is not for me to decide to leave."

Tulley waved off that objection. "The count has agreed to release you into my service."

Yves' anger rolled to the fore once more and his tone sharpened. "You spoke to the count of this before addressing me?"

Tulley shrugged, though his gaze was unnervingly steady. "It was an objection you were bound to make."

Yves forced himself to hide his feelings and heard only an edge of annoyance leak into his words when he continued. "I know nothing of this Philip de Trevaine beyond your own accusations. Surely you do not expect me to engage an unknown foe?"

Tulley's lips quirked. "Must you have made the acquaintance of one you would kill?"

Yves was not amused and he spoke curtly. "No. But I must know the strength of his forces, the number of blades pledged to him, the quality and quantity of his military alliances. Similarly, I must know of your own intent—do you plan that I should ride alone against an invading army of unknown size?" Yves scoffed deliberately. "Perhaps I am to be an assassin, by your plan, instead of a warrior."

Tulley's lips thinned. "Your mockery makes little of a great deal. This man is dangerous. Naturally, I will support

you fully with my own forces, as well as those ousted from
Perricault itself.''

Yves spread his hands. "Yet still I have no idea of the
comparative forces. It seems that you would appoint me to a
fool's errand.''

"Insolent *bastard!*" Tulley pushed himself to his feet with
the aid of his cane, but the charge was too familiar to hold
any sting for Yves. "I grant you an opportunity to aid one
of the most powerful lords in all of Christendom—myself!
You would be a fool to abandon this opportunity to make
more of your life!''

Yves, unimpressed, stretched out his legs and took another
sip of his wine. Tulley's gaze dropped to the cup before meeting Yves' again, and for once, Yves enjoyed that Gaston had
been absent and thence had not offered the guest a cup.

Yves cleared his throat. "I fail to see what you might offer
for this service that I might be inspired to foolishly risk my
hide.''

"Gold!" Tulley declared, his fists clenching on his cane.
"I shall pay you in *gold.* You name the price.''

"I have no use for gold." Yves gestured to his tent and
shrugged politely. "My needs are simple, as you noted, and
already well met.''

"Land, then!" Tulley leaned forward with gleaming eyes.
"I will grant you a property within Tulley, if you are successful. That is more than you will gain from the count's
hand.''

"A knight has need of land only if he desires the obligation
of wife and family," Yves countered calmly. "I am content
with my circumstance as it stands.''

The men's gazes locked once more and silence stretched
taut within the silken enclosure. It appeared that Tulley
ground his teeth silently as he glared at Yves, but the knight
remained unmoved.

"I have one thing that I know you will want," Tulley
growled finally.

"I do not believe that."

The older man's white brow arched high. "But you will."

Tulley leaned back to eye the roof of the tent, his expression curiously reflective. "You see, once upon a time, your father was beholden to me. The circumstances do not matter particularly, but suffice it to say that Jerome de Sayerne had to placate me and win my confidence in him anew to secure his hold over his hereditary estate of Sayerne."

Tulley smiled in reminiscence over that day of power, and Yves knew the old lord had savored that moment. "I could have ripped the estate out from beneath him that time," he mused, "and the miserable wretch knew it all too well."

Yves' throat constricted with this unwelcome reminder of the past and all its emotional turmoil. He had refused to think about his father since his death and was not going to begin thinking about him now.

Tulley's bright gaze landed on Yves once more. "Jerome put quill to parchment and concocted a declaration, signed before witnesses and dutifully stamped with his seal." The old lord paused for effect.

"Indeed?" Yves fought to sound indifferent and heard himself fail.

The old man's white brows rose high at the sound of curiosity in Yves' voice. "It is a declaration," he whispered with evident delight, and Yves hated how he strained for the words "that one bastard Yves, born in the year 1086 at Château Sayerne, is indeed the blood of Lord Jerome de Sayerne."

Yves' heart skipped a beat.

Tulley's gaze did not waver, though a tiny smile played on his lips.

Yves loathed how he was tempted, hated that the manipulative old lord had guessed the one thing that eluded him despite his success. Illegitimacy was not a taint a man could erase by virtue of his own deeds, regardless of how well he fared in this life.

And Tulley, curse him, offered a respite.

Tulley's voice dropped conspiratorially. "It further declares that this child's mother, one Eglantine de Chalome, should be recognized as the second wife of Jerome de Sayerne, for he took her as his common wife."

Wife? Yves had known no such thing and doubted its truth. But Jerome had pledged to it.

Respectability could be his! Yves' heart stopped cold and he could not summon a word to his lips. The promise of Tulley's document dangled before him like a carrot before a sullen mule.

Tulley leaned closer to press his case. "This document makes you legitimate," he whispered. "This document wipes the taint of bastardy from your hide, Yves de Sant-Roux. Meet my price and it can be yours."

Legitimacy! There was something Yves had never thought he might call his own. No longer would those highborn guests of the count's have reason to sneer at the birthright of the count's marshal.

The count consistently declared that he had selected Yves by that knight's skill alone, but Yves knew that the disapproval must trouble his patron. This document would eliminate any shame Yves unintentionally brought upon the man who had granted him so much.

Tulley straightened, a smile playing over his lips with the certainty that he had successfully cornered his prey. "All you have to do," he continued mildly, "is retrieve Perricault from Philip de Trevaine."

Suddenly, Yves realized that Tulley had had this document for the better part of his own life and not revealed its presence until now. Tulley had been content to leave Yves twisting in the winds of fortune until it suited the old cur to reveal what he had.

Wily Tulley, after all, only played to his own advantage.

Who could say what other scheme Tulley had in mind?

Would the old lord continue to change the conditions necessary to win the document?

And what precisely did the document say? Was it even genuine? For all Yves knew, Tulley might have another document hidden away that repudiated this one!

One thing was clear—once Yves stepped into the Lord de Tulley's web, he would never break free of the old man's will. The tangle would grow tighter and tighter, leaving him as soundly trussed as a fly who ventured unwittingly into a spider's web.

No, Yves would not venture back into the quagmire of the past simply to serve Tulley's ends. This mission smacked of whimsy, of the decisions made by men on virtue of emotion alone, decisions oft doomed to failure. Yves was a knight possessed of too much good sense to take Tulley's bait.

Yves set the cup of wine aside deliberately and rose slowly to his feet. Tulley's eyes were bright with the certainty of victory and his smile broadened.

"I refuse your offer."

Tulley's jaw dropped and he gaped at Yves. "What is this?"

Yves folded his arms across his chest. "I respectfully decline."

"But, but…" Tulley sputtered in outrage. "You *must* want legitimacy! What thinking man would not?"

Yves shook his head. "Not at your price."

"This is madness!" Tulley flung out his hands. "I had understood that you were a man with your wits about you!"

"All the more reason not to accept a fool's errand for uncertain reward."

Tulley glared at Yves, his breathing labored and the first hint of color staining his pallid cheeks. He straightened and jabbed the cane through the air that it very nearly hit Yves in the chest.

"Insolent bastard! I should have expected no less." Tul-

ley's eyes narrowed and his voice was no more than a rasp.
"I shall see that you regret this."

He waited, but Yves unflinchingly returned his stare. What
could the old lord do to him? Yves was outside the realm of
Tulley's power. Yves caught a fleeting glimpse of the realization of that truth in Tulley's bright eyes.

Then, with a snort of dissatisfaction, the old man spun and
hobbled from the tent. His voice raised imperially outside,
sounding much more petulant than it had earlier.

"Didier! We leave this place with all haste! Didier! Get
yourself to my side *now!*"

Long after Yves had calmly topped up his cup of wine and
returned to his stool, the ghost of Annelise lingered in his
mind. Silence filled the tent, the sounds from the field so
muted they seemed to carry from another world. Yves tried
again to push the past into the locked corner of his mind
where it belonged.

Annelise was dead. Sayerne had fallen to his elder brother
Quinn's hand and was undoubtedly managed with the same
cruelty as his father had shown. Was not Quinn said to be
the very echo of Jerome?

But none of that had anything to do with Yves' life any
longer. His part was over and done, for better or for worse.

From the fields came the sound of the crowds cheering with
renewed vigor. Someone had won a contest, evidently, but
Yves did not care. He swirled the wine in the cup and stared
into its scented depths.

The past had been successfully sent away from his door,
he told himself, and would never return. All would continue
in his life as it had these past years. Yves would once more
be the man within the count's hall who had no history, and
gratefully so.

But the image of his last sight of his sister would not fade
away as easily as it had before.

The sunlight had darkened to a deep gold when a rustle

came at the tent flap. Yves did not look up. "See that I am not disturbed, Gaston," he said, running a tired hand over his brow. A good sleep would see Annelise's ghost banished once more. "I have need of some sleep."

"It is too late for that."

Yves' head snapped up at the sound of a woman's voice.

The lady hesitated on the threshold, a shadow against the shadows, her resolute words echoing in Yves' ears. She was cloaked so that her features were hidden, the brown, homespun wool covering her from head to toe. She was tall, but beyond that and the firm resonance of her words, Yves could discern little about her.

He guessed by her accent and distinct manner of speech that she was nobly born. And she stood straight, like a princess.

That such a woman came here was odd, indeed, but the knight merely waited for explanation. As Yves stared at her, the lady lowered her hood, and he looked into the determination shining in her violet eyes.

She was a woman tending more to plain than beautiful, he judged, with her dark hair fastened tightly back in a way that was less than flattering. Her features were balanced and pleasant enough, but unadorned by carmine and kohl.

Those eyes, though, snapped with an intelligence that could not be denied.

"My name is Gabrielle de Perricault," she said. Her voice was slightly melodic, her tone firm, yet pitched low so that none might readily overhear.

Yves stared back at her, intrigued. He had never met a woman who gave no quarter to feminine charms and their powers over men. Was this one of the women that Gaston was certain were ready to cast their favors his way?

Surely not!

The lady's lips thinned before she continued, her blunt speech surprising him yet further. "I have need to hire a

knight and leader of men." Her gaze did not swerve from
Yves' own. "I hear tell that you are the best."

Yves arched a brow, unwilling to give any evidence of his
interest. "You make your choice based on rumor?"

Had she been a man, he would have called her response a
snort. Certainly her gaze sharpened. "Rumor may have
brought me to these tournaments," she retorted. "But it is
my own assessment that brings me to this tent."

"You watched the tournaments?"

"Of course. You show both strength and cunning on the
field." The lady arched a brow in turn. "It is a combination
most lethal, as was well proven on this day."

That revealed such clear thinking that Yves could not argue
with her. Indeed, he was quite astonished to make the acquaintance of a woman possessed of a sensible mind. It was
so far beyond his experience at the count's court, where
women chattered of clothing and embroidery and children's
smiles, that he momentarily did not know what to say.

The pair stared at each other for a long moment. The crowd
roared in the distance once more and she started, glancing
back over her shoulder with unexpected nervousness.

"None must see me here," she murmured.

Yves responded before he thought. "I will tell none of your
visit," he assured her.

The small smile of appreciation that curved the lady's ripe
lips caught at Yves' heart in a way he could not explain. How
could he have imagined, even for a moment, that she was
plain?

"I heard you were a man of honor, as well," Gabrielle
said, her low voice pleasant upon his ears. "How agreeable
to find that true."

Yves felt his pulse quicken, but frowned into his cup to
hide his response. "And why would you have need of a
knight?"

The lady's expression turned grim. "To reclaim my home,
the estate of Perricault, from one Philip de Trevaine."

Perricault again! Belatedly Yves recalled the lady's name and cursed himself for not paying more heed to her words than her smile. What had possessed him this day?

Pretty compliments to his abilities were well and good, but Yves had to consider the practicalities of Perricault's situation. Still, he was not inclined to take a challenge against an unknown foe.

"You should know that I have just declined the offer of the Lord de Tulley to regain your lost holding," he said, surprised to hear the gentleness of his own tone.

The woman lifted her chin proudly. There was a gracious strength about her that could stir a man's blood.

Yves' own blood was stirring, after all.

"I have something to grant that Tulley cannot," she said firmly. Yves thought he saw her inhale quickly, but knew he must have erred, for such a possessed creature could not have been uncertain of anything she meant to do.

"I offer myself to you in exchange for your winning back Perricault."

Yves blinked, but the lady stubbornly held his gaze, challenge bright in those violet eyes.

She was right. Tulley had not made an offer nearly as tempting.

But would Yves be just as much of a fool to accept?

Chapter Two

Gabrielle eyed the knight opposite her and could not imagine what was in his mind. It was disconcerting, to say the least, that he was so good at hiding his response to her brazen offer.

It seemed he had not even blinked.

Did women make such offers to him all the time? That he was such a handsome man did nothing to bolster her confidence. The legendary Chevalier Yves de Sant-Roux, champion and marshal of the Count of Burgundy, was reputed to be both uncommonly bold and uncommonly good-looking.

Gabrielle had thought herself braced for the truth, but rumor had fallen far short of reality. The knight was blond of hair and square of jaw; he was tall and broad of shoulder. There was a vertical cleft notched into his chin and his lips were drawn in a decisive line befitting one who made his way with his blade. The hands that cradled his cup were large and strong, yet toyed with the cup with a gentle dexterity.

That might have been troubling enough, had he not been half-disrobed. His linen shirt hung open to reveal a tangle of tawny hair on his chest, the garment clinging damply and lovingly to each muscle of his shoulders and arms. His hair was wet and disorderly, as though he had dunked his head and shoved his fingers through its thickness.

Gabrielle's task would have been much easier if the man had been mailed and armored for battle.

Yes, and helmeted as well, so that she could not see the calm consideration in those amber eyes. Or their steady perusal of her inadequate store of charms. Her father's long ago condemnation echoed in Gabrielle's ears though she fought against it.

The fading afternoon sunlight painted the interior of the tent in alternating stripes of light and dark gold, echoing the pattern woven into the silken walls. Gabrielle could smell the knight's skin, the cloves in the spiced wine he drank and the dampness of the earth beneath the tent's floor. There was also a whiff of leather and horse and wet steel, achingly masculine scents each and every one.

And each and every one was a reminder of the void in her life. Gabrielle felt more aware of her widowed state—indeed, more aware of her femininity—than she ever had before.

Had there been a flicker of something in the knight's eyes when she made her bold offer? Surely an estate was what most men wanted to call their own?

But there was something about this man unlike the men Gabrielle had known. He had been so quick to pledge his silence, and for nothing in return.

And he was so still.

Fear of failure made Gabrielle's palms damp. It was not like her to be so bold, she who had always been the obedient daughter, and later, the dutiful wife.

At least, until the most precious thing in her life had been stolen away. And that loss revealed a determination within her that she had not known she possessed.

A determination that had brought her all the way here.

But that determination, however demanding, did not make any of the challenges she faced, such as winning the support of this knight, any easier. Gabrielle's words fell from her lips in uncharacteristic haste, propelled by the need to convince this man to aid her.

"Should you win back Perricault, I will wed you. That will make you Lord de Perricault."

The knight shrugged. "I care nothing for lands and titles."

No! His indifference to something she had expected him to hold dear enraged Gabrielle, especially as it was all she had to offer. He must accept the terms!

For if he refused, what else could she do?

"How can you not care to hold a prosperous estate?" She stalked across the tent and flung out her hands, taking care to keep her voice low. "Surely you have some ambition?"

A slight smile flickered over the knight's lips, and Gabrielle burned with the knowledge that she was providing his amusement. Heaven knew such a handsome man would look to her for nothing else.

"As I told the Lord de Tulley just moments past, I am content with my lot," he said, his voice a pleasant rumble.

Then his gaze flicked away and he pushed himself to his feet, bending to fetch another cup. Gabrielle caught herself noting the strength of his legs, artfully revealed by his chausses when he bent, before she tore her gaze away.

What was in her mind?

"Wine?" he asked, and Gabrielle glanced back to find him offering cup and flagon. His scrutiny was so searching that she felt her every emotion was laid out for his perusal.

And entertainment.

Cheeks burning with self-consciousness, Gabrielle took a deep breath and nodded. "A cup of wine would be welcome indeed." Anything to make her forget the worries that stalked her every step.

He poured the ruby red wine into the brass cup with an easy grace, then offered it to Gabrielle. Their fingers brushed inadvertently in the transaction, the heat of his hand making Gabrielle step backward.

Honestly, how many knights had she faced, even since Michel's death? It must be the import of this request that jangled her confidence and made her aware of so many minute details.

Gabrielle sipped her wine quickly before speaking again. "Surely any knight longs to have a cadre of trained men at his command. If you fear the fate of idle comfort, Perricault offers none such. Being as it is on the periphery of Tulley and no small prize in itself, the lands are oft contested."

The quirk of his lips was so fleeting that Gabrielle barely noted its presence before it was gone. "I do not fear boredom," he said, his gaze locking steadily with her own. "It is only that material gains hold no allure for me."

That could not be true! All the same, Gabrielle would provide him with a more noble reason, if he needed it as an excuse.

"Then fight for the justice of it!" She stepped forward once more to argue her point. "Philip de Trevaine attacked unprovoked and without warning." Bitterness echoed in her tone. "No attempt was made to negotiate. No opportunity for peaceful surrender was made."

"It is oft thus with war," the knight argued carefully. But had his tone turned more considering? Certainly his eyes had narrowed and his gaze was fixed upon her.

Was it possible that Gabrielle was persuading him?

"No, this war was uncommonly cruel. I have seen war, but never like this." She recalled that fateful night, and her voice fell to a flat monotone. "They came in the night, slaughtered all in their path and in the village outside the walls so that a cry of warning could not be raised."

Gabrielle looked to the knight, to find his gaze bright. "We found women and children, unarmed and cut down as they rose from their beds at the sound. We found men, attacked from the rear and granted no chance to defend themselves."

"And the Lord de Perricault?"

"My husband was cut down from behind." Gabrielle's voice was hostile with the injustice of it. She had not loved Michel, but that had nothing to do with his having the opportunity to honorably defend his holding. He had been a good man, a decent husband, and there had been honesty between them.

It was all a woman could reasonably expect from marriage, after all.

"He never saw his murderer," she admitted tonelessly, "nor did he have a chance to defend himself."

The knight's blond brow arched skyward. "Then you have no army with which to return the attack."

"There is more to this than the count of men left standing!" Gabrielle pounded her fist into her palm. "What of the injustice?"

"Injustice will not be served by sending more men to their deaths," the knight countered calmly.

Gabrielle hated that he was right.

"I have a dozen men-at-arms and two knights loyal to my house," she declared proudly. "They have seen the worst Philip has done, and still hold fast." She looked the knight right in the eye and jabbed a finger through the air toward him. "Such commitment cannot be bought at any price!"

"That is true enough," he acknowledged. "But what of this Philip's forces?"

Gabrielle had to drop her gaze, for this news would not win her any favor with this obviously practical knight. "He bolsters his forces nearly daily. Our last count is fifteen knights at Perricault."

She sighed, then swallowed, knowing she would have to be honest with him. "The men-at-arms are too numerous to count accurately."

"Then you have spies abroad?"

"Yes."

Silence fell again in the tent. Gabrielle hoped with all her heart that despite the odds, this knight would take on her cause. She had made the best argument she could.

When the silence drew long between them, she knew she would have to appeal to his pride, as well. It disappointed her to find him so obviously like other men, after all, but Gabrielle made the argument that would be telling.

"I understand the odds are not as favorable as a lesser knight, or one of less experience than you, might like," she began, lifting her chin to meet his gaze once more. "And the task will not be an easy one. I have restrained my men from attack for want of a strategic plan and an effective leader."

And that under protest, though Gabrielle did not admit as much. It chafed her to know that she must trust another to regain all she held dear.

Since Michel's death, Gabrielle had come into her own in a way she might never otherwise have anticipated. The reins of leadership fit readily in her grip—yet the knights of Perricault were reluctant to follow a woman. Though Gabrielle had become a woman well used to resolving matters herself—with considerable success—the respect such behavior usually commanded had been denied to her.

Simply because she was a woman. That the stakes were so terribly high only made the insult worse.

But Gabrielle gritted her teeth and continued. "I have been advised that if any could win Perricault back, it would be you."

The knight said nothing.

Why did he not agree?

Or was he of the ilk of man who liked to see a woman beg? Curse him! Could the man not see what this appeal cost her?

But she truly had no choice.

Gabrielle took a deep breath and looked up once more, refusing to be daunted by the knight's steady and dispassionate gaze. "I beg you, Chevalier, grant my offer the consideration it deserves before making your decision. Perricault is not a poor prize."

She waited, but he still said nothing. The knight merely peered into his chalice, a slight frown marring his brows.

Had he forgotten her?

This interview was not progressing exactly as Gabrielle had expected. Indeed, he was supposed to leap at the prize of Perricault.

But this man had not.

Perhaps he needed time to consider the matter. The silence pressed so against her ears that she could not stand it. Gabrielle set down her cup and stepped toward the flap.

"If you could decide this evening, I should appreciate knowing which way the wind blows." She made to step out into the afternoon, but his low words brought her to a halt.

"There is no need to wait. My decision is made."

Gabrielle spun to face the knight, her heart in her throat, her fingers clenched tightly on the silken tent. To her consternation, she could not discern his conclusion from his expression.

Then the knight shook his head minutely and Gabrielle knew.

No! Her heart plummeted to her toes, even before his words found voice.

"I decline your generous offer, just as I declined the Lord de Tulley's offer to take this cause."

Rage erupted within Gabrielle, and she closed the space between them before she paused to think. "You cannot do this! I must have your aid in this matter!"

"You do not have it," he countered calmly.

"Then I shall lead my troops upon Perricault myself!" Gabrielle propped her hands on her hips, content to see the knight's eyes narrow slightly.

At least it was some sign that he had heard her.

"You cannot do that," he argued coolly. "You cannot have the experience to plan a successful strategy."

"I am sick to death of that argument, and believe me, Chevalier, I have heard it more oft than was welcome!" Gabrielle retorted. "There is no reason why I should not lead an attack, for I know that keep better than all others!"

The knight, though, shook his head, evidently unconvinced.

"Men will not follow you, or if they do, you will not be able to rely upon them. Should you proceed thus, my lady, you will only bring about your own demise and that of your followers."

"I shall *have* to do so, despite your arguments, and do so without delay!" Gabrielle retorted, her patience with men and their reasoning completely expired. She had tried to solve this problem without letting her emotions muddle matters, but this pushed her too far. "With or without your aid, I will save my son and I will do it soon!"

The knight pursed his lips and folded his arms across his chest as he scrutinized her. His eyes blazed like molten gold and Gabrielle knew she had said something that had securely snared his attention.

"Your son?" he echoed.

"Yes, my *son!*" Once uncorked, it seemed Gabrielle's passion could not be contained. "My son was captured by that miserable, scheming Philip and I will not tolerate his being used as a pawn in Philip's plans. He is just a child!" Gabrielle wagged a finger at the knight before her. "One way or the other, I shall see Thomas free, even if it is the last thing I do!"

The knight frowned, looked away, then impaled Gabrielle with a bright glance. "Is he your only child?"

"Yes! Yes, he is!"

To her own dismay, Gabrielle began to cry. Hers was not the delicate weeping of a refined woman, but the manner of crying that comes from the heart and leaves a woman looking her ravaged worst.

"He is only six summers of age!" she blurted out, without knowing why she confided this particular fact. "He will not understand what is happening!"

To Gabrielle's relief, the knight did not rush forward to console her or touch her with a familiarity undeserved. He simply stood back and let her cry.

And watched, a concerned frown marring his brow. To her

astonishment, his expression had softened slightly. Their
gazes locked and held for a breathless moment, then the
knight stepped closer and offered her a linen handkerchief.
Gabrielle gracelessly blew her nose and mopped up her tears
as he stood just a step away and watched her avidly.

"How can you risk your own life?" he asked with low
urgency. "Should you perish and your son survive, he will
be alone."

Gabrielle's chin shot up. She had not thought of that.

The unexpected pain glowing in the knight's amber eyes
stole her breath away. Gabrielle stared at him for a long moment before she could summon a word of explanation to her
lips.

He was right. If Thomas lost both his parents as a result
of her deeds, Gabrielle would be tormented by that for all
eternity.

"But I cannot leave him in such danger," she whispered,
and her telltale tears threatened to spill forth once more at the
very thought. "And none will aid me."

"You cannot risk the only parent remaining in your son's
life," the knight argued with quiet resolve.

Gabrielle turned away, torn by his certainty that she would
perish trying to retrieve Thomas herself.

But what else could she do?

"I have to try," she whispered brokenly. "I have to try to
help my son." Gabrielle looked back to the knight and was
snared anew by the intensity of his gaze. She took a deep
breath and squared her shoulders. "I can only hope your pre-
diction of my certain failure proves wrong."

The knight's lips tightened, but he did not speak. Gabrielle
inclined her head slightly and lifted her hood once more. "I
thank you for your time, Chevalier," she said quietly, and
left.

Gabrielle stepped out of the tent and took a deep breath of
the spring air. It was comparatively quiet here among the
tents, with all the other guests and their staff enthusiastically

cheering the competition on the tourney field. She forced herself to note the new grass pushing through the earth, the few flowers making their appearance after the winter.

Spring was a time for rebirth and renewal, after all. Easter was a time for faith, and her faith had sustained her thus far. It would see this matter through. Gabrielle had to believe that she could accomplish the impossible or she would have no chance of success.

"Wait!"

Gabrielle glanced back, not at all certain she wanted to hear whatever the knight might say. He stood framed by the tent flap he held open, his features painted golden by the rays of the sinking sun, and she was amazed again that a man could be so finely wrought.

And so different from the men she had known. Who would have guessed a knight would have declined the prize of Perricault?

"My lady," he said quietly, "I will accept your offer."

Gabrielle stared, stunned by the change in his decision. That hint of a smile tugged at the corner of the knight's mouth again and her heart began to pound loudly.

Surely he did not jest?

Surely he could not be concerned for her welfare? Certainly, the way he looked at her made her blood heat, made her feel achingly aware of the fact that she was a woman and he a man.

"For the sake of your son," he added.

The words hit Gabrielle like a douse of ice water.

It was an unwelcome reminder, particularly at this moment when she felt so vulnerable. Gabrielle knew full well that she was not the kind of woman for whom men risked their lives in tournament, nor for whom troubadours composed their odes. To be told so to her face was the last thing she needed on this day.

The knight's words were a reminder that all men looked to their own advantage alone. Yves de Sant-Roux wanted Per-

ricault, just as Gabrielle had guessed he would and despite
any coy games he played.

She was a fool to feel any disappointment that matters had
resolved themselves precisely as she had expected them to
do.

Gabrielle lifted her chin and stared back at the knight, determined not to let him glimpse how his words had stung. If
he wanted Perricault alone, then that was what he would stand
to win.

And that alone.

"Then, Chevalier, you should have no difficulties with a
minor condition, made purely for the sake of my son."

The knight sobered immediately. "Which is?"

"That our match be one made in name alone," Gabrielle
stipulated, suddenly having an idea of how to remove the
apparent whimsy of her request. "I would not have my son's
suzerainty over Perricault meet with challenge one day by a
younger sibling."

The knight's lips set and Gabrielle enjoyed the possibility
that he was displeased that she would not welcome him to
her bed. "It would be a marriage most unnatural," he commented, and Gabrielle's ire rose.

Trust a man to think no further than his own pleasure!

It was better, Gabrielle told herself savagely, that matters
were clear between them from the outset. This was a match
she would enter with eyes wide open to the truth. It was better
that she understood him to be no different from any of the
others.

"I will care nothing for your indiscretions," she declared,
hearing an unexpected bite in her tone. "My sole desire is to
have my son returned to my side and his estate regained.
Should you keep that estate in good trust for him, I shall be
well pleased by our match, be it *natural* or no."

The knight surveyed her silently for a long moment, and
Gabrielle realized that she would have to grow accustomed
to such calm consideration if she were to live with the man.

Then he stuck out his right hand to her. "We have an agreement, my lady."

She stared at his hand, uncertain how to proceed. Certainly, no man had ever cemented an agreement with her in such a way, or even with another woman, in her experience. Did he treat her as a partner in this task?

Or did he mock her?

But nothing could be discerned in his stony expression. And he stood, waiting for her to respond.

Reluctantly, for she was uncertain of his intent, Gabrielle slid her hand into his.

The knight's fingers closed securely over her own, with no jest or mockery reflected in his eyes. Gabrielle's hand was lost within the breadth of his warm palm and her traitorous heart skipped a beat beneath his steady perusal.

"Rest assured that I have no more interest in emotional entanglements than you," he confided, the deep rumble of his voice launching a tingle over Gabrielle's flesh.

Oh, she had been alone overlong, that much was certain.

"Know also, my lady, that I understand the problems garnered by a man populating an estate with his bastards. I never have and never will stoop to such behavior myself."

Gabrielle stared up at him, secretly amazed by this concession. Truly he would deny his own pleasure, to ensure the suzerainty of a child who was not his own? Had she heard aright?

But the knight's eyes were filled with a certainty that could not be denied. Gabrielle's mind worked furiously, but she could find no reasonable explanation beyond the highly unlikely one he had given her.

What manner of man was this knight?

Gabrielle realized belatedly that he still held her hand captive and she forced a laugh. "You shake my hand as though we were knights of equal."

A half smile crept over his lips as slowly as the dawn, and Gabrielle's heart skipped a beat at the sight. "You make an

argument, my lady, as compellingly as any man I have met."
He gave her fingers a minute squeeze. "This gesture seems
only fitting, given the circumstance."

Gabrielle, not often at a loss for words, did not know what
to say to that. She was not usually treated to the full impact
of a man's charm, much less a man as handsome as Yves de
Sant-Roux.

She hastily extricated her hand, resisting the impulse to
wipe off the seductive warmth of his touch. "The knight who
has been longest with my household has accompanied me
here," she said in her most purposeful tone. "I suppose you
should meet with him."

"Certainly." Those blond brows pulled together thought-
fully. "And I must confirm the count's agreement to my decision."

Gabrielle's expression must have revealed that she had not
considered this angle, for the knight immediately shook his
head. "There is nothing to fear, my lady. Evidently, the Lord
de Tulley has already made a case for my departure on this
very mission."

"Tulley!" Gabrielle sneered before she could help herself.
"That wily creature seeks only his own advantage!"

The knight chuckled, and she realized too late the foolishness of so clearly stating her opinion.

"Of course, he is a very skilled overlord..." Gabrielle
added quickly, hating how accustomed she had become to
being among those who thought similarly. How could she
have been so careless with her speech?

The knight silenced Gabrielle's explanation with a wave of
one strong hand, and his eyes twinkled for the barest instant.
"I harbor no fondness for your overlord," he confided, set-
ting her fears to rest again with an ease unexpected.

Their gazes clung for an electric moment of mutual understanding. Gabrielle realized that she now shared more than
one secret with this man, for none could know that she had
hired his services lest Philip hear tell of it.

"It would be best if none knew of our arrangement," she suggested softly.

The knight nodded in immediate agreement. "Yes." He folded his arms across his chest and held her gaze with disconcerting determination. "You might consider addressing me by my first name."

Gabrielle licked her lips, quickly discerning the direction of his thoughts. "That others might think something already is afoot between us and not be surprised if we wed upon regaining Perricault," she guessed.

He nodded again, a glint of approval in his eyes that made her heart warm. "Precisely, my lady."

Gabrielle struggled to quell her dissatisfaction with such mechanical planning, knowing it was beyond reason under the circumstances. She had wanted a strategist, after all, and should not have been surprised to find that this man reduced even the issue of marriage to a series of tactical moves.

All the same, she did not like it.

Which made no sense at all, for Gabrielle knew that marriage was not the pairing of two hearts of which the troubadours sang. Marriage was an arrangement made for mutual gain. And here, the gain for each party was clear as crystal.

Gabrielle knew she should have found this honesty reassuring, but oddly enough, she did not.

Clearly, being so far from Thomas was addling her wits.

She shook her head and summoned a pert smile. "I agree, Yves." His name clung to her lips in a most disconcerting manner, but Gabrielle forced herself to continue in the same confidential manner. "Shall we meet later?"

"After the evening meal." His tone was matter-of-fact. "I shall seek you in the hall, meet your knight, then between us, we can find a place to talk."

We. Gabrielle's heart sang with the possibility of being included in his planning, then she chastised herself.

The knight—*Yves*—was obviously a man who calculated with reason alone. He would want to know all that she knew, all that she had seen, all the recollections she could share of the attack. Then he would cast her out of the process of planning, assuming, as men always did, that a mere woman had nothing to add.

He was no different from the rest.

"Fine," she said, hoping no vestige of her disappointment showed. "I shall see you there."

Yves frowned quickly, as though he might say something else, but Gabrielle was more than ready for this troubling encounter to end. She had not planned to cry—weeping was a tool for weak women to win their way, after all—and she had not expected to be moved by this steadfast knight.

At least the meeting had ended the way she had expected, and doubtless matters would continue precisely as planned.

Gabrielle spun away, took a deep breath and strode back to the festivities, well aware of the weight of the knight's gaze resting upon her.

No doubt the next time she and Yves met, she would be better prepared to deal with him. Indeed, she would not have been surprised to find that his allure diminished markedly with further acquaintance.

At least, she sincerely hoped that it did.

Yves could not stop thinking about the boy.

He paced the width of his tent over and over again, sipping his wine, unable to shake the image of Lady Gabrielle fretting over the fate of her son. Evening fell, its inky shadows claiming the corners of the tent, yet still Yves paced and did not light the lamp.

Gabrielle de Perricault's appeal for her son had struck a powerful chord within Yves, probably the only one that could have induced him to accept this mission. A young boy, lost to his mother and played as a pawn in a game over property, was a tale that hit too close to home for Yves.

All the same, he did not like that he had been powerless to refuse Gabrielle once he knew of Thomas' plight.

Reason had succumbed to passion, for the first time in his recollection. Yves grimaced and set the wine aside.

It was Tulley's fault.

The first bell for the evening meal chimed, and Yves finally noticed the lateness of the hour. With dismay, he realized that he had paced and thought away the time when he should have been making arrangements with the count.

How unlike the methodical knight he knew himself to be! "Gaston!"

Yves whistled and called again, but his squire had evidently found other pleasures to pursue beyond his assigned labor. Though Yves strained his ears, he heard no running footsteps. Resigned to seeing to his own needs—again—he dressed with impatient gestures.

Gaston would not miss a meal, that much Yves knew without doubt. He stepped out of his tent and whistled for him once more, even knowing the futility of the gesture.

The mauve streak lingering in the western sky after the sunset made Yves suddenly recall the shadows in Lady Gabrielle's violet eyes. He thought of the vulnerability that had stolen over her features when she spoke of her son.

Indeed, young Thomas had something in his life more precious than all the gold in Perricault. He had his mother's love and protection.

Yves had had no such thing.

How different might his own life have been if he had had someone who cared for his welfare as passionately as this lady did for her son? It was true that Yves had made his way well enough, but how much easier it would have been to have had someone to turn to when his fortunes looked dark.

What would he have given to have even seen the visage of his own dame? All he knew of that lady was her name, Eglantine.

As Yves stared at the sky, lost in his thoughts, a longing awakened in his heart for something as alien to him as the most exotic eastern perfume.

Yet the Lady Gabrielle had made it clear that any affection in her heart was not for Yves. Theirs would be a match—if indeed, they did retrieve Thomas and Perricault—made in name alone. Yves felt a surge of irritation at Gabrielle's demand.

He was not that foul to look upon, after all. Other women invited him to their beds, even if he did not accept their offers. Yves scowled and whistled anew.

Where *was* Gaston?

The second bell for the evening meal was sounded as the knight propped his hands on his hips and surveyed the grounds with mounting irritation. There was no sign of the squire.

Curse the boy! Yves pursed his lips once more, just as Gaston came hurtling around the corner.

Chapter Three

Gaston, all flailing arms and legs in his haste, was tousled from head to toe, and there was a suspicious smudge of dirt down the left side of his tabard. He wiped something red from his cheek, his eyes widening when he glanced down at the resulting crimson smear on his hand, then bowed deeply to his lord.

"Sir!" Gaston straightened, then licked his lips nervously. Evidently Yves' displeasure showed, but he neither softened his pose nor greeted the boy. Let Gaston sweat the results of his inattentiveness! "I hope you have not been waiting upon me, my lord."

"Of course I have. The dinner bell has sounded twice."

Gaston glanced to the hall and shuffled his feet. "I would apologize, my lord."

"And so you should." Yves arched a brow. "You are fortunate that I am not too proud to garb myself."

Gaston flushed, then caught his breath as Yves stepped quickly forward and slid a thumb across the line on his cheek where the blood was beading once more. Their gazes flicked as one to the stain on Yves' thumb, then met.

"Again?" Yves asked mildly. "I should have guessed."

Gaston's complexion turned a deeper crimson. "My lord,

it was simply a jest. I had to prove to them that I had learned much in your employ...."

"Them?" Yves' tone was chilling.

Gaston fidgeted. "The other squires, sir. There was Richard from—"

"I care nothing for their names," Yves interrupted tersely, fixing the boy with his most stern glare. "Were you sparring without supervision *again?*"

Gaston's eyes opened wide in appeal and Yves knew the answer before he spoke. "My lord, it was only for a moment! And they challenged me! What else could a man of honor do?"

"Keep his pledge to his knight," Yves retorted, and the boy hung his head.

"I am sorry, my lord," he mumbled.

The boy looked so contrite that Yves did not have the heart to stay angry with him. It was, after all, only Gaston's enthusiasm that continually undermined his obedience.

If only Gaston did not want to be a swordsman so badly. If the squire's impetuousness could be curbed—his concentration improved, his inattention to detail remedied—he might make a good knight.

If nothing else, he had an interest in the task.

Yves laid a hand on Gaston's shoulder. "Do not be so impatient, Gaston. You will master all the skills in time." He gave the boy a minute shake, but Gaston was inconsolable.

Perhaps Yves had been too harsh with him. Perhaps he had let his own experiences of this day spill over into this encounter, which would have been beyond unfair.

Perhaps a little encouragement was in order, instead of criticism.

Yves continued in a more gentle tone. "Time will give you more than ample opportunity to swing a blade, for you do have an aptitude for the task."

Gaston looked up in wonder, his eyes shining. "Truly?"

The boy's enthusiasm was engaging, but Yves gave him a

strict glance all the same. "Truly. But you must do as you are bidden! I had you pledge to not use my weaponry for your own safety, for you still have much to learn and I would not see you wounded in foolish horseplay. That was no small promise you granted me and broke."

Gaston colored anew, but his smile was filled with proud delight. Oh, the boy had a gift for hearing only what he desired to hear!

"I shall not repeat the offense, my lord."

Yves did not believe that for a moment, but he let the matter be. "You need to have this washed so it mends cleanly. The healer at the keep will manage it." He rumpled the boy's hair. "We would not want you to frighten the ladies with your scars before you even earn your spurs."

"No, my lord, no, sir."

The third bell sounded and they turned as one, matching steps as they strode toward the keep, the squire fairly bouncing with delight at Yves' meager approval.

"You think I shall earn my spurs then?"

"With diligence."

Gaston shot a glance at Yves, and the knight braced himself for a question that would doubtless be impertinent. "Might we spar later this evening, sir?"

"Gaston!" Yves used his most forbidding voice. "You know well enough that the count has granted me many responsibilities in his household and that such numbers of guests will add even more to the weight of that burden."

"Yes, my lord." The disappointment in the boy's voice was almost tangible.

"And if there is any time to spare, we must make arrangements to depart." Yves kept his gaze fixed on the ground ahead, even as Gaston's head shot up. He knew the boy's eyes would be bright with curiosity, but had not yet decided how much of a role Gaston would play in pending events.

Certainly Yves would have to see some improvement in basic discipline before granting Gaston any further responsi-

bility. As it was, he sometimes despaired of leaving his faithful steed in the boy's oft forgetful care.

It was good fortune indeed that great black Merlin was as
tolerant of Gaston's failings as Yves was.

"Depart?"

"Yes. We leave with the dawn."

"But where will we go, my lord?"

Yves considered for a moment how readily Gaston spread
news among his fellow squires. There was a good chance that
someone here for the tourneys might have a connection with
Philip de Trevaine. A careless word could easily return to
him from here.

Lady Gabrielle had seen matters aright. Yet again, Yves
was reassured that he was dealing with a woman who was
clearly possessed of uncommon good sense.

"We take a missive for the count," Yves said casually.

"Aha!" Gaston's eyes gleamed. "A declaration of war!"

"No. It is a mere formality, a wedding agreement, I believe," Yves lied. "Indeed, it is more of an excuse for you
and me to have a leave from the business of war."

Gaston blew threw his teeth. "I have no need of a leave,"
he muttered. "I would rather attack castles and save maidens
in distress! Perhaps scale a wall!" He turned on Yves excit-
edly. "Have you ever scaled a wall, my lord? Perhaps over
a dark and dangerous moat?"

"Once or twice," Yves acknowledged, and Gaston sighed
with longing at the very thought.

"I should like to try that! And match swords with a fiend-
ish foe at the summit!" Gaston lunged back and forth, feigning a very active battle. "Ha! Take that, you villainous oaf!"
He gave the death blow of his mock engagement. "Then the
damsel in distress would be so grateful to me," he declared,
pursing his lips for a great, puckering kiss that nearly made
Yves smile.

The boy's words prompted Yves to try and put Gabrielle
de Perricault into the role of despairing damsel in distress.

He failed utterly.

And that did make him smile.

Gabrielle would not be the kind of woman to wait patiently for rescue, by any means. And even if some knight did save her, she would not fall on her knees in gratitude.

No, Gabrielle de Perricault would coolly review the rescue strategy, making suggestions as to how the goal could have been achieved sooner and more effectively.

Yves smothered his unwilling smile. There was something refreshing about a woman with her wits about her. He patted Gaston on the shoulder. "Perhaps we will have time to match blades on the journey," he said consolingly.

The way Gaston's face lit up provided all the confirmation Yves needed of the idea's appeal. When the boy hooted and danced ahead, Yves shook his head at such enthusiasm.

Moats and damsels in distress, indeed.

An hour later, Yves entered the hall just before the count, that man's hand heavy on Yves' shoulder and his typical monologue rumbling in Yves' ear.

"...Fine decision, my boy, though you always showed a ready ability to assess a situation. I am most pleased to find you taken with Gabrielle de Perricault. She is a supremely fitting choice for you."

Yves slanted a glance toward his patron. "It is early days to talk of the fulfillment of her offer. I have not yet won the challenge."

The count smothered a smile. "Ah, but you will, my boy, you will. I have seen well enough over the years the kind of determination you bring to a fight even when your heart is not engaged." He winked, a hint that, as always, he was aware they were likely overheard as they waded through the assembly of bowing nobles. "This lady has no chance."

Despite the crowd in the hall, Yves easily picked out the figure of Gabrielle de Perricault. She was garbed in simple indigo, a color that he guessed would favor the curious shade of her eyes, though where that unbidden thought had sprung from, he could not say.

Her dark hair was hidden, its ebony hue securely pulled behind a sturdy veil. That veil was anchored in place with a silver circlet of a simplicity that Yves found oddly pleasing.

The cut of her surcoat was uncomplicated, the wool unadorned with embroidery. The garment's simple lines accentuated her slenderness and her height, though Yves found the result far from displeasing. She wore no jewelry, yet the starkness of her attire suited her direct manner well.

All in all, the lady was not hard upon the eyes. Yves liked that her slender figure was neither plump nor painfully thin and that she was tall enough to look a man in the eye.

Yves suspected they would not have to slow the pace of their ride to suit Lady Gabrielle. This was a lady who would ride as long and as hard as most of his men. Indeed, he would guess that she would be the last to concede to hardship or handicap of any kind.

"And it is time enough that one of our noblewomen has caught your eye, Yves." The count squeezed Yves' shoulder companionably and the knight glanced up to find his patron's eyes sparkling with mischief. "There were those, you know, who expressed certain concerns about you and, shall we say, your *taste* in partner, for you are getting no younger and there have been no rumors of any liaisons in your tent."

Yves glared at the count. "My taste is perfectly orthodox," he stated coldly, and the count chuckled.

"So I said myself, my boy, so I did. I knew you were not of that persuasion. Similarly, I knew well enough that you were the kind of man who would not sully himself with this cheap piece of baggage and that, but who would wait for the right woman to come along. I knew you would wait until you were *smitten* before taking a lady's cause to your own."

Smitten?

The count leaned forward and whispered in Yves' ear. "And Lady Gabrielle is perfect for you. A fair estate, good breeding, not unattractive but not a beauty by any means. Not spectacularly marriageable but definitely in need of a spouse..." The count's voice wavered slightly as he considered this, then he continued with confidence. "She is a solid, good-hearted woman upon whom you can depend."

He clapped Yves on the shoulder, and Yves was surprised to realize that he found it offensive to hear this lady discussed in such a callous way.

More than good-hearted, Gabrielle de Perricault would sacrifice her very life for her son. And that was a rare trait indeed, especially among the noblewomen Yves had met these many years. Such creatures were unfailingly pretty but lacked an interest in anything beyond themselves and their own comfort.

Gabrielle was of a different breed, and it was startling to think that she was less eligible as a result.

But *smitten?* Yves eyed the lady in question, curiously unsettled by the count's assumption that he accepted this charge purely to gain the lady's favor. He had never been taken with a woman—indeed, that would have been sorely illogical!—and could not imagine why the count should assume he was now.

"By the way, I must congratulate you on what you have already accomplished with Gaston," the count continued in a low murmur. "My sister is quite amazed by his progress beneath your hand and has come to believe the boy might make his spurs."

"I have no doubt he will." Yves silently added provisos to that assertion in his mind, knowing that the count wanted to hear only good news about his once-errant nephew.

"But his discipline!" The count clucked his teeth. "He was so unruly before you took charge of him." The nobleman's grip tightened momentarily on Yves' shoulder. "I truly am pleased by the changes you have wrought in the boy."

Yves held his tongue, not in the least bit certain there had been an appreciable change in Gaston's behavior.

The count rolled his eyes and lowered his voice. "I had begun to fear, I must say, that my sister's ambitions for him might prove his only hope." He shuddered visibly. "To think that any blood of my own might become a troubadour!"

"I believe they earn good coin," Yves felt obliged to say.

The count grimaced. "But in such a way! No home to call their own, no bed two nights in a row, no certainty from whence one's next meal will come."

He shook his head and doubtless would have continued in this vein, but in that very moment Gaston himself appeared.

The boy's garb was remarkably neat, Yves noted, and Yves' cup and linen were in hand. Evidently Gaston had dashed off to change once it became clear that the count would sequester himself with Yves and dinner would be delayed.

The only sign of disorder was a smear of carmine on Gaston's cheek, undoubtedly bestowed by one of the cluster of adoring female relatives who now watched his progress. The boy stood so straight and tall as he approached that his demeanor was all that could be hoped for and more.

Yves wondered suspiciously whether his Gaston had a twin he knew nothing about. This was most unlike the boy he chided all the day long.

Yves even glanced over his shoulder, silently marveling when Gaston fell demurely behind him as he had been bidden to do dozens of times without success. The female relatives whispered to each other with obvious delight, and Gaston's ears pinkened.

Perhaps Yves should promise the opportunity to spar more frequently.

"Lady Gabrielle!" the count boomed, and chatter ceased as all turned to see what transpired. That lady dropped gracefully to one knee as they approached, with nary a flicker of a glance at Yves to hint that they had already met.

"My lord Count."

"Rise, lady! I have found the perfect companion for you

on your journey to the convent of the Sisters of Ste. Rade-
gund.''

This was the story concocted by the count to disguise Gabrielle's and Yves' true intent. Yves scanned those gathered
and wondered whether any guessed the true nature of their
journey.

Were there those here committed to the fortunes of Philip
de Trevaine? Or any who sought to win his goodwill? Yves
could not say, and that uncertainty troubled him.

He would hate it if Lady Gabrielle's mission was jeopar-
dized before it was truly begun.

''My marshal takes a missive for me in that direction—a
mere agreement for Lord de Rumiens' marriage, that all the
same must be delivered by hand. The Lord de Rumiens takes
offense with wretched ease—'' the assembly twittered with
laughter at that ''—and Yves would be delighted to accompany you, at my behest, as far as the convent.''

For the first time since he had entered the room, Gabrielle's
glance flicked to Yves. No expression crossed her features
before she inclined her head slightly. ''As you wish, my lord
Count.''

Yves bowed deeply before the lady in turn. ''I am at your
service, my Lady de Perricault,'' he said formally.

Gabrielle nodded, then turned to the count. ''I thank you
for the grace of your thoughtfulness, my lord.''

''And I for yours in seeking my advice,'' the count responded. ''I believe,'' he continued with a firm glance at each
of them that spoke volumes, ''that this decision is the best
one by far for all involved.'' The count coughed into his hand,
a sure sign to Yves that he meant to publicly utter a lie. ''The
sisters will be most pleased with your contribution to their
coffers.''

Yves and Gabrielle nodded assent simultaneously, then the
count gestured to the board. He raised his voice and flicked
a finger to the musicians.

"Music! Please! Come join the repast. Make merry and celebrate our fine day of festivities!"

Chatter broke out around them once more, and the count stepped away to offer his hand to the countess, just now descending from the solar. That lady smiled and the two proceeded to the dais, arm in arm. Yves found Gabrielle's gaze bright upon him, then noted the older knight standing slightly behind her.

"My escort thus far, Chevalier Leon d'Aquilare." Gabrielle introduced the man and he stepped forward. His grip was firm, his brown eyes unerringly bright. He looked to be about forty summers of age, the first few strands of silver touching the temples of his dark brown hair.

"It is my pleasure," he mumbled, obviously a man of unpolished social graces. "You fought well this day."

Yves nodded acknowledgment of the gruff compliment, then gestured to the board in turn. "Perhaps we might dine together this evening and take the opportunity to plan our journey."

"A fine plan," Leon said with approval.

Gabrielle nodded. "I requested places be held at the end of the dais." Her violet gaze was darker in this light and seemed filled with mysterious shadows. "I had thought that anywhere above the salt would be fitting."

There was a question in her tone, so Yves nodded immediately. "I am certain your arrangements will suffice."

They turned together, and Yves marveled at the difference between Gabrielle's impassioned argument this afternoon and her cool formality on this evening. It was true that the hall was full of seeing eyes and listening ears, but all the same—and against all reason—he missed the Gabrielle he had glimpsed earlier.

Yves could only hope that once they left these walls behind, the lady would speak her mind with him once more.

"The count's own marshal!" whispered someone within the assembly as the small group made its way to the board.

Yves' ears pricked with interest, though he gave no outward sign of listening.

"To escort such a minor noblewoman." The speaker clucked his tongue.

"And one without lands."

"One would think the count's marshal would have larger fish in the skillet than to escort her to a convent, the count's concerns about Rumiens aside."

"Aye, something is afoot, you can be certain of that."

"Of course, you *know* about his parentage...." The voice dropped to a confidential whisper, though Yves had no doubt how the conversation continued.

But it was the earlier words that made his flesh creep, so close were they to his own concerns. He had to do something to allay suspicions.

He recalled suddenly the count's certainty in Yves' own attraction to Gabrielle, and knew something could be made of that. A witnessed kiss, a glance too long, and nothing more would be said.

The lady, being as clear thinking as she was, would see the sense of it all, Yves was certain.

The candles had burned low when the count retired, and Yves, anxious to set rumor to rest, immediately turned to Gabrielle.

"Might I accompany you to your chambers?"

Gabrielle blinked, as though confused. "Of course," she said after a moment's hesitation, then offered her hand that he might aid her to rise.

Yves, well aware of the many eyes upon them, bent and brushed his lips across the back of her hand.

Gabrielle's flesh was surprisingly soft, as was the sharp inhalation of her breath. Her remarkable eyes widened, but Yves swept her to her feet undeterred. A whisper of speculation rose around them, but Yves still detected a current of skepticism.

He also felt the hostility emanating from the lady beside him when they gained the corridor. She directed him toward her chambers with a flick of her wrist, not deigning to speak until they stood outside her door. The torch in the sconce flickered orange overhead, and Gabrielle's eyes flashed with anger when she turned on Yves.

"I had thought you were a man of honor!" she raged in an angry undertone. "What manner of trouble do you mean to make with such gestures?"

Yves barely heard her words, so intent was he upon his task. If only there was someone to note this "tender moment," all would be well.

A maid ducked out of the adjacent room at that moment, her gaze flicking between the pair before she curtsied low. Yves had no doubt she would be the perfect vehicle for news.

It would be news that would ensure he could save Gabrielle's son.

Gabrielle seemed not to notice the maid, her tirade continuing uninterrupted. "Surely you can see that—" she continued, before Yves caught her in his arms.

Gabrielle was strong and supple, long and lean, just as he had imagined she would be. The top of her head came to just below his chin. She frowned up at him and opened her mouth to argue further, but Yves granted her no quarter.

He captured those lips securely beneath his own and kissed Gabrielle de Perricault with all the artfulness he could muster. She tasted like wine, yet had a sweetness of her own that flooded his senses. Her curves fit against him in an intoxicating way that nearly made Yves forget his motive for kissing the lady.

Then the maid gasped audibly, recalling him to his senses. Gabrielle quivered within Yves' embrace in a most bewitching manner, while the echo of feet scampering away filled his ears.

The news would be on every tongue within the hour!

Yves tore his lips from the lady's with a decidedly unexpected reluctance. It had been a long time since he had kissed a woman, after all, let alone one as alluring as Gabrielle de Perricault.

Perhaps once she understood his intent, the lady would kiss him again. Yves lifted his head, well satisfied with what he had wrought.

He was stunned by the force of Gabrielle's slap across his face.

By the time he blinked, the lady had ducked into her chamber and slammed the solid oak door in his face. He stared at the door uncomprehendingly and heard a bolt slide securely home. His annoyance followed quickly on the heels of his astonishment.

What ingratitude the lady showed for his foresight!

A man of honor. Ha!

Gabrielle was still seething as the first gray light of the morning crept through the small window of her room. Rain beat against the walls, the gentle rhythm of its pattering making her shiver beneath her bed linens.

It would be a miserable day for traveling, one well suited to the company she was destined to keep! But the sooner she began, the sooner Thomas might be safely back within her care. And that was more important than any nonsense she might have to tolerate from the likes of Yves de Sant-Roux.

And his behavior was nonsense, indeed.

Gabrielle gritted her teeth and swung out of bed, more than ready to be moving after her sleepless night. Why could men never be satisfied with what they already had to call their own?

Oh, Gabrielle could just spit at her own stupidity! She should know by now that all men were selfish brutes!

Yet she had dared to trust a stranger—even against her instincts—when he had asked to accompany her to her chambers. She had thought he was being gracious—ha!

He had wanted only to warm her bed!

And that after accepting her condition for a match in name alone! Now she understood the import of his pledge to seek out no others—he meant to bed her despite granting his word!

What kind of man broke his vow within hours of taking a pledge? What kind of man launched a campaign of seduction after agreeing to set his needs aside?

Gabrielle should have recognized that lie from the outset. She should have anticipated this amorous assault! She had been seven kinds of fool to let a man's thoughtful manner disarm her!

But it would not happen again, regardless of what charm Yves de Sant-Roux used in his pursuit. Gabrielle folded her arms stubbornly across her chest.

She would *not* let that knight between her thighs, either before or after Thomas was safe and sound. Gabrielle had given her word, and that was worth something, even if Yves' pledge was not. Should Yves save Thomas, she would wed him.

But he would never warm her bed.

Though the memory of his short, impassioned kiss was tempting, indeed. When had Michel's kisses ever stirred such trembles within her?

Never.

The truth was enough to make Gabrielle squirm. Unwillingly, she lifted her fingers to her lips. She could still feel the imprint of Yves' firm lips against hers, and her heart skipped a beat at the recollection of his sure touch. With shaking fingers, Gabrielle traced the outline of her own mouth, feeling as though it had somehow been changed by that brief embrace.

Would everyone within the hall be able to tell that she had been kissed?

And by whom?

What a weakness she had! It would have been so simple to deny Yves any response, to stand stock-still so he would know exactly how unwelcome his embrace had been. But Gabrielle knew she had not done so.

Had Yves known how his touch had weakened her? Had he felt her quiver in response?

Was she doomed to repeat her mother's mistake?

No! Gabrielle closed her eyes and prayed fiercely that Yves had not noticed, that he had been so fixed on his needs that any response of her own did not matter.

Surprise had been against her, she resolved firmly. Now that she knew the manner of tricks Yves was inclined to play, he would not catch her off guard again.

The issue resolved, Gabrielle dressed in haste. Her dark green surcoat was wrought of heavy wool, simple in line and warm beyond all. She unfurled thick knitted stockings, donned them and fastened the garters high above her knees.

The sturdy leather boots she had had made were more like a man's riding boots than those made for ladies, but Gabrielle liked their solid strength. Her thoughts of Thomas grew stronger as she braided her hair into a single plait, and her fingers stilled with a sudden realization. It was as though she girded herself for a battle and a journey that would leave her life changed.

A pang shot through her heart at that thought. Surely she could not lose her beloved Thomas? Surely the boy would be saved?

Surely it was not too late?

Unable to bear the thought, Gabrielle fastened the end of her braid with hasty fingers. She hurled her homespun cloak over her shoulders, gathered her possessions into her saddle-bags and strode from the room.

The keep was stirring to life, a rustle of activity in the hall revealing those who had already risen to break their fast. Gabrielle took a piece of bread and an apple wrinkled from a winter spent in storage.

A cluster of pretty noblewomen, obviously rousted at this

early hour by the demands of travel alone, chattered together
in one corner. One pointed to Gabrielle and they giggled, their
whispers now exchanged behind their hands.

Gabrielle refused to give them the pleasure of a response.
She stoically finished her bread and drank her ale, achingly
aware of the sensitivity of her lips. Could they see? Did they
know? Her cheeks burned with the possibility.

"Well, good morning to you, Gabrielle."

Gabrielle glanced up to find a tiny, angelically beautiful
woman sliding onto the bench opposite. Gabrielle forced a
polite smile, wishing it could be anyone other than Lady Adelys de Mornay who chose to make conversation on this morning.

Adelys had visited Perricault for the first time while Gabrielle was roundly pregnant with Thomas. Adelys' charming
company and her love of the hunt had made her visit a welcome distraction for Michel, but Gabrielle had felt the noblewoman's six week visit had been overstaying her welcome.

And twice a year for each year since—at least until Perricault had been lost—Adelys had paused at the estate, purportedly en route to one place or another. The way she settled
in with a vengeance, not to mention the expenditure of hous-
ing and feeding her retinue, made Gabrielle suspect the
woman came specifically to Perricault.

Though what Perricault's appeal might be Gabrielle could
not have said. Certainly, the hunting was renowned at Perricault, and Adelys had a lust for the hunt, rare in a woman.

Perhaps that was the sum of it. Undoubtedly, Gabrielle
would never know more. She looked now at her companion,
amazed once more that a woman could be so perfectly
wrought.

The winters had been kind to Adelys, for she did not look
the thirty-five years that Gabrielle knew she had seen. Though
her features were shaped with an unearthly beauty and her
long blond tresses were of the shade so many envied, there

was a brittleness in her green eyes that made Gabrielle wary of this widow.

Had Adelys' eyes always glittered like ice?

Adelys smiled coyly. "Tired this morn, Gabrielle?" She leaned across the board before Gabrielle could respond. "Well, it is no wonder. I heard you had a guest last evening and simply must congratulate you upon your fine taste in men."

Chapter Four

Gabrielle nearly choked in shock. "I had no guest last night!" she finally managed to say.

But even before the words left her lips, she saw that Adelys would not easily be persuaded of the truth.

Adelys chuckled throatily. "Come along, Gabrielle." She waved to the hall with an assurance that made Gabrielle's cheeks burn. "*Everyone* is talking about it."

The other noblewoman rolled her eyes appreciatively as Gabrielle's stomach churned self-consciously. Surely *she* could not be the subject of gossip?

"And what a way to spend a journey to the convent! I can imagine that our Yves will easily convince you not to abandon the pleasures of the secular world."

Gabrielle tore her bread with a savage gesture, but fought to hide her response. "Can you?" she restrained herself to saying.

Her skepticism must have shown, for Adelys leaned across the table and captured Gabrielle's hand beneath her own cold one. The tiny woman's gaze was more piercing than Gabrielle had ever seen it.

"Now, listen to me, Gabrielle. You are making a fool's choice in joining the convent. You are a sensible woman, after all. I understand that you are upset about the loss of Michel, but—''

"And of Thomas," Gabrielle interjected. Adelys looked at her blankly. "My son, Thomas," she clarified firmly.

Adelys frowned for a moment, then nodded impatiently. "The boy, yes, of course. I had forgotten." She dismissed this loss with an easy wave of her hand, and Gabrielle was stunned by the woman's callousness.

"But your circumstance as a widow is a good one for seeing to your own needs." Adelys released Gabrielle's hand to gesture to herself with evident pride. "Why, simply look at me! Ten years a widow and more gifts and romps than any woman needs to keep her happy. I am more wealthy than my poor dead Eduard ever dreamed of being and more spoiled than I undoubtedly deserve."

Adelys chuckled, almost daring Gabrielle to agree. "I take lovers as I choose, I answer to no one." Adelys' gaze locked steadily with Gabrielle's own. "It is not a life to readily cast aside, my dear, and I would have thought that you would have the wits to realize it."

To think that this coldly calculating woman had imagined Gabrielle to be one of her own ilk was galling indeed. Gabrielle stood carefully, fighting all the while to keep her thoughts to herself.

"I am not certain that your life would suit me well," she said, but Adelys' eyes widened in mock surprise.

"Truly? You have sampled it and laid it aside after just one night?" Her smile turned coy. "Or perhaps I should say, after only one *knight*." Adelys smirked when Gabrielle gasped, then examined her fingernails with feigned concern. "I seem to recall that Yves de Sant-Roux performed rather better than that."

Gabrielle's cheeks flamed, but before she could argue further, the knight in question stepped into the hall. All eyes turned to him, and there was silence for the barest moment before the whispers began once more.

Gabrielle hated that she was not the only woman who took note of his arrival.

"Here comes the man himself," Adelys cooed. "Perhaps we should ask *him* about last evening's activities. He will be looking for you this morning, I wager, for he has never been a man for casual liaisons." Adelys smiled anew. "I suppose it is no fault for a man to finish well what he has begun."

The twitter of feminine laughter grew louder as Yves strode farther into the hall, though he seemed indifferent to the women's obvious attention. His glance flicked to Gabrielle, and he caught her eye almost by accident. Once their gazes met, though, his sharpened and he did not look away.

And his footsteps turned in her direction.

Gabrielle swallowed the dryness in her mouth and knew full well that Yves would expect an accounting for her blow the night before.

Just as she expected one for his bold kiss. Yet as he drew closer, Gabrielle knew she could not face him before so many interested souls.

Adelys made a little growl of appreciation in the back of her throat. "Surely, Gabrielle, you cannot want to sacrifice the pleasures of the flesh quite so soon?"

That this woman believed her to be made of such loose mettle was insulting, indeed! Gabrielle spun away, not in the least interested in continuing the conversation. She could not even summon a word of dismissal, so distraught was she to find her sterling reputation cast in shreds about her feet so quickly.

Adelys apparently did not even notice her departure. "Good morning, Chevalier!" she purred, her voice carrying to Gabrielle's ears.

Despite herself, Gabrielle glanced over her shoulder to find Adelys sliding to her feet with a sinuous grace that promised pleasures to be had. Yves bent over the lady's proffered hand.

Just as he had bent over her own. Gabrielle's heart lurched to see how readily he made the courteous gesture.

The cur! He had probably bedded Adelys at least once for her to give him such a glowing reference!

Yves had probably bedded *all* these women who watched him so adoringly, and left each with the impression that she was the only one to hold his heart. He might even have gone to the bed of one of them directly after stealing that kiss from her!

Gabrielle tossed her saddlebags over her shoulder and headed for the stables in poor temper. She should have guessed that as soon as she refused Yves rights to her bed, he would try to seduce her. Trust a man to see no further than the contents of his chausses!

But Gabrielle was not going to become another of Yves' conquests, regardless of what he thought of the matter.

And that was final.

A light drizzle caressed her face as she stepped through the portal and into the courtyard before the stables.

Gabrielle had forgotten the rain, so upset had she been by Adelys' words, yet she halted for a moment beneath its soothing caress. The sounds of trap and buckles carried from the stables opposite and Gabrielle simply listened for a long moment.

It was only when she heard a step in the corridor behind her and feared Yves himself might appear that she hastened onward.

Methuselah seemed to be watching for her, for the gray stallion gave a snort of welcome as soon as Gabrielle stepped through the portal into the shadows of the stable. His breath made puffs of steam in the cool morning air and he stomped impatiently in his stall, his velvety nostrils quivering in anticipation of the treat he knew she would bring him.

The beast was too clever by half.

"Well, good morning to you, sir." The stallion nosed her saddlebags impatiently and investigated her pockets. Just being with the great, gentle beast vastly improved Gabrielle's spirits, especially when he snorted disdain at not finding a gift of any kind and fixed her with a skeptical eye.

She produced the apple from behind her back, and Methuselah's ears flicked with definite interest.

"This, sir, is in exchange for an easy saddling this morn," Gabrielle said, offering the apple. The stallion gave it an assessing sniff, then lifted his head proudly, apparently spurning the offer.

Gabrielle laughed under her breath. She would have been surprised if Methuselah had taken the bribe. The contest with the saddle was part of their routine, after all.

"All right then, we shall do it your way," she conceded easily.

Methuselah snorted again and laid claim to the fruit, chomping noisily as Gabrielle scratched his ears. He made short work of the token, then nuzzled her playfully when he was done.

"So, he *is* your steed."

Gabrielle looked up to find the dark-haired squire who had attended Yves the night before watching her from the end of the stall. He looked as rumpled as if he had slept in his clothes, but his glance was keen.

"Yes, that he is." Her acknowledgment seemed all the encouragement the boy needed.

"They told me that he was yours, and I must confess that I did not believe it." The squire stepped into the stall and Methuselah granted him a thoroughly disdainful survey. "I have never met a woman who rode a stallion and could not believe that one would ever do so."

Gabrielle spared him a glance. "Well, I do." The boy's confusion was so obvious that she softened and gave him more explanation. "Methuselah was my husband's horse," she added gently. "When he died, I thought to keep the steed."

"Oh! Well, he is a fine beast, my lady, there is no disputing that." The boy's grin was genuine, and Gabrielle warmed to him. It was refreshing to meet someone sincere enough to be taken at face value. "I would have saddled him for you this morn, for Chevalier Yves bade me make all ready, but as I said, I was not certain—"

"It matters little," Gabrielle interrupted, "as I prefer to saddle him myself."

The boy's eyes were round. "But, my lady! Surely you cannot!"

"Surely I can," Gabrielle countered firmly. She was not a small or delicately wrought woman like Adelys, and her new-found self-reliance was becoming a welcome habit.

Well aware of the boy's amazed gaze, Gabrielle laid the blanket on Methuselah's back. His nostrils quivered and she knew that this day, as most other days, he would make a show of fighting the saddle.

Gabrielle lifted the weighty saddle, gritted her teeth and heaved it onto the stallion's back. Methuselah took a few tempestuous steps, but she had had the foresight to make his tether short.

He granted her a chiding glance, as though he thought she had taken some of the sport out of their little game, but defiantly snapped the reins all the same.

"Careful, my lady! He looks to have a fearsome temper!"

"It is all show, you will see."

As soon as Gabrielle passed the strap beneath Methuselah's belly, she heard the stallion take a deep breath. Sure enough, by the time Gabrielle tried to fit buckle to strap, his belly was as round as a barrel, and the cinch could not be brought together.

The sight of this noble steed holding his breath thus always tempted Gabrielle to laugh, but she did not. He would have been sorely insulted if she had deigned to laugh at him.

Instead, she poked one finger hard between his ribs.

Methuselah exhaled in noisy surprise and Gabrielle buckled the cinch with a speed born of practice. It was a good thing for her that Michel's squire had confided in her the trick.

Yves' squire laughed aloud and clapped his hands. "Brava, my lady! That was a task well done!"

But the steed gave Gabrielle a glance that spoke volumes about the next time they matched wits this way. Gabrielle suspected there would come a day when the stallion bested her at this contest of wills.

"A task well done as yours was not," a familiar masculine voice interjected sternly, and Gabrielle's heart leaped to her throat.

She spun to find Yves framed in the doorway of the stables, a hand propped on his hip as he glared at his squire.

The glint of his mail hauberk could be spied beneath a tabard that she knew to be so deep an indigo as to be virtually black. The hauberk fell to his knees, a skirted tunic beneath of the same indigo hue extending to his ankles.

A fur-lined cloak of the same dark shade was fastened to one shoulder, a sword buckled to his hip, a helmet tucked beneath his arm. Even in the darkness of the stables, his fair hair gleamed golden and the brightness of his eyes flashed like twin flames.

Gabrielle, to her dismay, felt suddenly much warmer than she had before. *Seven kinds of fool!* she chided herself silently. She had no business responding to the allure of this man! What had happened to her resolve?

Her traitorous lips burned anew with the memory of the firm imprint of his kiss.

"Gaston, did I not send you here this morning to ready the horses?" the knight demanded.

Gaston hung his head with a dejection that might have been comic under other circumstance. "Yes, my lord."

Yves gestured to Gabrielle with evident annoyance, though his tone remained remarkably even. "Yet I arrive to find the lady saddling her own beast, and not a mere lady's palfrey at that! What explanation do you have for this behavior?"

Gaston shrugged, but before he could speak, Gabrielle

stepped forward to defend him. "I told the boy that I prefer to saddle my steed myself."

"Indeed?" The knight seemed unmoved by this confession. "And was this made clear *before* Gaston came to perform his labor or when you arrived to find the deed not completed?"

Lady and squire exchanged a glance, knowing full well that they could not talk their way around such reasoning. Had Gaston followed his knight's bidding, Methuselah would have been saddled before Gabrielle even reached the stable this morning.

"Methuselah is difficult to saddle," Gabrielle said, hearing the weakness of the argument even as it was made.

"Yes, sir! He blows out his stomach to avoid the cinch!" Gaston stretched out his hands in an attempt to show the span. "He must have been this wide before the lady tricked him!"

"Indeed." Yves glanced pointedly to the steed in question, and Gabrielle followed his gaze, only to find the silver stallion looking as innocent as could be. Methuselah nibbled meekly at the hay in his stall, but Gabrielle noted the mischievous gleam in his eye.

There were days when she imagined this beast was more clever than most people she knew.

"*This* steed?" Yves asked skeptically.

"This very one," Gabrielle said firmly. "Even now he endeavors to let you underestimate his wiles."

"Indeed." Disbelief lingered in Yves' tone, but instead of arguing the point, he turned to his squire. "But now that you know the steed's trick, there will be no excuse on the morrow. Am I understood?"

"Yes, my lord." Gaston bowed low.

"And Merlin?"

"Awaits saddled and caparisoned in his stall, my lord."

"Your own palfry?"

"Ready, my lord, and waiting with Merlin." The boy took a deep breath. "I made provision with the cook that a midday meal be provided and have only to fetch it from him. I do hope this meets with your satisfaction.''

Yves lifted a brow, and Gabrielle enjoyed the fact that he was surprised by this news. "Very good," he acknowledged with new warmth. "Other than the preparation of the lady's steed, you have shown foresight and planning this morn.''

Gaston flushed as he bowed low, a delighted smile at this praise threatening to ruin his attempt at a somber manner.

"Though you might lay hands on a tabard that looks less disreputable. The lady, no doubt, is accustomed to riding with a party appropriately garbed.''

Gaston looked to Gabrielle in alarm, as though he feared she had taken insult at the mere sight of him. Gabrielle could not help smiling in reassurance, and some of Gaston's cocky manner was immediately restored.

Yet he bowed low to his knight. "Yes, my lord.''

Gabrielle was forced to admit that the knight was not unfair with the boy. Michel might well have seen Gaston whipped for his failure to fulfil all his tasks.

But Yves sought to win her approval, that much Gabrielle knew, if only to prove that he could have whatever he desired even if she chose to deny it to him.

And likely *only* because she chose to deny it to him. Gabrielle knew full well that a man like Yves de Sant-Roux would never pursue a plain woman like herself of his own volition.

That was what she had to remember.

"I should fetch the meal, my lord.''

Yves nodded dismissal and the boy scampered away, leaving knight and lady alone together. Methuselah eyed the knight with some of the suspicion Gabrielle was feeling. The steady beat of the rain on the roof, the distant sound of squires working and the swish of the horses' tails filled the silence between them.

The shadows were such that Gabrielle could not see Yves' expression clearly, and she disliked how much that troubled

her. She kneaded Methuselah's heavy leather reins between
her fingers and could not find a thing to say to this taciturn
knight.

Gabrielle wondered whether his cheek still burned from her
blow.

Her own lips felt swollen and she barely restrained herself
from raising a finger to touch them anew. Gabrielle heard her
pulse hammering in her ears and wished suddenly that Yves
would seek out his own steed.

"We have only to await your staff, then," he said finally.
The practical words stood in such marked contrast to the turmoil of Gabrielle's thoughts that she felt her cheeks flush
scarlet.

"I have no staff," she said with a proud lift of her chin.
"There is only Chevalier Leon who accompanies me, and I
am certain he is already somewhere within the stables. His
squire will be with him."

The knight folded his arms across his chest. "No maids?"

"Not a one." Gabrielle shook her head, well aware of the
unconventionality of her choice, and deliberately kept her
voice haughty. "I have no need of such luxury, especially in
these times." She reached for her saddle, but the knight was
quickly beside her.

Once again, she could smell the heady masculinity of his
skin, and nervous butterflies took up residence in her belly as
a result. Curse the man for the way he unsettled her!

"Is something amiss?" she asked as coldly as she could
manage.

Yves stiffened immediately, his eyes narrowing as he
glanced at her. He looked as though he might say something,
but then shook his head and knotted his fingers together. Gabrielle saw now that he had already donned his leather gaunt-
lets.

His glance flicked to hers and she caught her breath at the
brightness of his amber gaze. "Might I have the honor of
giving you a hand up?"

Oh, he had charm, that much was certain! Though Gabrielle's heart lurched to find him so close, never mind to have his handsome features etched with concern apparently for her, it was time to end his attempts to charm her.

"No!" she retorted, more firmly than was certainly warranted under the circumstance. "No, you will not touch me again!"

His lips thinned briefly before his features were composed once more. "Perhaps you mistake my meaning," he said with dangerous calm. "I merely offer you assistance to mount."

Gabrielle snorted. "My point exactly, sir, though I doubt we have the same manner of mounting in mind."

Yves straightened abruptly. "There is nothing inappropriate in my offer."

"And I should say that there is!" Gabrielle snapped. "Indeed, I shall have your promise, sir, and have it this very morning, that you will never endeavor to lay a hand upon me again!"

"Not even for common courtesy?"

"Not for any reason whatsoever!"

The knight folded his arms across his chest and glared down at her. He was too close by far, but there was no room within the stall for Gabrielle to back away. "It is long indeed since a lady found me so offensive that she would not even let me aid her to mount her steed."

Oh, he would not fool her with his pretty words! This touch would be but the first of many, and if she ceded in this, she had no doubt his sensory assault would be relentless.

"And it is long indeed since I met a man reputedly of honor who moved to break his vow on the same day as making it!" she declared. Her words clearly stung, for he inhaled so sharply that his nostrils nearly pinched shut.

And then the knight was perfectly composed once more. It was as though she had imagined his fleeting response, but that realization was an unnerving one. All the same, Gabrielle would not back down.

"What flight of womanly fancy is this? I have never broken a pledge!"

"That kiss last eve was no flight of fancy and neither was it welcome! You swore agreement to a match in name alone, and only a potential one."

The knight glanced to either side, then he leaned closer and lowered his voice. "My lady, this is neither the place nor the time appropriate for this discussion."

"Ha! I wager that you will *never* find the time or the place to discuss your breach of our agreement."

"Breach?" Yves visibly ground his teeth, then continued with low urgency, his gaze boring into Gabrielle's own. "I made no breach of our pledge—"

"No? That kiss was far beyond the terms."

"That kiss," Yves said through his teeth, "was for your benefit alone."

Gabrielle nearly gasped aloud at his audacity. That he would put such a thought into words astonished her. "Well, you do have a lofty opinion of your allure, sir!"

"And I had thought you a woman of uncommonly clear wits!" the knight muttered in frustration. He shoved one hand through his hair and glanced down at her once more, irritation now blazing in his amber gaze.

"You remarked yourself on the need for confidentiality." His tone had dropped to a low rumble that made something deep within Gabrielle quiver.

She would have rather died than give any sign of his effect upon her, though. "You take your idea of confidentiality rather far for my taste, sir!"

"My lady!" The knight audibly ground his teeth, then leaned even closer and spoke in a low murmur. "There are those within this keep who might suspect the count's tale. Indeed, I heard whispers of as much last eve."

Gabrielle could not tear her gaze away from the intensity of his own.

"The count, you may have noted, is convinced that I take

your offer because I am smitten with your charms." Yves' lips twisted, as though they shared a secret. Gabrielle's stomach plummeted to her toes with the certainty of what that secret must be.

"We both know that is not true. However, it seemed fitting to promote the tale," he concluded.

But Gabrielle's pride would not let the matter pass so readily. They might both know how completely ridiculous the count's belief was, but it was beyond churlish for Yves to have stated the truth so flatly. So annoyed was she with his poor manners that it took her a moment to realize the import of what he said.

Then she glared at him. "You kissed me on purpose," she hissed with incredulity. "You did that purely to fuel gossip."

Yves nodded, evidently proud of what he had wrought. "It seemed best for you. We would not want speculation to travel beyond these walls."

"Knave!" Gabrielle slapped the smile from the knight's face for the second time in less than a day. "How *dare* you tarnish my reputation purely to serve your own ends? Have you any idea what people have said to me this morn? What manner of woman do you imagine they think me to be, taking a lover en route to becoming a bride of Christ?"

Gabrielle spat on the stable floor, and the knight took a step backward in obvious astonishment. "Take *that* for your favor! And spare me any further ones of its ilk!"

With that, she grasped the pommel and stuffed her foot into the stirrup. She hauled herself into Methuselah's saddle by force of will alone. It certainly was not an easy task, but Gabrielle was angry enough to accomplish the deed.

She looked down at the knight to find his hands on his hips once more, his cheek blazing crimson from her blow. "You are not thinking reasonably about this," he said with unexpected calm. "Gossip will inevitably come and go, but the greater good will be served by some speculation on our—"

"I do not care about your ideas of the greater good!" Gabrielle raged. Methuselah pranced impatiently, the steed evidently responding to her mood. "My reputation is the one thing of merit I had left to call my own, and I will not stand by and watch you destroy it for your own ends!"

His frown deepened. "I mean no harm, my lady, but—"

"But you have done some, nonetheless!" Gabrielle was in the most fulsome rage of all her days, though she did not dare examine why this man earned such a measure of her anger.

Instead she jabbed a gloved finger in the direction of his chiseled nose. "I have spent my entire life being told how I might be useful to one man's needs or another's, and I am well and done with the role! I shall *not* dance to your tune, Chevalier, regardless of how sensible you might think it to be. There will be no such contact between you and me again. Do we understand each other?"

Yves' lips thinned as he stared up at her, and Gabrielle's pulse pounded like thunder in her ears.

What had she done? Oh, she had erred in granting her tongue such full rein—especially before a man she did not know well! What had possessed her to make her thoughts so clear to Yves de Sant-Roux?

But Yves merely donned his helmet with an impatient gesture. "We most certainly do, my lady," he said savagely.

"Then let us depart." Gabrielle touched her heels to Methuselah's sides and the steed sprang away, anxious to be on the road after his days in the stable here.

But Gabrielle could not outrun her own unwilling response to the knight she had taken to her cause.

To Yves' mind, it was not a good portent to have a trip—let alone a mission upon which they would each need the other—begin so poorly. The party rode in awkward silence and were drenched to the skin within a matter of moments from leaving the count's abode. The gray weather was fitting, he concluded, for the lady certainly was in foul temper this morning.

Surely he could not have wrought such results with a single
kiss? He had only intended to protect her from rumor spreading to Philip, to ensure the security of their mission, but Lady
Gabrielle certainly had not shared his view.

Yves had not intended to insult Gabrielle, much less tarnish
the reputation she so carefully guarded, but why could she
not see that the greater good would be served in this? Any
speculation would be forgotten within days, when some more
titillating rumor captured the imagination of idle minds at
court.

Gabrielle's garb and manner were more earthy than those
of most women, but in the end, her heart sang the same whimsical, emotional tune. Yves chastised himself for his foolishness in expecting her to be different.

He had been so convinced that she was a woman of good
sense. He flicked a glance at her, but she rode with her chin
high, those unexpectedly sturdy boots locked into her stirrups.
An errant thought made him straighten abruptly.

Would Gabrielle's response have been different if his birthright was legitimate? Was the kiss the root of her response,
or was it his issue?

Yves scowled at the road. It had taken precious little time
for Gabrielle to show that she was no less conscious of blood-
lines than any other noblewoman.

Indeed, Gabrielle was apparently even more afflicted by his
issue than others were! To think that his illegitimacy made
him unworthy of even aiding her to mount her steed.

Now that was beyond unreasonable! In light of this, it was
all too clear why she wanted a match in name alone—the
lady could not bear the thought of a man who might be
half-common touching her noble flesh!

Yves hunkered down beneath his cloak and glared at the
road unfurling before them. And all this fuss launched by a
simple kiss. His impulse had been a good one and he knew
it well. And the kiss...well, Yves had found the kiss itself

rather pleasurable. He might not have been adverse to sharing another sometime.

But not now that the lady had shown her true colors.

And that was more disappointing than Yves thought it should have been.

Chapter Five

They rode in virtual silence for ten entire days.

On the morning of the eleventh, the small party plunged into a thick forest. Gabrielle led an unerring line through the trees, though no path could be readily discerned. At any given moment, Yves could not have easily determined precisely which way they had come. Yet she rode decisively, her carriage tall and proud, and his admiration for the lady he escorted grew even greater.

Surely it could be no more than admiration that compelled him to watch her so closely, to admire the tilt of her chin, the decisive glint in her eye, the firm grip of her slender, gloved hands upon the reins.

Surely it could be no more than that.

Deliberately, Yves turned and looked at the forest about them. These trees, vestiges of snow clinging to their branches despite the eruption of vibrant new leaves, made him deeply uneasy. It was all too easy to recall the fateful autumn day that he had ridden into a similar woods, indeed one not far south of here, and lost his only sister to a pack of hunting wolves.

It seemed the past, so long laid to rest, would not now let Yves be, and he spurred Merlin onward in uncharacteristic frustration. The silence of his companions only granted those memories more time to unfurl within his mind. His emotions were unsettled, and Yves, as a man used to having his emotions conveniently locked away, was decidedly at odds with this state.

He slanted glances toward Lady Gabrielle, respecting despite himself the way she rode without complaint, and did so as long and as hard as he, Leon and the horses were able. There was no fussing from her—not over her hair, her toilette, the food or the accommodations.

Each night Gabrielle made do with what opportunity offered. Indeed, Yves knew many knights who could have learned much from her manner.

It was curious how quickly her one emotional outburst had come to the surface, then disappeared. Yves conceded wryly that bastardy must be an issue of particular import to her, and he felt his lips thin to a taut line.

Gabrielle wheeled her steed at that precise moment, giving Yves the eerie sense that she had heard his thoughts and did not approve. She halted her destrier, her gaze colliding with Yves' in challenge. He reined in Merlin, well aware of Leon's assessing gaze upon him.

The place they halted was unremarkable, being indistinguishable from the forest they had already seen. A small clearing, it was carpeted in a thick blanket of pine needles, and a minute patch of sky was visible overhead. There was not even a place for the horses to take a drink.

It must be near midday, Yves decided, by the sun.

The lady watched Yves survey the place, evidently waiting for his gaze to settle upon her once more. A pale finger of sunlight fell upon her face, her hood having slid back slightly during the ride, and the pallor of her skin made her features look wrought of stone.

Certainly her expression was uncompromising. Yves was aware once more of being measured against some invisible standard and found lacking. That it was the circumstance of his birth Gabrielle held against him was frustrating beyond all, for it was one thing that he could not change.

The lady eyed him as though she could read his very thoughts. Yves doffed his helmet and stared back at her, feeling his own expression become uncompromising beneath her steady stare.

"Why do we halt here?" he asked, when it was clear she would explain nothing of her own volition.

Gabrielle lifted her chin, though her gaze did not waver, and Yves knew he would not like whatever she intended to say. "You cannot progress farther without a blindfold."

"What is this?" he demanded, hearing the steel of disapproval in his own tone. Such a breach of trust between the two of them was unfounded! This was beyond unreasonable!

"You must be blindfolded to continue," Gabrielle repeated, without any inflection in her tone.

"Why?" The word cracked like a whip between them.

"I cannot risk having any witness the location of those troops loyal to my house." Gabrielle's lips thinned. "Surely you, who warned of listening ears, can understand the necessity of that?"

That the woman's prejudice against his birthright should extend to not trusting in his word was appalling beyond all! Yves fought to keep rein on his suddenly explosive temper.

Never had he been so insulted!

Never had he been treated with such disrespect!

Regardless of his father's games, Yves had earned his spurs honorably and by his own labor! The woman owed him the respect due to his accomplishment, especially as it had been made against such odds!

With an effort, Yves kept his tone level, though his words were terse. "But you have hired me to your cause."

"And you were pledged first to the count's hand," Gabrielle countered with enviable ease. "How could I say what causes the count may have taken to his heart? You said yourself that the Lord de Tulley had already appealed for your aid in this cause. How could I know what truly governs your hand?''

That she could cloak her opinion in logic was more infuriating than he might have thought possible. Despite the hammering of his pulse in his ears, Yves was determined to match her argument in kind.

"The count released me from his service," he observed with forced calm.

Gabrielle shrugged with an indifference that made Yves long to give her a shake. His cheek chose that moment to heat in recollection of the blow she had dealt him and he gritted his teeth at the way this woman could make his blood boil.

"This I know by your claim alone," she said mildly.

Again his guarantee was worthless in her estimation! "I grant to you my most solemn word of honor," Yves said, spitting out each word with precision.

The lady was still unimpressed. "Which means naught without knowing to whom it has been granted first." She snapped her fingers and gestured to Leon. "Have you a cloth to blindfold him?"

That was enough.

"This is outrageous!" Yves dismounted with a grace born of fury and closed the distance between them with quick strides. He glared up at Gabrielle.

"How *dare* you question my word and my honor simply because of the taint of my birthright?" His anger, given rein, could not be checked once the flow of words had begun. "I have earned my spurs by deed alone, and my word of honor is not something to be readily discarded!"

"Your birthright?" Gabrielle looked perplexed by his words, but Yves was not fooled by her feminine tricks.

"Play no games with me, my lady! I am not so witless that I cannot see your revulsion in being touched by a man of bastard birth!" Yves gestured angrily to her booted foot. "Why else would you refuse to let your noble foot be sullied by my aiding you to mount your steed? Why else would you insist I never touch you, even in courtesy?"

He propped his hands on his hips. "Why else would you not even deign to speak to me, a man whose parentage might be half-common?"

"I am not certain—" Gabrielle began, but Yves did not let her finish whatever lie she was concocting.

"I have been shunned by many nobles, concerned for the propriety of their social relations, by virtue of my tainted pedigree," he informed her, and was vaguely aware that the lady looked slightly dumbfounded, "but never, my lady, *never* has anyone treated me with such rudeness and disrespect as you have done on this day. Perhaps you might recall that you have hired me to your cause by virtue of the kind of warrior I am."

Yves folded his arms across his chest stubbornly, all that needed to be said on the matter clearly expressed, to his mind. "I will *not* bow my head to be blindfolded simply to suit the whim of your illogical prejudice."

His tirade having run its course, he glared up at Gabrielle.

She blinked, cleared her throat and glanced at Leon, before looking back to Yves.

"You were born out of wedlock?" she asked quietly.

Yves felt his lips thin. "Do not feign ignorance now!"

Gabrielle stiffened. "There is no need to feign ignorance, for I quite simply knew nothing of your birthright."

What was this?

Yves stared at her in shock, but Gabrielle continued in the same relentlessly steady tone. There was something about the lady's manner that, despite his conviction in his own conclusion, tempted him to believe she told no lie.

"Though I can understand how you interpreted my actions, I assure you that I would never have cast such aspersions upon your character even if I had known of your birthright." Gabrielle met Yves' gaze pointedly. "A man can scarcely control the circumstance of his own conception."

Yves opened his mouth and shut it again, so unexpected was the lady's concession. That it so admirably echoed his own opinion of the import of his bastardy was no consolation.

But he was not so readily convinced of her innocence in all of this. "Why, then, did you refuse my aid in the count's stables? Why decline my assistance in such a simple matter?"

To Yves' surprise, Gabrielle's cheeks stained a light pink. She glanced nervously toward her knight Leon—who took to examining the foliage of the trees with marked interest—then looked back at Yves. She seemed markedly younger when she flushed, much softer and more innocent than was the norm with her, and Yves warmed to her anew.

"I...I have never been the target of gossip before," she said haltingly. "It was most distressing."

"And I apologize for my role in your embarrassment," Yves interjected quickly. "Truly, my lady, it was never my intention to see you hurt. I fear I saw only the need to disguise our true mission from prying eyes for the sake of Thomas."

The lady smiled. "Yes, I understand that now."

Yves recalled suddenly how sweetly Gabrielle's lips had curved beneath his own and the delightful shiver she had given beneath his touch. Desire flickered to life within him, and not for the first time since he had made the lady's acquaintance.

"I apologize if I have behaved poorly in this and caused you anxiety," she said in a low voice. Her color heightened yet further in a most bewitching way. Yves wanted suddenly to pluck Gabrielle from her saddle and taste her sweetness once more.

What madness did this woman inspire in his mind?

His own confused silence seemed to compel the lady to explain herself further. "You see, Chevalier, I have had one husband." She paused and licked her lips, evidently having difficulty finding the words to explain her thoughts. "And we have made an agreement, you and I. Even if we should

wed…'' Her voice trailed away and Yves realized suddenly
the import of what she was saying.

"We pledged to a match in name alone," Yves said quietly.

The lady nodded and looked away, her cheeks crimson.

And that condition had been on her insistence. Yves saw
now that that had not been because of the taint of his birth,
for Gabrielle truly had known naught of that.

Gabrielle de Perricault was still in love with her deceased
husband.

There could be no other explanation. The anger that had
raged through Yves abandoned him callously, leaving him
feeling curiously despondent.

The lady loved a dead man.

That the explanation was perfectly logical did nothing to
mitigate the undeniable disappointment that Yves felt weigh
on his heart.

Disappointment? But that made no sense at all! Just days
past, he had been perfectly willing to accept the terms of a
match in name alone. Indeed, he had welcomed it!

Surely nothing could have changed?

He looked to Gabrielle and saw sympathy shining in the
violet depths of her eyes. "I would not mislead you," she
said softly.

It had been his kisses, Yves saw, too late to repair her
mistaken impression. She had thought—not unreasonably, he
supposed—that he meant to push the boundaries of their arrangement, like some base knave. But he had not intended
any such thing.

Had he? Yves felt completely at a loss in this newfound
tangle of emotion unleashed by Tulley's visit. Undoubtedly,
he would be his own self once Sayerne was farther behind
him.

And that was the most encouraging thought Yves had had
in a long time.

"I granted you my word once already on this matter," he conceded, surprised to hear his flat tone.

Gabrielle nodded but did not look at him, bittersweet memories evidently engulfing her thoughts. Yves frowned at that, not nearly as pleased with this turn of events as he thought he should be.

He should be relieved that the lady had no interest in him, that her heart still beat for the memory of a man long gone. He should be delighted that she would make no emotional demand upon him, that any relationship they might have would be based on the purity of reason alone, that any marriage they made would not be flooded with complicated entanglements.

But seeing Gabrielle ache for the loss of her husband irked Yves. He was not disappointed—no, that would have been unreasonable considering how little he knew the lady.

He must be feeling sympathy for the loss she had endured. Yes, that was it! It made perfect sense, even if it was the strongest bout of sympathy Yves had yet felt.

Curse Tulley for opening old wounds and giving Yves' heart free rein!

Gabrielle turned suddenly and impaled Yves with a bright glance. "Surely you can understand that I cannot risk revealing the location of my troops to you, as little as we are acquainted at this point."

There was an appeal for understanding in her tone now, instead of the demand that had been there earlier, and Yves felt himself responding to the lady's allure.

Somehow he had to win her trust, for in this campaign they could ill afford a lack of understanding between them. The very thought was so sensible that Yves was immediately reassured.

And with reassurance came inspiration. Yves knew suddenly that there was but one way to resolve this thorny issue. The lady held her son's welfare in highest esteem, after all.

Yves unsheathed his blade with a smooth gesture. As Gabrielle watched, he dropped to one knee, laid his naked blade across his palms and offered the weapon to her.

"I pledge that the count did release me from his service and grant me the freedom to swear my fealty elsewhere," he said solemnly. "On this day, in this place, I pledge my blade to your son, Thomas, heir to Perricault. I vow not to rest until both he and his legacy are retrieved from Philip de Trevaine."

Gabrielle's eyes flashed a warning that Yves did not understand. "To my *son?*"

"It is he who lies at the root of this, is it not?" Yves asked. "And he whose position as heir you do not want to see compromised. My pledge would be evidence of my commitment to your path."

If he had thought this would please her, it seemed that Yves had been wrong, though he could not fathom why. Gabrielle stared down at him, motionless upon her destrier, and Yves could not read her thoughts to save his very hide.

Leon cleared his throat. "If you cannot accept the sworn pledge of a knight of honor hired to your cause, my lady, then who will you trust?"

"And who *hired* that knight, Chevalier Leon?" Gabrielle demanded coldly.

The older knight looked to Yves and his lips twisted. "Surely, my lady, you do not expect the man to pledge his blade to *you?*"

Gabrielle's violet eyes blazed, but before Yves could make sense of that, much less respond, she dismounted impatiently.

Leon followed suit, but Yves had eyes only for the lady who halted before him. She stood tall and straight, lifting the blade from his hands with the grace of one familiar with the weight of the weapon. She kissed the blade, her gaze unswerving from Yves' own, then handed the sword to Leon.

It irritated Yves that she only did so at her loyal knight's behest. She had chosen Yves to take her errand—surely she more than any should trust his word!

Surely that distrust—coming from a woman of sound good

sense—was at the root of Yves' annoyance. Poor reason could be the only explanation for his most uncharacteristic emotional turmoil.

Yves folded his hands together, as though in prayer, and remained on his knees. Gabrielle's hands closed over his, her grip firm and sure.

"Swear it before me, in lieu of my son," she urged in a low voice.

Yves did not hesitate. "In the name of the Father, the Son and the Holy Spirit, I pledge the weight of my blade and the loyalty of my heart to Thomas de Perricault, heir of Perricault and its environs, from this moment forth. I pledge to serve the Lady Gabrielle de Perricault in the place of her son until such time as my lord Thomas is restored to Perricault and Perricault is liberated from the invading hand of Philip de Trevaine."

"So be it," Gabrielle said. Her clasp tightened slightly and she urged Yves to his feet with a minute pull. He stood and she kissed him once on each cheek, her lips brushing against his skin as softly as the first snow.

The subtle scent of her flesh teased his nostrils, and Yves felt a primal desire to kiss the lady anew, to make her forget this Michel who had planted his seed within her, to convince her to abandon the shadows of the past to welcome a new future.

But what was he thinking? Yves would never risk caring for another person again, as he had foolishly done once before.

Especially a woman whose heart was securely held by a dead man.

Leon bowed low before Yves, then returned Yves' own blade. "Your pledge changes matters between us two," the older man said with a sharp glance. "I was pledged to the Lord de Perricault, and serve his lady and son since his death. Know that my service follows your lead in the retrieval of the lord's son."

Yves looked to Gabrielle as she stiffened slightly. "My lady? Does this meet with your approval?"

Her eyes flashed, but she turned to mount her steed so quickly that Yves wondered whether he had imagined she might be angry. Leon quickly offered his interlaced hands and Gabrielle mounted without looking back. When she looked down at Yves from her saddle, her expression was coolly dispassionate.

"It is why you were chosen, after all," she conceded tightly.

Though that was the truth and matters seemed resolved in a most sensible way, Yves could not dismiss the impression that, beneath her calm expression, the lady was infuriated with him.

Before he could ask, Gabrielle turned her steed adroitly. "Daylight wanes, Chevaliers, and we still have far to ride this day," she concluded with the crisp manner he had come to associate with her.

The lady wasted no time with frivolous nonsense, that much was certain. Indeed, he had never met another like her. Though in this moment, Yves was not certain whether that was a compliment or a curse.

Gabrielle did not wait for their agreement, but touched her spurs to the destrier and plunged into the forest, leaving the men to scramble into their own saddles and follow suit.

"Women," Leon muttered under his breath, and Yves very nearly agreed aloud.

Men!

Gabrielle ground her teeth in frustration as she rode, determined not to give a single clue that might let the annoying knight guess at her anger. If Yves de Sant-Roux could hide his thoughts, then so could she!

Yet she had very nearly lost her composure when he had pledged his blade not to her—not to the Lady de Perricault who had chosen his blade—but to her son. How dare he assume that she was a simpering fool, like all those decorative women one found at court?

She was the Lady de Perricault! She was the one to whom the knights should have pledged in Michel's stead, but though those who remained had served her, they did not pledge to a woman's hand. That was one circumstance Gabrielle had been forced to accept.

But to have a knight choose to pledge to a mere child— whatever his gender or status as heir—instead of to her was galling, indeed.

And it was worse, far worse, for Yves to be the knight who made that choice. The one asset of which Gabrielle was unduly proud was her intellect. That this purportedly perceptive man had failed to note that characteristic was insulting.

It could not be that his opinion of her mattered in the least. This was merely a question of respect, deserved but unfairly withheld. She had held the inhabitants of Perricault together; she had provided for their welfare and safety; she had sought out the leader they needed to reclaim Perricault.

And Leon, curse him, had immediately bent his knee to Yves! Since Michel's death Leon had evidently never even imagined that he might pledge his fealty to Gabrielle!

Men!

Gabrielle rode Methuselah hard that afternoon, diving recklessly along the unmarked trail she knew as well as the palm of her own hand. Let this cocky knight keep pace with her, worthless woman that he deemed her to be!

Long after they left the road, a stream danced across their course, its water sparkling in the fading light. Vestiges of ice clung to the rocks that lined its banks, for the shadows were long here even at midday. Methuselah, well accustomed to this spot, bent to drink from the stream, while Gabrielle examined the opposite bank.

There was not a sign of another being, which was precisely as it should be. She noted how the moss had turned green on the rocks, glanced at the deceptive shadows of the rushing stream. The water ran surprisingly fast and deep here. It was cold and many of the stones were slick with moss.

One must know one's way to cross here without incident. Yves drew alongside her and his steed followed Methuselah's suit. The boy started to speak, but Yves held up a hand for silence and fixed his gaze upon Gabrielle.

Without even glancing his way, she knew that he realized this was a place of import. She wondered whether he would be surprised when he saw what lay beyond, and noted that Leon's expression was carefully impassive.

Perhaps this bold knight would soon have to reassess her intellect, after all!

Though, no doubt, he would grant the credit to Leon, despite whatever explanation was given. Irked at that thought, Gabrielle pursed her lips and gave a long clear whistle.

Two heartbeats later, an owl hooted from the forest on the far side of the stream. At least it sounded like an owl, but Gabrielle knew it was Franz acknowledging her cry.

And granting her leave to proceed.

Well aware of the way Yves' glance darted from her to the apparently uninhabited forest, Gabrielle urged Methuselah across the stream. He chose his footing carefully, having taken more than one plunge into these icy depths, and gained the far shore with a nicker and a stomp of his hooves.

Despite herself, Gabrielle turned to watch Yves follow suit, fully expecting that he might discover the stream's icy depths. A wicked part of her wished he would fall and lose some of his cursed composure, if only for a moment.

He did not plunge forward, though, but granted his steed time to pick his way across the precarious rocks. Once the black beast would have misstepped, but with a subtle click of his tongue and a touch on the stallion's neck, Yves directed him to the precise place Methuselah had stepped.

When the pair gained the shore, Yves slanted Gabrielle a

knowing look that made her flush. He had guessed she had wanted him to stumble! Curse his powers of observation!

"Yah! Comet! Make haste!"

Gabrielle glanced up, just in time to see Gaston plunge recklessly into the current with his palfry. "No!" she cried, seeing disaster the instant before it happened.

Leon and his destrier leaped from the far bank in pursuit, just as Yves jumped from his steed's back.

And the boy's palfry stumbled.

Gaston yelped in terror as the palfry struggled furiously to regain its lost footing. Before Gabrielle could summon another word, Yves strode into the rushing water. The palfry nickered in fear and the boy screamed.

Then a curtain of water obliterated all from view.

Chapter Six

Gabrielle was almost afraid to look at the result.

But there was naught to fear. A displeased-looking Yves stood thigh deep in midstream. He held his abashed and sodden squire by the scruff of his tabard and gave the boy a hearty shake even as Gabrielle watched. A shower of river water was loosed by Yves' shaking and scattered about the pair like falling crystals.

To Gabrielle's relief, the palfry had regained her footing only eight feet downstream, though she looked shaken and wet, as well. She had retreated of her own accord to the riverbank and stood shivering in the wake of her fright.

"How many times have I told you to look before you leap?" Yves growled.

Gaston clearly bore the full brunt of his attention now, and Gabrielle did not envy the boy, even though he was unharmed. Even Leon's squire squirmed in sympathy on the far bank, for the knight's brow was dark with disapproval.

Yves shook Gaston again, releasing another torrent of water from the boy's tabard. At least, Gabrielle reasoned, the boy's clothing had had a good rinse. She barely managed to restrain her smile at that, for it was clear Gaston was not one who showed much concern over such matters.

And the boy was in dire trouble with his knight.

"The most witless fool could see that this stream would be beyond difficult to cross," Yves growled, "yet you plunge forward as though you would trod a garden path!"

The boy's head hung even lower. "I am sorry, my lord."

His contrition lasted but a moment though, before his head snapped up and eyes shone brightly. "But I thought of great knights dashing through rapids and storming to battle, like Percival rushing to the keep of the Fisher King, determined to find the Holy Grail...."

"You did not think at all," Yves retorted. "And therein lies the problem. If you have no care for your own well-being, then at the very least, you should spare some consideration for your steed."

The boy looked to the palfry, whose accusing glare and periodic shivers might have prompted guilt in the most recalcitrant soul. The squire's lip trembled and he looked as though he might cry. "I am sorry, my lord."

The knight's voice lowered. "Gaston, mere words will not make compensation if you lose a steed through foolhardiness."

It seemed Gaston had nothing to say to that.

Yves strode to the shore, set the boy down and surveyed him sternly. Gaston shuffled his feet and took great interest in the state of his toes until Yves sighed and shoved one hand through his hair. He squatted down so that the boy could not avoid meeting his eyes.

"Gaston, I beg you to begin using what is between your ears for more than the recollection of fanciful tales."

"Yes, my lord."

"And on this eve, you will see that palfry thoroughly dried before you tend to your own needs."

"Yes, my lord."

Gaston sneezed then with a startling vehemence. He shivered, then turned obediently to collect his beast, his chin nearly dragging on the ground. It was clear to Gabrielle that

Gaston held Yves as his hero and anything that knight said
to him was taken directly to heart.

Yves shook his head, then strode back to his own mount.
Leon and his squire crossed the stream in silence. Even knowing the rebuke she was likely to earn, for the knight's lips
were still drawn in a tight line, Gabrielle felt obliged to in-
tervene.

"The boy will catch his chill if he does not abandon that
wet garb in short order," she counseled in an undertone.

Yves did not look at her, but his brows tightened and she
knew he attended her words.

Gabrielle braced herself for an ugly exchange, yet continued. "Let him at least take some hot broth before he tends
the palfry."

Yves swung into his saddle and granted her a look that
might have burned through steel. To Gabrielle's surprise, his
tone was level once more, though his words were clipped.
"The nights are cold in these parts?"

Gabrielle blinked to find her protest considered with evident seriousness. She hastened to continue, before Yves decided not to listen to her. "The chill comes down from the
mountains, even this late in the spring. And our accommodations, as you will see, are less than luxurious."

Yves took a deep breath, frowned at his squire, then
glanced back to Gabrielle. "You make good sense, as usual,
my lady," he admitted with a faint hint of that heart-
wrenching smile. "Forgive me for losing my temper with
Gaston."

Gabrielle blinked at his ready concession and unexpected
apology. In her mind's eye, she saw her father watching a
disobedient squire be whipped at his own command some
long-ago afternoon, his regal features tight with a disapproval
not unlike Yves'.

And she recalled Michel raging at young Thomas when the
child had accidentally broken a crock, not ceasing even when
the boy wept in contrition.

Men Gabrielle had known neither softened their stance nor apologized. She marveled that this knight did both so readily, yet could not help but wonder why.

"He has a rare enthusiasm," Gabrielle said gently, surprised by the pang that shot through her at the fleeting memory of her son. "And places great weight on your advice."

Yves made a sound that might have been a wry laugh. "That enthusiasm is the trouble. He thinks of nothing but romance and battle and scaling castle walls."

Gabrielle urged her steed to keep pace with Yves' destrier. "Surely it is harmless?"

"For one other than a knight, it might well be," Yves conceded, flicking a glance fraught with concern at the cowed squire. "But I fear that one day such distraction will cost Gaston his very hide."

Gabrielle's heart wrenched to see Yves' fears for his squire. But no! Men looked to the fulfillment of their own needs alone! That was one thing Gabrielle had learned only too well.

An unexpected disappointment in that certainty made Gabrielle's tone harsher than it might have been otherwise. "And you would have to train another boy," she said tartly, "at much inconvenience to yourself."

Yves glared at her, his golden eyes burning with anger. "My lady, I understand that you hold my character in low esteem, but such thinking would be beyond base. Surely it is not so preposterous that I should care for the boy's survival?"

Gabrielle stared into the knight's eyes and saw a sincerity gleaming there that humbled her. She had never imagined that any man could look beyond himself in concern for another's well-being, but evidently this one did for at least his squire. Gabrielle did not know what to think, much less what to say, in the face of such unexpected consideration.

"I am sorry," she said softly, feeling the words were hopelessly inadequate.

Yves nodded crisply. "In truth, none of this is your con-

cern, my lady, and I apologize in turn for burdening you with
my troubles.'' His tone was so devoid of emotion that they
might have been discussing the weather.

Gabrielle felt suddenly that Yves had firmly closed a door,
one that had momentarily gaped open and granted her a
glimpse of his inner thoughts. And now she stood decisively
outside that door.

She felt oddly bereft by that change.

But Yves merely arched a fair brow. ''Shall we continue
before boy and steed do catch that chill?''

Gabrielle clicked to Methuselah, noting only moments later
that Yves had spared no concern for his own welfare, though
he was as wet and undoubtedly as cold as the boy left to his
charge.

Was it possible that all men were not quite the same?

Gabrielle gripped her reins and forced herself to recall what
experience had taught her. Oh, she knew better than to be
swayed by a handsome man's charm!

By the time they left the riverbank, the shadows were beginning to grow long beneath the budding trees. Yves found
himself shivering, the chill of his mail permeating the wet
wool of his garb in a most troubling fashion.

He hoped they were not far from a site to camp, so that he
could make a fire in short order. Gaston sneezed repeatedly
and even the palfry seemed to be sniffling.

But Lady Gabrielle showed no signs of halting soon. All
around them, trees and shrubs rustled slightly in the breeze,
as though they whispered to each other of the company's
passing. Gabrielle led her stallion sharply to the right and
toward what looked to be an impenetrable wall of forest
growth.

She whistled once more, and again an owl answered within
a pair of heartbeats. It could be no coincidence, yet Yves had
no chance to consider the matter further.

He watched in astonishment as the wall of foliage parted

cleanly and opened like a pair of gates. A tall man garbed in green and brown stepped forward and separated himself from the shadows of the trees almost as though he had appeared by magic. He grinned and waved a greeting before disappearing behind the gates to open them more widely.

Gabrielle clicked her tongue and hastened her steed, Leon following suit from behind. Yves and Gaston were hustled through the amazing portal and it was shut securely behind them in a twinkling of an eye.

Yves looked back and found a gate woven of vines and adorned with leaves that helped it blend into the trees. It was opened with ropes, much as any other gate.

As his eyes adjusted to the long shadows, he perceived the woven vines that climbed to the top of the trees on all sides. Adorned with living growth, they made an effective shield between this place and anyone happening to wander past.

Marveling, Yves turned to find a valley he would not have guessed was there spread out before his very feet.

And the camp sheltered within was busy at this hour.

For a camp it most certainly was. There were horses tethered on all sides—destriers, palfrys and plow horses sharing feed bins. A pair of cows was being milked by two robust and warmly garbed woman. A trio of other women similarly dressed turned a spit of venison over the single fire.

Men of all ages and classes stomped their feet and blew on their hands, evidently waiting for the meat. Peasant farmer stood alongside knight and mercenary, squire and cowherd, each exchanging comment with the other. Tents and makeshift cabins were scattered beneath the trees, each draped in leaves and vines to hide it from prying eyes.

Stunned at the artfulness of this hiding place, Yves looked at Gabrielle, only to find assessment in her eyes.

"What remains of Perricault, village and keep, is sheltered here," she said firmly. "These people are what remain of my responsibility, and should you be fool enough to betray the confidence vested in you on this day, you will have to answer directly to me.''

There was a new thread of steel in her tone, yet Gabrielle's protectiveness of those beneath her hand only made Yves admire her even more. And he already was impressed with this camp, for it was no small accomplishment to have conjured this place from the forest itself.

''It is astonishing,'' Yves said simply, and unable to help himself, he scanned the camp wonderingly again. ''I never would have guessed it was hidden here, and I have made a career of discerning such concealment. Your husband was wise indeed to contrive this place before his untimely demise.''

Gabrielle's gaze did not waver, though her lips twisted wryly for an instant as though the idea was unspeakably ludicrous. Yves was momentarily confused, for such a response did hold true with her regard for that man. But then her words surprised him.

''Michel had nothing to do with this refuge.''

Yves frowned. ''I do not understand.''

Gabrielle lifted her chin proudly. ''We built it, after Perricault was lost, by the labor of our own hands.'' She dropped her voice and glared at him, as though daring him to believe her. ''And at my design.''

The import of her steady gaze stunned Yves. She told no lie.

But to think that a woman unversed in war had created this place! He scanned it once more, unable to hide his awe.

Too late Yves saw that he had not given Gabrielle and her quick mind the credit either deserved, and he resolved to do better in future. The lady was an asset he could not afford to ignore.

When their gazes met again, hers had not softened.

Yves inclined his head. ''I salute you, my lady, for this is no mean feat. Clearly I spoke too soon in telling you that a noblewoman could know nothing of the art of war.''

Gabrielle flushed and turned away at that, gesturing impatiently toward the blaze. "There will be a fire for only a little longer, for we light it for short duration. You should make haste to ensure that you and Gaston are dry before it is smothered."

Before Yves could respond, a heavyset man strode to the lady's side and grasped the stallion's reins. He was dressed as simply as the others, but was uncommonly tall and broad. Yves thought he might have been the man who opened the gates.

"Lady Gabrielle!" he cried. "Your return is welcome indeed!" He reached up and she shook his hand.

"I thank you, Franz," she said with a smile more sunny than any Yves had ever seen from her.

Noting the change in her manner when she greeted the gatekeeper irritated Yves, though he knew his response to be completely unfounded. What matter to him if the lady greeted another with a smile?

As Gabrielle inquired after events in her absence, talk began to spread through the ranks of those encamped there. One could almost watch the news of their lady's return spread through the assembly.

People left their tasks to come forward and greet her, and Gabrielle, to Yves' surprise, dismounted to meet them. Many of them were clearly common people, but Gabrielle greeted them as old friends. She kissed cheeks and shook hands, inquired after ailments and passed gentle fingers over troubled brows.

And Yves saw the relief of one and all that she had returned safely to them. To find such emotional ties among those carving their living from an estate was something unknown to Yves. To be sure, the count was always anxious to hear Yves' news when he returned, but there was a warmth among these people alien to him.

This was their home.

Just when Yves was certain their party had been forgotten, Gabrielle turned and gestured to him.

"I have brought the count's own champion to aid our fight," she said clearly, and all eyes turned to Yves in expectation. "Make way for both him and his squire, for they have need of the fire."

A small man stepped forward to take Merlin's reins, and Yves liked how the man paused to scratch the steed's ears. Merlin also seemed to approve, for he gave the man a thorough sniffing.

The assembly looked Yves over, and one villein nudged another when he spied the water dripping from Yves' boots. The pair both grinned, and again news went from ear to ear with the speed of the wind.

Franz grinned crookedly, displaying a gap in his smile where a tooth ought to have been. "Swimming at this hour, my lord?" he jested, as though the knight were indeed one of them.

Yves glanced pointedly toward his flushing squire. "Fishing, more like."

The assembly laughed, one or two pointing out the squire's sodden state, and Gaston colored even more deeply.

"Do not be worrying, wee laddie." A burly matron bustled forward and plucked Gaston right out of his saddle. The boy gave a yelp of protest, but had no chance against her sure grip. "You were not the first to take a misstep in that stream and you will not be the last." She fixed him with a stern eye. "Next time, you will be watching your way more careful like, I am certain."

Before the squire could respond, she tucked him under her arm and carried him off to the fireside as though he were no more than a wayward sheep. "What you are needing, wee laddie, is a bit of something hot in that stomach of yours," she chided.

Gaston's expression was so surprised that Yves nearly

laughed aloud. "My lord!" the squire cried, but Yves simply shook his head.

"No doubt she is right, Gaston," he called after them. Gaston struggled, but to no avail. The matron plopped him down in front of the hearty blaze and bade him stay put.

Gaston, quite remarkably, did precisely as he was told.

Yves' gaze flew to Gabrielle, only to find her lips quirking with suppressed merriment. Her smile made Yves suddenly feel as though he was not a foreigner watching from the outside.

It was a rare and welcome sensation for him.

"You had best be quick, for make no mistake, Eileen will be back for you," Gabrielle advised. Yves must have looked skeptical, for she continued, her eyes twinkling in a most enchanting way, "She has tossed me over her shoulder once or twice."

"Oh, my lord! I have no doubt Eileen could wrestle you to the fire!" The man holding Merlin's bridle jested with a conspiratorial wink. "Shall we take a wager?"

The others laughed, a welcoming and friendly sound, but Yves needed no further encouragement to dismount quickly. He hesitated a moment before leaving his faithful destrier, but the man gripping the reins shook his head reassuringly.

"You need not worry about this fine beast, sir," he said in a gentle tone. "I am Xavier, Perricault's ostler. Time was that we had many such as he in our stalls." The ostler sighed, then smiled when the stallion granted him a sidelong glance. The expression on the man's face as he looked up at Merlin told Yves more than words that the steed would be in good care.

"Then I shall be delighted to entrust him to your hand."

"It is fortunate for you," Xavier whispered to Merlin, "that I saved a bit of oats just in case the lady persuaded a fine knight to take our cause."

Merlin's ears twitched and he snorted as though he understood what was said. He followed the ostler's lead without protest. Another man led Gabrielle's silver stallion in the same direction, and that beast nosed Xavier from behind.

"Oho! Trying to make friends again now that there are oats to be had!" The ostler laughed and playfully brushed Methuselah's nose away. "You have not forgotten that old Xavier keeps them hidden away, have you? What about your tricks with the saddle, Master Methuselah? Have you forgotten *those* while you were away?"

"You have no need to worry," Leon counseled Yves. "The beasts love him as much as he loves them."

Yves nodded and felt a smile slide over his lips. "Yes, I can see it."

"I shall ensure that he knows about Gaston's palfry, for you have much to do this eve." The older knight winked at Yves. "Rest assured, the creature will be so spoiled that she will likely leap into the stream as soon as she sees it again."

Yves glanced toward the fire, but Gaston had been bundled up and was sipping broth. It was clear the boy could not tend his steed himself, but Yves would ensure he did some extra labor on the morrow to encourage him to think before he acted.

Yves thanked the knight and strode toward the welcoming fire. Children trailed behind him, each and every one surreptitiously examining his weaponry and garb as they whispered to each other in excitement. Gabrielle fell behind, surrounded as she was by those with stories to share.

When the meat was gone, all eyes turned to Yves, seemingly of one accord. He stepped forward and the men closed ranks about him. Yves squatted down and laced his fingers together, bracing his elbows on his knees as he surveyed the circle of men about him.

Each face was somber.

"Tell me what you know of Perricault," he invited quietly. One man stepped forward and drew a snaking line in the dirt before Yves. "The river is here," he said, and drew a rectangle along the east side. "The château is here."

"How high is the riverbank?" Yves asked.

"There is a sheer drop to the river, with the walls rising high above it." The man flicked him a level glance. "They are mercilessly smooth and the wall is always staffed with archers.

"And the barbican is there," the man added, leaning forward to add two circles to the north end of the plan as Yves watched. "With a pair of towers on either side of the gate."

"And this wall?" Yves indicated the east side, and the man frowned.

"A tributary of the river runs there, meeting the main stream at the south end of the keep." He drew another line so that Perricault was nestled in the fork of the river. Yves grimaced just as the man glanced up at him. "It is a smaller river and the bank less steep, but it is no less treacherous for all of that."

"And behind the gates?"

"An outer bailey with another set of walls and gates that surround the high tower and inner bailey."

Which was almost certainly where Thomas was being kept. Yves frowned anew at the drawing. "Tell me about this."

"Wood gates on the exterior, then a portcullis, then a smaller interior pair of steel gates." The man ran a gloved finger over the line that indicated the northern wall. "There is no way to approach the gates without being observed, for the curtain wall is rife with observation points."

"You seem to know Perricault well," Yves commented, looking into the man's weatherbeaten face. Yves had learned to be leery of those anxious to share what they knew, but this man looked to be one who had long earned his way with his blade.

The man appeared to be thirty summers of age or so, though those years had been hard-won. His face was tanned, a long healed scar snaking a line across one cheek. In other circumstance, he might have been considered a handsome man. As it was, he looked to be an effective warrior.

His dark hair was long and tied back with a length of rawhide. His lips were set in an uncompromising line and his gray stare was piercing. There was not a measure of fat on his flesh, from the look of him, yet his muscles strained at the shoulders of his tunic. A veritable armory of blades hung from his heavy belt.

This man would be no small opponent.

His armor was odds and ends, purloined from this battle and another, Yves was certain. His boiled-leather breastplate was colored with age and wear; his woolen chausses were laced above his boots with leather thongs. All of his garb was of various browns, and Yves guessed he would fairly melt into the shadows of the forest.

Not a knight, but a fighting man nonetheless. Yves would have need of every ready blade, be it wielded by a nobleman or no, to see this task done.

The man shrugged. "Retrieving the heir of Perricault is a problem we have all sought to solve for the past six months. There is something about a puzzle like this that seizes a man's mind."

Yves watched the mercenary's gaze flick over the sketch, as though he sought to solve the puzzle on the spot, and appreciated his determination to aid Gabrielle. "What is your name?"

"Seymour de Crecy, sir."

"You were pledged to Perricault?"

"To Lord Michel de Perricault himself," Seymour acknowledged, and his eyes narrowed as he met Yves' regard. "May the Lord bless his soul."

Yves held the man's gaze, letting him see that he already knew the circumstance of Michel's unfortunate demise. "Yet you did not seek other employ when that man met his end?"

Seymour's lips twisted in a crooked smile. "There is something about a boy stolen from his mother's side that seizes the heart of even one hardened by battle, is there not?'' he asked softly.

Yves was suddenly glad to have this able warrior on his side. It was beneficial to have like-minded men raise blades together, for their responses under duress could be more readily guessed.

Yet despite his instinctive approval and the man's history of loyalty to the house of Perricault, Yves knew better than to trust those he had just met. And there was one certain way to test the reliability of Seymour's word.

"I would have you pledge your blade to me," Yves said.

Seymour glanced up suddenly, then flicked a glance to Lady Gabrielle, who stood slightly to one side. The move made the firelight catch the old scar on his cheek. Yves might have been troubled by the sudden reaction, had the man not obviously nursed a primary loyalty to Gabrielle.

"The lady agrees with this course?" Seymour asked with obvious concern.

"I have already pledged to him," Leon interjected from behind Yves.

That seemed to be all the assurance Seymour needed. The mercenary stood and proudly unsheathed his blade, offering its hilt to Yves. "I am but a man hired for warfare, my lord, but I should be honored to serve both you and Lady Gabrielle in the task of retrieving the heir of Perricault."

He dropped to one knee, and Yves could find no fault with the pledge. He looked up from Seymour's bent head to find the other men in a line before him, ready to pledge to his hand. Lady Gabrielle still stood to one side, the firelight painting her impassive features with golden light.

Yves caught a glimpse of unhappiness in the curve of her lips before she pivoted and stalked into the shadows of the night. He frowned in confusion. Nothing could be amiss—indeed, all went better than Yves might have hoped.

Then why was the lady troubled?

Yves looked to the men before him, then at the lady, unable

to explain his desire to lend chase and discover the root of
her dismay. Surely his task was here, with the men? Surely
there was no reason to be torn by a woman's whim?

What had Tulley's visit done to his decisive thinking?

Chapter Seven

"My lord?" Seymour appeared at Yves' elbow when the fire burned down to embers, his voice low. "I did hear something of late that might be of assistance."

"Indeed? Why did you not speak sooner?"

The man shrugged. "I thought it wiser to mention it to you in privacy first." Seymour grimaced. "You see, my lord, I did not want to speak of this matter before the others, because I cannot say whether it might be true or not."

Yves was intrigued. "And what is this matter?"

Seymour leaned closer. "I overheard that Philip de Trevaine intends to return to Château Trevaine soon and leave Perricault with a very small defending force."

Yves frowned. "Why would he do such a thing?"

"I do not know." Seymour spread his hands. "Perhaps he is reassured that none have come to avenge his attack upon that keep. Perhaps another covets his own holding of Trevaine and he fears for its security."

Yves considered this for a long moment, wondering whether any man could truly be surprised that no retaliation had come in the dead of winter. It was traditional, after all, to wage war only in the summer months.

Surely Philip would be expecting an attack only now?

But then, if a man had to choose between his primary holding and a recent acquisition, who could say which way he might bend? And truly, what did Yves know of the strategic workings of Philip de Trevaine's mind?

The man might well be an impetuous fool. Yves had met many of that ilk in his days.

"Where did you hear this?"

"Outside Perricault." Seymour's words came low and quick. "We go almost daily to keep a watch. There is a garrisoned bridge across the river to the north of the walls, but it is close enough to the forest that one can sometimes creep sufficiently near to hear the guards talking."

"Which branch of the river?"

"It spans them both and in truth is an ideal spot to assess the strength of the forces there. It is where we hide to count Philip's men." Seymour's eyes gleamed. "It was there, just yesterday morn, that I overheard two guards discussing the imminent departure."

Yves stared at the ground, thinking about this morsel of news. It seemed indeed to be a gift from out of the blue.

Could Philip truly be such a fool?

"It could be the opportunity we seek, my lord!" Seymour whispered.

Yves considered the man's shining eyes for a long moment. "Yes," he said carefully. "That it could be." He shrugged. "Or it could be a ruse, designed to deceive us all and lead us into a trap."

"That would not be so unreasonable," a voice declared from the darkness behind. "Philip won Perricault with deceit, after all."

Seymour jumped in alarm, and Yves pivoted smoothly to face a shadow behind them. Lady Gabrielle could be vaguely discerned, her arms folded across her chest.

"I thought Perricault was won by force," Yves said carefully.

"That is what we were all meant to think," Gabrielle ac-

knowledged. "But I have always wondered whether there was
one inside to make matters easier."

"My lady!" Seymour scoffed, recovering from his surprise. "I was on the wall that very night! There was no one
inside. They took the gate by surprise and viciousness alone."

Gabrielle, Yves saw, looked unconvinced, though she said
nothing else. She studied the other man, then looked to Yves
wordlessly. He was sorely tempted to put weight in her assessment of the situation. Had the lady not shown she was
keen of wit?

And Seymour did not seem the kind of man who had an
appreciation for subtlety. He might well have missed the flickering shadow of someone opening the gate.

Now Seymour laughed mockingly. "My lady! With all due
respect, I beg you leave matters of war to those who know
them best!"

Gabrielle stiffened, and the glance she fired Yves' way was
beyond hostile. "Of course," she said tightly, then turned to
walk away.

But Yves was not quite so ready to dismiss the lady's per-
ceptions. He waved off Seymour and gave chase.

Would there ever be a man in all of Christendom who
could acknowledge that a woman might have something of
merit to say?

Gabrielle stalked through the darkness, knowing her way
well enough, though she doubted she would be quite in the
mood to pray for Thomas by the time she reached her favored
spot.

In truth, Gabrielle was angry with herself for daring to hope
that Yves might show some regard for her opinion. Fool! Of
course he had not! Was he not a man like all the others?

"My lady?"

Gabrielle spun and was astonished to find the knight in
question pursuing her with undue haste. She halted and he
stepped up to her, his expression guarded.

How she hated that she could discern so little of his thoughts!

"I would hear more of your thoughts about Perricault," he said, but Gabrielle spun away.

"So, now my counsel is considered useful!"

The knight hesitated, then continued chase. "Your counsel was always considered useful," he commented, his tone bland.

"Only after you had learned all you could from the men in this camp," Gabrielle muttered. "Never mind that I have lived in that keep for longer than any of them, never mind that I could likely tell you the very room in which Thomas is held, never mind that I have actually met this base knave of an invader!" Gabrielle ground her teeth. "Obviously *men* have more of import to contribute than I."

The knight cleared his throat. Gabrielle stole a glance in his direction to find a slight frown marring his brow. "Make no mistake, my lady, I have learned a keen appreciation of your intellect. It simply seemed fitting to me to have the loyalty of these men pledged as soon as possible."

To Gabrielle's annoyance, she could make no argument against that, so she strode onward in silence.

"I wished also to see them and hear them speak, to listen to what they thought of import." He flicked a telling glance in Gabrielle's direction, which she steadfastly ignored. "You were there as well, my lady. Tell me what you can about these men."

Gabrielle shrugged, not yet ready to willingly provide the information he sought. "They are men of war. I know them little."

"You know more than you admit," Yves chided. "Were they all in your husband's employ?"

"Yes."

"For how long?"

Gabrielle sighed and faced the determined knight with her

hands on her hips. It was clear he would pursue her until he had the information he wanted.

"Those pledged longest to the house were killed in the attack, it seemed, with the exception of Leon. He was sworn to my husband long before we were wed." Gabrielle frowned, trying to remember. "The others came over the years, though I cannot clearly recall which ones came when."

"How long were you wed?"

"It would have been seven years at the last Yule."

"And you knew both Leon and your spouse before?"

"My father did." Gabrielle was surprised to hear the flat tone of her voice, so closely an echo of the knight's usual monotone. "I met Michel at the altar and Leon shortly thereafter."

"And Seymour? When did he come?"

Gabrielle had to consider that. The knight waited patiently, evidently guessing that she was trying to recall. The new leaves rustled in the trees far overhead and a few stars could be discerned through the nearly barren branches. A cool wind lifted Gabrielle's skirts and the sounds of the camp had faded slightly behind them.

"Last Yule," she acknowledged finally, lifting her gaze to meet Yves'. "I remember him coming into the hall with snow on his shoulders and Michel welcoming him to the board on such a holy day."

The knight frowned and looked back over the camp. "Is he reliable?"

Gabrielle shrugged. "As he said himself, Seymour was on the wall that night and fought valiantly for Michel's forces. It was he who stood over Michel when he had fallen so that he might be laid decently to rest."

Yves turned and his gaze locked with hers. "I take it that was no small risk."

Gabrielle nodded agreement, reluctantly conceding the honor of Seymour's action. She had never liked the man,

though she knew that was due more to his opinions of women
and his rough manner than to anything he did.

"Many others would have fled," she admitted, and shivered in recollection of the carnage she had witnessed. "Indeed, many others did."

Her words hung between them, though the growing silence
made Gabrielle uneasy. She was well aware of Yves' assessing scrutiny and did not dare to flinch beneath his regard.

"Yet you do not like the man?" he asked finally, his voice
low.

Gabrielle sighed and ran one hand over her hair. Indeed,
she should have guessed that Yves would discern the truth.

Before answering, she fought to separate emotion from reason and failed utterly. "I must confess that I cannot be ob-
jective about any man who believes women are useful for one
matter alone," she admitted in a low voice. "And Seymour
de Crecy is less than subtle in his opinions."

Yves' chuckle thrummed in the darkness, the unexpected-
ness of the sound making Gabrielle glance up. He was somber
by the time her gaze reached his visage, though a suspicious
twitch was evident at the corner of his mouth.

"I can well imagine that you cannot," he acknowledged
with a slight bow. "Yet that has little bearing on either the
man's value with a blade or his trustworthiness."

Gabrielle sighed again, well aware of the reason of the
argument. "I suppose it does not," she agreed hesitantly.

Yves waited.

Gabrielle considered the matter for a long moment, then
looked to the knight again. Fairness demanded that the mercenary be given his due.

"Michel trusted Seymour, this much I know," she confided. "Certainly there were never any complaints about him
within the household, except perhaps from the occasional
maid who found him too friendly for her taste. And, as you
say, it was without concern for his own safety that Seymour
guarded Michel's body during Perricault's attack."

Yves studied her, then nodded. He pursed his lips and scanned the undergrowth about them as he thought. When he spoke, his voice was low and his words came slowly. "So the question remains as to whether the news he overheard is true."

Gabrielle took a deep breath, preparing to speak her mind yet again. Indeed, the very fact that this man seemed to give credit to her opinions emboldened her to share them.

It occurred to her that she could readily grow accustomed to such discussions with this man. A thrill of anticipation raced through her at the idea of Yves becoming her spouse, before she stomped determinedly on it.

Theirs would be a match in name alone, and that at her dictate. And Yves would undoubtedly cease to be interested in her opinion once—or *if*—he retrieved Perricault and was installed as its lord.

Gabrielle cleared her throat, refusing to admit how those thoughts had dampened her spirits. "Do you not think it odd that Philip would consider leaving Perricault just when there is the best chance of someone avenging his attack?"

"Yes." Yves nodded and his gaze burned into hers. Gabrielle felt herself flush slightly beneath his perusal, though she knew she was a fool to take his agreement as anything other than that. "That is *precisely* what I find strange about this news. You are astute to recognize that inconsistency."

Gabrielle shrugged, not in the least accustomed to praise for her thinking. Indeed, no man had ever even listened to her before! "It simply makes sense," she demurred, though Yves' gaze was unswerving.

"Only to one who thinks matters through, as you do." He paused, and Gabrielle glowed silently with his praise.

"What will you do?" she had to ask.

Yves glanced at her and a smile danced across his lips so fleetingly that it was gone before she fully realized it was there. "Very little until I know more," he said. "On the morrow, I will go to Perricault myself to see the situation. Is it far?''

"An hour's ride."

"I shall walk, for it will be more quiet that way."

"I can show you the way."

Yves' eyes flashed golden. "You will remain here! There is no need to risk your hide any more than you have already done!"

"I will not be left behind!" Gabrielle retorted, outraged to be dismissed from the planning yet again. "Thomas is my son!"

"And you are his only parent left in this world." Yves' tone was as stern as it oft was with Gaston.

Gabrielle gaped in surprise that this was his reason.

Yves glowered at her, evidently anticipating that she would argue. "Understand, my lady, that I shall *not* be responsible for that child being left alone in this world."

The ferocity of Yves' concern for Thomas so astonished Gabrielle that his words silenced any protest she might have made.

He was denying her the right to accompany his mission purely to ensure her own safety?

The very idea was stunning for Gabrielle, whose survival had been taken for granted by those around her all her life. No one had ever troubled to worry about her safety. It was only after she had absorbed that astonishing fact that she wondered at the root of Yves' concern.

"That is not the first time you have spoken thus," she observed carefully, having already noted how hesitant he was to speak of his own history. Gabrielle recalled suddenly his tirade at the river, a rare show of emotion from this man, and his confession of bastardy.

The knight looked away and frowned into the dense shadows of the forest. He said nothing.

But he did not immediately walk away. Yves lingered as

though he would confess his reasoning to her, had he only known how to begin.

Compassion welled within Gabrielle, for she guessed that Yves had not been blessed with an easy road in this life. In that moment, she decided to press the issue.

The gentleness of her tone surprised even Gabrielle herself. "Am I wrong to guess this a matter of particular import for you?"

Yves scuffed his boot in the dirt as he shook his head, then glanced at her anew, as though he was afraid of some censure he might find in her eyes. Gabrielle knew she showed none, for she felt none, and their gazes clung.

"I was alone," Yves admitted in a low voice. "Indeed, I have been alone virtually every day and night of my life."

"Have you no siblings?"

Yves shook his head. "A sister, who was lost through my own youthful folly."

It was clear he blamed himself for this sister's demise, and Gabrielle rushed to reassure him. "But—"

"But nothing," Yves interrupted firmly. "Although I have fared well enough, my lady, mine is not a fate I would see bestowed upon any other." He flashed a glance toward her. "Let that explanation suffice for the moment."

It was not easy for him to speak of himself, Gabrielle saw. She smiled reassuringly at him as she nodded. "As you wish," she said, not wanting to make him feel he had made a mistake in confiding in her. "But know that I will listen whenever you wish to talk of your sister or anything else."

The knight stared at her, as though amazed by such an offer.

Then, ever so slowly, an answering smile crept across his lips.

The tentative smile made him look much younger than Gabrielle had ever seen him. Her heart wrenched to have that smile turned upon her, for Yves was infinitely more attractive this way than with his lips drawn in a stern line.

"Make no mistake, my lady," he said with resolve. "Your welfare in this matter is of equal importance to me as that of Thomas."

The intensity of his amber gaze made Gabrielle's heart skip a beat. Surely he could not mean as much as his glance implied? Surely this man, convinced to join her cause only of late, could not truly care whether she lived or died?

No! Yves' concern was only for Thomas. It was to Thomas he had pledged his blade; it was the retrieval of Thomas that he had sworn to see done.

All the same, Gabrielle could not seem to draw a full breath into her lungs. With difficulty, she tore her gaze away from his and studied the forest with feigned fascination.

The man had an appeal, that much was certain. Somehow it was becoming increasingly difficult to recall that such a finely wrought man would have learned to use that appeal as effectively as every other weapon in his arsenal.

Her father certainly had known such skill.

Gabrielle must focus upon the duty before them. She was the key to Thomas not being alone, a state he had admitted to finding important. She was the one who knew most about Perricault and these men pledged to the house. She was the key to Yves' attaining lordship of the estate.

A lordship Yves had said he did not desire.

Confusion reigned within Gabrielle at that recollection and she knew she had to be free of this man's dizzying presence to sort fantasy from fact.

"I thank you for your concern," she said, and hated the breathlessness of her voice. What had happened to her usual matter-of-fact tone? "If you will excuse me, I have an errand."

And Gabrielle, much to her own shame, fairly fled into the forest.

It was decidedly unlike Lady Gabrielle to turn tail and run, but that was exactly what it appeared she was doing.

For the second time in short order.

Yves could not imagine what he had done to frighten her. He watched her retreating figure with confusion that slowly melted into curiosity.

What kind of errand could she have up there in the woods? She had long ago passed the latrines, but showed no signs of slowing her course. Yves lent chase yet again, determined to set matters between them to rights.

Suddenly, Gabrielle halted, and it appeared she fell to her knees. Yves leaped forward, realizing too late that she had done so deliberately.

The lady looked up and Yves froze, feeling like a child caught with one hand on the sugarloaf. They stared at each other for a long moment while the wind rustled through the new growth overhead.

"I must apologize," Yves murmured finally. "I have interrupted your prayers."

Gabrielle seemed embarrassed and that tempting flush rose over her cheeks once more. Yves could not help but take a step closer. It amazed him that the same woman who could argue a point with vehement logic could moments later flush with a softness that made him want to taste her kisses anew.

"Yes, I pray for Thomas each night. You likely think my efforts wasted...."

"On the contrary."

Gabrielle's gaze flew to his, and Yves closed the distance between them. "I would have expected you to be a skeptic," she admitted.

"And so I have been," Yves acknowledged with a rueful shrug of his shoulders. "Yet there must be some effect to your prayers, for you alone were able to persuade me to take your cause, and that against all odds. Do not forget that Tulley tried to force me to his will only moments before your own arrival."

"And he failed."

"Most definitely."

Gabrielle's violet gaze clung to Yves' face. He had the sense that there were none but they two in the world, and recalled yet again the sweet press of her lips beneath his own.

The wayward thought awakened a heat deep within Yves that made it very difficult to follow the thread of the conversation.

"While you, my lady, succeeded," Yves concluded. "Surely that must be of import."

"You do not mock me in this," Gabrielle whispered.

Mock her? "Of course not."

"Then you will not keep me from my prayers any longer." Gabrielle's tone was dismissive.

But Yves was not quite ready to turn away. He looked back over his shoulder toward the slumbering camp and his heart ached at the homecoming that had greeted Gabrielle here.

For the first time in all his days, he felt that there was someone in whom he could confide. Gabrielle had not judged him for sharing the tale of his bastardy, after all.

She deserved the truth.

All the same, such confessions did not come easily to an independent man like Yves.

"My lady, this place is unlike any I have known," he said with less than his usual grace, his words falling more quickly than was his wont.

Gabrielle seemed to force a polite laugh. "It is not the accommodation any of us are accustomed to—"

"No, I do not mean that." Yves interrupted her with a terse shake of his head. "It is a home, as no place I have ever called my own has been."

Gabrielle's lips parted with surprise. "You have never had a home? What about Sant-Roux?"

"A fiction, created by the man who knighted me long after I fled my father's abode." Yves glanced toward her and then away, fearing her censure. "He had to knight me in the name of some estate and was reluctant to use his own, lest others think me *his* bastard."

"But your mother…"

"Died but days after I was born," Yves supplied tightly. He could not look at her, so frowned into the shadows of the forest. "And my father was less than delighted to have a bastard son underfoot."

"But surely at the count's court…"

"I was a bastard, tolerated for my abilities," Yves said savagely. "The count, to be sure, has always been gracious about my birth, but few others share his grace." He shook his head then and forced his tone to become cool once more. "I apologize, my lady, for none of this is your concern."

Gabrielle, to Yves' surprise, rose and laid a hand upon his arm. Reluctantly, he looked into her eyes, relief flooding through him at the compassion that shone there. "No, I apologize doubly for any offense caused," she said quietly. "I can well understand why you find the issue of your birth a troubling one."

Yves shook his head. "You did not know." He looked back toward the camp, his eyes narrowed against the darkness. "Just as you cannot know what a pleasure it is to be welcomed in such a home as this."

Gabrielle's grip tightened on his arm, the slight weight of her slender figures sending a tingle over Yves' flesh.

"I have never raised my voice in prayer, my lady," Yves admitted hoarsely. "But it seems that on this night I have something to be thankful for."

She inhaled sharply in surprise. "You have never prayed!"

Yves studied his boots and shook his head. "Indeed, I do not know how to begin," he confessed. "But since our objectives are as one in this, I would appreciate if you would permit me to lift my voice along with yours."

Gabrielle said nothing and Yves feared she would refuse him. He glanced at her and their gazes locked once more. "I would add my entreaties for your son's safe return to your side."

Gabrielle could not have declined Yves' simple request for all the riches in Christendom. She stared into the amber depths of his eyes, marveling that he had not been more severely scarred after all that he had endured.

It was so easy to imagine Yves as a young boy, a boy not unlike Thomas, all alone in an unkind world. Gabrielle's heart ached for what Yves must have endured. It was a credit to the strength of his character that he had become the success he was, for certainly the world had not granted him any favor.

"It is easy enough," she said huskily, and offered him her hand. The warmth of his grip closed securely over her own. Gabrielle began to pray, and Yves haltingly echoed her words, lending his voice to her appeal.

And for the first time since she could remember, Gabrielle felt she was not alone in battling the forces arrayed against her and her son.

Chapter Eight

The mist was still clinging to the surface of the river when Yves had his first sight of Château Perricault.

True to rumor, the keep rose high and unassailable above the river, which noisily raged at spring heights. A tributary joined the river at the south end of the massive rock that rose to support the keep itself, and the water boiled there against the great boulders scattered at the base of the steep cliffs. The walls that capped the cliffs were unsurmountably high.

A natural wonder had been transformed into a fortress that would not be readily assailed. The river's swift flow and the volume of water made it impossible to even consider crossing anywhere other than the bridge.

And Yves could see the men pacing its length even from here. Similarly, men could be spotted on the high curtain walls above, and there were more lookouts for archers than Yves would have preferred.

How he had hoped that Seymour had overestimated the keep's strength! It was doubly defeating to see that its formidability had been understated.

"It does not look good, does it, my lord?" Leon murmured by Yves' side. He was the only man to accompany Yves this morning.

"Not from this side," Yves acknowledged. "Though it

would be a fine keep to defend.'' Which made Yves marvel
anew that Philip had claimed Perricault so readily.

Could Gabrielle's suspicion be right? Just the thought of
her, and the shadows lurking in her violet eyes when she
spoke of Thomas, distracted Yves from the puzzle before him.

Never had he met a woman with whom he could so readily
talk, who grasped so easily the full import of strategy and
planning. Yves had told her more than he had ever confided
in another, yet the awareness of that did not make him feel
exposed. He felt more calm than he certainly had of late, as
though the burden of his history was not the weight he had
long believed. For a man who had always kept his thoughts
to himself, that was remarkable enough in and of itself.

But Gabrielle listened without judgment. She took Yves for
what he was and did not hold his bastardy against him. Gabrielle only succumbed to the emotion that ruled most
women's lives when she feared for Thomas, and that was
sentiment Yves could readily understand.

He wondered suddenly what it would be like to hold a
place in that lady's esteem. An unfamiliar longing rushed
through him with such dizzying speed that Yves banished the
thought and forced himself to consider the dauntingly high
walls of Perricault once more.

Certainly it seemed against the odds that any surprise
would be great enough to win access to the château without
inside aid, for this keep could be defended with very few men.

But perhaps he misjudged its situation.

"Closer," he urged Leon, and the pair crept toward the
bridge in silence. The thick forest undergrowth hid them from
view, especially wrapped as they were in brown, homespun
cloaks. The fog over the river similarly aided their mission.

The bridge was surprisingly active for such an early hour.
Yves could hear men's boots stomping on the wooden planks
even before they drew alongside. Noting how readily the
sound carried through the mist, he silently advised Leon to
move yet more quietly.

The sky had just barely lightened to gray in the east, but gradually Yves could discern great numbers of men mounted and armed on the road to Perricault's gates. Heavily laden wagons and carts spilled through the high gates even as they watched.

Could Seymour have spoken aright?

Yves and Leon exchanged a glance and settled in to the last outstretched finger of the forest to listen and watch.

"Hail, Reynaud!" bellowed one guard. "Have you enough ale in that cart to warm the Lord de Trevaine's belly in his home estate?"

The man driving the cart flicked his whip at the donkeys harnessed before it. "That and enough even for the thieving likes of you!" he retorted.

The men on the bridge laughed, then ushered the cart towards the bridge that crossed the opposite branch of the river. Yves drew a crude map in the dirt, placing Trevaine to the east of that river before looking questioningly to Leon.

That man nodded emphatically, then pointed back to the activity on the bridge.

A caparisoned steed of obviously fine breeding pranced down the road, the knight upon him garbed in fine mail and cloaked in crimson. A pair of squires trotted their palfrys before the destrier, one holding a standard of similar red hue high before the knight. A bevy of knights followed behind, their trap clattering in the morning light, their virtual army of squires trailing behind.

Yves looked at Leon, who traced a mark on his chest where the knight displayed his emblem. He moved his lips so that the name was clear without him uttering a sound.

"Philip de Trevaine."

Yves narrowed his eyes and scanned the obviously departing party once more. This was his opponent. It was impossible to discern much of Philip, for that man was fully helmeted and cloaked. He seemed of a build and carriage suitable to a man not much older than Yves.

Philip rode down the road from the castle gates and led his retinue across the far bridge. As soon as he reached the far shore, he gave his destrier his spurs. The party galloped along the road and were swallowed by the forest in mere moments.

And silence reigned.

Seymour was right, it seemed, for Philip looked to be abandoning Perricault. Yves scanned the walls once more and spotted only three or four archers lining the summit. Perhaps Philip, too, thought the keep could be defended with few hands.

But where was Thomas? Yves scanned the stragglers, scrutinizing each horse that passed, and could not find evidence of a small boy anywhere within their ranks.

And no child had ridden with Philip, Yves was certain. There were no women, either, not even any whores trailing behind the knights and men-at-arms, leaving him to wonder whether Philip had abandoned them within the keep, purportedly to care for the boy.

All the same, it was most odd.

Horses' hooves clattered on the bridge to the far side and, to Yves' amazement, the better part of the guards on gates and bridges turned to follow Philip's departing company.

By the time the sun crested the horizon and dispelled the mist from the river's surface, only a handful of souls remained in residence at Perricault.

Yves leaned back in the shrubbery and scowled at the keep etched against the morning sky. It seemed that his opponent was a more trusting fool than Yves could have imagined possible.

Seymour *had* been right. This was the opportunity they needed, and Yves knew he would be a fool himself if he did not take advantage of Philip's certainty that Perricault was securely his own.

Rumor, after all, of Yves' departure with Gabrielle might await Philip at Trevaine. It was imperative that Yves act now, while he yet had the elements of surprise and Philip's cocky confidence upon his side.

Had Yves known that a whistle echoed to mark his departure from the river valley, he might have been less certain of Philip de Trevaine's folly.

No less if he had witnessed those same departing troops quietly filtering back through the gates of Château Perricault. By noon, the keep looked precisely as it had when he left, with the marked difference that its walls sheltered a formidable army on full alert for Yves' next move.

Darkness had fallen on the forest camp by the time all of the horses were mustered. Gabrielle surveyed the armed troops and approved of their restlessness. They were anxious to strike a blow for her son, ready to avenge Philip's crimes against Perricault, and she would not have missed riding out with them.

The trick was that Yves de Sant-Roux must know nothing of her presence until it was too late to turn back. She could imagine full well that he would not take kindly to a woman in the ranks, but Gabrielle was determined to have the earliest possible glimpse of her son.

Seymour had been more than delighted to accept her offer of his riding Methuselah, though that destrier had been less than impressed to find an unfamiliar rider in his saddle. Indeed, the steed might be the one to give Gabrielle away, for his accusing glare was locked unswervingly upon her.

Curse the beast!

Here Gabrielle had thought the plain rough garb she had filched—including men's heavy woolen chausses—hid her identity remarkably well. The chestnut palfry she had quietly commandeered was not worthy of note. With mud smeared on her face, Gabrielle had prided herself that she blended readily into the company of miscellaneous troops.

At least until Methuselah fixed his stare upon her. Gabrielle fought to show no signs of discomfiture, and hoped against hope that the night would conceal any telltale hints of her identity.

It seemed that Yves at least was unaware of her presence.

"Where is Lady Gabrielle?" she heard him demand of Leon, who shrugged and looked about the camp. "I had expected she would see us off on this mission."

There was an obligation Gabrielle had nearly forgotten! She caught her breath. Methuselah stared stubbornly at her, as though he would answer the question for all.

"That beast seems taken with your steed," murmured the man beside Gabrielle.

She made a gruff sound and nodded as the man chuckled to himself. "They are a horny lot, those stallions, regardless of where they find themselves."

He leaned over and tapped her saddle with a knowing finger. Gabrielle's heart stopped with the certainty that he would look into her face and see the truth.

"Mind you watch your steed's back, lest that one take it into his mind to pursue another conquest than the one we all seek this night."

Rough laughter echoed about Gabrielle, and she tried to look comfortable with the man's earthy conversation. She grunted acquiescence, as he seemed to be awaiting an answer, and to her relief, he nodded and looked away.

Gabrielle exhaled as silently as she could manage and prayed her heart would cease its erratic pounding. Surely someone would hear the thunder of her pulse?

"She complained of a sour stomach when she offered me her steed," Seymour recalled, much to Gabrielle's relief. He smirked. "Women, you know, seldom have the constitution to face adversity."

Before Gabrielle's blood could boil, Yves slanted the man a glance that spoke volumes. "Lady Gabrielle is a rare breed in many matters," he said sternly. "I should hope you sent a healer to her, for she is not a woman given to nervous ailments.''

A healer! Would Yves check upon her welfare himself? At the prospect, Gabrielle did not dare to breathe. He would find her missing, he would search for her and she would be discovered hiding in these ranks.

And Yves would ensure that she was left behind.

"Of course, my lord," Seymour lied, and Gabrielle's lip curled with scorn.

Trust a man to see no further than ensuring his own reputation with his lord! Though the lie had served her purposes well, Gabrielle's estimation of Seymour's character was not improved in the least. He was typical of the men she had known in her life who saw to their own concerns alone.

"Well done!" Yves pivoted and faced the troops, his gaze darting over them all with such intensity that Gabrielle was certain he would spot her.

When he raised his voice to muster the spirits of the troops, Gabrielle felt her own heart stir with excitement. "We ride out to a battle that will not be easy, despite the apparent odds," Yves declared. "Remember that you avenge a wrong, for not only has the Lord de Perricault been struck down without cause—" the men murmured displeasure at this crime "—but those beneath his protection have been ruthlessly slaughtered—" the murmur became an indignant muttering "—his lady has been cast from her home, his heir and son has been taken hostage!"

Several men shouted outrage at this last and the horses stirred anxiously. Yves' eyes flashed and his black destrier snorted impatiently. He unsheathed his own blade and held it high, so that it flashed wickedly.

"Justice is on our side this night!" he bellowed, thrusting his sword toward the sky.

The troops roared and waved their weapons in the air in turn.

"Ride on!" Yves cried, and he pulled on his helmet. "Ride on and let Philip de Trevaine taste the bite of our swords!"

He spurred his great black steed and the destrier sprang toward the gates, Leon and Seymour riding fast on his heels. Franz cranked open the gates and ran to leap upon his own palfry, even as the raiding party passed into the forest like wind rushing through the trees.

The air was crisp on their faces as they left the valley, and once they had gained a narrow path, the horses thundered down its length toward Perricault.

The path turned onto the broader road and several horses galloped abreast. Gradually, the forest began to thin, and Gabrielle felt that Thomas was close to her grasp. The familiar sound of the raging river filled her ears and she could barely contain herself.

The promise of seeing Thomas again made her feel vibrantly alive. She chanted her son's name beneath her breath. Thomas would be securely within her arms before the sun crested the horizon once more!

Yves was fulfilling the pledge he had made to Gabrielle with a vengeance unexpected. Her heart fairly burst with the certainty that she had chosen the right knight to champion her cause.

Gabrielle's excitement made her urge the palfry faster and faster. So intent was she upon reaching her son that she was directly behind the knights before she realized what she had done.

She made the mistake of gasping aloud.

Yves fired a glance over his shoulder at the sound, and she saw anger flash in his eyes. Clearly her disguise did not even begin to fool him at closer quarters.

"My lady! What is this you do?"

The knight hauled his destrier to a merciless halt, ripped off his helmet and snatched at her palfry's reins. Destrier and palfry halted unceremoniously, while the other riders streamed around them and faltered to an uncertain stop just ahead.

Gabrielle swallowed carefully and looked into the molten gold of Yves' eyes. "I ride with you, of course," she said as casually as she could manage.

Yves muttered something decidedly unflattering under his breath, but Gabrielle chose to ignore it. "My lady," he growled with deliberation, "this is no place for a woman, much less for one nobly born."

Gabrielle lifted her chin. "You will not retrieve my son without me!"

Yves' eyes flashed. "I will do precisely that."

"You will not find him," Gabrielle insisted, determined not to be left behind. "Perricault is a keep rife with hidden nooks and crannies."

Yves' grip tightened on the steeds' reins. "I will move every single stone of that keep with my own hands, if necessary, to find your son and return him to you."

So great was his conviction that Gabrielle was almost swayed.

But still she would not stand aside and let another fetch her boy. "He will cry out," she argued. "Should you need to escape the keep stealthily, he might inadvertently reveal you."

Yves hesitated and Gabrielle pressed her case.

"This night is sure to remind him of the night Perricault was taken. He is a boy of good sense and will have learned to fear strange knights who snatch him up in the night." Her voice faltered. "He will be afraid."

Yves' lips thinned and he glanced to the waiting party, then back to Gabrielle. He was clearly not pleased with whatever conclusion he had drawn, or perhaps with Gabrielle proving troublesome in this matter.

"As much as I hate to admit it," he said in a low voice, a warm glint lighting his eyes, "you speak good sense in this."

Gabrielle caught her breath.

Yves' gaze bored into hers. "Understand, my lady, that you ride by my side alone."

Gabrielle did not dare to show her relief. She nodded.

"And you will give to me your solemn vow that you will follow my dictate precisely and immediately."

"But—"

"But *nothing!*" Anger fleetingly crossed the knight's visage. "My lady, if matters should go awry, I will not tolerate having anything happen to you." He fixed her with a quelling glance before she could ponder the import of that. "Do we understand each other?"

Gabrielle took a deep breath and held his gaze, knowing full well that this was not an argument she could manage to win. Should she not agree to his terms, Yves would send her directly back to the camp.

And as much as she hated to admit it, she had hired the man because he did understand warfare better than she. His dictate would undoubtedly be sound.

"I agree," she conceded quietly.

Yves nodded and pivoted, his grip still tight on the palfry's reins. At his urging, Merlin cut a clean path through the wondering troops, back to their head.

Gabrielle ignored the assessing glances of the knights. She lifted her chin high and stared straight ahead, not caring what any of them thought of her. When Yves donned his helmet anew and waved the party onward, she dug her heels into her palfry and remained steadfastly by the knight's side.

Yet in a secret corner of her heart, Gabrielle felt a thrill of victory that her desire had been granted by this unexpectedly sympathetic knight. Perhaps taking such a man to husband would not be a terrible burden, after all.

Perhaps she might find something in this match that had been so woefully lacking in her first.

Perhaps she was a fool to even think along such lines.

* * *

How Yves hated that Gabrielle had conjured an argument he could not refute! Having her in the party, even riding close to his side, was unsettling at best.

Yet here she rode, chin high and eyes bright, directly into the thick of the battle.

What was he to make of such a woman?

Yves had little time to consider the matter, for they drew near the river itself. The party halted beneath the shelter of the trees and Yves eyed the vast bulk of Château Perricault etched against the sky.

Not a single light illuminated its walls. He silently dispatched a pair of soldiers on foot, who flashed a light as prescribed mere moments later.

The bridge was taken.

Already.

It looked as though this task would be more than easy.

The party streamed silently from the forest, moving onto the bridge like shadows. The silver crescent of the moon rode high overhead, shedding enough light that the steeds could find their footing, but hopefully not enough to reveal their attack.

As Yves had decreed, padding was unfurled on the bridge to muffle the horses' footfalls on the wooden planks. They crossed and Yves drew his blade as Merlin began the ascent up the road to the gates.

The abandoned town crouched on either side of the road, its doors ajar, its windows hauntingly vacant. Even the chapel was filled with only shadows. The town had once been of considerable size. Yves wondered how many of the men in his party had memories of this place in better times.

He wondered how many had deaths to avenge from that fateful night.

Though it seemed there might be none to fall prey to that vengeance. Not a cry was raised from Perricault's walls, the silence of the massive keep more oppressive than Yves could have expected.

Nothing moved.

It was beyond eerie to find not a single sentry on the walls. Surely Philip could not have completely abandoned Perricault? The party eased closer and Yves felt a shiver of uneasiness slide through the ranks.

He halted when he saw that the gate was ajar.

This was not right.

Seymour frowned beside Yves and pointed to the gate, his brow furrowed in uncertainty. "I will check," he mouthed.

Yves nodded, watching silently as the man-at-arms urged Methuselah toward the gates. Seymour dismounted and peered cautiously around the open portal as the entire army seemingly held their breath.

Then Seymour disappeared into the château.

Methuselah nickered and Gabrielle sat up with a jolt, her wide eyes fixed on the gate. Yves straightened, his gaze darting between lady and destrier. Gabrielle knew the horse, knew well the sounds it made.

Clearly something was amiss!

Yves got no further in his thinking before a full assault was launched from Perricault's walls.

Two cauldrons of burning oil were poured from the towers high above as a war bellow broke from within the keep's walls. The fiendishly hot oil splashed on the road and the horses reared and screamed in fear.

The beasts darted backward of their own accord, just as a barrage of arrows was loosed from above. The shower of missiles found more than one mark among the surprised invaders. Men yelled in pain, horses shrieked and confusion reigned just a heartbeat after silence had filled Yves' ears. One steed even fled the scene, the wild echo of its hoofbeats carrying to Yves' ears.

As he gathered his knights about him, he noticed more of Philip's forces riding out from the forest to close the bridges behind him.

They had been deceived!

Just as Gabrielle had feared. But the truth was no solace now.

For the second time in a troublingly short span of days, Yves had let his passion rule his reason! He had desired too much to please Lady Gabrielle, and passion had steered him false.

Curse his stupid trust! Yves could only hope that his folly did not bear too heavy a price.

Gabrielle was stunned by the speed and brutality of the counterattack. One moment all was peaceful, if tense; the next, chaos had erupted on all sides.

The knight to her right glanced up at the whistle of the arrows and caught one right in his throat before he could look away. He fell from his destrier as Gabrielle watched in horror. Men shouted on all sides and flames erupted from the oil spilled on the road just before them.

It was bewildering to be suddenly in the midst of battle, especially when Gabrielle had never experienced the like. She looked toward Yves, finding him as composed as ever.

Only the narrowing of his eyes revealed his anger at Philip's deception. No doubt he was furious with himself for being tricked, but Gabrielle felt twice a fool for not making certain Yves understood Philip's duplicity.

"To the gates!" Yves roared, and those who could, followed his lead. Gabrielle was shocked at how many stalwart souls had already fallen, but she kept her head down.

"Take this," Yves muttered, shoving his quillon dagger at her. Gabrielle gaped at the wicked weapon, so much more heavy and lethal than anything she had wielded before.

She began to thank the knight, glancing up just in time to see him savagely cut down an attacker. That man fell to the ground, joining the first opponent to have reached Yves' side.

While she made sense of matters, Yves had already been at battle! Merlin jostled her palfrey and the knights gathered around, trapping Gabrielle in a tight circle.

On all sides, blades rose and fell with sickening regularity and blood danced in the air. Moans and shouts intermingled with the clash of steel on steel. Just when she thought matters could grow no worse, Gabrielle heard the creak of the portcullis being let loose from above.

"The portcullis gate!" she cried, looking up to see those dangerous spikes descending with frightening speed.

The men fought with renewed vigor, trying to win space on one side or the other, but Philip's troops fought to keep them trapped beneath the gate's wicked and quickly descending spikes. The blows of battle reached a crescendo.

Then, suddenly, the gate groaned overhead. Her heart in her mouth, Gabrielle looked up to find it frozen in its path.

But why had it stopped?

The answer came immediately. In bone-chilling slow motion, the wide-eyed gatekeeper tumbled out of the doorway that led to the gate room.

There was something decidedly odd about his stiff pose as he rolled bonelessly out onto the road. Philip's other troops still beneath the gates were so stunned by this development that they were quickly cut down. The destriers stepped instinctively out of the way, and the dagger embedded in the gatekeeper's back caught the light.

"Ha ha!" Gaston cried. The squire jumped out of the stall in close pursuit as Gabrielle gaped at the dead keeper. The boy's eyes were shining with excitement as he plucked his blade out of the man's back with a flourish.

He bowed deeply to Yves. "The gatehouse is ours, my lord!"

To Gabrielle's surprise, the knight scowled in disapproval. "You were bidden to remain with the party," he scolded the boy, whose smile faded to nothing. "You must learn to do as you are bidden, Gaston. What if there had been more than one within the gatehouse?"

"I would have taken them all," Gaston retorted defiantly.

Yves shook his head. "You could have been killed," he

muttered, so low that only Gabrielle heard his words. Again she marveled at his concern for the boy's welfare. "You *would* have been killed, for none knew where you were."

Gaston pouted.

Yves flicked an exasperated glance at the suspended gate and evidently was moved by the boy's disappointment.

"But your success is appreciated all the same," he conceded with obvious reluctance. "Though it would have been more so had you been following dictate."

Gaston grinned anew, apparently unaffected by the stern proviso, and leaped astride his palfry. "Bring them on!" he declared with a jaunty wave of his blade. "We shall slaughter them all!"

"You will do as you are bidden from this point on, understood?" Yves growled, though Gabrielle saw that the knight's demand had less impact than his praise.

"Yes, my lord."

Gabrielle belatedly realized that there had been a temporary respite in the fighting. She looked up to see a cadre of troops heading directly toward their valiant party. Philip's knights had formed a tight cluster within the outer bailey and drove toward the gates in a formation reminiscent of a wedge.

"Look!" Gabrielle cried, and she pointed.

Yves' head snapped up. "Look to the bailey!" he shouted to the knights.

"My lord, they come from below!" shouted another knight, and Gabrielle's heart sank to see that it was true. Another force rode toward the gates from the bridge below. Philip's men must have been hidden somewhere in the forest.

They would be caught between the two forces and slaughtered like pigs at the harvest!

Yves glanced to all sides, but still despair did not cross his features. "Choose your side! I will not compel you to fight to the death," he told his men. "May the grace of God be with you."

The men would flee while they yet had a chance, Gabrielle

realized with dismay. And those remaining would be lost in the inevitable slaughter. Thomas would be abandoned to Philip. She blinked back tears of disappointment at the failure of their quest.

Would they ever have another chance to save her son?

But Gabrielle did not need to fear. The men rallied closer, a determination she had not foreseen gleaming in their eyes.

"My lord, we follow you!"

"My lord, we will not leave alive without you and Thomas!"

The men roared approval of this and clashed their blades together over Gabrielle's head. Their enthusiasm for the fight was more than Gabrielle might have expected. She glanced about herself, amazed that Yves had won their loyalty so quickly.

"Which way, my lord?" demanded one of the knights.

"Lead on!" cried another.

What if Yves chose to leave Perricault this night? Gabrielle feared suddenly that Yves' strategic mind might choose against her heart. Even if the troops stayed to fight, they might still all be killed, for they were sorely outnumbered.

Yet if they fled, Thomas might pay the price of Philip's wrath. Gabrielle ached to continue onward in pursuit of her son. Before she could plead her case, Yves lifted his sword high and pointed directly at Philip's troops advancing from the bailey, his gaze locking with Gabrielle's own.

"I go for Thomas!" he declared.

Gabrielle's heart leaped.

The men bellowed agreement. "We are with you, my lord!"

The horses turned as one and plunged toward the bailey of Château Perricault. They met the oncoming forces with an earth-shattering clash of armor that shook Gabrielle to her bones. She barely had time to note that the two leaders had squared off before a swing of an ax hacked her palfrey out from beneath her.

The beast screamed. Gabrielle gasped.

Yves swore and swung hastily about, snatching Gabrielle in midair and slinging her across the front of his saddle. He never missed a stroke, though Gabrielle's head spun with the speed of his response.

It seemed all the breath had left her lungs.

But Yves took all in stride.

"Leon!" he raged.

That man was beside his lord in a heartbeat, his own blade swinging with a deadly rhythm against their foes.

"Take her!" Yves muttered, evidently unwilling to name Gabrielle in the present company. "Flee this place!"

"But, my lord—"

"Do it!" Yves parried a particularly vicious swipe before firing a significant glance at the other knight. "And do it *now*." He gave Gabrielle's rump a smack more fittingly delivered to an errant squire. "Go!"

Leon glared at Gabrielle when she hesitated, but she could see the wisdom of Yves' thinking.

And she *had* pledged to follow his dictate, as much as that recollection burned.

The horses bumped alongside each other and Gabrielle managed to clamber onto the back of Leon's saddle. That knight pivoted smartly, even as she struggled to sit behind him, and his destrier stepped away.

Gabrielle looked back, but Yves was deeply engaged with the leader of Philip's troops. It was not Philip himself, for the knight did not wear the colors of Trevaine, but still his skill was deadly, and Gabrielle feared for Yves' survival.

To her dismay, a shadow lunged into the gatehouse even as Leon headed in that direction. The gate creaked anew and began its descent once more.

"No!" She clutched at Leon's shoulder. "Yves cannot be left trapped inside!"

"My lady! He knows full well what he does."

"We must warn him!"

"There is no time!" Leon gave his steed his spurs.

Gabrielle looked back, wishing desperately that she could alert Yves to the danger, but now two knights engaged him simultaneously in battle.

Unfair! Gabrielle wanted to cry, but then she heard a sound that stopped her heart.

Somewhere, far above her, a child was crying.

Thomas!

Chapter Nine

Thomas!

Gabrielle could not think any further than that. She slipped from the back of Leon's horse before they rode through the gates, determined to reach her frightened child. She fell heavily to her knees in the bailey of Perricault.

Mercifully, no one seemed to notice her move. Leon rode on, blissfully unaware that he did so alone. His shadow galloped beneath the falling portcullis and he was gone.

Thomas cried with renewed vigor and Gabrielle knew she could not afford to linger. He would be in the solar, if he had his choice, in the southern corner where the sun's rays played in the morning.

A lump rose in Gabrielle's throat as she pictured her son trying to grasp a fistful of sunlight in days long before these troubled times. Her cheerful Thomas, always ready with a smile.

Now he wept, as he never had then. She blinked back her tears and shoved Yves' blade into her stolen chausses.

Her son needed her.

Gabrielle gritted her teeth and crawled through the melée toward the nearest wall. Stallions stomped on all sides, men slid limply from their saddles and blood fell like rain.

And one who listened closely would have heard Gabrielle

whispering the prayers that had become a part of her life, the prayers she had taught Yves to recite just the night before.

When she gained the wall and stood to sidle around its perimeter, Gabrielle was too focused on her goal to note that another pair of footsteps echoed stealthily behind her own.

Deceived, deceived, deceived!

The word echoed in Yves' mind like a litany and resonated with every fall of his blade. He could not believe his own foolhardiness, but at least the lady was clear of this place.

Regardless of what befell Yves within these walls, he could not have countenanced a failure to see Gabrielle safe.

The gate creaked behind him once more and Yves' lifted his head to find the portcullis descending again. His opponent dealt a blow to his shoulder that bit despite his chain mail.

Curse them! Another gatekeeper sought to imprison the rest of his troops within the walls. Yves thrust with renewed vigor and saw the knight who had wounded him fall in the dirt.

He spun Merlin adroitly and took stock of the situation. Only five men were left to his hand within the bailey, at least that he could see. Great numbers had fallen and lay still.

Yves grimaced, his heart sinking when he did not spy Seymour. That man had paid dearly for his bravery in sliding through the gates alone.

And where was Gaston? Yves scanned the bailey once more. The boy would turn him gray before his time. Imagine! Taking the gatehouse singlehandedly! The combination of bravery and impetuousness was dizzying.

But Gaston was nowhere in sight. A sick feeling rose in Yves' throat, but the portcullis was descending with relentless speed. He could only pray that Gaston had already left the bailey, for there was nothing Yves could do. He had to try to lead these remaining knights back to the camp.

Otherwise they all would perish.

"Retreat!" he roared. Those knights who could clustered their steeds about him.

Yves reached down and hauled a lamed man into his saddle before him as he passed, several of the other knights following suit. He waved the knights onward, scanning the fallen while the man he had rescued murmured relieved prayers.

When Yves was certain they had claimed all who still breathed, he headed for the gate. Too late, he saw that he was the last of the party and the portcullis was falling with dangerous speed.

Yves spurred Merlin, but the beast needed no urging for the task. Yves' heart rose in his throat as the gate creaked downward and Merlin lunged forward.

They would not make it!

The man before him moaned in fear. Yves lay across his saddle, certain they would be impaled. Merlin hunkered low and ran.

Cloth tore as Yves' cloak was snagged by the wicked spikes. Then he saw the lighter indigo of the night sky beyond the gatehouse and dared to breath a sigh of relief.

And the gate clanged home behind him, barely missing Merlin's heels. The pursuing troops roared in protest at the obstacle, but Yves spurred his destrier onward.

Far across the river, he glimpsed a rider that must be Leon riding with all haste, his cloak billowing out behind him and obscuring the lady Yves knew rode to safety there. Relief flooded through Yves at the sight. A flurry of battle greeted their eruption from the gates, but the knights who had closed the path behind them seemed more content to let them retreat than risk further injury.

Yves could not yet begin to think of the men they had lost.

Yves had not counted upon the orange flicker of flames shining through the night shadows of the forest. He stood in his stirrups, incredulous as the smell of burning assaulted his nostrils.

"The camp burns!" muttered heavyset Franz, his tone echoing Yves' disbelief.

But who would do such a thing? Surely they had left all of Philip's troops behind?

And what was the fate of those they had left in the camp?

Fear clutched Yves and he urged the tired destrier onward at all speed. They reached the gates, which had been wreathed in greenery just hours past, only to find them ripped open and cast in flame. Their skeletal remains framed the raging fire that burned recklessly in the camp.

In the midst of it all stood Leon, his helmet tossed aside. The knight looked bewildered, though he held the reins of both his destrier and silver Methuselah.

Methuselah. With lightning speed, Yves made the connection he had missed thus far. He had heard *one* horse flee the confusion of the attack. Yves slowed Merlin to a canter as the men following him did the same.

"Wait here. Something is sorely amiss."

Yves waved the men back as he dismounted. He surveyed the vestiges of the walls, the hungry flames and the surrounding woods, but could see no one other than Leon. Now he saw that Leon had been divested of his weapons. Yves took a deep breath, fully certain of who he would find within but seeing no other way to resolve matters.

He stepped through the burning gates alone.

"My lord, welcome home." Seymour greeted him with a cocky bow.

Just as Yves had suspected! It was Seymour who had purportedly overheard Philip's plan. He had slipped back here during the confusion of the attack, having known full well that Yves was destined to lose.

Seymour was Philip's spy.

"It was you," Yves declared, sick at his own gullibility. "You laid Philip's trap, both this time and the last."

Seymour pulled his sword from its scabbard and the menacing blade reflected the orange light of the flames. "He sent me to Perricault to learn its weaknesses."

"The lady was right about there being someone inside."

Seymour smiled coldly and shrugged. "It can matter little to admit the truth now."

Yves' gaze flew to Leon, only to belatedly note that the lady was not present. Where was Gabrielle?

"Leon?" he demanded, and the knight looked shamefaced.

"Thrice made a fool in one night, my lord. Once by Philip, once by the lady, who slipped from my steed at some point, and once by this upstart, who surprised me here."

Seymour smiled. "No doubt she is being adequately entertained at Perricault," he murmured. "Philip has an inexplicable fancy for her charms."

No! Rage burst within Yves. It was unthinkable that Gabrielle should be so poorly used! This man was the one whose deception had put Gabrielle at risk. A cold desire to see this wrong avenged settled around Yves' heart, and he knew Seymour would not leave this place alive.

"You granted your pledge to me, and earlier to Michel de Perricault," Yves said, hearing the low thrum of anger in his voice. "Is your word worth nothing?"

Seymour laughed. "Words are but words, Chevalier, and easily uttered. You are a fool if you put stock in a man's pledge alone."

"An honorable fool, then."

"Ah, and where does that honor see you in the end? No less dead than otherwise."

Clearly Seymour was one of those whose loyalty could be bought in hard coin alone.

Yves stepped farther into the camp, his heart sinking at the extent of the willful damage. What had happened to those women and children left here, supposedly in safety? Oh, he had failed Lady Gabrielle, and more spectacularly than his worst nightmare.

A clash of steel upon steel rang from the other side of the gates and men cried out in surprise. Yves pivoted at the sounds of swordplay, then turned back on Seymour.

That man's smile broadened. "A small reception for your

compatriots,'' he purred, and Yves hated that yet again he
had stepped into this man's trap.

"You wanted me and I am here," Yves said. "Release the
others."

Seymour shook his head and turned his blade in the firelight. "No one will leave this place who is not pledged to
Philip de Trevaine. Those are my orders."

It was outrageous to see men slaughtered for no good reason, but Yves controlled his temper with an effort. "This fire
is of your design, as well?" he asked, forcing his tone to
remain even.

Seymour nodded acquiescence. "An assignment from my
true liege lord, and sadly for you, not the last." Seymour
hefted the weight of his blade and eyed Yves assessingly.
"You see, Yves de Sant-Roux, I have been commissioned to
ensure that you in particular do not live to see the dawn."

Yves unsheathed his own blade, more than ready to duel
this snake to the death. "And is your sworn word worth as
little to Philip de Trevaine as it was to me?" he taunted.

The mercenary laughed. "That we shall have to see." He
swung his blade and stepped closer. "*En garde,* Chevalier."

The hall of Perricault was abandoned, only the remnants
of a meal scattered on the boards. The place looked as though
men had risen quickly to take to arms and left all as it stood.
A fire reduced to embers glowed on the hearth, and despite
the roar of warfare coming from the bailey, the sound of the
child's weeping echoed more loudly here.

Gabrielle carefully looked to either side. There was no sign
of another living soul. Even the dogs were absent. She crept
up the stairs to the solar on silent feet, hesitating in the long
shadows at the summit.

Again, nothing moved but the flickering flames of the
torches. The corridor ran straight to the solar itself, though
that door was closed.

And the sound of tears came from behind it.

It could be another trap of Philip's design, but it was one artfully baited. Gabrielle could not leave Thomas alone.

She looked about herself once more, then darted down the corridor. A great oak bar had been mounted across the width of the door like a drop latch, so that the door could no longer be opened from the inside.

Gabrielle struggled to lift its weight, well aware that Thomas' weeping had stopped at the sounds of her struggle. Had he learned to dread any arrival? Gabrielle's heart wrenched, but she did not dare to whisper reassurances to him lest she be overheard.

Thomas sniffled uncertainly.

With herculean effort, Gabrielle lifted the bar and flung open the door. She swept into the room and immediately saw the small boy huddled beneath the window, where she had guessed he would be.

He shrank back, as though he would disappear into the very wall, and Gabrielle froze in place.

There was no candle in the room, but moonlight fanned through the window above Thomas, painting his fair hair silver. The solar brooded in silence, the dust thick on every surface. The braziers were gone; the stone walls radiated cold. This was a far cry from the warm and inviting room Gabrielle had maintained here.

Thomas eyed her uncertainly.

Gabrielle feared suddenly that her son might not remember her. Six months was an eternity for one his age. She ached to check his fingers and toes, ensure that he was not injured, marvel over how much he had grown, stare into the dark eyes he had inherited from Michel, and discover what he had endured.

But she must not frighten him more than he already was.

"Thomas," Gabrielle whispered, creeping carefully into the solar as she spoke. "It is *Maman*."

Silence greeted her confession. She saw the shadow of

Thomas' fist rise to his mouth. He had chewed his fist as a babe and still did so in those rare times of great duress.

"*Maman?*" Disbelief echoed in Thomas' words, but he straightened slightly with curiosity. Gabrielle could feel his gaze upon her as she cautiously continued.

What had the poor child suffered in her absence?

"I have come for you," she whispered, her voice reassuring and low. "And only regret that it has taken so very long."

The moonlight painted a panel of light on the floor, and Gabrielle, intent on her son's response, did not realize when she stepped into its ethereal light.

"*Maman!*" Thomas cried when he spied her face.

He hurled himself suddenly toward her, arms outstretched and legs running as fast as they could carry him. Gabrielle noted fleetingly that his hair had darkened to a tawny gold, before she snatched him up in her arms and held him close against her pounding heart.

Thomas buried his face in her tunic and locked his arms around her neck. "*Maman,*" he whispered against her throat and his tears soaked Gabrielle's garb.

"Thomas! Oh, Thomas!" She rocked his precious weight in her arms and murmured reassuringly to him. He was too heavy for her to carry now, but she did not care.

Gabrielle felt her own tears slip down her cheeks. She cuddled Thomas close as she led him to his window, nestling him in her lap as she sat down in the moonlight.

Her child.

He was whole and, as far as she could discern, unscathed, though he was more slender than he had been before. Thomas had grown a little taller, for Gabrielle could see that his sleeves had become short.

When she checked behind his ears, then tweaked them with a click of her tongue—as she always did when he was sorely in need of a bath—Thomas smiled through his tears for the first time. The moonlight showed the wet spikes of his lashes as he looked up at her, and the pair smiled at each other for a long moment.

"I am here," Gabrielle whispered, and brushed her fingertips over the tiny line of concern between his brows. "Do not think any more of what has happened."

He said nothing, but gnawed on his fist and nestled anew against her warmth. Gabrielle stroked his hair back from his brow. For once, he was tolerant of her maternal caress as she wiped the tears from his cheeks.

And he was safe in her arms again. Gabrielle bent and kissed her son's temple, marveling that this moment should finally be hers.

"Such a touching scene!"

At the echo of a man's voice, Thomas quaked in fear. Gabrielle locked her arms protectively around the boy and sat up with a jolt.

Only to find Philip de Trevaine lounging in the doorway to the corridor.

Before Gabrielle could say anything, a smaller shadow leaped atop Philip from behind. Philip cried out, swore and struggled before another shadow loomed behind the pair. The new arrival hit Philip's attacker over the head with a bludgeon.

The small figure fell limply to the floor.

Philip pushed his inert form aside with a careless foot and stepped back into the corridor. His profiled features were burnished gold as he reached for a torch, the down-turned curve of his mouth etched with a clarity that could not be missed.

Gabrielle's mouth went dry when Philip turned back to face her, his expression filled with purpose. What would he do to her? Or to Thomas?

Then the golden torchlight fell on the boneless figure on the floor and Gabrielle's heart leaped in recognition.

"Gaston!" she cried before she could stop herself.

Philip flicked a scathing glance Gabrielle's way. "Fool,

more like!" He spat and kicked the squire's limp form into the solar.

Philip de Trevaine was as fastidiously attired as Gabrielle recalled. His crimson tabard was cut of the finest damask from the East and hemmed with silvered embroidery so rich that it must have taken a team of women a year to stitch. A scarlet cloak lined with ermine was clasped to one shoulder, its ornate pin catching the meager light.

His dark hair was neatly trimmed, his beard fashioned to an artful point below his chin. He had a pointed face, a sharp nose and small eyes the color of which Gabrielle had never tried or desired to determine.

And his mouth was turned down at the outer corners in a permanent expression of displeasure.

Philip was tall and slender of build, and might have been considered a handsome man by one who gave no account to his despicable character. Gabrielle had witnessed the cruelty of his ambition firsthand and was not surprised that he himself had not taken sword in hand to defend his newly acquired keep.

No, Philip was a liar and a cheat, who preferred to keep his rich garb unsullied by achieving his ambitions underhandedly.

"You have killed the boy for nothing!" Gabrielle struggled to her feet, Thomas huddled close against her as he watched Philip approach. Gabrielle hugged her son tightly and glared at the man responsible for her woes.

"He is not dead." Philip's lip curled as he looked down at the squire. "But he should have known better than to dare to touch me." Philip glanced back at the great hulk of a man behind him and smirked. "Especially with Algernon in residence."

Oh, Gabrielle remembered this Algernon's visage well enough! Philip's personal guard stood so tall that the top of his bald pate brushed the arch of every doorway he strode through.

Algernon's black beard grew thick and fell halfway down his chest. A single dark brow marked a line across his brow from temple to temple. A heavyset brute of a man, Algernon was not keen of wit by any account, but was reputed to be able to rip open a man's chest with his bare hands.

Philip smiled with the feigned charm Gabrielle recalled all too well. "It seems you have an admirer, my lady," he mused, and turned to give the squire's shoulder another nudge with his elegantly shod foot.

Gabrielle longed to determine Gaston's state herself. She did not dare draw closer to this lethal pair, though. Thomas, by the way he clung to her, was definitely of like mind.

The sardonic smile she remembered all too well curved Philip's lips as he assessed her. "It has grown quiet," he mused. "Obviously, your champion's assault on Perricault has met with failure."

He craned his neck to eye the location of the moon through the window, then clicked his tongue chidingly. "And somewhat earlier than anticipated, I must say. What manner of warrior did you hire, my Gabrielle?"

To have this man insult Yves' abilities was too much! "One who did not anticipate your lies!" Gabrielle retorted. "You deceived us!"

Philip smiled with cold charm. "But of course! Lies are an integral part of a successful man's arsenal." He strolled closer, his manner confidential, and Gabrielle drew back against the wall. "If your champion survives this night, that might be a lesson he could afford to learn."

No! Yves could not have been killed in this assault!

"He retreated!" Gabrielle cried, not nearly as certain of that as she would have liked to have been.

Philip's cold smile did not waver. "One could say that, my Gabrielle, but the sad truth is that he abandoned you here, just moments past." Philip's brows rose with mock disdain. "Such a champion!"

"He escaped." Gabrielle breathed a sigh of relief, though that consolation was to be short-lived.

"Well, for the short term, at least." Philip examined his fingernails with apparent fascination as Gabrielle caught her breath. "You see, arrangements have already been made."

Gabrielle's heart jumped, for it was clear Philip meant no good. "What do you mean?"

Philip smiled and glanced at her. "How hungry you are for details, my Gabrielle! Do you have a soft spot in your heart for this fool knight?"

"He is no fool!"

Philip's gaze sharpened. "No fool? Even though he has been fooled twice in one night?"

Twice? A sick feeling rose within Gabrielle. "What have you done?"

Philip's smile was cold. "All in good time, my Gabrielle, all in good time."

Before she could demand an explanation, he continued. "For now, you have other concerns." He assessed Gabrielle's figure so boldly that she felt naked beneath his perusal. For the first time she was aware of how much these men's chausses revealed. "Such unfeminine garb, as alluring as it might be, is hardly fitting for a bride."

Gabrielle's mouth went dry. "A bride?"

Philip arched a brow. "But of course. Perricault was not the only property of Michel's that I long coveted."

Philip would wed her? After what he had done? Revulsion made Gabrielle's flesh creep. "I will not wed you!"

Philip's lips thinned with impatience. "You most certainly will wed me, for that is the best way to assure my suzerainty over Perricault."

Trust a man to think to his own advantage alone!

Anger roared to life within Gabrielle, but Philip strode closer. He fingered the end of her long braid, the heat in his eyes decidedly predatory. "When shall we wed, my Gabrielle?" he whispered.

"Never!" Gabrielle spat the word.

Philip hid his annoyance so quickly that she nearly missed it. He snatched at Thomas and the boy cowered against his dame. Gabrielle retreated, but found the stone wall of the keep behind her back far too quickly.

"What have you done to my son?" she demanded wildly.

Philip feigned mild surprise. "I? Nothing, Gabrielle, nothing at all." He leaned closer, and she could see the gleam of malice in his eye. "You see, Thomas has proven to be a most useful lure." His gaze flicked to the boy. "At least, thus far."

Gabrielle's heart leaped to her throat, but she had to have the truth clear between them. "Thus far?" she echoed fearfully.

Philip smiled. "I would tolerate him within my home, simply to satisfy a wife's whim," he said with what he apparently considered great indulgence.

Gabrielle did not believe Philip. Had he not paved his way through life with lies?

"I cannot wed a man who holds both me and my son in such low esteem," she declared.

Philip's eyes flashed. "My *esteem, madame,* will be earned on your back. What I want from you are a few simple words before a priest, and then a son, the second provided in short order."

Gabrielle lifted her chin, unable to imagine permitting this man to climb atop her. And what would happen to Thomas once Philip had an heir of his own blood? Even Philip's vow of indulging her whim would likely end there.

"And if I refuse?"

"You may take a swim." Philip gestured to the window behind her. "It is a long fall to the River Perricault from here," he purred. "Do you not think so?"

Despite herself, Gabrielle glanced over her shoulder. All too well she recalled the long, straight drop from this window to the rushing river and the rocks that marked the river's confluence.

"You may rest assured, my lady Gabrielle, that I will let you watch your precious son take his leap first."

"No!" Gabrielle cried.

Philip snapped his fingers and Algernon advanced on Gabrielle. Thomas bellowed fit to wake the dead, clearly sensing what was going to happen. The little boy locked his arms and legs around Gabrielle, and she clung to him with all her might, but Algernon parted the pair far too easily.

"No! Do not take Thomas!"

Algernon swung Thomas over his shoulder, the boy wailing mightily, and Gabrielle lunged after her son.

Only to find Philip blocking her path. He was taller than her and when the weight of his hands landed on her shoulders, she could not push past him. Though she certainly did try. Desperation gave her renewed strength. "Let me go! Bring Thomas back to me!"

Philip's grip tightened on Gabrielle's shoulders so that his fingers dug into her flesh. "Do not test me, my Gabrielle," he counseled in a low voice. "Both you and Thomas could quickly outlive your usefulness to me."

Gabrielle looked into the icy pallor of Philip's eyes and recognized the threat in his words.

But she could not surrender so easily!

"No!" She lunged at Philip with all her might, but he slapped her face hard and pushed her away. Gabrielle fell against the wall, but was back on her feet in an instant.

It was not quick enough. Philip had already crossed the solar. He savagely slammed the door behind himself before she could cross the room.

She fell against the heavy oak panel just as the bar dropped into place on the opposite side. Gabrielle pounded desperately against the wood, even knowing that her efforts were futile.

"In seven days, we shall meet at the altar, Gabrielle, or you and your son will leave this solar by the window alone," Philip called. "I will give you some time to consider your

choice, but hope that you will not be foolish when the dressmakers come to fit your nuptial gowns.''

"What will you do to Thomas?" Gabrielle asked breathlessly.

Philip chuckled. "The brat will be safe in my tender care,"
he said, waiting a moment before he continued.

"For now."

These words sent panic through Gabrielle and she hammered on the door with renewed vigor. "Bring my son back
to me!"

Philip chuckled. "After the wedding, my dear Gabrielle,"
he said. "After your pledge is mine. Do not fear for his welfare. As I said, the boy is still *useful* to me."

With that, Philip strode away, the echo of his footfalls fading.

"No!" Gabrielle cried. Faintly, she could hear Thomas
crying and hated that she could not console the boy. Her own
tears welled up, her frustration enough to nearly overwhelm
her, and her fists fell against the door more and more slowly.

Thomas! How wretched for him to see her only for a moment, then to be torn away from her side again. Her anger
spent, Gabrielle sank down and buried her face in her hands.

What a mess this evening had wrought! Thomas was stolen
again from her side. Some foul fate awaited Yves, she was
certain. The bile rose in Gabrielle's throat at the very thought
of that knight being killed trying to win her cause.

It was unfair. It was wrong.

And it was all Gabrielle's fault. Too late she saw that she
had put too much faith in the honor of battle fairly met. Philip,
it was clear, saw no merit in such tactics.

She truly might have to wed him to see those she held dear
safe from his malice, even for just a short while.

That was a galling thought.

But what future could there be for her in bending to such
a man's will? Philip would always hold the threat of her own
demise over her head—or that of Thomas—when there was

something he wanted. This would not be the first or the last concession he demanded of her, of that Gabrielle was certain.

Her life would be a living hell.

What would she do?

What *could* she do?

Gabrielle looked at Gaston and deliberately blinked back her tears.

For now, she could aid Yves' squire. She leaned over his limp form and was encouraged by the faint whisper of his breath.

He *was* alive! And he had valiantly come to her aid. Gabrielle bent to gently assess the size of the lump rising on Gaston's head.

The squire was a credit to the knight he served. Gabrielle found herself thinking of Yves and hoping against hope that he had foiled Philip's plans and survived this terrible night.

Certainly, Yves de Sant-Roux had surprised her more than once. Perhaps he would surprise Philip as well.

Gabrielle could only pray that it would be so.

Chapter Ten

The fire that consumed the camp crackled on all sides, the flickering orange flames casting Seymour in a diabolical light. The challenge had only just left that man's lips and his eyes glowed with the blood lust of a contest he evidently guessed would not be easily won.

"If your sworn pledge means nothing to you, then why serve Philip de Trevaine with such loyalty?" Yves demanded.

The mercenary laughed. "Because we are two of a kind," he confided. "He understands what I desire of this life and rewards me accordingly."

"With what?"

"Gold!" Seymour's eyes gleamed at the very thought. "And when he is done with this campaign, I shall have estates and a title to call my own. No one—*no one*—will ever consider Seymour de Crecy unworthy of account again!"

"What campaign?" Yves asked, as the pair began to circle each other.

The mercenary smirked. "Philip will become the next Lord de Tulley. The secrets that miserable old cur has locked within his vaults will supply opportunities for a creative man like Philip for years to come."

Seymour laughed, apparently unaware that a secret of Yves' own was locked within those very vaults. Yves found it loathsome that one would use those secrets purely to fund his own financial gain. That was even more reprehensible than Tulley's use of his knowledge to manipulate people to his will.

"Philip will prosper, and I—I shall be at his right hand through all of it."

Yves gripped his blade and stepped forward, knowing that this was one time he would take delight in striking the killing blow.

"And what of Lady Gabrielle? What are Philip's plans for her?"

"He will wed her, of course, to ensure his suzerainty over Perricault and silence any protest from Tulley before his time is come."

Something tightened in Yves' gut at that. "And if the lady is unwilling?"

Seymour laughed harshly. "She will have no choice. Indeed, I would truss her ankles to the bedposts myself to aid my lord in seeing his will consummated."

Yves' stomach churned that Gabrielle might be already suffering such a fate. "What of the boy?"

Seymour sneered. "He is useful as a tool only until the lady shows the wit to bear my lord a son."

The bile rose in Yves' throat. "And then?"

"Once Philip's heir is born, the lady and her son might well prove to have no use whatsoever to my lord." Seymour shrugged. "I see no reason why they would not be…disposed of."

What a treacherous man this mercenary served! No one could ever count himself secure as long as Philip drew breath. Gabrielle had been right to be leery of that man's intent!

And now she was securely within his grasp.

If he managed to survive this battle, Yves pledged silently, he would see the lady freed, regardless of what price he must pay. She had known Philip's ruthlessness before they even attacked Perricault and had cast her fears aside solely for the sake of her son.

Such courage could not go unrewarded.

But first, he had to dispatch this mercenary to the hell he undoubtedly deserved. Yves eyed his opponent and decided Seymour was a man of passion.

And impassioned men never fought well or for long.

"Philip will never take Tulley," Yves insisted, his intention purely to goad the other man.

Seymour thrust with his blade as his eyes flashed, but the blow was poorly aimed. "He will take Tulley and easily!"

"And then what of your own usefulness?" Yves dodged another feint easily and let his tone turn taunting. "When all the dirty work is done, Philip may well dispose of *you.*"

"Never!" Seymour bellowed, and dove at Yves. "Philip de Trevaine will never betray me!"

Yves lunged forward at the same moment, their blades meeting with a thunderous crash. Yves felt the impact of the blow right to his shoulder, but he parried and thrust again with even more force. Seymour fought recklessly, his anger driving his attack, yet he was strong enough that he might not quickly be spent.

Yves deliberately reined in his own anger and resolutely waited out the fury of Seymour's attack.

The flames crackled and drew yet closer, the greedy fire leaping from tree to tree overhead. The two men's blades clashed again and again, each strike countered by an equal blow. There was a cry from beyond the gates as someone struck a death blow. Seymour made the mistake of glancing up at the shout and Yves saw his chance.

He leaped forward, but Seymour parried with an unexpected speed. The mercenary's blade caught Yves across the cheek. Pain flared and Yves grimaced as he struck angrily at Seymour's blade.

The sword flew from that man's grip and landed on the forest floor some feet away. Seymour dove after it, but the fire swallowed it first with leaping orange flames. Yves gave chase, jumping backward when Seymour spun to face him anew.

The mercenary had a dagger in each hand.

The fire claimed the last untouched link in the circle about them and began to creep across the forest floor, the dampness of the leaves only slowing its progress minutely.

"Leon! Save the steeds!" Yves cried.

Seymour chose that moment to dive forward, his daggers slashing at Yves' knees. Yves dodged the blades in the nick of time and pivoted with an ease that denied his exhaustion. Seymour stumbled and Yves swung his sword downward.

The blade caught Seymour's shoulder and the man bellowed before he twisted from beneath its weight. He leaped up, his daggers leading the way, and steel grazed the chain mail covering Yves' hip. Yves kicked and they sprang apart.

The pair circled each other slowly. Yves noted the trickle of red flowing from the other man's shoulder. He narrowed his eyes against the sting of the smoke and fought the urge to cough. The heat of the encroaching fire pressed against his skin.

Suddenly a burning branch fell behind Yves with a resounding crash. The flames crackled and jumped, the fire blazed even brighter and sparks danced into the night sky.

And Seymour closed in for the attack. Steel echoed on steel, and Seymour tried to force Yves back into the raging flames. Yves twisted and dodged. When Seymour pivoted, Yves elbowed him, sending him sprawling on his backside.

Yves quickly stepped over the mercenary. He slashed at Seymour's wrist, cutting the leather glove so cleanly that the flesh cleaved directly beneath. The mercenary's hand fell open and the dagger dropped to the bed of damp leaves below.

"God's blood!" Seymour bellowed.

"Hardly that," Yves muttered through his teeth.

Seymour's grip tightened on the other blade, but Yves stepped on his wrist so hard that that blade fell aside as well.

Seymour roared and lunged to his feet, nearly toppling his opponent in the process. Yves pulled out his own dagger with a flick of his wrist just before the mercenary was upon him.

A sigh escaped Seymour as the small blade was buried deep in his belly. He went limp.

Then his hands locked around Yves' throat with startling speed.

The blood cascaded from Seymour's wrist as he squeezed with telling strength. Yves struggled against the mercenary's inhuman grasp and saw the flames cavorting in dizzying colors all about him. The pair staggered across the clearing in a lethal embrace as the fire drew ever closer.

Suddenly Yves could not see and knew he would soon be lost. In a last bid for survival, he shoved his knee skyward as hard as he could manage.

Seymour's groan of pain revealed that the blow had met its mark.

The mercenary's grip loosened enough for Yves to strike another blow. Seymour staggered backward and Yves filled his lungs as he dove after the man. He punched Seymour in the face and the man fell bonelessly backward, blood erupting from his nose.

Seymour's head cracked hard on a stump and his mouth lolled open. Yves watched and waited, his breathing still erratic, his fists clenched, but Seymour's chest did not rise again.

The traitor was dead.

Yves lifted his head and wiped the blood from his cheek, only to find the flames closed tightly about him. He spun wildly, seeking a means of escape, but was surrounded by a wall of flame.

Too late, Yves realized that neither he nor Seymour would leave this place.

"My lord!" Leon cried, and Yves' head snapped up.

He faintly discerned the shadow of a line descending through the woods and immediately understood the other knight's intent.

A rope! Yves sheathed his sword and snatched the rope out of the air when it swung into the small clearing he occupied. It hung at an angle, obviously slung over some high bough beyond the curtain of flame. He scrambled up its length, grateful to be among thinking men.

Yves spotted a trio of shadows on a broad branch of a great oak, before all three of them leaped down to brace themselves against the trunk of the tree. They hauled with all their might, pulling Yves' weight skyward, and lifted him just barely over the encircling flames.

But moments later, Yves stood on the branch above Leon and two other knights of Perricault. The four looked as one to the advancing blaze.

"How many of us are there?" Yves asked the dreaded question.

Leon shook his head. "We are the last, my lord, along with Franz, Xavier and a pair of squires." Stalwart Franz grinned before wiping a grimy hand across his brow. "The boys guard the destriers at the road."

The news was worse than Yves had hoped, by far.

But there was nothing for it. At this point, he had to formulate a plan to save Lady Gabrielle and her son before Philip could do his worst. Time was of the essence, for Philip could wed Gabrielle and rape her in but a matter of moments, if he so chose.

Yves could only hope that that man would be so certain of his victory that he would take time to woo the lady.

But to retrieve her from Philip's clutches, Yves would need more troops. He needed aid, most logically from another who stood in the line of Philip's wild ambition. Mercifully, that estate was not Sayerne.

"What is the closest estate beneath Tulley's hand to the west of Perricault?" Yves asked.

"Annossy, of course," Leon responded, the other knights nodding acquiescence.

"And the name of its lord?" Yves asked.

"Quinn de Sayerne," Leon supplied, and Yves' heart plummeted like a stone.

Quinn de Sayerne? He was going to have to ask his own brother to aid him in this task? The fates could not be so cruel as to force him to face the man reputed to be the very echo of their cruel sire. "Surely not?" he demanded, hearing the strain in his voice.

But Leon nodded confidently. "Surely so. Lord Quinn gained suzerainty over Annossy when he wed Melissande d'Annossy, the only daughter of the house. He rules both estates now."

Yves took a deep breath and scanned the burning forest, bracing himself for an ordeal he had never expected to endure. For all he knew, Quinn might enjoy seeing his bastard brother twist in the wind.

But Yves knew that his trepidation in facing his malicious brother was nothing compared to what Gabrielle undoubtedly already endured.

The worst Quinn could do would be to decline his request. The worst Philip could do to Gabrielle was unthinkable.

Yves took a deep breath and looked into the eyes of his faithful remaining cadre. "We ride to Annossy," he said flatly, no hint of his own fears in his tone. "We will seek the aid of the lord there and do so with all haste."

Gaston awoke to a relentless pounding, like a battering ram landing against heavy gates. A despairing damsel was trapped in a tower, the château was besieged by the forces of good and it was up to him to scale the high wall, let them in and save the lady. He winced at the onerous task before him, but valiantly forced open one eye.

A brilliant ray of sunlight made him squeeze his eye shut once more. The pounding grew more diligent and Gaston re-

alized belatedly that the hammering came from within his
own head.

He had been dreaming his usual dream.

Gaston sighed, disappointed that there truly was no damsel
to save, no heroic deed to accomplish, no loathsome wound
gracing his brow as a trophy of his heroism. Only a headache,
likely the result of some overindulgence the night before.

"Just lie back," Lady Gabrielle urged quietly.

The sound of her voice launched a flood of recollections
in Gaston's mind. To his delight, his dream had not been far
from the truth. The forces of good—led by his own knight
and lord—had besieged a château by night, though the gates
had not been barred against them.

And the lady had come with them, but she had ventured
into the high tower alone and unprotected. Gaston had known
he had to follow her, that his lord would have done the same
if he had not been so heavily occupied in battle that he had
not noticed the lady's departure. But Gaston could recall little
beyond following the lady to the solar.

He forced both eyes open this time and found that same
sunlight flooding the room. The lady crouched before him,
watching him with concern. Gaston feared suddenly that he
had fallen asleep and failed her while she needed his aid the
most.

And that would be most disappointing. Surely he could not
have failed so miserably at his first chance for valor?

"How long have I slept?" Gaston asked, surprised to find
his voice a rough croak.

The lady almost smiled. "You did not sleep, Gaston," she
corrected mildly. "You were hit on the head from behind.
Do you recall attacking Philip?"

Gaston shook his head, then winced anew at the pain that
simple movement launched.

"You have quite a nice lump to show for your gallantry."

Gallantry. That sounded more promising than having fallen

asleep. Gingerly, Gaston explored the back of his head, yelping aloud when his cautious fingers encountered said lump.

"I put cold water on it all the night long," the lady informed him. "You may be surprised to learn that it has already become smaller."

"But it is bigger than a goose egg!" Gaston protested.

At that, the lady did smile, though the cheer did not reach her eyes. "Your fingers tell lies," she said. "It is much smaller than that." She rose then and moved gracefully across the room, wringing out a cloth in a basin formed within the wall.

The lady returned and pressed the cloth against Gaston's wound. He flinched at the coldness of it, but she grasped his chin and granted him no quarter.

"It will help to shrink it even further," she insisted, and Gaston acquiesced.

Indeed, after the first shock of contact, the chill of the cloth felt good. The pounding even seemed to diminish slightly.

"There is no food, I am afraid," the lady continued grimly. Gaston's stomach growled at the reminder of its emptiness. "No doubt Philip intends to win agreement through weakening me."

"But how long have we been here?"

"It was only last evening that we arrived here at Perricault."

Only one night. Gaston was reassured that he had not left the lady unprotected for too long. He sat up and surveyed the solar of Perricault.

His first impression was that the place was far from welcoming. No embroideries hung from the stone walls; no braziers burned near the lady's feet. There were no tokens of battle or friendship adorning the space, as was characteristic in the solars of his own home estate and that of the count's. The great pillared bed was devoid of mattress or bedding, and the strewing herbs were so dry they looked unfit for mouse nests.

Suddenly, Gaston realized that he and the lady were alone.

"But where is your son?" he asked with a frown. "I recall seeing him with you last night, I am certain of it."

The lady's lips tightened and she turned away, but not quickly enough to hide her dismay. "Philip took him," she said in a wavering voice, far from her usual firm tones.

"He took him from Perricault?"

"No." The lady shook her head. "Philip simply took him from my side, to win my approval to his scheme."

"The fiend!" Gaston jumped to his feet more hastily than might have been wise. He paid the price with a renewed throbbing between his ears, but was so outraged that he ignored it. "What dastardly scheme has he in mind?"

The lady folded her arms across her chest and studied her feet. Her voice was low when she spoke. "He would have me wed him and make his suzerainty of Perricault legitimate."

How despicable! "But a lady like you cannot be forced to wed such a man!" Gaston argued heatedly. "Your overlord will protest!"

The lady shook her head. "Tulley may have no chance, if the nuptials are performed and the match consummated before he hears of it."

"That is not fair!"

The lady's expression turned wry and she eyed Gaston once more. "Fair has little to do with the actions of men seeking their own advantage," she said gently.

While Gaston tried to make sense of that declaration, the lady retreated and sat on the stone ledge beneath the window. Her expression was more bitter than Gaston had yet seen. Clearly, she was discouraged by their circumstance, but Gaston knew he could reassure her.

He crossed the room to stand before her. "My lord, Chevalier Yves de Sant-Roux will not stand by and see such a wrong committed," he declared proudly. "He will come to your aid before Philip can do his foul deed."

"No, Gaston." The lady shook her head and her voice was oddly flat. "He will not come."

"Of course, he will!"

"No, Gaston. Your knight has seen his pledge fulfilled and will turn to other tasks."

"What pledge?"

"He vowed only to aid me in retrieving my son."

"But that is not done!"

"No," the lady acknowledged. "But your knight made a valiant effort and barely escaped the attack upon Perricault with his life. It would be foolhardy to return to almost certain death, even to see a wrong set right."

"You say as much only because you do not know the manner of man he is," Gaston insisted hotly.

The lady surveyed him for a long moment, and Gaston was surprised to see the resignation in her steady gaze. Finally, she lay a hand upon his arm and spoke with quiet conviction.

"Gaston, you are yet young and have much to learn of men. What you did for me last evening was beyond brave, though you could have seen yourself killed for your efforts. Perhaps, even now, with the lump upon your head, you would not make the same choice again."

"But I would!"

"Then, you have much still to learn. Gaston, men of war do not take such chances with their own hides. They see to their own gain alone."

That she could even give consideration to such a thought was appalling to Gaston. "Not *knights!* Not men pledged to protect those weaker than themselves and uphold the cause of righteousness!"

"Yes, *knights,*" the lady insisted grimly. "And they worse than any others. Knights have more to lose and more to gain than most in this world."

"My lord is not like that. He will return to see his mission complete. Yves de Sant-Roux will not rest until you and your son are safe."

Indecision crossed the lady's features, and Gaston sensed that she wanted to believe him.

Then she abruptly shook her head. "No. He will not."

Before he could argue further, the lady turned and looked out the window, a small frown tightening her ebony brows. "Perhaps I erred in this," she murmured, almost as though she spoke to herself. Her fingers drummed on the sill. "Perhaps I should have wed him first."

Gaston could not curb his impertinence. "What do you mean?"

The lady's gaze flew to his once more. "Had I wed your lord sooner, there would be more at stake than his pledge to aid me. Perricault would hang in the balance, as would the possibility that I might bring him an heir."

She grimaced and turned to the view once more. "But I did not do that," she said quietly. "And now it is too late."

"It is not too late! Do not despair as yet!" Gaston protested, but the lady did not even acknowledge his words.

It was clear enough that she would not be persuaded to abandon her view, though Gaston knew she was wrong about his lord.

"You will see," the squire said finally. "He will come and then you will see."

Gaston retreated to the far side of the solar and hunkered down. He propped his aching head upon one hand and watched the lady, wishing there was some way he could raise her hopes.

But Gaston knew, deep in his heart, that only his lord could fulfill that task.

Yves' mission proved to be even worse than he had anticipated.

Upon the party's arrival at Château Annossy the following morning, Yves learned that Quinn and his lady were not resident, but taking their leisure at Château Sayerne.

Sayerne, where Yves' father had barely tolerated his pres-

ence; Sayerne, where his dame had died, unacknowledged by
the man whose child she bore; Sayerne, the ravaged estate
that Yves and Annelise had abandoned to the wolves and the
wind when word of Quinn's return came to their ears.

Yves would have to return to the very place he wanted to
avoid at all costs.

The knights looked to him expectantly, and Yves thought
of Gabrielle, caught in Philip's web for a full night and a
morning. Who knew what could have already transpired
within those high walls of Perricault?

No, this was not a task he could lay aside.

"To Sayerne," Yves commanded, his own fears as naught.
Somehow he would face his ghosts squarely. Somehow he
would convince his malicious brother to aid his course.

Somehow Yves would find aid for Lady Gabrielle and her
son.

All the same, it was with some trepidation a day later that
Yves crested the rise that he knew marked the division between the lands of Annossy and those of Sayerne. He braced
himself for the sight of those abused fields and impoverished
villeins that had been the most obvious evidence of his own
sire's cruel hand.

But the fields of Sayerne that unfurled before Yves' eyes
proved so different from his recollections that he wondered
briefly whether he was on the right estate.

Much of the village that clustered outside the château walls
had been rebuilt, a fact that furthered his amazement, and the
mill was new. Villeins bustled purposefully. The first green
growth could be spied in kitchen gardens alongside each
house. Children shouted and ran in the streets, and a plump
woman burst from the alehouse, calling back a laughing re-
crimination to her spouse, who was evidently still within.

This prosperous and happy village was a far cry from the
shadowed ruin that Yves remembered here. It certainly did
not correspond with the rumor of his brother's character.

As they passed through Sayerne's great gates, a shadow crept over Yves' heart. The bailey was nearly as barren as it had been long before, the chill rising from the stone in the evening light enough to bring back a barrage of memories.

His sire had beat him in that corner. Yves mouth went dry and he looked away, though memory was not so readily dismissed as that.

Childhood feelings of failure and inadequacy assaulted Yves. The entrance to the stables beckoned, as always it had, and he wondered if the old ostler yet lived. Those afternoons playing with the ostler's hounds had been the only glimmer of childhood he had ever had, but knowing those moments were secret and stolen had cast a pall over them.

But this was not the time for such whimsical recollections. Yves had to go to the hall and convince his brother to ride to Gabrielle's aid.

He dismounted, hoping against hope that he appeared nonchalant even while his heart pounded in his ears. He followed a squire's polite gesture to Sayerne's portal, took a deep breath and stepped over the threshold he had never intended to darken again.

Yves was shown to the solar, where the lord and lady were taking their leisure. The hall he strode through was quiet, a few men drinking before the embers glowing on the hearth, the shadows just as Yves recalled.

The chatelain mounted the stairs briskly before Yves, obviously unaware of the churning in Yves' gut. Yves half expected to find his father lurking in the darkness at the apex of the stairs.

The door to the solar was slightly ajar, with warm, golden candlelight spilling through it onto the wooden floor of the corridor.

"I shall beat you soundly, woman, and then you will regret that move," a man growled.

Yves stiffened, for the words were what he would have expected to hear fall from his brother's mouth.

The chatelain, though, rapped on the door, clearly untroubled by the prospect of domestic violence. Sayerne had not changed! Yves thought. Abuse was so common here that all took it in stride.

And Yves had been fool enough to come back.

Chapter Eleven

A woman within the solar laughed. "You will have no such chance," she retorted with a cheeky bravado that seemed decidedly uncalled for under the circumstance.

The chatelain smiled thinly and rapped again.

"Come!" bellowed the man.

"A visitor, my lord," chirped the chatelain. "One Chevalier Yves de Sant-Roux." He then moved back and gestured to Yves to enter.

Yves stepped into the golden light of the room just as Quinn pivoted in surprise. Though Yves and Quinn had never met, Yves having been born after his brother's early departure, this man could be no other than his own blood.

Golden eyes so like his own returned his appraisal boldly. Russet hair like Annelise's was threaded with a few lines of silver. This man was larger and broader than Jerome de Sayerne had been.

"Yves de Sant-Roux?" Quinn demanded.

A shiver crept through Yves, for he was certain nothing good would come of his brother's guessing his true identity.

"The count sends his own champion to me?" Quinn asked, and Yves silently exhaled in relief. "Something must be sorely amiss, but the count should know that he can rely upon my aid."

The chatelain slipped from the room on silent feet, and Yves struggled to appear poised. "It is a matter closer to home that brings me here this night."

"Then come!" Quinn said, and offered his hand. "I am Quinn de Sayerne. Your men and steeds have been attended?"

"I believe your chatelain has matters well in hand."

Quinn gestured to the table where he had been sitting. "Come and share of the wine, then. Tell me your tale."

"Aha!" the woman seated at the table declared. Yves looked at her for the first time, surprised to find such a mischievous smile upon her face. Had his brother not just threatened to beat her? Her eyes danced as she plucked something from the table and skipped it over two similar dark shapes.

"I shall beat you yet, Quinn de Sayerne!" she declared, then popped one of the shapes into her mouth.

Belatedly, Yves understood that they played draughts.

"Melissande! You will eat all of the dates!" Quinn protested, though a merry twinkle lurked in his own eyes. The woman chortled and ate the second date she had skipped.

"Only if you insist on playing so poorly that you lose," she retorted, then wiped her fingers as she smiled at Yves.

"Welcome, sir. I am Melissande d'Annossy. I must apologize for the casual state of matters this evening." She flicked a glance full of import at her spouse. "But *someone* will eat all of the dates alone if unchecked, and I must confess to a fancy for them myself."

"A fancy?" Quinn snorted in disdain, and Yves understood that this was an old game between these two. "That someone who eats all the dates is hardly me."

The lady laughed in a most delightful fashion. "At least I eat them at the board," she jested, her eyes glowing.

Yves could readily guess where else the dried fruits were consumed, for the pair exchanged a glance so smoldering that he felt momentarily awkward in their presence.

This was the brother he had avoided meeting all these

years? This was the man whose cruelty had sent him and his sister fleeing Sayerne in the dead of winter?

Yves decided to reserve judgment upon his brother's character until his tale was told—and Quinn's response was clear.

Melissande smiled and gestured Yves to a seat. "Please, join us." She turned to the door, but before she could call, the chatelain ducked into the room with another goblet. He also brought a flagon of wine to join the one already on the table, and a platter of bread, cheese and olives.

"I took the liberty, sir, of providing a repast for our guest's company in the hall and bade them make themselves comfortable there."

"Most admirable, Rustengo," Quinn declared amiably and took his own seat once more. "What would we do without you?"

Rustengo flushed slightly but looked pleased by the praise all the same. "If that will be all, sir?"

Lord and lady looked inquiringly to Yves, who could find no fault with their hospitality. Indeed, the smell of the bread made his stomach growl. He nodded to the chatelain and discarded his gloves. "I thank you."

Melissande pinched a date from the draughts board and popped it into her mouth. The conspiratorial wink she granted Yves and the impish curve of her lips when she glanced toward Quinn told Yves that she had not won that particular fruit yet.

It was not behavior for a woman wed to an abusive man.

No sooner had Rustengo disappeared than Quinn leaned forward and braced his elbows on the table. "Now tell me, if you will, what matter brings you to Sayerne's gate?" His amber gaze was so steady that Yves wondered again how much Quinn knew.

"Quinn, let the man eat," Melissande chided.

But Yves leaned forward as well, his mission of greater import than filling his belly. "What do you know of Philip de Trevaine?"

Quinn grimaced. "Little good. Michel de Perricault fell at his hand, from what I hear."

"And both Michel's widow and his son are Philip's captives," Yves added grimly.

"No!" Melissande protested. "I thought Gabrielle escaped."

Yves shook his head, once again feeling the full weight of his failure. "She did," he admitted. "And she won my support for her cause to see her son free from Philip."

Quinn's gaze sharpened, and both he and his lady leaned closer, keen to hear the news.

"Last night we attacked Perricault, after I witnessed Philip's withdrawal from the keep without Thomas." Yves swallowed and laid the bread aside. "We were routed severely and the men who ride with me are the sum of those who managed to escape."

"Deceitful dog," Quinn muttered under his breath. "He must have returned to the keep."

"That he did."

"Does he have a confidant within your ranks?" Quinn hissed.

Yves met his brother's gaze squarely. "No longer."

Quinn nodded, his glance unswerving. "Good."

The word hung between them for a long moment, then the lady leaned forward to pour Yves some wine. He sipped at it slowly, choosing his next words with care.

"But that man confided in me Philip's plan." Yves looked to lord and lady. "He means to make Tulley his own."

Melissande hissed through her teeth, then took a draft of her own wine. "Annossy will be next," she said, then looked toward Quinn with worry in her eyes.

Quinn covered her hand with his own and gave her fingers a squeeze. "We have kept foes from Annossy's gates before, Melissande," he said in a low voice. "Do not fear that we will see your family holding secure once more."

Then he looked to Yves, his expression decisive. "What is

mine is yours," he said. "Together we will see Lady Gabrielle and her son safely out of Philip's grasp."

"And Philip dead," Melissande added savagely. "Such a villain cannot be permitted to live."

A child cried out from the curtained corner of the solar and the lady was immediately on her feet. No wonder she felt such sympathy for Gabrielle and Thomas!

"Hush!" she murmured. "You will wake your brother." As she turned, her surcoat pulled and revealed the ripe curve of her belly.

Two children at least, Yves realized, and another en route. His brother had not only an estate to his name, but a family, and a wife who clearly adored him. As Melissande excused herself to console the child, Yves looked at Quinn.

He found his brother watching him with appraising eyes that he suspected saw much more than he would have liked. Yves stared back, finding himself unable to look away. There were no shadows in his elder brother's eyes, and the lines traced in the tan of his visage were those drawn by laughter, not anger.

Could Yves have been wrong about Quinn?

It was remarkable to question the truth of tales that had been fed to him from the cradle, but this man did not match expectation in the least. He had pledged his aid to Yves' cause with the alacrity of a decent man. Indeed, now that Yves considered the matter, who had spread the tales of Quinn's cruelty?

None other than Jerome de Sayerne.

Could Quinn's departure from Sayerne have been enough to turn their sire against his firstborn? Certainly, Yves had no doubt of Jerome's malice, having felt its bite repeatedly upon his own flesh.

Quinn cleared his throat, drawing Yves back to the present. "Once I heard a tale, Yves de Sant-Roux, that I was quick to discount in those days," Quinn admitted slowly. He flicked a sharp glance to Yves, then stared into the depths of his wine.

The fire in the brazier crackled and wax slid down the side of the fat beeswax candle reposing on the table. Yves did not dare to move or even to ask what that tale might have been. Faintly, he could hear Melissande crooning a lullaby.

"You see," Quinn continued, "the tale was so fantastic that I could not imagine it to be true. At least, not until now, when I see you before me and detect a hint of my sister's visage in your face."

Yves' throat clenched as Quinn impaled him with a bright glance. "Could it be, Yves de Sant-Roux, that once upon a time, you were the bastard of Jerome de Sayerne, a son also named Yves?"

Yves' grip tightened upon the chalice of wine, but he could not have lied to save his very life. Not to the man who had pledged his household to aid Gabrielle so quickly.

"I still am that man," he admitted quietly.

Quinn studied him silently. Yves suspected that the turmoil loosed within him by that confession was readily discernible by that perceptive gaze.

"Perhaps," Quinn said finally, "I did not dare believe because Yves de Sant-Roux was precisely the kind of man I would be proud to call my own brother."

Yves blinked in astonishment at that. But Quinn slowly smiled. It was a welcoming and warm smile, a smile that just hours past Yves would never have expected to receive from this man.

"Do not look so surprised! You have come far, brother of mine," Quinn acknowledged. "And done so honorably, despite the harsh legacy we both share. I know well enough the lies our sire told about me. Thanks be to Dame Fortune that you were undeterred by both those lies and whatever memories you must have of this place."

Quinn scanned the room before looking back to Yves anew, his expression somber. "It took me some time to banish my ghosts before I could again consider Sayerne my home. I would have that for you, as well."

As Yves struggled to absorb his brother's amazing words, Quinn set his wine aside and offered his hand. "Welcome home, Yves. Welcome home to Sayerne."

Yves stared at his brother's hand—so like his own—for only a moment before he responded. And as he grasped it and felt the sincere strength of that man's grip, he knew that at least one haunting ghost from his past faded to no more than a wisp of harmless smoke.

"Look," Melissande said, her return making both men look up. "What about this?" She crossed the room, a slumbering child cradled against her shoulder, offering a small drawstring bag made of crimson velvet to her spouse with her free hand.

"I had forgotten about it," Quinn admitted, and rose to his feet. He lifted the sleeping cherub from his wife's arms, then took the bag and offered it to Yves. "This belongs rightly to you."

Yves accepted the bag and felt the weight of something small within it. He looked inquiringly to lord and lady, who gestured simultaneously for him to open it.

"We found it in the treasury," Melissande confided. "Oh, this place was in terrible shape, and I, for one, was certain there was nothing of merit left within its walls. There was nothing, except that."

She lowered herself carefully onto her seat again and reached for the dates. "Quinn thought that one day you might return here, so we saved it for you."

Yves sank onto his stool, surprised yet again. He had been certain there would be nothing here for him at Sayerne and was being proven wrong for the second time in short order. He loosened the string and a tiny circle of silver spilled out onto his palm.

It was a ring, and one for a lady, judging by its size. It was patterned in some way, the surface catching the light. Yves studied the ring more closely and realized there were words carved into it.

À mon seul désir it read, the words making a complete circle around the outside of the ring.

To my one desire.

Yves looked to his host and hostess, not knowing quite what to make of this token.

"It was marked as having been the only jewelry that Eglantine wore," Quinn confided, and Yves' heart tightened at the familiarity of that name. "I will give you the scroll that was with it, for it told of how Eglantine died bearing Jerome a son."

Eglantine. Her ring burned a circle in Yves' hand.

"It is not an easy document to read." Quinn frowned. "The chronicler was quite opinionated about children born out of wedlock, not to mention their dames."

Quinn cleared his throat as Yves stared at him, willing his brother to say what he already suspected. "I am quite certain that this ring belonged to your dame," Quinn concluded.

This ring had adorned the hand of the mother he had never known. A lump rose in Yves' throat as he marveled at the ring's minute perfection. He had never had any token of his dame, nor even any hint of what kind of a woman she was. He did not even know what she looked like, but this ring, this very ring that he held now, had once graced her finger.

To my one desire.

He wondered what his mother's one desire had been. Could it have been to have a healthy son?

Yves thought suddenly of Gabrielle and the strength of her determination to see Thomas free.

Gabrielle was a woman unlike any other Yves had ever met. There was a woman who knew what she desired of life, a woman determined to win the return of her son, regardless of the price. He wondered whether Gabrielle and his own dame would have seen eye to eye.

The thought made him smile. Yves ran a finger around the perimeter of the silver ring and knew with sudden clarity what he would do with this token.

He would put this ring upon Gabrielle's finger once Philip de Trevaine drew breath no more. This would be the ring to seal the troth between them.

It was only fitting.

Yves slid his mother's ring to the second knuckle of his smallest finger and looked at Quinn with newfound determination. "We have need of a plan," he said firmly, "and must implement it quickly."

Three days and nights of silence had reigned in the solar by the time the dressmakers came. The gates of Perricault were unassaulted and Gabrielle's belly echoed hollowly. The trio of women smiled as Algernon let them through the heavy door, his bright glance pinning Gaston to a corner with an unvoiced threat.

That they brought hot food was an enticement Gabrielle did not even need. She knew full well what she had to do.

Gaston refused the food stoically, but Gabrielle frowned at him. "Come and eat," she bade him sternly, sitting to do so herself. "You have need of a good meal in your belly."

"But, my lady," Gaston hissed, darting a glance toward the waiting women. "It could be *poisoned!*"

"At this point, a lack of sustenance may kill you just as quickly," Gabrielle said matter-of-factly. She took a bite of rich rabbit stew and closed her eyes against her body's response.

Gaston still hesitated, she noted.

"Gaston, do not fear the food," Gabrielle urged quietly. "We are yet too useful to Philip for him to want us dead."

And that was the simple truth. The argument evidently made some sense to the boy, for he sidled closer and accepted a bowl.

"We have brought the finest red samite for your wedding garb," one of the women chirped, displaying the fine fabric for Gabrielle's approval.

"And pearls to adorn it," contributed another.

"Cloth of gold for your veil, and wondrous golden embroidery for the hems," cooed a third.

"And look!" The first threw open a tiny chest filled with gleaming gems. "Our lord sends fine jewelry for your selection."

Gabrielle waved a disinterested hand. "Do whatsoever you think fitting," she said, and concentrated on eating her meal.

"Then you agree to be fitted for the nuptial gowns?" the first woman asked anxiously.

Gabrielle looked up to find all three of them, as well as Algernon, watching her avidly. From the corner of her eye, she saw Gaston freeze halfway to lifting a piece of bread to his mouth.

"Yes," she said quietly, knowing there was nothing else she could do.

As difficult as it was going to be, wedding Philip was the only way that she could ensure Thomas' safety. Even that was a tenuous proposition, but Gabrielle had no other choice. The rush of the river beneath the window was a haunting reminder of Philip's threat. She had lain awake long into the first night, just listening to the water as she came to terms with what she must do.

It was clear that Philip meant what he said.

Gaston's jaw dropped, as did his bowl of stew. The bowl clattered to the floor, and the women clucked in disapproval, but the squire rushed to clutch Gabrielle's arm. "Surely, my lady, you are not considering wedding this cur?"

The three dressmakers inhaled simultaneously and Gabrielle shot the boy a quelling glance. "Mind your tongue, Gaston," she said sternly. "Your opinions are not wisely shared here."

The boy frowned, looked to the women, then leaned closer to Gabrielle to whisper, "But, my lady, I told you my lord would come to aid us."

Gabrielle smiled mockingly, as much for the attentive dressmakers and Algernon as anything else. "And I know you are wrong." She added in a more gentle tone, "Eat your meal, for there may not be another for a while."

Gaston, however, waved with indignation. "But this would be a travesty of a marriage! Have you not heard the minstrels sing of love between partners?"

This time Gabrielle's wry smile was genuine. "Gaston, Gaston, such thinking has a place only in the troubadour's chansons."

The boy's eyes widened in astonishment. "But did you not love your husband?"

"Michel?" Gabrielle shook her head. "No, we had respect for each other and honesty between us. That is more than most can boast." She noted the boy's chagrin and chided him gently. "Gaston, ours was an arranged match and worked out better than most such marriages."

"But he treated you with honor?"

Gabrielle nodded.

Gaston leaned closer, his gaze burning with conviction. "Then why can you not believe that my lord will do the same? Why do you insist that men follow their own advantage alone? Did your husband do as much?"

Indeed, Gabrielle could see why Yves had a difficult time in disciplining Gaston, for even when he exceeded the bounds of propriety, he did so with such genuine charm that she was tempted to answer.

"You are impertinent," Gabrielle scolded, because she felt she should, and the boy's ears heated to a dusky red.

But Gaston did not back down. "Did he?" he asked again, and Gabrielle could not help but smile at such persistence.

"No," she conceded, "but he was spared the curse that makes men beyond selfish."

Gaston frowned. "What do you mean?"

"Michel was not a handsome man, indeed he was most plain, and therein lies the reason for his solicitude."

Gaston considered this for a moment, then obviously realized that his lord was fair of countenance. "But—"

"Enough!" Gabrielle said, more curtly than she intended. "You have had more answers than was likely wise of me to confide." She set her bowl aside and turned to the waiting women, taking note of the avid curiosity upon their faces. "I would bathe before you begin."

"Yes, my lady." The three curtsyed low and one was dispatched. Algernon locked the door behind her, and Gabrielle had little doubt that man stood resolutely in the corridor beyond.

"Did you trust your husband?" Gaston demanded in a low voice.

Gabrielle turned to the boy to find his conviction still burning brightly in his eyes. His idealism was so strong, it touched her heart, and she hated that she must be the one to destroy his illusions about the ways of men.

"I trusted him to see to his own best interest," Gabrielle said gently, "as do all men." Gaston held her gaze stubbornly, as though he would will her to continue. Gabrielle sighed. "Gaston, I should have wed your lord when I had the chance. Then, coming here would have been in his best interests. But I did not and it is not, and now I must bear the price of my own folly."

"He will yet come," the boy insisted in a low voice.

Gabrielle shook her head. "We have had this argument before."

Gaston's shoulders sagged with the disappointment of his failing to convince her. Gabrielle thought she saw tears glisten in his eyes before he turned away and folded his arms across his chest. He looked much younger from the back, his tabard rumbled and his hair disheveled.

He picked up his bowl with disinterest and morosely picked at its remaining contents. "He will come," Gaston whispered as he hunkered over his meal, almost murmuring to himself. "He will come and you will see that not all handsome men think only of themselves."

And Gabrielle, to her own dismay, ached with the hope

that the boy was right, though she dared give no sign of her foolishness.

A full week had passed by the time Yves and Quinn reached Perricault once more. The sky was sullen overhead when they reached the perimeter of the estate, and Yves feared what might have happened to Gabrielle in those seven days and nights.

In this moment, his own confidence in their plan faltered, and it no longer seemed as destined to succeed as it had within the firelit solar of Sayerne. All the same, he did his part, secreting himself within one of three wagons.

From the outside, the wagons appeared to be bearing gifts, instead of armed knights. One seemed to be piled high with spoils of the hunt, though in truth only the slain peacock and the stag at the peak were genuine. Beneath the festooned straw was a false bottom and knights hidden in the space below.

The two other wagons were similarly outfitted—one sporting a pair of tapestries and hints of many more below, one apparently piled high with trunks and chests. These were all false sides and tops, and Yves crept into the darkness beneath. The men were packed elbow-to-elbow, and the wood cart groaned with the addition of Yves' weight.

Yves could never have imagined he and Quinn might have raised an army of such magnitude. Fully fifty knights were hidden in the cramped quarters within the carts and another fifty trailed behind. These would reinforce the attack, along with those men-at-arms and others who wanted to lend their support. Yves had glimpsed more than one face familiar from Gabrielle's camp.

It warmed his heart to find so many supporting the cause of Gabrielle, and Yves shook hands with all the men in his own cart before it lurched into movement. They jostled and bumped against each other, silencing the clatter of their weaponry with gloved hands, more than one murmuring a prayer for protection as they drew nearer to Perricault's gates.

What seemed long hours later, words were exchanged outside, the cart halting, then moving forward once again. Its wheels rattled across wooden planks and the rushing of the river filled Yves' ears. The men exchanged resolute glances in the tight space as the carts began to mount the incline to the gates themselves.

"Hail there! Who arrives at Perricault?"

At the gatekeeper's call, the men within the wagon straightened silently.

"Lord Quinn de Sayerne," Quinn replied without hesitation. "I came to parlay with Philip de Trevaine."

"Does he expect your company, sir?"

Quinn chuckled easily. "I doubt as much, for I do come unannounced. I bring gifts for your lord, as proof of my true intent in welcoming him as my neighbor."

Yves hoped full well that any irony he detected in his brother's tone was due to his own imagination alone.

There was an indistinguishable murmur, then Yves' heart pounded at the familiar sound of Perricault's portcullis being raised.

"Welcome, Quinn de Sayerne!"

The carts lunged forward again, the tired old mules Quinn had set to yoke straining against the weight. Yves thought he felt the chill of the gates fall over them, then the wheels rattled on cobblestones. An eternity later, the portcullis creaked again.

They were inside Perricault.

"Quinn de Sayerne," cried another voice. "Come! My lord will meet you within the hall."

Footsteps echoed and faded. The men eyed each other as silence fell around the cart once more, and settled to the difficult business of waiting for their signal.

Yves gripped his own blade and heard Gabrielle's prayers echo in his ears like an anthem. By all that was holy, he

thought grimly, if Philip de Trevaine had harmed a hair on
that woman's head, Yves would dispatch that man with his
very own hand.

Would that he had the chance.

Chapter Twelve

The sound of horses on the morning of the wedding sent Gaston running to the window. His dismay that the opening faced away from the bailey was immediately evident.

"You are wrong," Gabrielle chided quietly, wishing the boy would face the simple truth that his lord would not come. One of the dressmakers clucked her tongue, turning Gabrielle to face her as she placed a last stitch in the hem of the lavish surcoat.

Gaston fired a glance to Gabrielle that spoke volumes, but before they could begin again the argument they had had a thousand times, a man laughed in the portal.

"Ha ha!" Philip himself swept into the solar, his smile more sunny than Gabrielle thought was warranted under the circumstances. A week without his company had certainly done little to improve his appeal.

He whistled through his teeth and circled Gabrielle, his gaze so hot upon her that she nearly fidgeted. "Are you not the most beautiful bride in all of Christendom?" he demanded gallantly, then bowed deeply to her.

Gabrielle folded her arms across her chest at this unwelcome display. "Good morning," she said crisply.

Philip's smile only widened, though he arched a brow as

he regarded her. "No smile from my fetching bride?" he taunted.

Gabrielle forced a facsimile of a smile, her patience stretched thin both by the fussing of the women and the sullen insistence of Gaston. Though the squire's faith in Yves was touching, it had certainly proven to be unfounded as the days went by and the knight did not appear.

Gabrielle did not blame the boy for his poor reconciliation to the truth, for she was surprisingly disappointed herself. Not that she had *truly* believed Yves would come—oh no, nor even that it would have been reasonable to hope as much.

Gabrielle told herself that that could only be because the prospect of wedding Philip was not a welcome one, or because she was concerned for Thomas.

Sadly, neither of those reasons seemed adequate explanation for the full weight of her disappointment.

Surely she could not have come to care for the handsome knight who had taken her cause? Surely Gabrielle knew better than to even wonder whether a man could truly care for something beyond himself?

Suddenly she became aware that Philip was watching her avidly. Had he guessed the direction of her thoughts? Her heart skipped a beat and she uttered the first words that came to mind.

"You seem in a fine mood this morn."

"And why not?" Philip swaggered across the room, dismissing the dressmakers with a sweep of his hand. They scattered like so many skittish birds. "On this very day, I shall wed the lady who has long held my heart," he continued, a mocking note in his voice.

"Surely the situation does not demand such empty flattery," Gabrielle replied, her tone more harsh than she intended.

Philip's eyes narrowed and his smile faded. "As you wish," he said flatly. "I am in a fine mood for I shall shortly

wed the lady who can secure my suzerainty over Perricault."
He arched a dark brow. "Better?"

Gabrielle shrugged. "It is at least honest."

"Oh, it is that," Philip mused. He examined his nails, and
Gabrielle wondered what else was afoot.

"Did I hear someone arrive this morning?" she dared to
ask.

Philip's smile flashed anew. "That you did, my Gabrielle,
that you did." A glint lit his eye, making Gabrielle suddenly
more distrustful. "Quinn de Sayerne has cleverly come to
plead truce."

Gabrielle had met the lord of Annossy and Sayerne only
twice, but he struck her as a man of uncommon principle, not
unlike Yves de Sant-Roux.

"Quinn de Sayerne would not! He has not!"

Philip fired a sharp glance her way. "He has indeed," he
insisted, with such confidence that Gabrielle could not doubt
his word. "He has, in fact, done precisely what I expected
him to do."

"I do not understand."

Philip laughed aloud at Gabrielle's confusion. "And so you
would not, my bride, because I have not told you the entire
tale." He folded his arms across his chest and leaned non-
chalantly against the wall, his lips quirking with self-delight.
"Indeed, this is the finest sign of my success thus far."

"That Quinn de Sayerne comes to make a truce with you?"

"Yes!" Philip's eyes gleamed. "Because I dispatched Seymour de Crecy to win precisely this truce—"

"Seymour de Crecy!" Gabrielle gasped. "Seymour de
Crecy was pledged to you?"

"Seymour de Crecy *is* pledged to me," Philip corrected
coldly.

"But he was the one who told Yves of your departure!"

"A lie, artfully planted, would you not say?" Philip asked
mildly.

Gabrielle was outraged by this news. "He bent his knee to Yves de Sant-Roux! He pledged to our cause!"

"He lied," Philip concluded crisply, then shook his head bemusedly. "Indeed, my Gabrielle, you have some fetching ideas about the worth of a man's word."

Too late, it all became clear. Seymour was the reason why Philip had known of their attack, and Seymour had been the weak link in Yves' receipt of news. Gabrielle felt sickened that she had not insisted that Yves accept her instinctive distrust of the man, and felt doubly responsible for all that had gone awry.

"And what is yours worth to Quinn de Sayerne?" she demanded bitterly.

Philip smiled anew. "Precious little, I am afraid," he admitted readily. "But I shall accept his gifts and play along with this game of truce for as long as it suits me."

His callousness appalled Gabrielle. "You will deceive him as well!"

"But of course. It is only a matter of time before all of Tulley comes under the weight of my hand." Philip watched as Gabrielle struggled to hide her response to this revelation. She thought she might have been successful until he spoke.

"Please do not tell me that you have changed your mind about our nuptials, my Gabrielle," he murmured in a dangerously low voice. "Or shall I have Algernon fetch your son? He might enjoy a swim on such a day."

"No!" Gabrielle cried, her tears threatening to choke her. "No, do not hurt Thomas!"

Philip smiled and offered her his elbow as though nothing was amiss. "Then come, and let our new ally witness our nuptials. We have, after all, a great deal to celebrate this day."

With a supreme effort, Gabrielle swallowed the lump in her throat, stepped forward and took Philip's elbow.

For Thomas' sake, she had no other choice.

Philip turned as his other hand locked over hers, and he

stared into her eyes. "You see," he hissed, "Seymour was bidden to go to Sayerne only after he saw Yves de Sant-Roux dead."

Gabrielle felt the blood drain from her face. Her mouth dropped open and she could not utter a sound, though Gaston gave a strangled cry behind her. Gabrielle stared into the cold light of conviction in Philip's eyes and felt the world had suddenly stopped.

Yves was dead.

"You had no need to do such a thing," she whispered unevenly. "He had already retreated from Perricault."

"A man in my position can take no chances," Philip asserted smoothly. "Indeed, one can never be certain what lengths a man of honor might follow to fulfill his word. They are a most curious breed."

"He would have come!" Gaston cried from behind them.

Gabrielle closed her eyes against the heartbreak echoing in the boy's voice. A warm tear broke free of her lashes and spilled over her cheek. It could not be that that knight was dead, and only because she had persuaded him to take her cause.

"He would have come, I know it!" Gaston insisted, his voice rising boyishly high.

"Shut up!" Philip snapped. "Or Algernon shall toss *you* from the window!"

He hauled Gabrielle from the solar, and she felt the brooding presence of Algernon before she saw him in the shadows of the corridor. The door to the solar was slammed behind them, Gaston trapped behind with his disappointment.

"Down to the hall," Philip commanded, emphasizing his words with a shove to Gabrielle's shoulders. She stumbled slightly until Philip's gloved grip landed securely on the back of her neck.

"And there will be no nonsense from the likes of you on this day," he hissed.

Gabrielle glanced over her shoulder, only to find his gaze

even more chilling than it had been before. Her heart went cold.

"Do we understand each other?" he demanded, and Gabrielle could only nod silently.

Philip gave her another shove toward the stairs. There would be no respite for her now, Gabrielle understood, for she would shortly become the wife of an uncommonly cruel man.

Would Yves have come if he had not been ruthlessly killed? she wondered. Now she would never know.

She stumbled along the hall, feeling that some spark within her had died with Philip's news. It mattered markedly less to Gabrielle what her own fate would be, but she hoped that her submission would win some concession for her son.

Otherwise Yves would have died for nothing, and Gabrielle could not bear the thought of that.

The owl call did not come nearly soon enough for Yves' taste.

All manner of fears darted through his mind, a thousand uncertainties raised their heads and countless foul possibilities that he and Quinn had never considered came to mind in the silent shadows of the cart.

Then the owl hoot sounded as clearly as a bell.

Yves was on his feet and out of the wagon in a heartbeat, his helmet slammed on his head, his blade swinging. The other knights followed with singular speed, and in a dizzying instant, the bailey of Perricault was once more filled with the clash of steel upon steel.

Yves dispatched three sentries, ensured that the gate was taken and the reinforcements on their way up the hill before he dove through the portal of the château. Twenty knights followed close at his heels. Yves blinked twice at the relative darkness, then plunged onward, following the sounds of swordplay to the hall.

Quinn struck down a mercenary with a savage blow just

as Yves burst into the room. His brother was sorely outnumbered here, for the hall was filled with Philip's men.

Torches smoked from sconces on the wall, painting the fighting men in flickering orange light. The table had been set for grand festivities, though when Yves roared a battle cry, his men lunged forward to engage the enemy, disregarding the spread of fine linens and candles.

A steely eyed mercenary came after Yves, but he had only to think of Gabrielle, and Thomas and Gaston, to see the man dead in a trio of quick strokes. Truly, Yves had never burned for vengeance as he did this day.

"No!" a familiar feminine voice cried.

Yves pivoted in time to see a slight but finely garbed man haul a crimson-clad woman toward the stairs on the far side of the room. She was tall and slender, though her features were obscured by a fine veil.

Could this be Gabrielle? Yves pushed his way closer, his heart leaping in recognition as the lady bit her assailant with a force that made that man bellow aloud.

Gabrielle, no doubt, he concluded with pride.

"Bitch!" the man that must be Philip de Trevaine cried out. He backhanded Gabrielle and she fell against the stairs with a gasp that wrenched Yves' heart. Her veil fell away, revealing the pallor of her skin and the bright red imprint of Philip's knuckles on her soft cheek.

The desire for retribution burned with the vigor of a newly kindled flame within Yves. Nothing could have kept him from Philip de Trevaine. He cut down one warrior after another, his stroke sure and lethal, even as Philip virtually dragged Gabrielle up the stairs.

The pair had disappeared into the shadows lurking above by the time Yves reached the foot of the stairs, but he plunged into the darkness all the same.

Silence greeted his ears from the upper floor and Yves instinctively slowed his pace. Silence seemed to be a warning sign from this Philip, for such a silence had greeted their attack upon Perricault's gates.

A woman fought to catch her breath, the sound cut short so quickly that Yves knew she had not fallen quiet willingly.

The sounds of battle faded behind him as he focused on the shadows ahead and strained for a sound that would reveal what awaited him.

Nothing carried to his ears.

Yves' pulse thundered with such vigor he was certain all would hear it. He tightened his grip upon the hilt of his blade and took another step.

And another.

And yet another.

Only four steps remained to the summit, then a yawning blackness stretched beyond. How long was the corridor? How many openings?

Where was Lady Gabrielle? A woman gasped and Yves braced himself for he knew not what. Trusting the lady, he lifted his blade, then cautiously stepped forward again.

Light flashed with sudden brilliance, blinding him with its intensity. He barely glimpsed a shadow coming for him. A blow landed so heavily against his sword that Yves almost fell to his knees. It would have killed him had he not been prepared.

But he had been warned.

A mere heartbeat after taking that near-fatal step, Yves was dodging a wicked blade. The newly lit torch illuminated a terrifying giant of an opponent, bald and bearded, who swung a great blade at Yves with savage accuracy.

Indeed, the expressionless giant never seemed to take a breath, his blade falling with steady regularity again and again.

Twice, three times, Yves evaded the weight of the sword, his mind working like quicksilver. Behind his opponent huddled a pair of shadows, undoubtedly the lady and Philip himself.

But before he could aid Gabrielle, Yves had to dispatch Philip's guardian. It occurred to him that the man, despite his obvious determination to see Yves minced, did not appear to be the sharpest blade in the armory.

Yves thrust at his opponent, checking his response, and earned a bone-shattering blow against his own blade. He faltered slightly, aware of the lady's gasp, and took a step down with apparent unwillingness.

The giant grinned and gave chase.

Yves thrust again and his opponent parried the blow with tremendous force. To Yves' delight, though, he noted that the much larger man leaned out over the stairs to make his play.

Yves took another step down, waited for the man to follow suit, then feigned another assault. When his opponent lunged forward to put his full weight behind his parry, Yves swiftly withdrew his blade and flattened himself against the wall.

The man's look of exultation changed to terror in the instant before he tumbled head over heels. His fall was halted with the resounding crack of his skull against the stone floor far below.

The only movement was of the blood spreading from his mouth.

Yves dashed back up the stairs, not surprised to find Gabrielle thrust behind a Philip who looked less certain of himself than he might have liked. Yves recalled only too well that Philip had not joined the battle for Perricault a week past.

This was a man who let others fight his battles for him. Philip's hand shook as he held his sword aloft, and Yves did not like that Lady Gabrielle was so close behind the villain.

A coward could be unpredictable when cornered.

Gabrielle shrank backward, her eyes wide with fear, and Yves realized suddenly that she did not know who came to her aid. After what she had endured, she might well fear another attacker within Perricault's walls.

And he had a perverse desire to have Philip know the name of the man who would see him dead. The shock of finding

Seymour's quest a failure might well lend Yves an advantage in this match.

Yves lifted his blade and stepped forward, well aware of the lady's gaze fixed upon him. She must recognize his colors, but her manner revealed her uncertainty. What had Philip told her?

"Philip de Trevaine, I would presume?" Yves demanded with feigned casualness. The lady caught her breath at the sound of his voice and her hand rose to her lips, though not quickly enough to hide a small smile that warmed Yves to his toes.

That man tossed his head. "Philip de Trevaine and de Perricault, if you please."

"I most certainly do *not* please," Yves growled. He lunged forward, catching Philip unawares. The other man parried with undue haste, nearly dropping his sword in the process, and failed to block Yves' strike.

A trickle of blood ran from Philip's cheek. Yves danced backward, watching Philip's hands quiver as he renewed his grip upon his hilt.

"And who might you be?" Philip demanded with bravado. "What manner of coward does not show his face in combat?"

Yves nearly chuckled aloud, the necessity of his helmet well proven by the nick in Philip's cheek. He noted that the other man wore no mail, an obviously undeserved confidence in the men that guarded his keep.

"By your standard, brave men would be fools who did not live long at all," Yves retorted easily. He attacked again with an agility that belied the weight of his armor. Philip hacked at Yves' blade, his eyes wild as he struggled to defend himself. He panted desperately, and Yves tried to back Philip away from Gabrielle.

"But perhaps it is defeating death that makes a man cautious in such matters," Yves continued. Philip's gaze flew to his face with alarm, almost as though he guessed Yves' next words. Yves hauled his helmet from his head and cast it aside.

"Yves!" the lady breathed with undisguised pleasure.

Philip looked from one to the other, a scowl darkening his brow. "You know this man?"

"Of course," Yves responded smoothly. "I am Chevalier Yves de Sant-Roux."

Philip blanched. "But you are dead!"

"Seymour de Crecy is dead, not I."

Philip's mouth worked for a moment, then he dove for Gabrielle.

"My lady, run!" Yves bellowed, even as he attacked the other man with renewed vigor. Gabrielle needed no such encouragement, for she had already fled into the darkness of the corridor.

She knew this keep, Yves reminded himself, hoping against hope that no other foes awaited her in the darkness. Philip snatched the air after her, but only caught at her veil. He swore, pivoted, and his eyes widened in alarm to find Yves so close behind him.

He barely raised his blade before Yves sliced it from his very hand. Philip gasped and Yves drove his sword into the villain's belly, determined that this man should torment the world no more.

"My wedding clothes!" Philip squealed at the sight of the blood spurting on his fine garments. He scrabbled at the blade with anxious fingers, though made no impact, for it was planted deep.

Then suddenly, he stilled.

His hands fell limp and his chin lolled against his chest. His body slumped against the wall and the blood coursing from his wound slowed to a trickle.

It was odd how much smaller Philip looked with the force of his anger stolen away forever. The silence of a battle won carried to Yves' ears from the hall below, and he had no doubt who had been victorious on this day.

Yves retrieved his sword and peered into the shadows ahead. "My Lady Gabrielle?" he called. "He is dead."

A faint patter of footsteps carried to his ears, then the silhouette of Gabrielle separated from the darkness. She rushed forward, disbelief in her eyes, her gaze fixed upon the fallen figure of the man who had so destroyed her life.

This was the man who had slaughtered the husband she loved, Yves realized. He watched her as she came forward, hesitation still evident in her movements, her pallor revealing the shock of events.

But Gabrielle came, despite her fear, and yet again Yves was proud of the woman she was. Gabrielle was daunted by nothing, much less her own trepidations.

The light revealed that she was dressed in a rich shade of crimson that highlighted her coloring marvelously, the ornate golden embroidery and fragile lace so suiting her that Yves was amazed she always dressed so simply.

Gabrielle's hair was dressed differently, more ornately, braided and set with pearls, its dark splendor framing her features in a way that her usual single braid did not. Her dark lashes looked longer and thicker; her eyes appeared yet more violet in her fear.

When she looked to him with wonder in those wondrous eyes, he marveled that he had ever thought the lady plain.

"He is truly dead," she whispered, then her lips curved in a tentative smile. She reached out one trembling hand, as though she could not believe Yves stood before her. "And you, you are not."

"No," Yves agreed, doffing his gloves and capturing the slender strength of her hand within his own. Her skin was so soft, her fingers so cold, that he closed his hand protectively about her own and pulled her closer. "No, I am not."

Their gazes clung and a heat kindled to life between them. Gabrielle parted her lips and Yves could not look away from their luscious curve, his mind flooded with recollections of their softness trapped beneath his own.

"And you came," she breathed.

Yves smiled. "You had my pledge."

Gabrielle shook her head minutely, as though she could not believe he stood before her. She raised a hand to the nearly healed scar Seymour had given him, and Yves' heart clenched at the concern in her eyes. "You are hurt!"

"No longer. It was but a scratch." Yves stepped forward, following his impulse before he thought. "And you?"

"Unscathed," she admitted breathlessly, and a tension within Yves eased.

Gabrielle's gaze fell to his lips, then danced back to his eyes, the gesture making Yves burn to taste her sweetness anew. He lifted his hand to her face.

"My lord!" came a muffled but familiar voice from the darkness beyond. The lady danced backward as Yves' head snapped up in disbelief. Could his ears be deceiving him?

Gabrielle's eyes glowed with amusement. "It seems I owe Gaston an apology," she murmured with a confidential air.

"Gaston?"

Gabrielle nodded, and relief flooded through Yves that his impossible squire had not paid the ultimate price for his impetuousness—at least, not this time. Only then did he consider Gabrielle's strange assertion.

"Why an apology?"

Gabrielle sobered as she stared up at him, her eyes so wide that Yves felt he could drown in their warm depths. "He was certain all along that you would come."

Her implication was clear, but Yves would have her say the words, even knowing how disappointing they would be. "And you were not?"

Gabrielle shook her head. "It was not sensible."

"I granted you my word," Yves reminded her sternly. "And that, *madame,* is no small matter."

"I know, but circumstances were not usual. The odds were too great against you, and you had already tried—"

"For a woman of faith, my lady," Yves interrupted her firmly, "you have surprisingly little of it in me."

The lady stared at him, apparently at a loss for words. She

opened her mouth, then closed it again and visibly swallowed. "I simply did not think," she began tentatively, then paused. She frowned and tried again. "I have never known a man who put his own well-being last."

"It is not a case of well-being, but of keeping a pledge given," Yves retorted, unable to completely explain his irritation with her. Others had expressed a lack of faith in him before and he had not been troubled as he was in this instance.

"I understand that now," Gabrielle murmured, and her lips curved in a most unsettling little smile. "Perhaps I owe you an apology, as well," she whispered.

And to Yves' amazement, she stretched to her toes and planted a chaste kiss against his cheek. Her fingertips fluttered against his face for a fleeting moment during which Yves thought his heart might burst. He longed to crush her against his chest and kiss her truly, but she seemed so vulnerable that he was loath to frighten her. In some way he could not begin to understand, his return to Perricault had shaken her expectations.

Then Gabrielle's fingertips quivered and the single word she uttered fanned across his flesh.

"Thomas," she whispered, and looked so uncharacteristically vulnerable that Yves' heart wrenched.

"Where is he?"

"I do not know. Philip took him away." She clutched at Yves' arm in sudden trepidation, those shadows claiming her eyes once more. "He could not have killed him, could he? Thomas must be here!"

Yves gripped her chilled hands and stared into her eyes, willing her to believe him. "I will find him."

Gabrielle's glance flicked away, then she took a deep breath and met Yves' gaze once more. "I know," she admitted unevenly. "I know." Twin spots of color burned in her pale cheeks, but she did not look away.

It was as though she, in turn, would will him to believe her.

The two simple words launched a surge of pride through Yves, for he had never expected this lady to rely upon anyone, much less himself, and certainly not in comparatively short order. He knew in that moment that he could not rest before all was set right within her world.

She swallowed again, her eyes wide as she looked up at him. Her words came so faintly that Yves had to lean closer to hear them, the move earning him a whiff of the warm scent of her skin. "I am so glad that Seymour de Crecy failed at his task."

Then she was gone.

Yves' heart thudded in his chest as he watched the lady flee into the darkness of the corridor. It seemed that he could not draw a full breath into his lungs. What was this witchery Gabrielle cast about him?

"Let me out! Let me join the fray! My lord, do not leave me imprisoned!" Gaston began to pound on the door of wherever he was captive. Yves snorted with the certainty that the boy could not be sorely injured if he could manage to make so much noise.

"I am coming, Gaston. I am coming," Gabrielle retorted brusquely, reminding Yves of the task that yet lay before him. He donned his gloves once more, scooped up his helmet and went in search of the heir to Perricault.

While the others tended the wounded and tallied the damage, Yves opened every door within that keep. He peered into every cranny, calling to Thomas, though he fully expected the child would answer to no stranger now. He worked the château from the ramparts down with methodical precision and terrifyingly lean results.

Finally, Yves ventured into the deepest dungeons of Perricault.

A sniffle alerted him to the presence of another. Yves lifted his torch high and peered into each cell in succession.

Through the sturdily barred window of the fourth door,

Yves could see a fair-haired child cowering in the farthest corner of the heavily padlocked chamber. His fist was raised to his mouth, his garb was dirty and his dark eyes were fixed on the door.

Evidently he had heard Yves coming and knew not what to expect.

Mercifully, the keys had been left close at hand, and Yves made short work of the locks, casting the door open with impatience. He jammed the torch into a sconce and stood in the portal. Yves faced the silent child, uncertain for a moment how to proceed.

"Are you Thomas de Perricault?" he asked gently.

The boy endeavored to take a step backward even though his back was already against the wall. He did not speak, but a wariness dawned in his dark eyes.

This could have been himself when he was six summers old, Yves thought suddenly. This could have been the way he looked when he was a child, lost and confused within his father's house. And oh, Yves well recalled how frightened he had oft been.

He squatted down in the portal, moving slowly so as not to alarm the boy. Yves set his helmet aside, propped his elbows upon his knees and laced his fingers together.

"I am Chevalier Yves de Sant-Roux," he said slowly. "Your mother convinced me to take the cause of winning back Perricault and seeing you safely by her side once more." Yves paused, noting how the boy's gaze flicked to the corridor behind him, then back to fix upon him.

Still he said nothing, though Yves had no doubt he understood. Though the color of his eyes was so different from Gabrielle's, the boy's gaze had a steadiness about it that echoed his dame's.

"Your mother is in the hall even as we speak, safe from harm." A light kindled in the boy's eyes and it seemed he chewed that fist with less vigor.

"Philip de Trevaine lies dead, and by my own hand," Yves continued.

The boy blinked and shuffled his feet with new restlessness. Evidently, he was still not convinced to come any closer.

But he had responded to the mention of Gabrielle. Yves made a point of looking about the dark and damp chamber, knowing full well that that avid gaze devoured his every move.

"I do not think your mother would be pleased to see you in such circumstance," he observed. "As men, it is our task to protect ladies from such troubling sights."

Yves removed his glove and extended his hand cautiously to the little boy. "Perhaps it would be best if we met her in the hall."

Thomas looked at Yves' hand, then met the knight's gaze once more. Yves did not dare to breathe. What if the boy refused him?

Slowly, almost reluctantly, Thomas lowered his fist from his mouth as he considered the knight before him. Thomas rubbed his fist on his tunic, nibbled at his lip, then stepped forward and tentatively put his small hand in Yves' own.

In winning a measure of this child's trust, Yves felt relief so great as to be staggering. But he dared give no sign of his response.

He nodded briskly and was careful not to close his hand over Thomas' lest he frighten the boy. He stood slowly, half-certain that his full height would make Thomas skittish again.

To Yves' surprise, the boy held fast to his hand as he peered out into the dingy corridor. It was clear Thomas expected nothing good to greet him there.

Apparently reassured to find them alone, he looked to Yves, his expression expectant.

"Shall we go?" Yves asked.

Thomas nodded, though he lingered as close to Yves as a shadow. They stepped out of the cell, but had only gone half a dozen steps down the lengthy corridor before Thomas stumbled on the uneven cobblestone floor.

Instinctively, Yves scooped up the boy, not knowing what manner of foul matter graced this floor. Too late, he feared that his quick move would betray all he had won.

Thomas stiffened for but a moment, then his tiny fist gripped Yves' tabard with a confidence that made Yves want to smile. This buoyant feeling could only be due to the satisfaction of a task well completed, he told himself, though it was true he had never felt so jubilant before.

And Gabrielle would undoubtedly be even more pleased. Yves took the stairs three at a time, unable to bring Thomas to Gabrielle's side quickly enough.

Chapter Thirteen

A ragged cheer broke from the ranks within Perricault's hall, and Gabrielle turned from the task of restoring order where mayhem had reigned. Her heart stopped at the sight of Yves de Sant-Roux carrying Thomas across the hall.

"Thomas!" she cried, and ran to meet them. Her son reached for her and Gabrielle swung the boy into her arms, delighted to have his weight against her once more. Thomas' little arms locked around her neck and she hugged him tightly, knowing she could never make up for the time they had lost.

She glanced up in the act of planting a kiss on her son's temple and found Yves' amber gaze fixed upon her. His smile was for her alone, and Gabrielle's heart lurched awkwardly in her chest.

Surely she was only delighted to find her son whole and hale? Though Gabrielle had to admit she was still shaken by the depth of her relief to find that this knight still drew breath. And she could no longer evade the truth. Chevalier Yves de Sant-Roux had not only kept his word to her, but had risked his own health to attack Perricault a second time. This man had acted contrary to all the men Gabrielle had ever known.

She took a deep breath and resolved to give the benefit of the doubt to this knight.

Surely she owed him no less.

"Chevalier, you have more than fulfilled my expectation," Gabrielle said, knowing that all within the hall attended her words. Yves watched her with a steadfastness she found no less unsettling than she had at their first meeting.

Indeed, her very flesh seemed to be afire.

Gabrielle's mouth went dry, but she lifted her chin and said the words she knew she was obliged to say. "I made you a pledge and my word is no less meaningful than yours."

Yet again, Yves' features were impassive, and Gabrielle wondered if she would ever be able to guess at his thoughts. Surely he found that she had some measure of appeal? She had thought he might kiss her in the corridor outside the solar just an hour past. Could she have erred?

Her pride pricked, Gabrielle turned to Thomas, who looked to the knight with open curiosity. "Thomas," she said quietly, "I pledged to this knight that I would take him to husband if he was successful in this endeavor. That will make Yves de Sant-Roux your new papa, but if you object, we shall have to find another solution."

To her surprise, the normally garrulous Thomas did not utter a word in response. The boy eyed the knight, who returned his regard unflinchingly.

"Have you any objections?" she prompted when he said nothing.

Thomas shook his head with unexpected resolve. Gabrielle blinked in astonishment, for Thomas had never been quick to take to strangers, and she had expected that tendency to have worsened given the experience he had just had.

But his agreement could not be mistaken. It could only be a good sign that he had taken to Yves so readily. But why did he not speak? It was most unlike Thomas to be at a loss for words. Gabrielle turned to the knight, her heart hammering with the boldness of her plan.

"The hall is already made ready for nuptials, Chevalier," she said in what she hoped was her most practical voice. "I would suggest that we make use of the preparations completed.''

No hint of surprise flickered through those amber eyes. Yves bowed and his fair hair gleamed like gold. Gabrielle was clutched by an unexpected urge to run her fingers through it, though even the thought shocked her with its playful intimacy.

"Whatsoever my lady desires," Yves agreed smoothly.

Gabrielle heard the cook's wife sigh with delight—she was a large woman and her heartfelt sighs were hard to miss— and felt her cheeks heat in self-consciousness.

"And may I be the first to raise my voice in congratulations," declared Quinn de Sayerne, whom Gabrielle had not noted among the company until that very moment.

Only now she saw that his eyes were of the same uncommon amber shade as Yves', though the men shared little other in their appearance beyond their height. He clapped Yves companionably on the shoulder, and to Gabrielle's surprise, that knight tolerated the friendly gesture with a rare smile.

Did they know each other?

"That stag and peacock we brought will have greater usefulness than expected," Quinn continued, then stepped forward and bowed low over Gabrielle's hand. "I will be most delighted to raise a glass to the return of our neighbors," he said.

"How does your wife fare?" Gabrielle asked, recalling her manners rather late.

Quinn smiled. "Well enough, though too close to the arrival of a fourth child to travel, much to her chagrin. She will also be pleased to hear that all has gone well this day, though disappointed, no doubt, to have missed a wedding."

"Which will not take place if we continue to chatter," Yves said amiably. He lifted a still-silent Thomas from Gabrielle's arms and set the boy upon his feet, tucking Gabrielle's hand into his elbow with a proprietariness that stole her breath away.

When he looked down into her eyes, Gabrielle was certain there was not enough air to be had in the entire hall. "Shall we?" he murmured, that familiar quirk of his firm lips making her heart beat a staccato rhythm.

"Of course," Gabrielle agreed, hoping against hope that she sounded as cavalier as he.

The chapel of Perricault was as glorious to Yves' eyes as the cathedral in the town outside the count's own court. To be sure, it was smaller, but the stained glass painted the sunlight a thousand rich hues and the gold laid upon the altar gleamed like a treasure just unearthed. The altar cloth was of linen, its hem embellished in heavy lace that he guessed had been wrought by the fingers of the ladies of the house.

They halted outside the doors as was traditional, and the priest came to greet them there. Yves' spirits soared in a most uncharacteristic fashion that he put down to the unusual circumstances.

After all, he had never wed before and the vow he was about to make to this woman—and she to him—was no small thing.

He turned to face Gabrielle before the open doors of the chapel. Her pupils were large and dark, her cheeks rosy, her gaze bright and full of the intellect he admired so deeply. She was to be his wife, he thought, and a lump rose in his throat.

"Now let him come who is to give away the bride," intoned the priest.

No one stepped forward. A slight rustle stirred the gathering of staff and knights who had followed them to the chapel. Gabrielle and Yves exchanged a glance.

"Have you sire or brother here?" Yves whispered, but Gabrielle shook her head.

"My sire is dead and I had no brother."

Yves looked to the priest, neither apparently having a quick solution to this difficulty. Surely such a detail could not bring matters to a halt?

To Yves' relief, Quinn stepped forward and took Gabrielle's hand in his own. She looked up at him in obvious confusion, but Quinn merely smiled.

"As brother of the groom, I suppose I shall have to suffice."

Gabrielle's frown deepened and she turned to Yves for an explanation, but the priest continued on as soon as he saw that the matter was resolved.

"And let him take her by the right hand," he declared in a booming voice. Quinn did so. "And let him give her to the man as his lawful wife, with her hand covered if she is a maid, with her hand uncovered if she is a widow."

Quinn dutifully passed her hand into the care of Yves. Yves admired anew the slender grace of her fingers, a delicacy that denied their strength.

The lady's hands were as good an indication of her character as anything else about her, for she was simultaneously finely wrought and as strong as the best Toledo steel.

His bride.

Yves slid his mother's ring from his own finger and slipped it onto the index finger of Gabrielle's hand, wishing it was wrought of the finest gold instead of mere silver.

"In the name of the Father—" he moved it to her second finger "—and of the Son—" he moved it to her third finger "—and of the Holy Spirit." Yves slipped the ring into place, then captured her hands within his own once more. He dared to look into her eyes and found a tenderness shining there that nearly stole his voice away.

"With this ring I thee wed," he pledged. "With this silver I thee honor and with this dowry I thee endow."

And when Lady Gabrielle smiled for him alone, Yves saw that the shadows were indeed banished from her lovely eyes. Knowing that she granted the credit for that to him was enough to fairly burst his heart.

The priest chose that moment to trace a cross on each of their foreheads with holy water, blessing both the couple and

their union. He urged the assembly into the chapel to celebrate the Mass.

Minstrels within, garbed in green and gold, raised their
voices in song as the priest crossed the threshold, and censers
of sweet incense were swung before the party. The tall candles on the altar were lit, their flames vying with the sunlight
to illuminate the space. Quinn's men and the people of Perricault jammed into the tiny jewel of a chapel, their faces
wreathed in delighted smiles.

Yves led Gabrielle down the aisle, marveling that such a
woman would be his wife, even if in name alone.

She leaned closer to him, her voice an excited whisper.
"The ring! It is so lovely. I never noted it on your hand
before."

"It was my mother's own," Yves confided in an undertone. "Quinn had kept it for me."

"Then he *is* your brother."

Yves looked down into her curious eyes and smiled despite
himself. "And one I would never have known, had it not
been for my pledge to you."

"I do not understand."

"Sayerne was my home estate, Jerome de Sayerne my
sire," Yves explained hastily, taking the liberty of brushing
a playful fingertip across the lady's nose. "And you shall
have all of the tale some other time, my lady. Simply know
now that I thank you with all my heart for bringing Quinn
and me face-to-face."

Gabrielle smothered a delighted smile, her fingers toying
with the ring's unfamiliar weight. "Do not fear," she whispered. "I shall take good care of your mother's ring."

"I know," Yves managed to murmur just before they
halted at the altar. The priest pivoted and lifted the Eucharist
high above them, even as Yves marveled at the truth of that.

He *knew* his sole token of his dame was in good care. The
priest's words flowed over him unheard for a moment, as
Yves considered the import of that.

He trusted this woman as he had never trusted another before. Already the change she made in a place was tangible at Perricault, despite the recent nature of Philip's dispatch. It was evident as much in the faces of the people around them as the mood of the place itself.

Gabrielle made a home wherever she was, here just as at the camp in the woods, and she did so effortlessly. And she had invited him to stay here, in the first home Yves had ever known.

He could only hope that time granted him the opportunity to show the lady the fullness of his appreciation.

This wedding was a far cry from the solemnly formal nuptials Gabrielle had celebrated once before. As soon as she and Yves left the chapel, she was hugged and kissed by people from every side—many of them strangers, but all delighted with the outcome of affairs. She lost her footing more than once, despite Yves' resolute hold on her elbow, and found herself laughing at the situation.

Laughter echoed all around her as the entire assembly lurched down the corridors and back to the main hall. Even Yves' amber gaze twinkled in a most uncharacteristic fashion. And back in the hall, the very cellars of Perricault seemed to have been emptied for the event—and perhaps those of Trevaine, as well—for there was ale and wine flowing in quantity and in short order.

Toasts were called and salutes drunk; songs were sung and dances enjoyed by one and all, without regard to rank or association. The minstrels made a merry noise; the jongleurs outdid each other with their tumbling and their mimes. Gaston sat transfixed by their tales, his obligatory duties to Yves completely forgotten.

Yves shook his head, smiled and took the remission in stride.

Thomas' eyes shone with excitement, though still he said nothing. He fairly bounced on the bench beside Gabrielle, periodically clutching her sleeve to silently point out one jongleur or another.

Yves was nearly as quiet as her son, the warmth of his thigh brushing periodically against hers and making her tingle from head to toe. When she spoke to him, he inclined his head toward her, his warm gaze and slow smile giving Gabrielle the feeling that she was the only woman in the world.

Was she repeating her dame's folly by wedding such a handsome man? The wine and the revelry combined to convince Gabrielle not to care. All was right in her world, and that for the first time in a long while, if not the first time ever.

She would savor the moment while she could.

Just when Gabrielle thought she could neither laugh nor drink anymore, a fanfare sounded and Perricault's cook promenaded with his helpers from the kitchens, proudly bearing a stag. The assembly, being mostly men, raised their voices in a robust cheer and hailed the arrival of such quantities of food with a toast and a ribald song that made Gabrielle laugh aloud.

Then they clanged their goblets on the tables and bellowed as one.

"A kiss!" they roared. "A kiss between the bride and groom!"

Gabrielle's face fell, her laughter silenced, and an awkward lump rose in her throat.

"Surely it is not such a dreadful thought," Yves teased, his tone light but his eyes filled with concern.

"Of course not." Gabrielle managed a pert smile, knowing the wine swimming in her veins would make it difficult for her to deny Yves' appeal. Could she manage to keep from responding to his touch?

Did she even want to? The traitorous thought was more appealing than Gabrielle felt it should have been. She was too clever to fall prey to a man's selfish games!

But Yves de Sant-Roux did not act like her father. As reluctant as she might be to admit it, this knight had done nothing to feed her suspicions.

She had trusted Michel. Perhaps Gabrielle could similarly trust Yves. She looked to the knight in question, only to find his amber gaze steady upon her.

"There is nothing dreadful about one small kiss," she said, hoping her voice sounded more carefree than she felt.

Yves glanced skeptically toward the roaring assembly. "I doubt one small kiss will suffice."

Gabrielle caught her breath, knowing the truth when she heard it. That languid warmth she had come to associate with Yves' presence grew within her at the prospect of a long, slow kiss from this man.

Could she manage to hide the response she knew was inevitable?

But before Gabrielle could voice an objection, Yves leaned closer to her. His golden gaze was so intense, so fixed upon her alone, that her trepidation evaporated.

"I must tell you this, my lady, while yet I have the chance," he confided in a low voice. "I have never had a home in this world—while it seems that you have a gift for creating a home wherever you happen to be. Perhaps you will not understand the import of what I must say."

Yves swallowed and his gaze flicked away, as though he could not find the words. His fair brows drew together and Gabrielle was surprised to see this bold knight so obviously unsettled.

She recalled the night in the forest when he had confided in her once before. Obviously, such confessions did not fall easily from his lips, and Gabrielle felt honored that he shared them with her.

Yves looked at her anew, sincerity gleaming in his eyes. "I would thank you," he said, his voice yet lower. "I would thank you from the bottom of my heart for welcoming me into your home."

And Gabrielle saw the depths of his appreciation shine in

his eyes. Unwittingly, she had given this man his one desire, even as he had taken great pains to grant her own. The ring Yves had given her weighed heavily on Gabrielle's hand, its inscription seeming more fitting than she might have imagined just hours past.

She stared at the knight, struck speechless by his words, and Yves slid closer. In one smooth gesture, he engulfed her jaw in the gentle strength of his hand. Gabrielle shivered in anticipation, but could not bring herself to move away.

He was going to kiss her, and thoroughly so, judging by the determination in his gaze. There was no need for pretence between them—after all, they were wed. And Gabrielle wanted this kiss more than she had ever wanted anything in all her days.

Indeed, she wanted far more from Yves de Sant-Roux.

With aching slowness, apparently oblivious to the hoots rising from the assembly, Yves leaned closer until his breath mingled with Gabrielle's own. He looked deeply into her eyes, as though expecting her protest, and when he found none, locked his lips over her own with a surety that made her heart pound like thunder.

Yves tasted of wine and an undeniable masculinity that fed Gabrielle's desire. One strong hand closed on her waist and the other slid to her nape, cupping her head and lifting her yet closer in his embrace.

Gabrielle sighed, vaguely aware that the assembly roared approval. She closed her eyes as the world spun giddily about her, though she knew the wine alone was not at fault.

Gabrielle felt her hands rise to Yves' broad shoulders, as if of their own accord. At her response, Yves gathered her closer, the firm caress of his hand making every fiber of Gabrielle's being come alive as it never had before.

Yves lifted his head, his golden gaze smoldering with sensual heat. "And know this, my lady," he whispered huskily. "I know well enough that I cannot replace Michel in your heart or in that of your son. Indeed, I would not even try to do so."

Yves paused, then frowned as though these words as well came to him only with difficulty. Gabrielle raised one hand to his cheek, wanting him to know that she understood, that she would not judge, that she wanted only to share what secrets burdened his heart.

That half smile that so affected her quirked Yves' lips as he looked into her eyes anew. He ran a finger down her own cheek and tipped her chin toward him. "Such compassion," he murmured. "You are the easiest person in all of Christendom in whom a man might confide, my lady."

Gabrielle felt herself flush and might have demurred, but Yves' thumb slid across her lips. That caress both sealed her words and raised her blood to boiling.

She wanted to feel his hands on more than her lips.

"My sire was both poor spouse and poor father," Yves continued quietly. "The only way I know to end the legacy of his cruelty is to deny it, as my brother Quinn has done."

Yves' gaze bored into Gabrielle's own and she knew these words came from the heart. She was achingly aware of the solid heat of his hand cupping her jaw and the imprint of his leg against her own.

What had possessed her to insist this match be made in name alone?

"I pledge to you that I shall be the finest husband and father that I can, and ask you only to be tolerant of my mistakes when they come." Yves arched one brow and his voice dropped yet lower. "Bear with me, my lady, while I master this new task."

He sealed his words with yet another kiss, this one even more languorously thorough than the last. The assembly hooted approval, but Gabrielle did not care. She opened her mouth to his embrace and wished with all her heart that this moment would never end.

This might well be folly, but it was not without its rewards.

When Yves finally lifted his head and the men applauded, Gabrielle was positively dizzy. She picked at her food, struggling to make sense of what Yves had just said. Despite the desire roaring through her, Gabrielle could not possibly bring herself to make the wanton suggestion her very flesh demanded.

Even if a consummation of their nuptials was what she desired beyond all else. Would that Yves pressed his case!

Gabrielle's thoughts prompted her to looked guiltily to Thomas. The boy was obviously becoming sleepy, but still smiled with delight at the jongleurs' antics. He must have witnessed those wanton kisses between herself and Yves, but seemed remarkably untroubled.

Gabrielle leaned over the boy, and he glanced up when her hand landed on his shoulder. "Do you mind having a new papa?" she asked quietly.

Thomas looked at Yves as though assessing the knight, then back to his mother. His gaze was clear when he shook his head.

"Will you not talk to me about it?" she asked gently.

Thomas eyed her for a long moment, then shook his head once more, turning back to watch the entertainment. Gabrielle straightened, knowing a worried frown creased her brow.

Why did Thomas not speak?

"Are you sleepy?" she asked.

Thomas shook his head, an obvious lie, but Gabrielle was encouraged that he did not wish to miss any of the festivities.

"Well, then, will you come and keep me warm, all the same?" she urged, delighted when her son immediately climbed into her lap as he had oft done before.

Still, he was troublingly silent.

"What do you think of the jongleurs?" Gabrielle hoped he would respond.

But Thomas simply grinned at her and nestled closer as he watched the antics of the entertainers. He did not seem to be unhappy about anything, let alone angry, so why did he refuse to speak?

"Do not fret, my lady," Yves murmured in her ear, his breath fanning her cheek in a most distracting manner. His voice was pitched low, evidently so that Thomas would not hear. "He will speak when he is ready to do so, and no sooner."

Gabrielle looked at her new spouse, seeing once again that concern in his eyes. "But it is most unlike him," she whispered, leaning closer to Yves and watching Thomas. Contrary to her son's assertion, his eyes were drifting closed now that he was against her warmth. Gabrielle tugged the end of her cloak to tuck around him. "He has always been such a talkative child."

"But that was before all around him changed so suddenly," Yves argued with quiet resolve. He slipped an arm around her shoulders with an ease that made Gabrielle warm all over. "It will take time for him to realize he is no longer alone, and that Perricault is safe once more."

Gabrielle brushed the fair hair back from her son's brow and wondered whether Yves was right. The knight's words made her recall his own tale of childhood solitude, and she knew that his understanding of Thomas was a result of his own experience.

"Do you really believe his confidence can be restored?" she asked worriedly, barely noticing how readily she turned to this man with her concerns.

Yves smiled reassurance. "Time heals much, my lady, as does your gift for listening without judgment." He nodded to the dozing Thomas. "Already he smiles."

It was true enough. Yet despite Yves' heady praise of her own talents, Gabrielle suspected it would be the knight's quiet confidence that would restore Thomas' faith in the world.

This was a man who could securely capture her heart.

In that moment as she watched her son sleep, achingly aware of the knight seated beside her, Gabrielle hoped desperately that she had the allure to win more than Yves' confidence in return.

Chapter Fourteen

A fortnight after his nuptials, Yves was restless.

Still.

His pledge to the lady that theirs be a match in name alone was proving most difficult to live by. When Gabrielle had kissed with such abandon in the hall—and before a veritable army of knights!—Yves had fairly been turned inside out by the unexpected heat of her response.

Which only made his pledge doubly difficult to keep. It had taken every vestige of resolve within him to leave the lady alone in the solar, once the priest had blessed the bed. Just the sight of that great pillared bed made him long to sweep Gabrielle into his arms and carry her there to make love all the night long.

But he had given his word of honor.

Every glance the lady gave him inflamed his desire for her more. Every confidence she whispered into his ear, every time she laughed or demanded an explanation for something he did within Perricault made Yves' burden all the worse. Never had he been so troubled by desire for a woman.

Yves barely slept, for his dreams were haunted by a certain lady's compelling violet eyes and the lilt of her laughter.

Despite his exhaustion, he was driven by his restlessness to keep busy. The knights of Perricault trained to the same ruthless discipline as had those at the count's own hall. Yves had made a point of personally checking each point of defense, each change of sentry and guard. It had done much to cement his relations with his men, but little to dissipate his impatience.

So, whenever time allowed, Yves rode. Never had Merlin had so much exercise, and for the first time, Gaston had no cause to complain at the amount of jousting the two of them did. But on this day, after a fortnight of furious activity, even Merlin looked indifferent at the prospect of yet another ride.

A snort of oats recalled the other destrier housed in Perricault's extensive stables. Yves turned to find Methuselah watching him with a wary, albeit interested, eye.

Not for the first time in these busy weeks, Yves felt the presence of another behind him and knew that Thomas trailed him yet again. Indeed, the boy was often as close behind Yves as his own shadow.

Yet still he did not speak. Gabrielle was near sick with worry. Though Yves knew the boy would talk in his own time, he hoped—for Gabrielle's sake—that time would come soon.

Yves never disclosed his awareness of Thomas' presence until the boy stepped out of hiding; then he invariably made time for him. He was a clever boy—not surprisingly, given his dame's intellect.

One morning Yves had shown Thomas how to properly hone a knife and was pleased to see immediate results. Thomas now proudly brought his own blade to the board and kept it in good care. The boy seemed to devour Yves' attention, and Yves suspected it was because of the time Thomas had been forced to spend alone.

And likely also the fact that Yves never pressured Thomas to speak.

Yves had taught Thomas to play draughts well enough that the child, albeit silently, insisted they play every evening. He won as often as Yves did, and Gabrielle took no pains to hide her amusement at the fact.

Her laughter only made Yves long to kiss her smiling lips anew, but he did not dare press his suit. On the day of their nuptials, such a display had been warranted, but now Yves was painfully aware of the burden of his cursed pledge.

The very thought renewed his restlessness yet again. Yves propped his hands upon his hips and confronted the stallion, well aware of his tiny audience.

"Well, Methuselah," Yves said calmly. "It seems high time that you had a long ride." He had taken to speaking his thoughts aloud, in a most uncharacteristic fashion, so that Thomas might understand what he meant to do and why.

The steed exhaled noisily, sending a shower of oats to the stable floor in a gesture of supreme boredom.

The echo of little footsteps carried to Yves' ears and made him smile when they halted just a short distance away. He did not look back, but fixed his attention on the gray stallion.

Perhaps it was time the boy learned something about destriers. Thomas frequented the stable enough that such a lesson might be well timed. The great beasts could be skittish, after all.

Methuselah's ears twitched with curiosity as he eyed the knight.

Yves took a step closer. "You must be impatient with this stall, though I am certain Xavier sees you exercised in the lower bailey."

Keeping one eye on the knight, the destrier nosed in his feed bin once more. Yves patted his rump and the beast did not step away.

Indeed, he seemed to lean into the stroke.

Yves smothered a smile and reached for the brush, watching the stallion's flesh ripple as he settled to work. He whistled between his teeth and continued his monologue, knowing that one small set of ears listened closely.

"Ah, Methuselah, you will get fat spending all day within

your stall,'' Yves chided in the soothing tone of voice he
always used with horses. It mattered little what he said, only
that he talked to the beast, brushed him and won his confidence before trying to ride him. He would be, after all, an
unfamiliar burden, and this destrier was no less clever than
Merlin.

"What you need is a good ride in the countryside, a run
in the forest. Sadly, there is no one to take you there but
me."

Methuselah granted Yves a skeptical glance that nearly
made the knight laugh aloud.

He shrugged. "It is true, sadly true. Xavier has far too
many steeds to his hand these days, and we have far too few
knights. Though I do my best to rectify matters, it will take
time, as all things of merit do."

He gave the steed one last stroke of the brush, finishing
with a flourish. "And my lady Gabrielle has much to resolve
these days, with the keep having been poorly tended for so
long." He shook his head with mock sadness. "No, my
friend, I fear that if you want to run, I am the only one in a
position to take you for a ride."

The stallion's nostrils quivered and he stepped impatiently
within his stall.

Yves chose to take the move as an agreement.

"Well, then, we are decided!" Yves brushed his hands
together with purpose and wondered suddenly whether he
could induce Thomas to ride with him. The change of view
might do the boy a world of good.

First, though, he would have to tempt Thomas to come out
into the open.

"And which blanket do you prefer, Master Methuselah?"
Yves mused, certain that if he talked enough, Thomas might
feel obliged to contribute an answer.

None came, although the hay rustled in the next, otherwise
unoccupied, stall.

"This one looks a popular choice by its wear." Whistling

through his teeth once more, Yves chose a blanket and spread it over the stallion's back. "And how is that?"

Methuselah spared him a wily glance and braced his feet against the floor. Too late, Yves recalled the beast's reputed tendency to fight the saddle.

No horse had bested Yves yet, however willful the creature had proven to be, and this destrier of Michel's would not be the first.

"You have need of a tether," he commented mildly, knowing he did not imagine the beast's baleful glare as bridle was fitted and buckled. Yves knotted the reins closely, giving the steed a stern glance of his own before he continued.

"And now the saddle." Yves hefted the saddle into place, bending quickly to fasten the buckle.

But Methuselah had blown out his belly to such proportions that the cinch could not be fastened. It seemed Gaston's tale had been true, after all.

"A surprise," Yves murmured with a frown. Methuselah held his breath with a vengeance. "The lady said you have need of a surprise to take the cinch, but I cannot recall what she did."

Before Yves could ponder the matter any further, a small shadow separated itself from the far side of the stall. Thomas dove beneath the great destrier with a bravado unexpected, his eyes sparkling with mischief as he reached up and gave Methuselah's testicles a hearty squeeze.

The beast squealed in outrage.

Yves saw one shod foot lift and his heart nearly stopped in terror. He lunged beneath the destrier and snatched up an astonished-looking Thomas just before Methuselah slammed that foot hard in the precise place the boy had been.

Thomas gasped and clutched Yves' neck as the gray destrier stamped with anger. Yves retreated with the boy until his back collided with the stable wall. Methuselah bared his teeth and finally settled with an outraged snort, his nostrils still quivering.

He granted the pair of them a baleful glance fit to curdle milk.

Yves' heart hammered in his chest, and the staccato of Thomas' pulse vibrated beneath his hand. Yves felt a cold trickle of sweat meander down his back at the thought of what might have been, but fought to control his tone before he spoke.

"I think," he finally managed to say, "that you surprised all of us with that."

Thomas grinned impishly, obviously unaware of the danger of what he had done, and squirmed to be released.

Yves swallowed, then marched the boy to Merlin's stall. He spoke soothingly to his destrier, watching the steed's ears flick in acknowledgment before advancing into the stall.

"You see," Yves explained with a mildness he was far from feeling, "it is not wise to surprise a stallion." He squatted down beside Merlin and set Thomas on his feet.

The stall was broad enough that they were well out of the range of the stallion's feet. "Stand back and look at the size of this creature. Methuselah is no less small. Here, give me your hand."

Thomas did as he was bidden, his smile fading when Yves placed both their hands against the expanse of Merlin's massive foot. Even Yves' own hand with fingers outstretched did not span the width of the hoof.

"These are great heavy beasts," he told the boy solemnly, "and their weight should not be underestimated." He then clucked to Merlin and stroked the horse's foreleg.

The destrier lifted his foot with a docility far different from Methuselah's response, revealing the crescent of steel beneath his hoof. Thomas' eyes widened at the sight.

"You could have been sorely injured," Yves informed him, then grimaced with mock fear, for he thought his point was made. "And your mother would have made mincemeat of me for that, you can be sure."

Thomas grinned again, then backed obediently away at

Yves' gesture, his hands folded behind his back. He watched with apparent fascination as Merlin's foot dropped heavily to the floor once more.

It was clear he had an interest in the steeds, and Yves decided to take advantage of that curiosity.

"Come out here into the corridor and let me tell you something of horses," he invited, pleased when the boy did not think twice before doing precisely thus. Yves hunkered down in the sweet-smelling straw, choosing a panel of sunlight for their place of discussion.

"You see," he began, noting that Thomas listened avidly, "if you mean to ride a steed, he must trust you. Surprising him does little to feed that trust. Did you see what I did before we went into Merlin's stall?"

Thomas nodded. Yves waited, but the boy clicked his tongue, mimicking the sound Yves had made. Then he raised his hand, as though he patted a steed's rump.

Yves smiled. "Exactly. You have a keen eye, Thomas." Thomas smiled at the praise and sidled closer to Yves. "I always make the same sound when I come to Merlin's stall, so he always knows it is me, even though I approach him from behind."

Thomas nodded in understanding.

"And I pet him so that he knows we are yet friends. Whenever I can, I brush him before we ride, because he likes that and he likes that I do it for him."

"Friends," Thomas said approvingly. Yves' heart jumped with surprise that the boy had spoken, but he dared not give any sign that this was unusual.

How he wished Gabrielle could have heard this first word!

"Exactly," he agreed. "We are friends."

Thomas squatted down beside Yves, his pose a perfect copy of the knight's, and Yves struggled not to smile. A tiny frown pulled Thomas' brows together, and Yves' inclination to smile died a quick death.

What was amiss?

Thomas laid one small hand tentatively on Yves' knee and looked up at the knight, uncertainty shining in his dark eyes. "Friends?" he asked softly, his fear of rejection so obvious that Yves' heart wrenched.

"I should like very much to be your friend," Yves declared, and Thomas smiled sunnily. Yves smiled back and closed his hand firmly over the boy's small one, amazed at how one child's smile could make so much difference in his mood.

But then, Gabrielle's smile had much the same effect.

Yves glanced to the other stall, only to find Methuselah watching them both with a vigilant eye. Yves leaned closer to the boy, deliberately letting his voice become teasing. "But I am guessing that neither of us will be friends with Methuselah anytime soon."

Thomas giggled and shook his head, clearly enjoying the fact that they two were in disfavor together. The sunlight in the stables seemed suddenly more golden with promise than it had before, and Yves marveled at the acceptance he had found within Gabrielle's home.

It was now his home.

And Thomas was his son, as well as his friend.

Would that Gabrielle could hear her son speak, too!

Yves watched Thomas' bright gaze as he eyed the destriers. Clearly the boy had an affinity for the creatures and it could be no coincidence that his first word had come here.

Yves recalled all too well how he had adored the wolfhounds in Sayerne's stables when he was a child. "When I was a boy, of about your size," he said carefully, "there were wolfhounds in the stables of Sayerne."

Thomas turned to Yves, his mouth round with delight.

But he did not speak again.

"I liked playing with the dogs," Yves confided, though still Thomas held his tongue. "Do you like dogs?"

Thomas nodded with enthusiasm and his fingers clenched

minutely over Yves' own. Perhaps the presence of dogs
would coax yet more response from Thomas.

But did Gabrielle desire dogs within her home? The absence of any such creatures gave Yves pause. He should ask
her thoughts before making any promises to Thomas.

Yves' heart skipped a beat. He guessed that Gabrielle had
been avoiding any private moments between them, but now
he had reason for such a moment. The news of Thomas' first
word and this idea to prompt more from the little boy gave
Yves the perfect excuse to seek out his bride.

The lady, after all, dearly loved to be asked her opinion.

And perhaps, if Yves were fortunate indeed, he might have
another chance to sample one of the lady's intoxicating kisses.

He could hardly wait to find her alone.

The afternoon sun had circled past the windows of the solar
and the late afternoon shadows were beginning to stretch long
in the room. Gabrielle stopped short at the sight of the great
bed already turned down. The servants were less than subtle
in their hints these days, and she knew that they had guessed
Yves did not share her bed.

And Gabrielle found the great bed uncommonly cold these
nights.

For a moment, she permitted herself to imagine Yves' lean
strength entangled with hers, mornings spent abed, nights
spent loving.... Then she gave her head a resolute shake.

By the terms of her own demand, that was not to be. Gabrielle unknotted her girdle and strode across the room to
fetch a finer one—her only concession to joining Yves at the
board each night. She steadfastly avoided glancing at the bed
again.

"Gabrielle?"

She pivoted smoothly at Yves' soft murmur of her name.
Her heart hammered to find the subject of her imagination
lounging in the doorway. Not for the first time, Gabrielle had
the odd sense that Yves could hear her very thoughts.

His golden hair gleamed and his eyes seemed uncommonly
dark. He was garbed in dark tunic, hauberk and tabard much
as that evening in the count's court, and Gabrielle was painfully aware of the intimate nature of the solar.

Indeed, the bed seemed to mock her. If Gabrielle had not
known it was whimsy, she would have been certain the pillared bed loomed even larger in her peripheral vision, its pristine linens inviting amorous play.

But she would rather die than let Yves guess how readily
he affected her. Why would he come here? He had not
crossed the threshold of the solar since their wedding night.

Gabrielle's heart skipped a beat. Was this some ploy to see
his own base needs satisfied, despite the terms of their marriage?

Would she be able to resist any approach he made?

Gabrielle straightened. "Is something wrong?" she asked
crisply.

Yves shook his head, and the smile she adored tugged the
corner of his lips. His gaze was warm upon her and suddenly
it seemed to Gabrielle that the solar lost its late afternoon
chill. "On the contrary, something is very much right."

It was nearly impossible to keep rein on her thoughts when
he watched her with such intensity. "I do not understand,"
Gabrielle admitted, feeling her cheeks heat.

Yves' gaze flicked across the solar—no doubt noting the
state of the bed!—then back to Gabrielle. "May I join you?
This will only take a moment."

Gabrielle took a deep breath, not in the least bit certain that
she could deny Yves even for a moment if he touched her.
"Of course," she said with a falsely bright smile.

Yves stepped into the room and pushed the door not quite
closed behind himself. He strode purposefully to Gabrielle's
side, his amber gaze locked with her own. Gabrielle's heart
began to race.

"It is Thomas," he confided in a low tone when he stood

directly beside her. Gabrielle could smell his skin and longed to have another of his heady kisses.

Yves flicked a pointed glance at her. "He spoke today, and—"

"He spoke!" Gabrielle grasped Yves' shoulders and gave him a shake, her own desires momentarily forgotten. "When? What did he say? What prompted him to talk?"

Yves dropped the weight of a warm finger against her lips, laughter dancing in the amber depths of his eyes.

Her son was talking again! Gabrielle looked to the man responsible for this change, her heart lurching to find his warm gaze fixed upon her and the half smile that melted her knees toying with his lips.

Her knees melted right on cue.

"He said the word *friend* twice. That was all."

Gabrielle frowned. "But…"

"I was explaining to him about tending a steed, that it is important to win the beast's trust before riding it." Yves' tone was low, and Gabrielle had a curious sense that he was not talking entirely about steeds. "He suggested that Merlin and I were friends, I agreed, and he asked if he and I could be friends."

Friends with his new papa. Tears rose unbidden in Gabrielle's eyes and she raised one hand to her lips as she stared at Yves. How could she have worried whether Thomas would take to this knight?

Yves chuckled beneath his breath at her expression, and he flicked an affectionate finger across the tip of her nose. "Do not fret, my lady," he said, his voice a low rumble that made Gabrielle tremble to her toes. "I told him that we were."

"Oh, Yves!" Gabrielle laughed despite herself, and a pair of tears splashed on her cheeks. "You are teasing me!"

Yves slid an arm around her shoulders so easily that Gabrielle barely noticed the gesture. The weight of his arm felt warm and right, no less the gentle fingertip that swept away her tears. Gabrielle met his gaze for a fleeting moment and found something there that encouraged her to lean ever so slightly against his chest. She dropped her gaze, and her heart throbbed with the certainty that Thomas could have no finer man for his father.

"I thought you should know," Yves murmured, his lips moving ever so slightly against her hair.

Gabrielle could hear the thunder of his heart. Did she dare to imagine that its pace was accelerated? Was he as affected by this simple embrace as she?

He pulled back slightly and Gabrielle feared suddenly that Yves would leave and this golden moment would end all too soon. "Do you think that this is just the beginning?" she asked hastily. "That maybe Thomas will speak even more?"

"I have an idea," Yves confessed.

Gabrielle looked up as he frowned slightly, and she marveled that he had taken her son to his heart like his own blood.

"Quinn has a litter of wolfhounds, and perhaps, if you are amenable to the idea, we could convince him to part with a breeding pair. I think Thomas has a great affinity for animals and that it is of import that he spoke first in the stables...."

"Yves, that is a wonderful idea!"

"It is just a thought," he countered with a smile. "When I was young, I played with the wolfhounds in Sayerne's stables. Seeing Quinn's pups reminded me of those times." His gaze sobered and Gabrielle knew his memories of those days were not all good.

She reached up and laid a hand tentatively on his cheek, surprised when he did not pull away. "Is that where your good memories are?" she asked quietly.

Yves nodded, his lips twisting in a sad smile before he pressed a kiss into her palm. "I hid there. When my father was in a rage and I had the chance to escape." He took a steadying breath and forced a smile. "The ostler and his wife were good to me."

Their gazes held for a long moment, and Gabrielle was

again amazed that this strong man showed her so much of his own vulnerability.

"Just as you are so good to my son," she whispered. An unexpected tear glistened on Yves' lashes. Gabrielle impulsively stretched up and touched her lips to his own.

She may have intended to offer only a chaste kiss, but any such inkling was soon forgotten. Yves' arm closed around her waist in a possessive demand that made her heart soar, and when his lips closed resolutely over her own, Gabrielle wanted all of him. She wound her arms around his neck with abandon, arched against his strength and surrendered to the majesty of his kiss.

This man loved her son. This man trusted her with the secrets of his heart.

This man had securely captured her own barricaded heart.

So lost were they in each other that neither heard the patter of little footsteps or the slow creaking of the heavy portal being pushed open.

An audible gasp echoed in the solar. Gabrielle spun from Yves' embrace, shocked to be interrupted in such a position.

"*Maman!*" Thomas cried out.

Before Gabrielle could discern his expression, the little boy turned and ran.

Gabrielle was fast on his heels, the sound of Yves' boots echoing right behind her.

Chapter Fifteen

No!

Terror gripped Yves' innards as he ran after Gabrielle's slight figure. What would he do if Thomas compelled her to choose between husband and son? Yves knew full well whose side Gabrielle would choose.

The power of her love for Thomas was, after all, one of the things he most admired about her.

Thomas dove into a storeroom at the far end of the corridor, Gabrielle in hot pursuit. She threw a glance over her shoulder to Yves, appeal in her wide violet eyes.

"Could you fetch a light?" she asked breathlessly, but Yves knew what she truly wanted of him.

He was not welcome here. She was already turning him aside, had already guessed the direction of her son's thoughts.

He should have expected no less.

Without a word, Yves turned and strode back to the solar, leaving Gabrielle to cajole her son. Yves struck a flint with impatient fingers and lit the lantern there as resolve grew within his heart.

No. He would not be dismissed from this discussion, when everything he had ever desired lay in the balance. He would not stand aside while his marriage was discarded.

If nothing else, he was Thomas' friend.

If nothing else, he would fight again for the bride he had so arduously won, even if her heart was always to be withheld from him.

Yves strode back to the storeroom, surprised to find Gabrielle still lingering in the doorway. Had she been waiting for him? She flashed Yves a smile of gratitude, then indicated a pile of spun flax in the far corner.

"He has climbed up there," she confided, leaning toward him as though they needed to solve the problem together. Yves lifted the lantern higher and caught a glimpse of a wide-eyed boy perched atop the spools.

"Thomas?" Gabrielle said softly. "Will you come down and speak with us?"

Us. Yves' heart glowed at her ready use of the single word. He dropped his hand to the back of Gabrielle's waist and stepped forward with her to face her son.

Their son.

Thomas shook his head adamantly and scrambled a little higher.

"The spools will not hold our weight," Yves murmured to Gabrielle, and she nodded, her gaze fixed on the boy.

"I cannot imagine why he is so concerned. He accepted you at the nuptials, and again on this day in the stables." Relief swept through Yves that Gabrielle evidently did not see their marriage as the root of the problem. A spark that had been kindled by her kiss raged to life once more in recollection of the kisses they had shared at their nuptials.

And it was true—Thomas had witnessed that embrace without incident.

Which meant something else was amiss. A weight slipped from Yves' shoulders at this realization, even while Gabrielle spared him a worried glance. "Do you have any ideas?"

"Perhaps he will talk." Hope gleamed in his wife's eyes, and Yves slid his hand reassuringly across her back.

Bolstered by her confidence in him, Yves handed Gabrielle the lantern and stepped into the room, hunkering down as he had when he talked to the boy before. Thomas watched every move from his perch.

"I thought we were friends, Thomas," he said gently.

Thomas nodded warily. "Friends," he whispered, and Yves heard Gabrielle inhale sharply.

It was only the second word she had heard her son utter, he knew, and she might not have trusted her ears the first time. Gabrielle held her tongue, though he guessed such restraint was not easily won.

"Friends can talk about what troubles them," Yves continued easily. "Could I tell you what troubles me?"

Thomas nodded and leaned forward slightly, as though he did not want to miss a word of what Yves said. Yves took a deep breath and wondered whether confessions from the heart would ever fall easily from his lips.

He cleared his throat, then locked his gaze with Thomas' dark one. "I know that you saw me kissing your mother. My concern is that you might not like that."

Yves held his breath and waited, sensing that Gabrielle did the same behind him. Thomas looked from one to the other, then moved slightly closer.

"Are you going to die?" the boy asked suddenly.

Die? Yves did not know what to make of that. Surely Thomas' dislike could not run so deep? "Do you want me to?" he asked quietly, fearing that matters were much worse than he had imagined.

Thomas shook his head vehemently, and Yves was momentarily confused. He felt Gabrielle's presence behind him, welcomed the weight of her hand on his shoulder. Perhaps she could guide him through this unfamiliar territory.

"Your papa did not want to die, Thomas," Gabrielle said softly. Of course! The boy was concerned about a repeat of the past. "Yves has made Perricault safe again and killed the man who killed your papa. Yves is not going to die."

"Not anytime soon," Yves added forcefully. He reached up and captured Gabrielle's hand within his own, hoping against hope that the potential loss of his new friend was Thomas' only concern.

To Yves' amazement, a tiny smile dawned on the boy's face. "I like having a new papa," he declared, "but only if you are not going to die."

Yves dropped to one knee in the pose of a man taking a pledge, his gaze unswerving from his son. "I swear to you, Thomas of Perricault," he said solemnly, "that I shall do my level best to live to a ripe old age."

Thomas grinned.

Then he giggled.

"Thomas!" Gabrielle chided, her admonition gentle in her relief. "I have told you time and again not to climb anything piled loosely. Now, come down here and be careful!"

No sooner had the words left her lips than the flax, not stacked for any such use, began suddenly to roll beneath Thomas' scampering feet.

He squealed; Gabrielle gasped and turned, anxiously seeking a place to safely set down the lamp. Yves leaped to his feet and plucked Thomas out of the tumbling spools.

Thomas threw his arms around Yves' neck, his shining face stopping any admonition before it was even uttered. "Yves is my new papa, just like you said!" he informed his mother.

Gabrielle took a deep breath and stepped closer to take her son's outstretched hand. She flicked a glance toward Yves, and he loved the smile that played over her lips. "I understand that you two are friends."

Thomas grinned. "He is my best friend ever, except for you, *Maman.*" The boy sobered and held his mother's gaze solemnly. "You found the very best papa," he informed Gabrielle, and Yves' heart lurched. "Now we are a real family again."

A real family. Little did Thomas know that this was Yves' first experience of a real family, and one all the more precious to him for that. He looked to the woman responsible and lost himself in the glow of her eyes.

Thomas' satisfaction with that circumstance was evident. Gabrielle dared to look at Yves, and something lingering in the golden depths of his eyes stole her very breath away.

Could they truly make a family?

"Can we really have two dogs, *Maman?*" Thomas demanded. It was clear that he had overheard something of their conversation, perhaps the part that interested him most.

"Do you think we should?" she asked with a mildness she was far from feeling.

"Wolfhounds!" Thomas exclaimed, his excitement at the prospect transforming him once more into the happy child he had been.

"Wolfhounds from Sayerne," Yves interjected. Gabrielle's heart melted at the way he bounced Thomas on his hip. "Just like the ones I used to play with when I was your size!"

Thomas inhaled with delight. "Can we, *Maman,* can we?"

"Well." Gabrielle struggled to focus on the question itself, aware of the considering weight of Yves' gaze. "Who will take care of these dogs?"

"I will take care of them, *Maman!*" Thomas spared an obviously adoring glance toward Yves, one not unlike those Gaston uncharacteristically granted his knight. "My *friend* and I will take care of them."

Gabrielle looked to Yves and saw his own pleasure at this outcome of events reflected in his eyes.

"I will make time for this," he assured her, his low voice launching shivers down Gabrielle's spine. "And Gaston has somewhat less to do these days, as well. I am certain the pups would scarcely be neglected."

Indeed, Gabrielle herself had missed the few hounds they had had within the hall before Philip's attack. Mere mongrels, they had not had the interest in children nor the gentle tolerance that Gabrielle knew was typical of large wolfhounds.

"Can we, *Maman? Can we, please?*"

Gabrielle smiled and touched her son's cheek. "I think it is a fine idea," she conceded, laughing when Thomas squirmed free of Yves' embrace and rained kisses upon her cheeks.

Gabrielle did not care that her gratitude for Yves' patience with Thomas showed when she met his gaze. Indeed, she could not have imagined that any other than this knight with his quiet confidence could have persuaded Thomas so readily that all was well at Perricault.

She owed him a debt for this, and Gabrielle knew suddenly the only deed that would suffice.

"Thank you, *Maman!*" Thomas pulled free of her embrace, his tolerance of maternal hugs expired for the moment. "I have to ask Xavier where they can sleep," he said, and looked inquiringly to Yves.

Yves ruffled Thomas' hair with an affection that made Gabrielle certain her decision was the right one. "There will be plenty of time to talk to Xavier before the dogs come."

"Can we do it now?" He granted his mother a sunny smile and took Yves' hand pointedly. Yves looked momentarily flummoxed, but Gabrielle gave him a minute push.

"Not everyone is invited to escort Thomas on his missions," she teased, knowing her eyes were sparkling. Oh, her suggestion would be forward, but in this moment she did not care.

And she had to make it before she lost her nerve. "Perhaps we could speak in the solar afterward?" she asked in a rush.

Yves smiled with the slowness that made her blood heat. "I will be just a few moments, my lady," he murmured, before Thomas fairly dragged him from the room.

"What color are Quinn's dogs? Are they big yet?" Thomas demanded, his volley of questions unstoppable now that they had begun. "Are they bigger than me? Will they like me? What do they eat?"

And when knight and boy disappeared down the stairs, Gabrielle hugged herself with delight. Who could have imagined that all would work out so well? Her heart pounded with anticipation of Yves' return and she paced back to the solar impatiently.

For then she would make him another bold offer.

It took Yves so long that Gabrielle's bravery nearly completely abandoned her. A real family. Her suggestion would certainly make them that, if Gabrielle could bring herself to give it voice.

When Yves' boots sounded in the passageway, Gabrielle jumped to her feet and tried to look nonchalant as her husband entered the solar once more.

He shoved one hand through his hair and granted her a rueful smile. "Now he will not stop talking."

Gabrielle could not help but smile. "I cannot believe it," she whispered, knowing her eyes shone when she looked at Yves.

"He said but two words in the stable," the knight confessed as he crossed the room to her side once more. "I never imagined he would speak so much so quickly."

"He is as he always was," Gabrielle admitted, her lips curving in a smile. "Likely he will talk your ear off, given half the chance—you can see now why his silence surprised me so."

Yves chuckled. "That I can." He stared at Gabrielle for a long moment, and beneath his heated regard, she could not summon her bold proposition to her lips.

"I suppose I should ride to Sayerne on the morrow and ask Quinn for the dogs." Yves' expression turned wry. "Pray that he does not refuse me, after all of this."

"He will not," Gabrielle said, and Yves' gaze clung to hers once more. She should ask him, now before he left, but the words abandoned her.

The silence grew between them, though the heat in Yves' eyes did not diminish. He cleared his throat suddenly and frowned. "You have no need to worry about the security of Perricault while I am gone. The men are in fine form."

"I know."

Yves stared at his boots. "I suppose I will not be gone more than a few days—"

"Do not go," Gabrielle interrupted, and Yves' head snapped up.

"You do not want the dogs?"

"No, not that." An unfamiliar nervousness claimed her and her words fell with a haste she did not like.

But they were not the words she needed to say.

"We could ride together," she suggested. "Then Thomas could choose the pups he liked, if Quinn did not mind." Gabrielle was babbling like a fool and knew it well, but could not stop. "It would be good to have a ride and for Thomas to see something outside these walls."

"That is a good idea," Yves conceded. "Would the morrow be too soon for you?"

Gabrielle shook her head and the knight took a step away. "I shall make the arrangements," he said, and turned away.

Not before she had said what must be said!

"No!" Gabrielle dove after Yves and latched on to his sleeve. He looked at her with surprise, but Gabrielle knew she had to make her offer before she lost her nerve.

She stared at the dark wool clutched within her own hand, for she could not bear to see rejection light those amber eyes. "What you have done this day, these past weeks, is beyond whatever I might have expected from a husband, especially one taken in name alone."

Gabrielle swallowed and drew a fortifying breath, achingly aware of Yves' watchful silence. "This is a match most unnatural, as you declared at the beginning, and I would rectify that situation."

Never had she made such a brazen offer. Never had Gabrielle permitted herself to believe that her charms might have an appeal for a man.

But Yves was different.

Yves was the man she loved.

Though still she knew she had to offer more than just herself.

Gabrielle dared to glance up, her fledgling confidence bolstered by the flame in Yves' gaze. "I would have ours be a match in truth," she whispered unevenly. "Out of gratitude for your deeds, I would bear you a son, Yves de Sant-Roux."

She barely had time to note the sharp way he inhaled before Yves bent and kissed her with a vigor unexpected. Gabrielle's heart sang and she locked her arms around his neck.

Yves lifted his head too quickly and his voice throbbed low against her awakened lips. His bright gaze brought her very blood to a boil and Gabrielle was exultant that her offer had been accepted.

"As always, your desire is my command, my lady," he murmured. Before Gabrielle could summon a word to her lips, Yves swept her into his arms and strode toward the bed.

She was surrendering to the allure of a handsome man, it was true, and that might well lead to an echo of her dame's unhappy fate. Gabrielle did not care. When Yves kissed her with such abandon, she could think of nothing but the promise of his touch. If this was the most gloriously misbegotten error of all her days, Gabrielle would regret it later.

In this moment—perhaps for this entire afternoon and evening—she had more important things to do.

Yves had not needed Gabrielle to issue such an invitation twice.

In fact, so surprised was he by her offer that he meant to leave the lady no time to change her mind. He could not reach the pillared bed quickly enough, even if it was only late afternoon.

Gabrielle flushed slightly, her eyes sparkling as she looked up at Yves, but she did not request that he stop.

That she should be so receptive to his touch was something unexpected. To be sure, there were noblewomen who had teased Yves in the past, but only until they knew his birth-right.

Gabrielle knew all of him, yet she did not turn him aside. That she was the sole woman he had ever desired with such vigor was a blessing indeed. It was almost too much to believe that not only was this woman of rare character his own wife, but that she would welcome him to her bed.

He took a deep breath and looked into the lady's eyes as he laid her on the bed. Gabrielle's lips curved in a slow smile that wrenched Yves' heart. They stared at each other for a long moment, then the lady lifted her lips in silent offering.

Yves could not deny Gabrielle's allure. He stretched out beside her and kissed her deeply, cradling her against his chest. Yves' desire roared with a vengeance, but this was a mating he would make most memorable.

This would be the consummation of their match, after all, and the first time he and Gabrielle touched each other in truth. This would be a day that would linger in their memories for a long while, if not forever. Yves would make it as leisurely and sweet as ever man and woman together could be.

Gabrielle deserved no less.

"A bath," he said huskily. "We have need of a bath."

Gabrielle flushed. "I bathed this very morning," she protested, but Yves kissed her into silence.

"Cleanliness is not at issue."

Gabrielle frowned. "Then why summon a bath?"

Yves deliberately let his gaze slide over Gabrielle's form and linger on every delightful feminine curve. His hand followed suit, and he felt Gabrielle shiver slightly beneath his touch. The very boldness of his plan made his voice husky.

"I would bathe you, my lady," he whispered. Yves heard the catch in his own voice, but could not look away from Gabrielle's bright gaze.

Gabrielle stared up at him and her lips parted invitingly. "There is no need," she argued softly, though Yves could see the idea had an appeal. "I can do the deed more quickly alone."

"Speed is not at issue, either," Yves countered quietly, letting his fingers mold to the curve of her breast. "I would take the cloth to your flesh with my own hand. I would bathe you slowly from head to toe, just so that I might learn all there is to know of you."

Yves watched as Gabrielle swallowed. She opened her mouth as though she would protest anew, but Yves granted her no such chance. He kissed the ruby ripeness of her lips with a tenderness aimed to reassure her.

She was so soft against him, so demanding in her own caress, yet vulnerable with an uncertainty Yves could not explain. Gabrielle's fingers slid tentatively into his hair and he savored the combination of her softness and strength.

Indeed, there could not be a woman like Gabrielle anywhere—and she was his bride. This was a lady Yves was proud to make his own.

Reluctantly, Yves lifted his lips from Gabrielle's, enjoying the way she looked slightly disheveled in the wake of his kisses. Her cheeks were flushed and her eyes bright—that combining with her smile to make her look young and fragile.

It was a side of her few had the grace to see and one that Yves would treasure.

"Do not move," he advised, ignoring the demanding ache in his loins. This could be no petty rutting, but a lovemaking that would tempt every possible nuance of response from the lady's flesh.

He would make this day fulfill every fantasy Gabrielle had ever possessed.

"I would not dream of it," the lady whispered throatily.

Yves crossed the room hastily and threw open the door. "A bath!" he cried. "Summon a bath for the lady, if you please."

"Yes, my lord," came a chorus of voices from below.

Yves turned back to meet Gabrielle's gaze and could not

resist the lady's shy smile. Surely she could not doubt her allure? Yves was drawn back to the bed as steadily as a fish caught on a lure. He sat on the edge of the broad mattress and captured Gabrielle's hand securely with his own, feeling it tremble in his grip.

An uncertainty lurked in her eyes that he wanted to banish beyond all else.

"I like that you are not afraid to show your desire," he murmured, and Gabrielle stared up at him. "It feeds my own as nothing else could." He looked deeply into her eyes, willing her to believe him, a confession he might have once found difficult to make falling readily from his lips before his lady's uncertainty. "I like that there is honesty between us, in this and all else."

Gabrielle's broadening smile lit all the secret corners of Yves' heart. "As do I," she whispered. Her hand landed on his chest, those slender fingers pressing lightly against him. Yves captured them within his grip and pulled her yet closer.

"I want this to be good between us," she added unevenly, as though she was not certain it could or would be.

Yves had no such doubts.

"It will be," he said with heartfelt conviction. "We shall make it be so, I pledge to you."

Her smile turned impish. "You do not need to pledge everything to me. I trust you to do as you say."

The words buoyed Yves as nothing else could have done. The lady trusted him! "It is my way to make a vow when something is of import to me," he explained quietly, his fingertips brushing her veil away from her cheek. Her skin was so very soft. "Does that trouble you?"

"No." Gabrielle shook her head, the heat in her gaze making Yves' chausses tighter by the moment. "I like very much that you are true to your pledge." Yves could have willingly drowned in the violet pools of her eyes.

The knock at the door could only have been called inopportune, to his mind.

Yves muttered a curse, the back of his neck heating when Gabrielle laughed at him. The merry sound of her laughter filled the solar as brightly as the sunlight.

Yves stalked to the door and she wagged a scolding finger at him from her perch on the bed. "Would you have such language leave Gaston's lips?" she teased. "Or Thomas'?"

"It is hardly the same," Yves retorted, hearing the smile in his own voice. The lady let him escape with nothing, and he liked her cleverness well.

Yves hauled open the door to find a trio of servants there, led by the indomitable Franz, none of whom could completely hide their delighted grins. Yves' ears burned with the certainty that all knew what they were about this day, but Gabrielle's laughter reassured him.

"We bring the bath, my lord," Franz declared.

"And time enough it took," Yves acknowledged gruffly, not in the least comfortable with providing fuel for gossip. His words launched a decidedly unladylike guffaw from his wife. Conspiratorial grins were exchanged all around as the bath was hauled into the room and filled with steaming water. Yves stood outside the circle of activity, fighting against his discomfiture.

It was Franz who handed Yves the soap. The tall man winked in the midst of the transaction and gave his lord a friendly nudge. "We shall not expect you at the board this night, my lord," he whispered, displaying the gap between his teeth as he grinned. His voice dropped to a whisper. "Enjoy!"

Then Franz winked again and the lot of them were gone.

"Do not look so surprised," Gabrielle chided.

"They are uncommonly bold," Yves retorted, not certain whether to feel pleased that he had been accepted or insulted that they did not fear his wrath.

Gabrielle laughed anew. "They are happy that all is well within Perricault once more. Do not fear, Yves, you have won their trust. Franz would not have dared say as much otherwise.''

The specter of the unknown Michel rose at this most inconvenient moment. Yves hated the reminder that another man had touched Gabrielle before him. No, it was not that, but the fact that Gabrielle loved Michel that rankled.

No, it was that she still *did* love Michel that lay at the root of his dissatisfaction. He looked at Gabrielle, sprawled upon the bed with her veil askew, her lips quirking with laughter.

Michel had undoubtedly seen her in such casual intimacy thousands of times. The very thought was sobering, the ghost Yves had fought to keep in the background forcing his way into the sunlit solar now, when he was least welcome.

Yves wished with sudden fervor that he had had the opportunity to win this lady's heart, for hers was one he would treasure beyond all else. But it was granted and lost, buried forever with a man who had died in the cruelty of war.

Had they two ever loved here in the afternoon?

Yves could not bear to think of it. In this moment, he loathed Michel as he had never loathed another being in all his days.

And he had not even known the man. His response made no sense.

''Would he have said as much to Michel?'' Yves asked woodenly, unable to keep the question to himself.

Gabrielle sobered, though her gaze did not waver. ''No,'' she said flatly, then rose to her feet to come to Yves' side.

Yves looked toward the floor and turned the soap in his hands, not knowing what to do with this tide of unruly emotion unleashed within him. Gabrielle looked up at him, even as her fingers landed on his arm. Yves could not look into her eyes and risk seeing her love for Michel still burning bright.

''Let us not speak of Michel again this day,'' she urged softly, and Yves could not evade the truth.

Her heart was yet lost to that man and likely always would

be. Though Yves enjoyed some measure of the lady's charm, still she kept her heart locked away.

But the lady desired *him*. Surely that could only be a good import for the future? He would prove to her that her desire was not misplaced and perhaps, in time, the lady would offer more.

Yves could only hope.

"I will not mention his name ever again," he pledged, fully meaning the words. Her fingertips rose to his face and desire rolled through Yves with new vigor.

Ye gods, but this woman fired his blood!

He met her gaze, and Gabrielle took the half step remaining between them. She reached purposefully for his tabard, but Yves evaded her grasp.

He grasped the ends of the girdle tied about her waist and hauled her so close that her hips bumped against his own. His fingers made short work of the knot, even as Gabrielle's hands landed on his chest.

"You wear too much garb for a bath!" he teased, bending quickly and taking his own teeth to the laces on one side of her surcoat.

Gabrielle gasped, but did not move away. She seemed surprised, and Yves took advantage of that rare state. He slipped his hands around the neat indentation of her waist, his teeth making short work of first one lace, then the other. He could smell the sweet perfume of her skin and feel the heat rising from her flesh, the combination feeding his desire.

When the laces hung loose, he could not resist sliding his hands through the open sides of her surcoat. The fine linen of her chemise met his fingertips; the soft warmth of her flesh curved beneath his hands. Yves straightened slowly, looked into the lady's eyes and let his hands slide upward until he cupped her breasts.

She gasped when the taut nipples came under the heat of his palms. In the same moment, Yves bent and captured Gabrielle's lips with his own.

He felt her hesitate even as his thumbs circled her nipples. Then slowly she stretched to her toes, her strength curved against his chest in a most intoxicating manner. Yves kissed her deeply, his tongue tangling with hers in an elaborate dance, and Gabrielle, to his delight, did not draw away from the flame they kindled.

Surely she could not be burning with the same desire that consumed him? Would she turn him aside once she knew the strength of his own need? Or would she merely tolerate his caress?

Yves wanted no less than overwhelming pleasure on the part of each on this night. Nothing else would suffice. His hands slipped to the pert curve of Gabrielle's buttocks and he lifted her against his arousal, so that she could not miss the fullness of his desire. If Gabrielle did not want him, this would be her chance to turn him aside.

But the lady rolled her hips against him without hesitation.

Chapter Sixteen

The fire Yves kindled beneath her very flesh was a sensation alien to Gabrielle, but still she knew her role well in all of this. She closed her hand over Yves' arousal when he drew away from her and he caught his breath, his eyes blazing into hers.

She worked his tabard loose and he aided her to lift it away. Gabrielle's hand fell immediately to his hauberk, with a purposefulness born of the familiarity of this task. But when Yves finally stood before her in loose chemise and chausses alone—the very image of his appearance that first day they had met—he caught her efficient fingers with his own.

Gabrielle looked to him in surprise, but Yves merely planted a kiss in each of her palms. "There is no rush, my lady," he charged softly, and uncertainty claimed Gabrielle once more.

She knew the ritual she and Michel had followed, but it seemed Yves did not. Mating with Michel had been an effectively managed rite—first Gabrielle undressed her spouse, making sure she touched him *there* at frequent intervals to maintain his interest in the deed. Then she washed herself hastily—and not before Michel's gaze—for he had been particular that she be pristine before they touched. Finally, she crept into the bed and Michel rolled atop her and spilled his seed.

The entire deed posed a very short interruption in the activities of the day or night.

Yves' call for a bath had not surprised Gabrielle, though his insistence that he would bathe her was confusing. And now he did not seem to want to quickly disrobe.

Gabrielle did not know how to proceed. And Yves' kisses sorely distracted her from what she knew she should do. Indeed, she had to fight every urge to simply lean back in his embrace and enjoy.

But to do so would have been grievously wrong.

While she fretted, Yves discarded her surcoat. His hands shook with an impatience Gabrielle had not guessed he could possess. Could this man possibly desire her for herself?

But no, that was foolish whimsy. Yves must want a son of his own, and desperately so. Did he not share an uncommon bond with Gaston and now Thomas?

When Yves grasped her chemise in two fistfuls and made to discard it as well, Gabrielle suddenly feared his response at the sight of her nudity. She stayed his hands and knew her cheeks burned when she met his questioning gaze.

Heaven knew she was not as finely wrought as he!

"You cannot bathe fully garbed," he chided softly.

Gabrielle felt her self-conscious flush deepen. "I am not a beauty," she whispered, her gaze fixed upon the floor. "And I can bathe myself more quickly. Go to bed and I shall shortly be there."

Yves lifted her chin so that she was forced to look into his eyes. A compelling sincerity gleamed there, and once Gabrielle looked, she could not turn away.

"My lady, is the thought of my bathing you so distressing that you would refuse?"

Gabrielle swallowed as she stared up at him, knowing she could not lie. The very thought of those strong hands sliding over her bare flesh was enough to make her knees weaken.

And they *had* pledged to have honesty between them.

She shook her head, unable to give further voice to her fears, and a slow smile curved Yves' lips. Despite that smile, Gabrielle's hands trembled as she reluctantly lifted them away from his own. Yves swept her chemise aside in one gesture, then stood back, the sheer linen spilling from his hands.

He looked upon her nudity in silence.

Gabrielle studied the steaming bath, not having the fortitude within her to face the disappointment that must light his eyes. Oh, this bold proposition of hers had been an error indeed!

"Gabrielle," Yves murmured, his low voice catching at her heart. "My lady, you have lied to me."

Gabrielle's head shot up, for she had never lied to him and she knew it well!

But the glow of admiration in Yves' eyes silenced her protest before it even began. He met her gaze steadily, then stepped forward, an uncharacteristic hesitancy in his manner. The chemise fell from his grip as he tentatively lifted a hand to her chin.

Then the heat of his hands was in her hair. His fingers worked methodically through her braids, and Gabrielle closed her eyes at the sight of his chest so close to her bare breasts. She inhaled deeply of his scent. She felt all atremble inside, as never she had before in such a moment of intimacy.

The pins scattered about her feet and her hair swung free. Gabrielle felt her hair brush against her hip as Yves spread its mass about her shoulders. He cupped her face in his hands then and smiled down at her.

"You are a beauty, indeed, lady of mine," he declared softly. "Never imagine otherwise." Gabrielle blinked in astonishment, but Yves bent to close his lips over her own.

Though Gabrielle knew he flattered her, she could not deny his touch. She wanted him, she loved him, and knowing that he wanted her—however fleeting that desire might prove to be—was a siren's call she could not ignore.

Gabrielle arched against his strength, feeling shameless but wanting no less than his all.

And now she knew once more what to do.

But before Gabrielle could reach for the tie to his chausses, Yves scooped her up and dumped her into the steaming tub.

Gabrielle gasped at the shock of his move, even as the warm water closed over her. Yves leaned over the tub and waggled his eyebrows at her in a mimicry of a stern tutor.

"Not yet," he scolded with mock severity.

Gabrielle splashed the water playfully in his direction. "Coward!" she charged, and Yves chuckled as he danced out of range. "You see me naked but will not bare your own flesh."

Yves grinned like a young boy and cast his chemise aside. He knelt beside the tub and propped his bare arms along its rim, the soap dangling from his fingertips.

"Better?" he breathed. He was disconcertingly close, the bronze of his bare skin overwhelming. It was not reassuring in the least to Gabrielle that the man was even more superbly muscled and lean than she had imagined.

Yves' fair hair was tousled as Gabrielle had never seen it before, his smile disarmingly confident. His bright gaze missed none of her perusal, she knew.

She was wed to a veritable Adonis. Surely he could only grow weary of her charms?

Yves leaned closer and his breath fanned in her ear. "What do you think, lady of mine?"

"I think you are as vain as ever a man was," Gabrielle retorted, feeling decidedly unsettled by her own uncertainties. "No doubt you think no further than your own satisfaction on this day," she charged, knowing the accusation was unfair but unable to keep it from her lips.

"Oh, no," Yves murmured. "I mean to see fully to your own pleasure first."

Her own pleasure? Gabrielle jumped as the wet heat of Yves' tongue leisurely outlined the curve of her ear. She might have pulled away from the unfamiliar but delightful sensation, but Yves' arm had slid across her back. His hand locked on her shoulder, holding her fast against his chest.

If she could not escape, she rationalized, she might as well enjoy this interlude while it lasted. That was an excuse and Gabrielle knew it well, but she did not care.

But, oh, there was much to be enjoyed!

She stretched her neck back as Yves nibbled a path of infinitely small kisses along her jawline. He paused at the corner of her lips, his own mouth but a finger's breadth away, and Gabrielle felt her head turn that increment toward him.

Their kiss was gentle and languid at first, as though Yves would coax a reluctant response from Gabrielle. Surely he did not imagine that she did not desire him?

Gabrielle knew how to dismiss that thought. She raised her hand from the heat of the bathwater and let it trail up his arm. She traced the outline of his shoulder with her fingertips, before grasping his neck. Then Gabrielle pulled Yves closer, demanding more of his kiss.

Yves hauled her more tightly against his chest with a vigor that made her heart lurch in anticipation. His mouth slanted purposefully over hers, and Gabrielle's blood boiled as his tongue tangled once more with her own.

She closed her eyes with a sigh and leaned back in his embrace. His arm gripped her shoulders like a safe harbor sheltering a ship in a storm; his other hand cupped her face with a tenderness unexpected. His thumb slid along her jaw in a caress that could melt Gabrielle's bones, and she forgot whatever she was supposed to do next.

Then Yves' fingertips slid down the length of her throat. The soap traced a path across her skin in a smooth caress that made each increment of flesh it passed resonate in its wake. Yves' other hand lifted from her shoulder, his fingers spearing demandingly into her hair.

And the errant hand slid beneath the surface of the bath-water.

Gabrielle arched backward, unable to help herself when those strong fingertips curved possessively over her breast. He worked up a lather with the soap that made his caress all the more gently seductive. Yves swallowed Gabrielle's gasp as his thumb and finger kneaded her nipple to an aching point.

Gabrielle was powerless against this sensory assault, so far beyond anything she had experienced before.

Yves' hand slid lower and she thought she would faint at the power of her desire. He abandoned the soap and it bobbed to the surface with a little splash.

But Gabrielle was aware only of the downward spiral of those exploring fingers. He traced the curve of the underside of her breast; he caressed the silhouette of each rib; he encircled her navel, then tickled inside it. Yves' fingers splayed and his hand flattened against the soft curve of her belly.

Gabrielle gasped, but Yves granted her no respite. His fingers slid through the nest of curls at the apex of her thighs and slipped into the sensitive flesh hidden beyond. That secret part of her throbbed with insistence, but Gabrielle sat suddenly straight in the tub.

She tore her lips from his. "Yves!" she gasped, certain this could not be right.

"I will not hurt you," Yves murmured soothingly. "Indeed, you may like this well." Gabrielle could hardly argue with that, for the weight of his hand, even where it rested now, was far from unpleasant.

"I have never done such a thing before," she said uncertainly. "I do not know what to do."

"You have nothing to do but enjoy."

Gabrielle frowned, for that made no sense at all, and reached for her spouse. "Let me touch you instead," she suggested, feeling that familiar ground would be welcome despite the temptation of this knight's touch.

"No," Yves said with quiet resolve. "A lady's pleasure must come first."

"But—"

"But nothing," he chided, silencing her argument with a quick kiss. Yves brushed the tip of his nose against her own and smiled that half smile that so disarmed Gabrielle. "Trust me," he urged quietly. "You will not regret this."

Gabrielle's resistance melted before his charm. She argued no more and did not protest when his lips lowered to hers again.

And for the first time since they had crossed the threshold, Gabrielle ceased to fight her intuitive response. She welcomed the heat Yves thrummed to life within her and trustingly parted her thighs before his gentle but sure touch.

She was rewarded by a surge of sensation that shook her to her core. The secret spot between her thighs hummed like a busy bee on a summer's afternoon, and Yves expertly cajoled it to yet greater heights.

Gabrielle moaned, but he did not halt his caress, his fingers coaxing and teasing as she writhed in response. His kiss stole her very breath away and she felt as if she floated in the warm water on a tide of sensation. The grip of Yves' hand upon her nape was the only fixture in Gabrielle's world.

The desire that had coursed within her veins ever since the first afternoon they had met rose to a crescendo. Her very flesh heated and she trembled in anticipation of something she could not name. She clutched at Yves' hair; she gripped his broad shoulders; she twisted and squirmed.

The heat rose increment by increment, each moment taking it yet further beyond what Gabrielle thought she could endure. She ached for something, felt a void deep within her and wanted only to have Yves fill her with his strength.

That thought made everything within her explode in a sea of brilliant light. Gabrielle cried out and felt herself strain ever higher as the tumult of her release swept through her.

And left her trembling in its wake.

Yves kissed her brow as she slipped limply into the bath-water once more. The hollow ache within Gabrielle still demanded to be satisfied, though, and she reached up to cup his jaw in turn, the soapy water dripping from her fingertips.

"I want you," Gabrielle whispered hoarsely, not caring if Yves saw the fullness of her desire. "I want you now."

Yves' amber eyes blazed into hers for a timeless moment. Then he shed his chausses, the turgid strength of him bare to her view for the first time. Gabrielle reached for him, belatedly recalling her role in all of this, but Yves brushed her hands aside.

"I cannot wait," he muttered, and she marveled that she could have such an effect upon this man.

Then there was no more time to marvel, for Yves plucked her from the bath. His hands locked upon her waist and he lifted her high above him, impaling her upon his strength as he stood, his powerful legs braced against the floor like ancient trees. Gabrielle quivered against Yves even as rivulets of water ran from her flesh to make a puddle upon the floor.

It was as though she coupled with some pagan god, bronzed and gilded, possessed of an immortal's strength.

Yves' gaze roved over her as though he marveled at *her* and Gabrielle's pulse accelerated anew. She locked her legs around his waist and twined her arms around his neck, determined to grant him as much pleasure as he had given her. Yves gripped her buttocks, then lifted her up and down in that ancient dance of mating.

His eyes glowed. "Gabrielle," he murmured, her name a caress falling from his lips. "You are my sole desire."

Gabrielle pressed herself against her knight and kissed him with a fervor she had not known she possessed, rolling her hips against his strength as her own need rose once more. Yves groaned and his grip tightened upon her, but Gabrielle in turn granted him no escape from the primal power of their mating.

She watched a flush rise across his flesh. The sight of his desire burning in his eyes and the strength of him within her fed her own hunger yet again. Insatiable, Gabrielle strained against Yves, kissing him demandingly, clutching at his hair, sending their passion escalating madly.

Suddenly Yves clenched her tightly.

Then he tipped back his head and bellowed her name. The heat of his seed raged within Gabrielle even as her own release flooded her veins with new vigor. They strained together, arching for the sky, then clung together as they plummeted from the heights they had won.

"Gabrielle," Yves whispered against her temple, his voice ragged.

Gabrielle closed her eyes and leaned against him, certain she could sleep for a week. "Never before," she managed to whisper, and she felt Yves smile against her hair.

"But soon again," he assured her. Gabrielle looked to him in wonder, liking the crooked grin that curved his lips. He arched a fair brow. "Next time though, it will be in the bed, my lady."

Gabrielle wanted to laugh, but instead she forced a sigh of mock contrition. "I *suppose* I could let you into my bed," she said, as though the concession was a trying one. She looped her arms around his neck and pursed her lips. "Perhaps once a month or so."

"Thrice a day, if not more often," Yves corrected, but Gabrielle laughed.

"We shall never get anything done!"

His golden gaze turned smoky with intent. "Tell me something more worth doing."

Gabrielle tapped her chin as though she had to consider the matter seriously. "Well, there is always some mending to be done," she mused, whooping in surprise when Yves swept her over his shoulder and made for the bed.

"Teasing wench!" he charged in a playful growl. He crossed the room with long strides and tossed her onto the feather pallet, following suit before she even bounced twice.

His hands were on her, tickling mercilessly so that she

laughed aloud. Gabrielle dove beneath the coverlet, still laughing, and loved how close he was behind her.

"I shall make you forget any mending!" Yves' arm locked around her waist and he hauled her against his strength.

"Will you, now?" Gabrielle looked over her shoulder to find a purposeful gleam in her husband's eyes.

Husband. Gabrielle's lips quirked at the thought.

"Give me but a few moments and then I shall show you what this bed is for," Yves teased threateningly.

Gabrielle snuggled against him in anticipation. Indeed, she could hardly wait.

Yves awakened to find the lamp extinguished and the darkness in the solar nearly complete. He stretched, smiling to find Gabrielle's softness nestled so tightly against his side. She still slumbered, her ebony lashes fanned against her cheeks. Yves ran an admiring finger along the gentle sweep of her jaw, marveling at the magic they had made together.

And would make again. He bent to tempt her awake with a kiss, just as a knock sounded upon the door.

The lady's eyes flew open in alarm. Yves did not move away and her gaze leaped to meet his.

And she flushed even as she smiled shyly up at him. Yves smiled back, then called out, not troubling to hide his impatience. "Who is it? I thought we would not be troubled!"

Gabrielle giggled and gave him a hearty poke in the ribs. "You will fuel the gossip in the hall!"

"It already runs rampant, no doubt," Yves murmured. He gave her shoulders a minute squeeze. "Do you care?"

Gabrielle shook her head, her eyes shining. "No. Do you?"

Yves grinned. "Not a whit."

"My lord, I am most sorry to disturb you," Franz declared from the corridor outside. "But a guest has arrived in the hall."

Yves looked to Gabrielle anew. "Do you expect someone?"

She shook her head and propped herself up on her elbows. Her breasts were laid delightfully bare by the move and Yves could not resist bending to kiss one pert nipple.

Though she did not pull away, Gabrielle's voice was uneven when she called out, "Who is it?"

"Lady Adelys de Mornay, my lady. Shall we expect you at the board?"

"Adelys?" Yves hissed, and lifted his head, not in the least pleased by the prospect of abandoning a merry evening for the sake of that woman's company. Gabrielle stiffened, and he feared suddenly they were confidantes. "Is she a friend of yours?"

Gabrielle shook her head. "She came often in the past, to hunt." She shrugged. "Perhaps that is why she comes again."

To Yves' dismay, the lady swung her legs out of the bed. "We shall come to the board," she informed Franz, much to her husband's disappointment.

Something of his thoughts must have shown, for Gabrielle shook a finger at him. "Shame on you! She is our guest and we must show her proper hospitality."

Yves grimaced and propped himself up on his elbows in turn. "I would rather stay here and let her find her own hospitality."

Gabrielle chuckled. "I thought you were the one so intent on always following proper rules of conduct. I shall have to tell Gaston of this lapse!"

"And I shall tell Gaston that there are times when rules of conduct well deserve to be broken," Yves replied. Gabrielle shook her head and turned her back upon him to reach for her chemise. The sight of her bare buttocks, so smooth and strong, was more than a man should be forced to endure.

Yves did not let the opportunity pass. He lunged across the bed and snatched up his wife, falling back upon the pallet even as she squealed with delight. Gabrielle did not laugh long before he kissed her soundly.

"You have but one thing upon your mind," she scolded, her eyes dancing at the thought of that very same thing.

"It is true," Yves conceded with a sigh. "As you say, I cannot think beyond keeping any pledge granted, especially to a lady fair."

"What pledge?"

"To show you the merit of a bed such as this," he retorted, permitting himself a wicked grin.

Gabrielle laughed and swatted his shoulder. "Incorrigible!" she charged. "There will be enough time for that later."

Yves caught her chin and she stilled as she stared up at him. "Yes," he purred. "Especially if we waste no time in sleeping this night." Gabrielle caught her breath but did not seem inclined to argue, her hand locking around Yves' neck as he bent to kiss her deeply.

Yves heartily hoped that Adelys de Mornay showed the good judgment to eat quickly and retire early.

Adelys wore an elegant sweep of embroidered sapphire wool that immediately made Gabrielle feel large and plain. The euphoric bubble that Yves' touch had awakened within her popped with an almost audible burst as the tiny, perfect blonde turned to smile at her approaching host and hostess.

How could Yves be immune to such beauty? How could he not look at the two of them and see the dearth on Gabrielle's end of the scale?

"Gabrielle!" Adelys cried with a delight that seemed undeserved. Her voice dropped with an appreciation Gabrielle knew she did not imagine as she offered her hand to Yves. "And Yves. How well you look!"

"As do you," Yves returned smoothly, his expression impassive. Oh, here was a time Gabrielle would have loved to read his thoughts!

Adelys preened as Yves politely kissed the back of her

hand, her bright gaze fairly devouring the sight of him. Sadly, Gabrielle needed no aid to read that woman's thoughts.

To his credit, Yves seemed to also be aware of Adelys' expression, though when he straightened, he looked directly at Gabrielle. The weight of his hand on the back of her waist was a possessive sign she more than welcomed.

"I shall check with the cook about the meal," he said. He winked at Gabrielle with such speed that she nearly missed it, though she could not mistake the firm stroke his thumb made across her back before he turned away.

Intuitively she understood his meaning. Gabrielle's fears to the contrary, her husband was disinterested in their guest's charms.

And he was interested in her own. Gabrielle glowed with pleasure at that, looking again toward Adelys as Yves turned away. That woman's lips were drawn in a harsh line, her gaze fixed upon Yves as he walked to the kitchen.

Then she forced a smile for Gabrielle and beckoned her to a quiet corner. "How thoughtful of Yves to grant us a chance to chat!" she exclaimed. She arched a fair brow. "You know, I never expected you to take my advice after our last discussion."

Gabrielle's mind whirled in recollection and she heard again Adelys' accusations. Gabrielle bristled anew at the woman's poor view of her character, but did not think it wise to disclose to such a gossipmonger the truth of what had been between herself and Yves.

Gabrielle managed to smile politely, hating that practicality demand she support a lie. "Yves is most persuasive, as you said."

Adelys chortled. "Oh yes, he can be that." Her lips curved in a knowing smile, her gaze trailing to the kitchen portal yet again. "You know, he is truly a catch. I must congratulate your taste once more."

Gabrielle fought to hide the way the woman's words made

her ire rise. "We seem well suited," she satisfied herself with saying.

Adelys laughed throatily at that. "Yes, you with a rich holding and he with a handsome visage! I cannot blame you for welcoming him between your thighs, Gabrielle, but you should never have taken the drastic step of wedding again."

"I like our situation well," Gabrielle said stiffly, painfully aware that as hostess she should not insult her guest.

"And so will he!" Adelys leaned closer and tapped a finger on Gabrielle's shoulder. "As do I, I must confess. As soon as I heard the news, I simply had to come and resurrect our old arrangement."

Gabrielle frowned, unable to see what one had to do with the other. "You came to hunt?"

Adelys smiled. "Yes, but in the hall of Perricault instead of the forest." She pursed her lips as though considering the matter. "Unless, of course, the weather is most fair."

In the hall? Gabrielle glanced up, only to find Adelys watching her closely, a curious knowledge in her gaze.

"Oh, Gabrielle, do not be coy! We have shared a man before, have we not? And that was without objection."

"I do not know what you mean," Gabrielle protested.

"I mean *Michel,* bless his heart, had the enthusiasm but not the technique in bed, if you will forgive me for speaking so boldly." Adelys nodded to the kitchen door once more. "Whereas Yves, well, I absolutely shiver at the thought of his touch."

"Michel?" Surely Adelys did not mean that she had...that she and Michel had...what Gabrielle thought she meant?

"Do not look so surprised, Gabrielle!" Adelys reached over and patted her hand. The gesture was obviously meant to be consoling, but the blond woman's hand was like ice. "You *must* have known."

Gabrielle could only stare at her guest.

Adelys chortled to herself. "I mean, Michel was so lusty, it was no wonder you needed relief. No one woman alone could have satisfied him." Adelys sighed in recollection as Gabrielle gaped. "Such a man he was." She sighed again. "I have missed Michel."

Then she met Gabrielle's stunned gaze and laughed anew. "Oh, Gabrielle, you play the wounded wife too well! Surely you saw us, at least once. Michel was far from discreet, after all. Why, the man had me in the gardens once while you sat on the bench and embroidered, not two dozen feet away. You must have known!"

Gabrielle looked down at her entwined hands and noted that they gripped each other so tightly that the knuckles were white. She recalled the day in the garden very well, though it was seven years past, on Adelys' first visit to Perricault.

Gabrielle could almost taste how ill she had been that morning, how grateful she had been for Michel's consideration. He had aided her to her favorite seat in the garden that she might enjoy the sunshine. He had been so thoughtful.

Surely Adelys was lying? Certainly, there had never been love between herself and Michel, but there had been honesty between them.

Or so Gabrielle had thought.

"In the garden?" Gabrielle echoed woodenly, unable to imagine that such an indiscretion would be carried out so boldly.

"Of course! He brought you to sit in the garden and whispered to me how he loved the threat of discovery." Adelys chortled behind her hand. "Oh, he was quite the enthusiastic mate that day, you can well believe. Quite outdid himself, in fact."

Gabrielle recalled the pair appearing with surprising suddenness, complete with giddy smiles and leaves clinging to Adelys' gown. At the time, Gabrielle had innocently swallowed some explanation of a fall on a loose stone, but now it all made a horrible kind of sense.

Gabrielle swallowed, but could not evade the truth.

Adelys had slept with Michel. Then Michel had returned

to Gabrielle's bed with nary a word of confession or a twinge of guilt.

And this had happened over and over again.

The revelation made Gabrielle's skin crawl with revulsion. How could Michel have dishonored her and the sanctity of their vows that way? How could Adelys have accepted Gabrielle's hospitality while committing adultery beneath Perricault's own roof?

Gabrielle had been a fool not to see the truth. A trusting, innocent fool.

Was she a fool again? It was all too easy to recall the way Yves kissed Adelys' hand with such grace, how Adelys seemed to *know* what kind of lover he was....

Gabrielle thought she would be ill on the spot.

Adelys leaned closer when Gabrielle said nothing, and her eyes glittered. "You *must* have known, but you did Michel one better by never acknowledging what you knew. Oh, he was so disappointed!"

Gabrielle forcibly swallowed the lump in her throat, well aware of Adelys' bright gaze upon her. "Of course," she lied, her voice tight in her throat. "It was as you say."

Adelys studied her for a long moment, then closed both icy hands over Gabrielle's own. "And now we shall repeat our delightful habit once more," she whispered. She nudged Gabrielle playfully and chuckled deep in her throat with delight. "I cannot tell you how pleased I am by your choice of spouse. My visits to Perricault promise to be long indeed!"

Adelys' head snapped up, her attention diverted too quickly for her to note Gabrielle's expression. When the other woman smiled with every vestige of her charm, Gabrielle knew who returned to the hall.

She looked up to find Yves crossing the room with purpose in his step. What chance had she of winning his heart, let alone in competition with Adelys' wiles? Her gut writhed as her father's condemnation echoed in her ears once more, and Gabrielle could not have remained in that hall to save her life.

She fled, avoiding Yves' puzzled gaze. Tears blurred Gabrielle's vision and she stumbled on the flagstones, but hurried onward, Adelys' cruel laughter ringing in her ears.

Chapter Seventeen

Something was wrong with Gabrielle. Yves watched her run, then turned on the woman he was certain was responsible. "What did you say to her?"

The woman smiled coyly and patted the bench that Gabrielle had abandoned. "Come and sit with me," she cooed, "and I shall tell you all you desire to hear."

Yves did not care for the woman's manner, nor for the way she had laughed while Gabrielle left. His wife was upset, there was no denying that, and Adelys was responsible. Oh, Yves had seen this one stir the pot for her own entertainment time and again at the count's court.

She would tell him nothing that even resembled the truth.

"The meal will be served shortly," he said tersely. "If we have not returned, please do not wait for us."

With that, Yves pivoted and went in search of Gabrielle.

"But you cannot leave me!" Adelys cried. "I am a guest."

Yves fired a glance over his shoulder. "An uninvited guest, and by your behavior already in this hall, an unwelcome one," he corrected sternly. "Enjoy your repast."

Adelys sputtered in indignation, but Yves had no time for her. Gabrielle was distressed and he could only hope that he could mend whatever damage had been done.

He found her in the gardens of the upper bailey, a shadow

against the shadows, her face buried in her hands. Yves stepped onto the pathway, knowing she must hear his step, but she did not acknowledge his presence.

"Gabrielle? What did Adelys say to you?"

"Nothing of import," she retorted, and Yves ached at the ravaged sound of her voice. She was weeping, and he knew that only something of tremendous import would draw tears from this lady. "It is none of your concern."

"It *is* my concern," Yves corrected gently and continued into the garden. These gardens were extensive, the herbs and flowers surrounded by an orchard of goodly size. The leaves were in the fullness of the summer now, a gentle evening breeze lifting Yves' hair as he progressed.

Gabrielle said nothing, but he thought he heard her swallow a sob.

"It is my concern if you weep, because you are my wife."

"Do not toy with me!" Gabrielle burst out. "Do not play your games—I know you would rather be with Adelys, so go! Go back to the hall and be with her!"

Yves folded his arms across his chest and surveyed his wife, not liking how little sense she made. She must be very upset to have abandoned her clear thinking.

"What did Adelys tell you? She is a troublemaker and a gossipmonger."

"She is a beauty!" Gabrielle retorted.

Yves snorted at that. "She is not!"

Gabrielle looked up at him, her pale features drawn in an expression so forlorn that he dared to step closer. "She is the most beautiful woman I have ever seen," Gabrielle said quietly, but Yves shook his head.

"She may have been born with pleasing features, but the blackness of her heart steals away any merit they might bring to her."

He was close enough now to see Gabrielle nibble her lip.

Then she tossed her hair and stepped away. "You do not need to lie to me any longer," Gabrielle declared proudly.

"You have wedded me to win Perricault and bedded me to plant your seed and surely there is nothing else that you can want from me now."

"I never wanted Perricault or any other estate," Yves said evenly. "And I never wanted to bed you solely to plant my seed. There is only one thing that I want from you and it is what I have wanted all along."

"What?"

Yves stretched out a fingertip and touched the lady's chest. Her heart pounded beneath his hand. "I want your trust," he said simply.

She stared at him, and as Yves watched, the tears gathered anew in her lovely violet eyes. "Trust is just another lie," she whispered.

Yves felt his lips set in a grim line. "What did Adelys say to you?"

Gabrielle's mouth worked as though she could not bear to give voice to what troubled her, then she blurted out the words. "She slept with Michel!"

And the tears broke loose in a ragged torrent.

Yves winced and clutched Gabrielle before she could flee. She did not fight him, only stiffened, then suddenly crumpled against his chest and wept like a child.

The man Gabrielle adored had been unfaithful.

And with the likes of Adelys. Yves could not blame Gabrielle for being so distraught. A cold anger erupted deep within him.

"Before you were wed?" Yves asked carefully, hoping the offense would be so minor, but suspecting not.

"No!"

"Perhaps Adelys lies," he suggested. "She has been known to tell tales merely for her own amusement."

"No!" Gabrielle retorted. "This is *true*—she told me of one day and I remember." She pointed a quivering finger to a stone bench to Yves' left. "I sat *there*, at Michel's dictate, for I was pregnant with Thomas and ill beyond all. He told me that the sunlight would improve my spirits, and I..." Her voice faltered. "I believed him." She swallowed, then pointed to the orchard. "But he wanted to bed her there, right beneath my nose."

What a tragic waste that Gabrielle had given her heart to such a man. Yves frowned and fought against his own impulse to respond angrily. He must remain calm, for that alone would aid Gabrielle. "Perhaps it was just the once...."

"No! She came here twice a year for weeks at a time, and he went between the two of us." Gabrielle took a deep, shuddering breath. "It makes me want to retch."

Yves could well understand that sentiment. He held his wife closer as her tears slowed, and was reassured when she did not pull away.

She inhaled raggedly and wiped futilely at her tears. "I am sorry." Her voice was soft and sad, as that of someone who had lost something precious. "Perhaps we reserve the full weight of our disappointment for those who shatter our dreams."

Yves closed his eyes against the import of her words. She still loved the treacherous wretch! Disappointment flooded through him, but he could not abandon the field so readily.

"Michel is dead, Gabrielle," Yves said quietly, feeling that it was more than time this point was made. "This betrayal is over and done, however newly discovered it is by you."

"You do not understand!" Gabrielle declared. She turned to face him, and Yves ached at the trail of tears marring her cheeks. "I *trusted* him," she said angrily. "There was honesty between us, or so I had always thought."

"There are many men not worthy of trust."

"*All* men are unworthy of trust! All men see to their own advantage alone. My mother warned me as much, for she had seen the truth. Indeed, she begged me not to repeat her mistake, but Michel persuaded me that he was different." Gabrielle folded her arms across her chest and stared at the garden. "And I was fool enough to think that he was different because he was not a handsome man."

Yves frowned, unable to follow the path of her logic. "I do not understand what difference that makes."

Gabrielle took a deep breath but did not look up. "My sire was beyond handsome, selfish and vain to match," she said tonelessly. "My dame worshipped the very ground he trod, but he made no bones of the fact that he had wed her for the richness of her estate alone. She always swore she loved him enough for both of them."

Gabrielle paused for a moment, but Yves did not rush her. "She was wrong. I remember that when she lay dying, he did not have the time to come and see her." Gabrielle flicked a telling glance toward Yves. "You see, he was being fitted for a tabard that showed his good looks to great advantage. The precise height of the hem was of greater import to him than my mother's life."

There was nothing Yves could say to that.

Gabrielle halted once more and swallowed awkwardly. "She realized on her very deathbed that he truly cared naught for her. It was a cruel blow and perhaps the one that stole the last breath from within her. Her heart was broken and she lost all will to live. Before she died, she begged me not to grant my heart to a man, especially one fair of face. She warned me of men, warned me not to be fooled that they could ever put anyone before themselves."

Gabrielle paused again, her lips tight.

"It was a lesson you took to heart," Yves suggested, and earned a sharp glance for his observation.

"Oh, my father gave me no chance to miss that lesson," she said bitterly. "It seemed that my mother's estate reverted to her own family on her demise and did not fall to my sire, much to his disappointment. There was no longer any holding to fund his wardrobe and his servants and his taste for every bit of frippery he fancied. He informed me that he had made arrangements for my wedding, the dowry being paid to him in gold coin.''

She cleared her throat. ''On the day of my nuptials, when he was paid, he berated me for not being more beautiful, for then he could have sold my hand for more.''

Yves felt his fists clench that Gabrielle had endured such insult from her own sire. It was incredible to him that she had gone through with those nuptials, let alone that she had come so willingly to the altar a second time.

But then, she had done so out of her love for Thomas, which Yves had already seen could not demand too much of Gabrielle.

This was a lady who had been poorly served for far too long.

''Where is your sire?'' Yves demanded, hearing the thread of anger in his own voice.

''Dead,'' Gabrielle said, so crisply that Yves knew she cherished no tenderness toward her sire. ''He cheated a tailor, who hunted him down and choked him with his own tabard. I like to think it was the one he had hemmed the day my dame died.''

She plucked at her surcoat with absent fingers and her veil fell over her face, hiding her thoughts from Yves' view.

''We have something in common in that,'' Yves said in a low voice. Gabrielle's gaze flew to meet his own and he smiled ever so slightly. ''Our fathers are undoubtedly both warming themselves in hell.''

Something flashed in her eyes, but Gabrielle turned quickly away once more. ''It is hardly an accomplishment to feed one's pride.''

''No, it is not that,'' Yves conceded, disappointed that he had not been able to make her smile. ''Tell me of Michel. Why did you trust him?''

Gabrielle sighed and frowned. ''Michel was not handsome, you see, and I thought that perhaps he had no cause to be vain or to see his cause won at the expense of others. He had his own estate, for Tulley had just invested him with Perricault. There was nothing I could give him that he did not have, save perhaps a son."

"You did that."

"Yes, though apparently that was not enough." Gabrielle frowned, then plunged on past the topic of Adelys' revelation. "I came to trust him. I thought we had a match based on honesty and good sense."

And love. Gabrielle had come to love the man who had so cruelly cast her affections aside, choosing instead the empty pleasures that one like Adelys would grant him.

It was far, far less than Gabrielle deserved.

"But it was all a lie," she said savagely. "My mother was right and I should never have ignored her advice."

Yves saw suddenly that this horrible pattern could be drawn to him. Did Gabrielle fear she had ignored her mother's words again? If Gabrielle tarred him with the same brush, he would never truly win her trust.

And that had no part in the future he envisioned for them both.

"No!" Yves gripped Gabrielle's shoulders, bending to snare her gaze when she did not look immediately to him. "Your mother was right about your sire, she may even have been right about Michel, but her words do not apply to all men."

"They must!" Gabrielle insisted.

"Why? Do you fear that I am no better than your sire?"

Gabrielle looked from side to side as though to somehow escape Yves' question.

"Do you?"

"I do not know."

Yves felt a surge of anger at that. She had no cause to doubt him, and he would prove it to her! Was Gabrielle not a woman of good sense? "Do you find me vain?" he demanded. "Do I fritter away the funds of Perricault on garb and useless frippery?"

"No. You have spent nothing to my recollection."

"Have ever I deceived you in any way?"

"No."

"Have ever I treated you with less than honor?"

Gabrielle shook her head miserably.

"Or broken my word to you?"

"But it is not the same," she argued, and Yves could not help but give her a shake.

"It is precisely the same!" he insisted, his temper wearing thin that she was so determined to align him with such sorry company. "Gabrielle, use the wits you are graced with! Is it more fair to judge a man by the deeds of others or by his own deeds?"

She slanted him a mutinous glance. "His own."

"And mine?"

Gabrielle sighed, clearly unable to avoid the concession. "Above contempt," she admitted. "At least thus far."

"Thus far! Thus far!" Yves stalked away from her in frustration, shoved a hand through his hair, then strode back to her side. "Am I never to win your trust? Must we spend the remainder of our days with you reserving judgment on my character?"

"Only until you have nothing else to gain!"

"And what have I to gain from you now?"

Gabrielle lifted her chin. "My indifference to your dalliance with Adelys."

"Adelys," Yves hissed, and felt his lips thin. "Let me review. I have wed you for Perricault alone, I have bedded you only to beget a son of my own blood and I am solicitous to you now only so that I may warm the bed of that bitch Adelys with a clear conscience." He snorted in disdain, certain a woman had never infuriated him more. "What a relief it is that you do not hold my illegitimacy against me!"

Gabrielle folded her arms about herself. "You make it sound so unreasonable."

"It *is* unreasonable!" Yves fairly bellowed. "I have done

nothing to earn your sorry opinion of my character!" He flung out his hands in frustration. "Surely it is not too much for a man to be judged by his own words and deeds alone!"

Gabrielle wiped away her tears and regarded Yves solemnly. To his dismay, he could not fathom a guess at her thoughts. "I have never seen you so angry before," she observed quietly.

"Oh, my lady, you have only to persist in such unreasonable obstinacy to see yet more," Yves retorted. "Never has anyone thought so little of me in all my days, with the possible exception of my own sire."

Gabrielle winced. "That is not company I would like to keep."

"Then you can appreciate that I do not appreciate being cast in the company of your sire and your faithless spouse!"

She looked toward her toes for a long moment, then glanced at Yves once more. He thought he saw a hopeful light in her eyes and dared to try to convince her to believe in him.

"Gabrielle," Yves said in a low voice, his gaze unswerving from her own. "I told you at the count's court that I had no desire for property. It was by your invitation alone that I came to your bed this evening. If perchance you conceive a child, I shall be as delighted with its arrival as I am with Thomas, whether that child be born son or daughter. And if you do not conceive, it matters little, for you have already given to me a son in Thomas."

A tear welled in his lady's eye, but Yves plunged on. "Yet if you imagine that I have any desire for that malicious creature sitting in the hall—" he jabbed a finger in that direction "—then you have much to learn of the manner of man that I am."

The lady said nothing, though the avidity with which she watched Yves emboldened him to continue.

"Gabrielle, there is but one woman in all of Christendom who fires my blood," he said firmly. "She is a beauty from the depths of her heart to the tips of her fingers, for the strength of her character shines in her eyes and makes her more lovely with every passing day. I never met the like of her..." Yves' voice dropped huskily "...and unless she insists otherwise, I would like to spend the remainder of my days and nights on this earth winning her trust."

Gabrielle's eyes shone beneath his praise and she stepped a little bit closer to him. "Who is she?" she whispered, though Yves knew she had already guessed. The fact that she did not turn away, let alone that she drew even closer, encouraged him as nothing else could have.

"I am going to kiss her this very moment," Yves murmured. "And then you will know the truth without a doubt."

Yves did precisely as he intended, relief sweeping through him when Gabrielle's arms wound around his neck. He kissed her soundly before he pulled away.

He stared down at her swollen lips and shining eyes as his pulse thundered in his ears. His loins tightened in recollection of the afternoon and he caught his breath at the promise of the night they would share.

But there were two things yet to be resolved before they returned to the solar.

"What would you have done with this place?" Yves asked gently.

"The garden?" Gabrielle bit her lip and looked over her shoulder. "I must confess that at first I wanted to destroy it all," she confessed with a wry smile. "I had the idea that I would tear every root from the ground with my own hands." She shrugged and looked back to Yves. "That does seem a waste beyond reason."

"This was a place you enjoyed, though?"

"Oh, yes. I always found it peaceful here."

Yves nodded, his mind made up. "Then we must make it a place of repose for you once more." He glanced about them, Gabrielle's hands firmly clasped within his own, then met her gaze steadily. "If nothing else, that bench should go."

"Go?"

"Franz and I could cast it over the walls, if you so desired."

Her eyes widened. "It would shatter on the rocks in the river!"

"Precisely."

Gabrielle chortled, her fingers rising to cover her mouth as though she feared she should not laugh at the idea. "It would be madness," she whispered, her eyes glowing.

"Would it make you feel better?"

"Oh, most definitely! The thought alone improves my spirits."

"Then it shall be done first thing in the morning," Yves decided.

Gabrielle looked at the bench, at the far wall, then back to Yves. Her expression was filled with wonder, as though she marveled that someone would do something so simple for her pleasure alone.

The lady had been ill used, indeed.

"Now, off to bed with you," Yves chided gently. "Adelys does not deserve more of your graciousness."

"But what of you?"

"I have one task to do, then I shall join you." Yves kissed his bride firmly. "I shall tell you of it only when it is done."

Gabrielle smiled tentatively. "Another surprise?"

Yves nodded, then shooed her toward the portal.

In time, she would trust him fully, he knew. Had she not confessed a tale so close to her heart? And he would never betray her. Yves would never have guessed she had endured such villainy, but the tale only increased his admiration.

"Now go," he urged, and Gabrielle did precisely thus.

She pivoted in the portal and wagged a finger at him. "You will not destroy that bench without my being present," she warned him.

"I would not dream of it."

Gabrielle grinned then and disappeared into the keep.

Yves waited until Gabrielle's footsteps had faded completely before he returned to the hall below. He schooled his temper as Adelys waved to him with playful fingertips.

"Yves! Yoo-hoo!"

A wave of loathing rose within Yves, but he did not dare give it voice. He stoically took the place opposite Adelys and did not miss her pout, even as he waved aside Franz's offer of a meal.

"I am so glad you came back without Gabrielle," Adelys cooed. "She is a sweet child, but you and I have so much to talk about."

"Indeed? I thought we had but one thing to discuss."

Adelys' eyes glowed and she leaned across the table in anticipation. "Oh, I do like a man who cuts right to the heart of the issue," she purred.

"Then let us not waste time with niceties," Yves said coldly. "You have distressed my lady wife with both your presence and your deeds. As a result, you are no longer welcome at Château Perricault."

Adelys' features froze in shock, but Yves continued on relentlessly.

"You will leave this hall before the dawn, so that Gabrielle is spared another sight of your sorry hide, and you will never darken the threshold of this keep again, for I shall make no bones of turning you away."

"But Yves! Is this any way to treat a guest?"

Yves let his lip curl in a sneer. "One such as you should be turned out into the woods at this very moment and not left within the walls for the night."

"One such as *me*? I could please you better than that plain stick of a wife you have taken!"

Yves smiled at the ridiculousness of the thought. "I think not."

Adelys inhaled sharply. "You would deny me?"

"As always I have."

Adelys' eyes narrowed as she pushed herself to her feet, and the vindictiveness of her nature showed with sudden clarity. "I shall make your life a living hell," she declared. "I shall tell everyone that I was abused here, that the bastard of Sayerne does not know how to conduct himself as a nobleman. I shall spread whatever lies about your wife that I can imagine."

Yves stood in turn. "If you do, I shall recount a tale to the archbishop in the count's court."

"I care nothing for the archbishop!"

"You would if he brought the charge of murder against your name," Yves responded calmly. He savored the way Adelys gasped. "To be an adulteress is one thing, and a crime not easily proved when the man in question is dead, but murder is another matter altogether."

"What are you talking about?" Adelys demanded in a strained voice. "What lies have you been told?"

"Oh, I have no doubt it was not a lie," Yves argued smoothly, though in truth he was not certain. "The man who told me the tale could certainly be found again if the archbishop wished to check the facts."

Adelys' face turned white as though she dreaded what Yves might say. "Tell me!"

"It cannot be news to you, Adelys, that Eduard de Mornay was poisoned." Yves watched the last vestige of color drain from the lady's face and knew the tale he had thought might be rumor was truth. "Or that everyone within the keep of Mornay believed Eduard's wife was responsible for the deed."

Adelys managed to laugh, though the sound was strained. "If that were true, the priest of Mornay would have seen matters put aright!"

"One would think so," Yves conceded, giving Adelys time to smile victoriously before playing his last card. "But then, if the lady had seduced that man of the cloth—as went the tale—then that priest would have had much to lose.''

The brittle green gaze locked with Yves' own, then Adelys' shoulders sagged in concession. ''What do you want?'' she demanded tiredly.

''I have already told you.''

Adelys' lips set in a sullen line, though she did not argue any longer. Yves would have to write the count so that the matter could be pursued, for he was certain the knight who had shared the tale could readily be found once more.

The count would ensure that justice was served.

''Franz!'' Yves called, and that man was immediately by his side. ''Regretfully, Lady Adelys must leave before the dawn on the morrow. Could you ask Xavier to have everything prepared for her party's early departure?''

''Of course, my lord.'' Franz bowed and was gone.

''You will, of course, forgive my lady Gabrielle and I if we do not see you off in the morning?'' Yves said politely.

Adelys visibly ground her teeth. ''Of course,'' she said tightly, then her eyes flashed as she made one last effort. ''But, Yves, would you not consider one little liaison before I go?'' she asked with a smile evidently intended to be winning. ''I shall make the dalliance worth your while.''

Yves bowed politely. ''My lady wife awaits me,'' he said firmly, then turned to leave the hall.

Gabrielle huddled beneath the coverlets, straining for the sound of Yves' return. Now that the truth was clear between them, she knew she had nothing to fear. His frustration in the garden had shown her what she should have seen all along. By her mother's own rule, there was no advantage to Yves in courting Gabrielle's favor. There was nothing else she had that Yves might desire.

Except her heart.

And it seemed the man had some interest in capturing Gabrielle's heart for his own.

That was a promise for the future that she could not deny. As she lay in bed awaiting his return, she dared to imagine a glorious marriage filled with love and affection. She caught her breath when she recalled the fire in Yves' eyes when he had called her beautiful.

On this night, she would show him the full extent of her love. She had nothing to risk and so very much to gain.

But what kept the man? What was this surprise he sought? Gabrielle was fairly bursting with curiosity by the time Yves' footsteps echoed in the corridor.

Their gazes met across the solar when he closed the door behind him, and Gabrielle felt more delightfully feminine beneath his regard than she had in all her days.

She watched as her spouse shed his clothes, unable to quell her response to the splendid sight of his nudity. Her fingertips itched to trail across his skin; her very flesh seemed alive with the promise of a repeat of this afternoon. Yves carried the lantern to the bedside, then climbed in beside Gabrielle as though they had slept thus for years, his smug smile feeding her curiosity.

Where *had* he gone?

"Curious?" he asked with mock innocence, and Gabrielle laughed that he understood her so readily.

"Of course! Where did you go? And why did it take you so long?"

Yves lay back against the pillows, sighed with satisfaction, then surveyed her lazily. "This is quite a comfortable bed," he mused. "Much better than the pallet I used to sleep upon."

"Tell me or I shall cast you back to it!" Gabrielle teased.

Yves laughed, the low rumble of his voice warming her to her toes. He gathered her against his side with an intoxicating possessiveness and pressed a kiss to her temple. Gabrielle's heart swelled as if it would burst and she hated that she had doubted him for as long as she had.

"You have nothing to fear, wife of mine," Yves murmured. "I merely ensured that Adelys saw the good sense of leaving Perricault before the dawn."

Gabrielle pulled back and looked Yves in the eye. "You did what?"

"I cast her out and bade her never to return here," Yves said, so solemnly that Gabrielle knew he spoke the truth.

"But she was our guest!"

"She lost those privileges when she insulted the lady of the estate," Yves said grimly. "She will not be back."

Gabrielle could not imagine how Yves had convinced Adelys thus, but his manner dismissed any possible doubt. A glow took up residence in her heart and she nestled against him again, amazed that he had done such a thing because she was upset.

No one had ever shown Gabrielle such consideration before. Indeed, the man went to great lengths to see anything that troubled her cast out of her life. She could well become accustomed to this man's ability to dismiss her every concern.

"Would you still ride to Sayerne on the morrow?" Yves asked now, giving her shoulder a minute squeeze. "Thomas is most anxious to choose his pups, but if you think you will be too tired, we could leave the matter for a few days."

"Tired? Why should I be tired? The hour is not late." Gabrielle looked toward Yves in confusion, only to find a devilish twinkle lurking in his eyes.

"I did give you my word about this bed," he said solemnly.

Gabrielle laughed and tapped a fingertip on his bare chest. "But will *you* not be too tired to ride to Sayerne on the morrow?"

Yves made a show of considering the matter, then shook his head. "No, I do not think so." He rolled over quickly, trapping Gabrielle beneath him, and cupped her chin in his hands. "You see," he murmured, his words fanning her lips "there are certain activities that tend to invigorate rather than fatigue." His eyes blazed into hers and Gabrielle had no doubt of what kind of activities he meant.

"Indeed?" She stretched up and provocatively traced the outline of his lips with the tip of her tongue. She liked how Yves caught his breath, and felt powerful in her femininity for the first time. "I should like to learn of such deeds," she murmured against his flesh.

"Oh, that you will, my lady," Yves growled with purpose, and grinned wickedly as he loomed over her. "That you will."

And when he bent to claim her lips in a bone-melting kiss, Gabrielle could not wait to learn more.

Chapter Eighteen

Two glorious days later, Gabrielle watched her son romp with a litter of wolfhound pups in the stables of Sayerne. She was well aware of Yves' gaze lingering warmly upon her and was happier than she had been in all her days.

Remarkably, Methuselah had not fought the cinch when they left Perricault two days past. Gabrielle had checked the destrier, but found nothing amiss—except for Yves and Thomas chuckling conspiratorially together. Something had happened, that much was clear, but Gabrielle cared little for the details. It was enough for her that Thomas had taken so well to his new papa.

And Thomas was not the only one enraptured by Yves de Sant-Roux. It seemed that all required of Gabrielle was to abandon her fear of Yves to have him charge boldly forward and conquer her heart. And by the bemused smile that seemed fixed to that knight's lips—and the ardor with which they met each night—Gabrielle guessed that his heart was falling prey to her allure.

She would never have expected such love to blossom between them. Perhaps it was sweeter to find something so unexpected, she mused, smiling herself as Thomas plucked one pup from the wiggling group surrounding him. The stall was deep with sweet straw and six rubbery puppies whose tails wagged so ferociously they frequently fell over.

Thomas was having a wonderful time examining each pup in turn and being licked by every one that could manage to reach his face. They were of goodly size, even for pups, and that was only a promise of how big they would become. The dame of the litter lay back in the corner, watching the antics of her brood just as Gabrielle and Yves watched Thomas.

"I like this one, *Maman!*"

Gabrielle looked toward Sayerne's burly ostler, who nodded agreement. "A fine bitch, Thomas," he said. "Now, come and pick a stud from this other litter down the way. There is one of brindle hue, much like the one Chevalier Yves favored as a boy."

Thomas grinned with excitement and struggled to both retain his grip on the wriggling puppy and make his way from the stall. Another pup latched sharp little teeth into his chausses and held on tight, tugging with vigor, the four others making a tangle of soft fur around the boy's knees. Thomas squealed with laughter and lost his balance, disappearing beneath a mound of affectionate pups as Gabrielle bit back her laughter.

Yves waded purposefully into the stall and tucked Thomas' puppy under his arm. The pup wagged her tail with vigor and squirmed against Yves, straining to lick his face as well. Meanwhile, the knight lifted Thomas by the scruff of his tabard and shook the determined puppy's teeth free of Thomas' chausses.

"I like him, too!" Thomas declared, but the knight shook his head.

"Go and see what you think of the brindle one."

As he spoke, Thomas leaned over to scratch the chosen pup's ears. She wriggled and lunged forward to lick his face. The boy squealed with delight, the pup wagged even harder in her excitement and the other pups jumped on Yves.

Yves visibly gritted his teeth and waded through wriggling

puppies to the corridor. Gabrielle fought against her laughter, knowing it would not be appreciated. Thomas fled after the ostler as soon as he was set on his feet, but Yves' eyes suddenly widened in surprise.

Before Gabrielle could ask why, she saw the wet stain spreading from the pup and knew she could not stop her laughter this time.

"It is not funny!" Yves declared. When he lifted the pup from his side and eyed the wet mark on his tabard, his indignant expression sent Gabrielle into greater gales of laughter. Never would she have imagined to see this knight in such a circumstance!

Yves' lips twitched, though he obviously fought to keep his expression stern. Before he could comment, someone cleared his throat.

Both Gabrielle and Yves pivoted toward the portal admitting the sunlight from Sayerne's bailey. Gabrielle's laughter was silenced by the sight of the familiar silhouette of the Lord de Tulley.

She and Yves exchanged a glance as the old lord harrumphed and peered into the stables. Gabrielle took the puppy from Yves, wondering what the old lord wanted here.

"Chevalier Yves de Sant-Roux?" Tulley demanded. "Is that you I hear?"

"Yes, my lord Tulley." Yves dropped to one knee as Tulley snorted.

The old lord advanced into the shadowed interior of the stables, blinking rapidly at the change in the light. "My lord Tulley, indeed," he echoed waspishly. "What made you imagine you could wed Gabrielle de Perricault without my permission?"

Tulley's gaze sharpened as he spotted Gabrielle. He wagged a finger in her direction, giving Yves no chance to reply. "*You* should have known better."

Gabrielle lifted her chin and endeavored to look dignified despite the puppy wriggling in her arms. "It seemed only fitting to wed the knight who retrieved Perricault and killed Philip de Trevaine."

Tulley's eyes gleamed as he glanced back at Yves. "Did you now?" he mused. "I had wondered." Then Tulley jabbed a finger at Gabrielle once more. "But you had no right to seek out the services of this knight without my permission."

"I had every right to see my son retrieved," Gabrielle retorted. "It was you who had no right to seek a champion for Perricault without *my* permission."

That was not precisely true, but the old lord seemed content to let that charge pass unchallenged. "You should not have wed him without asking me first," he declared. "The decision was mine to make! For your presumptuousness, I shall annul this match this very day!"

Gabrielle gasped, but before she could summon a word to her lips, Yves straightened and looked the old lord in the eye. "The match is consummated," he said with precision. "And should you try to see it annulled, I shall battle your will all the way to Rome."

Gabrielle's heart sang at this endorsement of their nuptials, but Tulley's slow smile made her leery of what that man might say.

"I shall expect your pledge of fealty before I surrender the seal of Perricault."

Yves did not hesitate to respond with characteristic resolve. "And you shall have it."

"Well, then," Tulley said softly. "I truly cannot complain at the outcome of this. Perricault reclaimed, Trevaine dead, a widow wed most satisfactorily and the count's own champion prepared to swear fealty to my hand in order to keep Perricault firmly held for me."

Tulley, to Gabrielle's amazement, produced a parchment scroll from within the folds of his cloak. "So, it is only fitting that I keep the terms of our original discussion. This document will be yours, Yves de Sant-Roux.'' Tulley paused. ''Or should I say, Yves de Sayerne?''

Yves took the document, and Tulley cast Gabrielle a smile that seemed mocking. She was bursting with curiosity, but did not want the old lord to see any sign of it.

Tulley watched her for a long moment, then he swept from the stables, muttering about mulled wine. As soon as the lord turned his back, Yves stuffed the document into his belt and would not meet Gabrielle's eyes.

''What is that?''

Yves' mouth drew into a grim line. ''Nothing.''

''It cannot be nothing if Tulley was so keen to grant it to you.''

''It is nothing of import,'' Yves said firmly. ''Let us find Thomas and see what other pup he has chosen.'' He reached for the pup Gabrielle held, but she lifted the dog before her like a shield.

''No.'' At her protest, Yves' gaze flicked to hers, then he looked away again. ''It cannot be nothing if you are so intent upon hiding its contents from me,'' Gabrielle accused. ''What is it?''

Yves shoved his hand through his hair. ''Gabrielle, it is not a document I ever wanted, so it means nothing to you or to me.''

Gabrielle did not believe him. Surely if Yves told her the truth, he would look her in the eye?

Suddenly she was not quite so certain that Yves had nothing to gain from her. Her heart went cold.

Yves reached for the wolfhound again, and this time, Gabrielle let him grip the wriggling puppy. When both his hands were occupied with holding the dog, Gabrielle snatched the document from his belt and danced away.

''Gabrielle!'' Yves roared. ''I told you that it means nothing!''

But she had unfurled the parchment and read enough to

feed her worst fears. She scanned its contents hastily, then looked to Yves once more.

Now he held her gaze, his own filled with a sadness that could only mean she had been played for a fool by a man yet again.

"This declares you legitimate," she observed as tonelessly as she could manage. "Was this the bait that Tulley offered in exchange for your winning Perricault?"

"Gabrielle, I declined his offer."

"So you said." Gabrielle felt her own lips thin. "Tulley seems to think otherwise."

"Tulley plays to his own rules, as you well know."

"Tulley plays as all men do," Gabrielle retorted savagely. "But I was fool enough to think that you were different."

"Gabrielle, it was not as you think...." Yves began, but she had no patience for whatever lie he might contrive.

"No! No, it was not at all as I thought and therein lies the problem! I *trusted* you! I thought you were different! I thought that you cared for me, or that at least you cared for Thomas!"

Gabrielle turned away so that Yves would not see her rising tears. Curse the man! She had trusted him!

She still loved him!

But she would not be used as a pawn again. "It was all for a wretched piece of parchment!" she said bitterly, then spun to face him anew. "Take it! Take it now! Take this declaration that is so terribly important to you!"

Gabrielle flung the document in Yves' face, taking advantage of the knight's surprise to snatch back Thomas' puppy. She felt her tears well up and buried her nose in the puppy's soft fur.

Yves said nothing. He stared at the document but did not pick it up. It was clear he had no defense to make in his own name. Gabrielle had called the matter right. Her heart ached so much she thought it might split in two, but she knew she should have known better.

All men cared for their own advantage alone. Her mother had told her so, but Gabrielle had been fool enough to ignore the advice.

Gabrielle stalked to the portal, hating how her voice quivered when she turned back to Yves. "There was something you needed from me, after all," she said unevenly. "I simply did not know fully what was at stake."

"Gabrielle, it is not as you say." Yves' voice was low and urgent. "You do not understand."

"No, *you* do not understand," she countered softly. Gabrielle bit her lip and looked at the parchment discarded on the stable floor. "This is the worst betrayal that I could ever imagine."

"It is no betrayal!" Yves argued. "I ask only that you give me the opportunity to explain. I never wanted Tulley's document!" Gabrielle felt the weight of his gaze land upon her but did not dare meet his eyes.

She had always been too vulnerable to this man's appeal.

"Spare me your pretty tales and your charming smiles," she said flatly, and felt suddenly very tired at the prospect of living her life without Yves.

No, it was only an illusion that she would miss. It was infinitely better to know the truth now than it would have been to spend her life believing a lie. That had been her mother's error, after all.

Gabrielle lifted her chin and looked directly at Yves, a part of her errant heart twisting at the sight of his dismay. But it was all for effect, and Gabrielle would not be swayed again.

"I loved you as I have never let myself love a man before," she confessed heavily. "And you could only destroy that, to see your own worldly end achieved."

If Yves looked dumbfounded by this confession, it was no surprise to Gabrielle. So few people saw their selfishness in its true terms.

All the same, she felt ill with what she must do. "I will take Thomas home to Perricault immediately, along with his puppies. You will not accompany us, nor will you return there.''

Yves took a deep breath. ''Will you give me no chance to explain?''

''There is no need to cover a lie with another,'' Gabrielle said sharply.

''A lie?'' Yves crossed his arms across his chest and surveyed her sternly. ''Gabrielle, I have never told you a lie and do not tell you one now!''

''Ha! Our entire acquaintance has been a lie from one end to the other!'' Gabrielle retorted. ''At least you were honest about showing how much it troubled you to be born a bastard! I should have guessed that nothing less than legitimacy could have won such a dedicated response from you!''

''There was no promise of legitimacy!'' Yves retorted. ''I declined Tulley!''

''By your account alone! Tulley seems quite certain that you had an arrangement.'' Gabrielle stalked to the door, glancing back over her shoulder to the obviously irritated knight. ''And Tulley,'' she added softly ''has nothing to gain in this, does he?''

''Gabrielle, you push me too far!'' Yves roared, but she was striding through the bailey of Sayerne. When Yves' hand landed on her shoulder, she froze but did not look back. ''What of the lie *you* tell this day?''

Gabrielle pivoted smartly. ''What lie?''

Yves' lips twisted. ''That you love anyone other than Michel de Perricault,'' he charged softly. ''Your heart might as well be buried with that man, for the relentlessness of his grip upon it.''

Gabrielle gasped, her denial dying upon her lips. Let Yves think she cared for Michel! If he had wounded her this badly thinking that, what would happen if he believed the truth?

Gabrielle's response was low and intent, for she knew that if she lingered she might change her mind. ''Do not come to Perricault. And do not talk to my son again.''

With that, Gabrielle shook off the weight of Yves' hand and returned to the hall of Sayerne. A few quick words to Leon sent that knight in pursuit of Thomas, and she retreated to the sanctuary of the women's chambers. She forced belongings into her saddlebags, not caring what was packed where.

And there, all alone but for an affectionate puppy, Gabrielle wept for what she had lost.

The hour was early when Quinn came to Sayerne the evening after Gabrielle's departure, but Yves was already feeling the effects of the wine. Indeed, Gaston could not refill the pitcher quickly enough.

Quinn dropped to one knee before Tulley, whose visit was partly responsible for Quinn leaving Annossy and the heavily expectant Melissande.

A cloaked person accompanied Quinn—a woman, judging by the slender build, though if so, remarkably tall. Yves could not have summoned the interest to care. He watched his brother survey the hall when Tulley dismissed him. Frowning, Quinn murmured something to his companion, then both came to share the board with Yves.

"Where is Gabrielle?" Quinn asked. The cloaked figure slid silently onto the bench, and Yves could feel a searching gaze from within the shadows of the hood.

But the hood remained drawn, and he had no interest in social games on this night.

"Halfway to Perricault, no doubt." Yves snorted and emptied his chalice once more. He flicked a finger to the pitcher, but Gaston shook his head.

"My lord, I believe you have indulged enough this night."

"You are impertinent," Yves charged, though the last word was less easily formed than usual. Still the boy hesitated, and Yves muttered a curse and reached for the pitcher himself.

He was well aware of the glance Quinn and Gaston exchanged, though neither of them could have guessed the magnitude of the ache within him. This was worse, far worse, than the pain his heart had endured before. The wine splashed on the board, the task seeming more difficult than Yves had recalled.

Quinn sat on the bench opposite, his concerned gaze going from Yves to the wine. "Do you not accompany your lady wife?"

"Not when I have been forbidden to do so."

Quinn frowned. "By who?"

"By none other than the lady herself!" Yves drank deeply of the wine, then reached for the pitcher once more. It was empty yet again, though he was certain Gaston had just filled it.

Yves sensed that the cloaked figure was following every word of their conversation. To his mind, not acknowledging this individual's presence was a fitting compensation for such rude eavesdropping.

Gaston, though, kept looking toward the arrival with open curiosity. He even offered refreshment to that individual, though he was declined with a gesture.

"Fetch another here," Yves bade his squire, treating the boy to a stern glance when he hesitated.

Gaston heaved a sigh, but took the pitcher across the hall.

"Why," Quinn asked carefully, "would Gabrielle forbid you to ride with her?"

"I am apparently not worthy of Gabrielle's company, even though the Lord de Tulley saw fit to bring this little token of his affections to me this day." Yves slapped the parchment responsible for his troubles onto the board, not caring that it landed in the spilled wine.

Quinn plucked the document from the wine and read it, his gaze rising to meet Yves' with new concern. "Legitimacy?"

Yves shrugged indifferently. "Tulley offered it as bait when he wanted me to retrieve Perricault. I refused, but when he heard the deed was done, he graciously granted it to me."

Yves grimaced and lifted his goblet to the lord in question before he took another draft of wine. "Directly before the lady."

"She thinks you took her quest for this prize alone."

Yves shrugged acquiescence. His chalice seemed to have a hole in it, for it was consistently empty. And Gaston was unreasonably tardy about refilling the pitcher.

Quinn's hand landed heavily on his own and Yves was forced to look into his brother's eyes. "Did you not tell her the truth?"

"She would not listen."

"Then go after her!"

Yves took a deep breath and frowned at his chalice. "She forbade me to return to Perricault." Yves felt suddenly as though he had not consumed a single sip of wine. He fingered his empty chalice and found the words thick in his throat.

"Because you are drunk?"

"I am not drunk and have not been drunk in twelve years," Yves retorted angrily.

Quinn looked skeptical. "Twelve years? *Precisely* twelve years?"

"It will be thirteen years on the week before the Yule, if you require precision," Yves clarified firmly.

Quinn arched a brow. "A date to remember?"

"A date I could hardly forget." Yves looked sternly at his brother. "And a date that you should also recall, for it was the day our only sister was killed."

Quinn frowned. "I beg your pardon?"

"It will be thirteen years this Yule that Annelise de Sayerne was killed by wolves in the forests south of Tulley. I fail to see what is difficult to understand about *that*."

"But—"

"But *nothing!* Our only sister died a savage and cruel death because *I* forced her hand." Yves jabbed a finger into his own chest, punctuating his self-recriminations. "*I* demanded she choose between two suitors when she was determined no to wed at all. *I* refused to back down from our argument when Annelise chose the convent, which I knew she hated. *I* led the party that was lost en route and it was I who found her remains ravaged by wolves.''

Yves blinked back unexpected tears and lifted his chalice, pounding it impatiently on the board when he found it empty, and discarding it. Gaston returned, his eyes wide.

''And yes, I was sorely drunk for a good week afterward,'' Yves continued. ''For I knew that Annelise's death was my fault as surely as though I had taken the blade to her myself.''

Yves shoved his hands through his hair, then buried his face in them, well aware of the accusation that must haunt Quinn's eyes. That man's silence said more than Yves could bear.

''She was our only sister,'' Yves confessed quietly, ''and the only one within all the length and breadth of Sayerne besides the ostler who treated me with anything other than disdain. I have never forgiven myself for not ensuring her safety better than I did.''

Yves took a ragged breath. ''The wound of her loss is one that has never healed. I vowed twelve years ago never to cultivate another wound like it, or even to take the chance that anyone else could deal me such a telling blow.''

Yves felt the weight of Quinn's hand on his shoulder. ''But you have?''

Yves nodded, unable to lie to his brother, whatever that man might be feeling for him now. ''But this—this is a thousand times worse.''

''Yves, look at me.'' Quinn's voice was low, but not filled with the condemnation Yves expected.

Reluctantly, he lifted his head and was astonished to find his brother smiling slightly. Before he could protest, Quinn spoke with resolve. ''Annelise is not dead.''

''Of course she is! Quinn, I found the remains myself!'' Yves saw the bloody sight in his mind's eye once more, and the bile rose in his throat, but Quinn shook his shoulders.

"Listen to me!"

Yves shook off his brother's grip, then saw from the corner of his eye that the cloaked figure had lifted a very feminine hand to her hood.

His heart stopped. Yves stared as the hood was drawn back to reveal his sister, Annelise.

Annelise. She was older, but the vivacity he remembered about her burned even brighter in her eyes.

"Annelise!" Yves whispered, the wine forgotten. "I thought... I was certain..."

She laughed. "And I thought *you* had been killed."

They stared at each other, then smiles dawned on their faces. Yves stumbled to his feet, knocking over the bench in the process, and Annelise bounced up to meet him halfway.

"Annelise!" he roared, and swung her in the air with an abandon he had never expected to feel again.

"I came to help Melissande with her birth," she said, her words falling with characteristic haste. Yves closed his eyes and savored the sparkling sound of her voice. "For she has done the same for me twice now. Quinn met me on the road, for Rolfe will not let me ride alone, and he told me that you were at Perricault. Perricault! So close..."

Annelise caught her breath and pulled back to survey Yves. Her hand stretched out to him as though she had to touch his face to know he was real. "He told me, but I never imagined it could be so."

The pair stared at each other for a long time.

"Look at you," Annelise whispered finally. Tears misted her eyes and she bit her lip. "You went and grew up, Yves," she continued unevenly. "You became a knight that I am so proud to call my brother."

Yves blinked a suspicious blur from his own eyes. "You did not die," he said, still marveling at this inalienable fact.

"My husband saved me from the wolves that night," Annelise confided. "My palfry died, though."

Yves cleared his throat. "Well, what of this husband? Is he good to you?"

Quinn chuckled. "You would like him. Rolfe de Viandin is a man of his word."

"Rolfe de Viandin?" Yves looked at Annelise with confusion.

She laughed, the sound as merry as tinkling bells. "Yes, exactly the man you wanted me to marry and I refused." She tapped a finger smartly on the end of Yves' nose. "Now, do not start telling me how perfectly logical the choice would have been or any of that nonsense."

Oh yes, Annelise was alive and much the same.

This was almost too much to be believed. For years, Yves had blamed himself for Annelise's demise, blamed Tulley for summoning Quinn home to Sayerne and forcing them to leave this keep, blamed Quinn for being the very image of their cruel sire.

But Quinn was not cruel and Annelise was not dead. The evidence was smiling up at him with all the impulsive charm he remembered.

Annelise tapped an impatient finger in the middle of Yves' chest. "Now, what is this? You said you cared for another. Is it your Gabrielle?"

His Gabrielle. Yves frowned. "She lied to me."

Annelise leaned closer. "But do you love her?"

"I am not smitten," Yves retorted, and backed away. He folded his arms across his chest. "But it is most frustrating that she will not listen to reason. The lady's good sense is one of many traits I admire."

Quinn folded his arms across his chest in turn, the glint in his eye promising little good to Yves' mind. He winked at Annelise, who smirked. "So, you *admire* the lady?"

Yves slanted a glance at his siblings, not trusting this cajoling tone. "Yes."

"But no more than that?"

Yves fidgeted, not in the least bit comfortable with the

direction of this conversation. "It does not matter what I think."

Quinn wagged a finger at him. "I think it does. And I think what you feel is what is making you drink for the first time in twelve years."

Yves' heart nearly stopped that Quinn could read his thoughts so easily, and he instinctively dreaded what his brother would say next.

But it was Annelise who chimed in with the conclusion. "I think that you are in love with your wife." She nodded. "And I think you should tell her so."

Yves stared at his long-lost sister. As soon as he heard the words, he recognized the truth in them.

He loved Gabrielle. It was so simple and clear.

"It does not matter what I feel for the lady," he argued hastily. "She lied to me and barred me from her home."

Quinn shrugged. "Lies can be set aright."

"Not this one!" Yves wagged a finger at his brother in turn, only now understanding why Gabrielle's lie had burned so deeply. "She and I pledged to have honesty between us in our match, and on this day, she deliberately lied!"

"What did she say?" Annelise demanded.

Yves took a fortifying breath. "She said that she loved me, but that this document dismissed all of that."

His sister shrugged. "And where do you find the lie?"

"She does not love me!" Yves argued. "She never did and never could! Her heart is firmly claimed by Michel de Perricault and always will be!" Yves plucked the pitcher of wine from Gaston's grip, since the boy showed no inclination to refill his chalice, and poured wine with a vengeance.

"She does *not* love Michel de Perricault!" Gaston protested. "She never did!"

Yves gave the boy a skeptical glance. "And what would you know about the state of the lady's affections?"

"Only what she told me," Gaston insisted proudly.

Yves blinked. "*Told* you?"

"She told me, when Philip held us captive, that she had never loved her husband."

"I do not understand," Yves said slowly, not daring to hope.

"She said there was trust between them and that that was more than she had expected from an arranged match," Gaston asserted.

Yves gaped at the boy, his interest in the wine completely gone.

Gabrielle had told him only that she had trusted Michel. Yves had assumed she loved that man as well, but the lady had never said so.

Could Yves have drawn a false conclusion?

Could Gabrielle have told him the truth?

And if Gabrielle had loved him, was there any way that he could win her love anew?

"Go!" Annelise urged, but Yves needed no such encouragement. Already he knew there was but one way to find out the truth. He stumbled to his feet, not caring how his brother grinned, and scowled at Gaston.

"And what is keeping you from your tasks?" Yves demanded of his squire. "We must ride to Perricault with all haste—do you not have Merlin saddled yet?"

Gaston laughed aloud and fairly danced on the spot. "Just like a *chanson!*" he declared with undisguised delight. "We ride in the middle of the night to win the damsel's reluctant heart."

"You are impertinent," Yves chided, though his smile took the bite out of his words. "Hasten yourself, or you will be the one to scale the high gates of Perricault."

Perricault was cold, to Gabrielle's mind, despite the heat of the summer sun. They had been home for but a half a day and already she missed Yves with a vengeance.

Thomas had little to say once he learned that his friend was not returning anytime soon to Perricault. He took his puppies and went in search of Xavier, leaving Gabrielle to her own resources. Everyone within these walls seemed less optimistic than just days past, and Gabrielle escaped the hall's brooding atmosphere by retiring to the garden.

The sun shone brightly on this June afternoon. Butterflies and bees were busy amid the plentiful flowers. The sound of rushing water carried to her ears, and Gabrielle attempted to stroll as though she were at peace.

But she was not. To her surprise, it was not the ghost of Michel's indiscretion here that haunted her, but the vision of Yves and Franz tossing the stone bench over Perricault's high walls. Gabrielle leaned on the wall and looked down into the rushing water of the river far below, imagining that she could pick out one or two shards of the bench.

A hollow ache resonated where her heart should have been. What had she cast aside in her anger?

A footstep sounded on the walkway and Gabrielle spun.

It was only Franz, looking apologetic to be troubling her. "My lady, a knight begs your audience in the hall. Will you come?"

"Who is he?"

Franz glanced away. "I know only that he is pledged to Perricault."

Responsibilities called. Gabrielle swallowed her dissatisfaction. Yves was not here, so the responsibility of administering justice for those pledged to Perricault was hers. She spared one last glance toward the broken bench, wishing she could remain in her own company alone, then forced herself to smile.

"I will come, Franz."

That man bowed and disappeared through the portal, leaving Gabrielle to follow behind. She took her time, not in the least bit interested in adjudicating some transgression or another. En route, Gabrielle noted that none of the servants seemed to be about.

That was odd for this time of the day.

She stepped from the corridor into the hall, only to find the reason why. Everyone who lived within the walls of Perricault was there, and a goodly number of those from the village now being restored.

They stood around the perimeter of the great hall, their expressions somber, the torchlight gleaming on their tanned faces. Thomas stood with Xavier, his gaze fixed upon a cloaked man standing in the middle of the room.

The familiarity of that man's silhouette made the breath catch in Gabrielle's throat.

But she did not turn aside from what she had said she would do. As she stepped into the room, Yves cast back his hood. He was paler than she recalled and uncertainty lingered in his features, though his glorious amber gaze bored into her own.

"My lady Gabrielle," he said, and his voice was uncharacteristically husky. "I ask only that you listen to what I have to say before casting me out of Perricault for all time."

Gabrielle could not find it within herself to deny Yves this one small request. She stared at him, not knowing what to say.

With a flick of his wrist, Yves produced a document that Gabrielle feared was familiar. "When last we were together, my lady, the Lord de Tulley granted me this document from his vast cellar of secrets."

"I remember."

Yves stepped forward and offered her the parchment. "Would you ascertain that it is the very same?" Gabrielle could do nothing but comply.

As they had so many weeks ago, in a tent at the count's tournaments, their fingers brushed in the exchange.

But this time, Yves' hands were cold. Gabrielle's gaze flicked to his and she saw shadows lurking in the depths of his eyes. What had happened? What had wounded him so? She barely spared the parchment a glance, so disturbed was she by his obvious dismay.

Yves must be sorely troubled for his thoughts to be so readily visible, but Gabrielle could not imagine what the reason could be. Had he discovered that Tulley's document was a lie?

"It is the same," she acknowledged.

Yves nodded and plucked the parchment from her fingers once more. He snapped his fingers and Gaston snatched up a torch from a sconce on the wall and carried it to his knight.

"It is the same document, the one that pledges my legitimacy, and the one that sent you fleeing from my side." Yves' glance was compellingly steady, and Gabrielle could not look away. His voice dropped. "I told you that I declined Tulley, that I did not take this quest for the sake of him or this document. On this day, I will prove it to you."

And Yves took the torch from Gaston as Gabrielle watched, touching the flame to the parchment so that it burned with vigor. He held the document until most of it was consumed, then cast it on the stone floor and ground the remainder to ashes beneath his heel.

Gabrielle gasped, then looked to her spouse to find his gaze burning with intent. "Was it genuine?"

"Of course."

"There must be another!"

"There is none," Yves said flatly. "This is the one and only, and it is no more."

As Gabrielle fought to make sense of his deed, Yves dropped to one knee before her. "Gabrielle, I love you as I never imagined I could love another in all my days. I would not have this nonsense of Tulley's drive us apart."

Gabrielle could not believe her ears. "But your illegitimacy!"

"Means nothing in the face of what we two could have together. I thanked you once for inviting me into your home. Now I would make a family within this home, a family with the love between husband and wife at its very core."

Yves cleared his throat and offered her his hand. "Gabrielle, I love you. Come and be my bride in truth."

It seemed that all within the hall held their breath as they waited for Gabrielle's response. She looked toward the ashes of the document and into the depths of Yves' gaze, then to the strong hand he offered her. She could trust Yves, rely upon him, confide in him.

And she could love him, as well. This man had already fulfilled her every desire, except for one.

That one desire, the one Gabrielle coveted beyond all others, Yves offered to her now. But one glance into his eyes told her that this knight's heart could be her own.

It was more, far more, than Gabrielle had ever hoped to claim.

She reached out and took Yves' hand, gripping his fingers tightly. "I love you, Yves," she declared, feeling tears of happiness rise to blur her vision. "I love you with all my heart and soul. I can imagine nothing I could desire more than to be your true bride."

The cook's wife sighed with romantic satisfaction, Gaston whooped with delight, but Gabrielle had eyes only for Yves. His smile was a flash of white against the bronze of his tan, his eyes gleamed with promise and he swept Gabrielle into his arms with rare abandon.

His kiss heated everything within her, though it was but a hint of what they would share later in the solar. Gabrielle returned his embrace wholeheartedly. The happy couple parted with a laugh as the assembly hooted and cheered, though Yves kept Gabrielle tight against his side.

Gabrielle felt a small fist clutch at her skirts. She looked down to find a pair of solemn dark eyes surveying them from below, Thomas' other hand gripping Yves' tabard.

"Does this mean that you have come back to stay?" her son asked uncertainly.

Yves ruffled the boy's hair. "Of course," he said firmly. "How else can I play with my friend and his new puppies?"

Thomas grinned with delight and clung to Yves' hand. "You have to see! Xavier found a stall for them and they like it, I just know they do. Come and see!"

Thomas darted off toward the stables, assured that all was right within his world once more. "Hurry!" he demanded.

Yves captured Gabrielle's hand in his own and gave her fingers a squeeze. "We simply have to go and see," he insisted, and Gabrielle laughed.

"Hurry!" she teased, and readily matched step with him. As they walked, Gabrielle turned the ring Yves had put upon her finger, then looked up at him with a smile.

"However did you guess my sole desire?" she whispered, knowing her love for this knight shone in her eyes. Yves smiled the slow smile she loved and halted in the corridor to possessively bracket her waist with his hands.

"I told you once that my lady's desire was as my own," he murmured, bending to brush his lips across her own. "So it has been and so it shall remain."

As he claimed her lips yet again, Gabrielle's heart sang with the certainty that her knight spoke the truth. He would be her sole desire, as she would be his, from this day forward until the end of time.

And that was no small thing to have between them.

* * * * *

Author Note

Rings, like Eglantine's, have long been considered to have magical power. The never ending circle of the ring has represented eternity to many peoples, as well as the circle of the year, and the wheel of fortune. Rings carried a man's signet—or signature—and in fabulous tales, protected their wearer from harm.

It's not surprising then that rings have been associated with marriage since at least Roman times. The Romans chose the third finger of the left hand as the ring finger because they believed a small artery (the *vena amoris*) led directly from this finger to the heart. There was no worse omen for a match than a broken wedding band!

Historically, marriages among nobles were not meant to be love matches, but strategic alliances. The troubadours patronized by Eleanor of Aquitaine in the twelfth century promoted the radical ideal of romantic love between a man and a woman—and because marriages had nothing to do with that happy state, they maintained that love was to be sought *outside* of marriage.

This was dangerous business, as a conviction of adultery—for a woman, at least—could mean death. Elaborate rules governed the interplay of these courtly lovers, many of whom concentrated on showing esteem for each other in public and did not sully their "pure love" with consummation.

Rings were given as surreptitious tokens of the man's admiration of the lady, in mimicry of wedding rings, but were worn on the small finger of the left hand. Over time, it became popular to give a ring engraved with a generic pronouncement of love, known as a poesy ring. Popular expressions included *A mon seul désir* (to my one desire) and *Amor Vincit* (love will conquer).

As it became acceptable in Western Europe to marry for love, the poesy ring evolved into the engagement ring, a token still given by a man to his lady fair as a symbol of his honorable intentions.

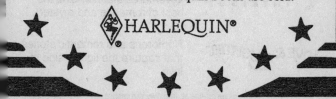

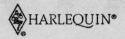

Not The Same Old Story!

Exciting, glamorous romance stories that take readers around the world.

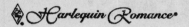
Sparkling, fresh and tender love stories that bring you pure romance.

Bold and adventurous— Temptation is strong women, bad boys, great sex!

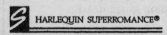
Provocative and realistic stories that celebrate life and love.

Contemporary fairy tales—where anything is possible and where dreams come true.

Heart-stopping, suspenseful adventures that combine the best of romance and mystery.

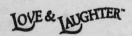
Humorous and romantic stories that capture the lighter side of love.

Look us up on-line at: http://www.romance.net   HGENERIC

Welcome to *Love Inspired*™

A brand-new series of contemporary inspirational love stories.

Join men and women as they learn valuable lessons about facing the challenges of today's world and about life, love and faith.

Look for the following April 1998
Love Inspired™ titles:

DECIDEDLY MARRIED
by Carole Gift Page

A HOPEFUL HEART
by Lois Richer

HOMECOMING
by Carolyne Aarsen

Available in retail outlets in March 1998.

LIFT YOUR SPIRITS AND GLADDEN YOUR HEART
with *Love Inspired!*™

Steeple
Hill™

LI498

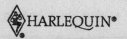

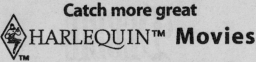

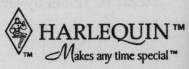